JUSTINE FIXES EVERYTHING: REFLECTIONS ON MORTALITY

AN AGRIPUNK THRILLER

THE PEOPLE OF THE MARTINIERE LEGACY

JOYCE REYNOLDS-WARD

1 / FIXER FOR THE MARTINIERES

JULY, 2086

"AUNT JUSTINE, WE'RE HERE," HER GREAT-NEPHEW AND WARD RON SAID.

Justine Martiniere startled awake from a murky dream featuring a character mix of her late brother Gabriel—*Gabie*—their father Philip, and—Philip's clone, Mike.

When had she fallen asleep on the drive from Moondance Ranch to the Double R?

Somewhere over northeastern Oregon's Blue Mountains, up top around Meacham most likely. She and Ron had been making the three-hour trek every other day over the past two weeks. They needed to update Mike regularly about everything that had happened in the Martiniere Group while he had been in pursuit of the killers of Ron's father Brandon. But Mike's physical and mental condition only allowed for short periods of work.

Justine groaned and pushed herself upright. Was she ready to deal with Mike right now? Fragments of that interrupted dream clouded her thoughts, especially since it was a continuation of last night's dreams.

She wasn't sure she was prepared for Mike today. An uneasiness

she couldn't quite place teased at her as she thought about seeing her
—nephew? Father?

Mike.

Michael Marcus Martiniere, *the* Martiniere, head of the closely-held
family conglomerate and the Family itself.

Mike.

Her father's clone. So unlike the father she hated—and yet, at
times, so much like him. Adopted and raised by Gabie and his wife
Ruby, after they'd rescued Mike when he was five.

Father? Nephew?

Neither?

Both?

Justine exhaled as Ron plugged in the electric truck. He extracted
her walker from the back seat of the crew cab and helped Justine out,
steadying her until she readjusted her sunglasses, put on her sun hat,
and took a firm grip on the walker.

Damn this getting old. The past was finally catching up to her.

"Thanks, Ron," she said, blinking against the mid-morning sun.

Eastern Oregon in summer was *so bright*, the sky a clear brilliant
blue. Especially here at the Double R Ranch in Thunder County. It
didn't have the dust and air pollution that Moondance Ranch, where
she and Ron lived, did during the summer.

Not unless wildfires flared nearby—always an issue.

"Tell Mike and JoAnn that I'll be in shortly," she continued.

"You okay?" Ron asked. He looked very much like Brandon and
Gabie, even though his skin was darker than theirs. Today was one of
those days when the timbre of his voice, his expressions, *everything*
about Ron reminded Justine of his father and grandfather. Even
though he was only sixteen.

Justine nodded. "Just need some time to wake up from the drive.
Get centered."

Plus her skin tingled, and she vaguely sensed Gabie's presence as a
digital clone—a digi. He wanted to talk, and *that* needed to be dealt
with before she saw Mike.

It felt urgent. A mental image came to her of Gabie with his arms crossed, glowering at her, tapping his right foot, muttering *hurry up, Tine, we've gotta talk.*

"All right," Ron said. "You give me a holler if you need help."

"I will," Justine promised. Sometimes it seemed as if their roles as guardian and ward were reversed, with Ron caring for her.

He glanced toward the family cemetery near the horse pasture. "Going to contemplate things for a little bit?"

"You're awfully damn perceptive for a kid your age," she retorted. Another likeness to Gabie and Brandon.

"I've been around you long enough to know your habits, Aunt Justine." Ron surprised Justine by kissing her cheek. "I worry about you." He swallowed hard. "And Mike. You two are the only living close family I have left."

"Oh, honey. I know."

Justine found it easier to be softer with Ron than almost anyone else—*Donald*—over the course of her long life. In the course of a few short months, Ron had endured his father's brutal murder, assumed the role of the Martiniere-in-waiting, temporarily *become* the Martiniere while Mike disappeared, and dealt with the appearance of the digital clones of dead members of his close family.

He had grown up fast for a sixteen-year-old. Like she did, only for Ron it was at a younger age.

Maybe that was why she could be soft with Ron. Shared trauma, plus the two of them had governed the Family and the Martiniere Group for a few weeks, as the Matriarch and the underaged Martiniere who needed her to approve his decisions. Her great-nephew, now her legal ward, was the closest Justine would ever come to having a child of her own.

Even more than Mike had been as a kid.

But Mike was not exactly reliable at the moment.

Illness, or something more?

That uneasiness about Mike fueled her reluctance to go inside. Especially since she wondered if it was a factor in her sense of Gabie's presence. She needed time to steel herself against what she might see in Mike.

Justine leaned against the truck for a moment as Ron left. Then she straightened up and rolled her walker toward the gravel path that led to the small family cemetery—once only for the Ryder family. But now it held Martinieres in addition to the Ryders.

A wry smile came and went. That was Ruby's doing. Ruby—and Gabie.

The automated cemetery gate latch opened with a light tap. Mike had installed it after Ruby's death, to give Justine easier access. She headed for the bench placed underneath the lilac bush, both Ruby's additions after Gabie's death. That gave her the best view of the Martiniere tombstones. A perfect place to deal with that buzzing *presence* that kept growing stronger.

Give me a moment, Gabie. I'm not as young as I used to be. I need time to get in the right frame of mind to talk to you, much less Mike.

She didn't say it out loud, though. That would summon her brother's digi.

Justine made herself study the markers before she did anything else. Contemplating her dead, except for Donald. She once thought her grandmother Donna was silly to do this years ago in the private Martiniere cemetery near Paris—now Justine understood why Donna-gran had chosen this particular form of meditation. Remembering who had come before. Acknowledging their legacy, so much a part of the Martiniere life.

And now, for her, a means to prepare to face their digis.

Gabie. Ruby. Gabie and Ruby's son Brandon. Brandon's daughter Lily, Ron's older sister.

Damn it, so many gone.

She sat there for a moment, considering each one. She had survived so many beloved members of her family.

Donald was the only one missing, and that was her own damned fault.

Justine took a deep breath. She had counted and acknowledged the dead who now lived in digital form. *Now* she was ready.

"All right, Gabie," she said, her voice half-exasperated. "Have you been poking at my dreams? What the hell is going on?"

A shimmer in front of her. Then the form of her late brother took shape, as he looked in his vigorous early middle age. A figure she only knew from pictures.

Still athletic, slender, unbent by advancing years and the G9 virus that later temporarily crippled him; gray infiltrating the black of his beard and hair, face beginning to show lines, brown skin darkened by sun exposure from working outside as he developed his Moondance Ranch during the era after his divorce from Ruby. And that piercing, predatory Martiniere gaze along with a sly *come-hither* twinkle in his brown eyes. She recognized the picture that image came from, a casual shot taken by Gabie's second wife Rachel.

Justine shivered. She still wasn't accustomed to the manifestation of Gabie as a digi. It hammered home the realization that their father had been a digi for years after his death, banished through the combined efforts of Gabie, Ruby, Mike, and herself.

And Mike's dogs and horses, she reminded herself.

Never a good idea to underestimate Mike's links to his beloved animals. Those links were amplified by Ruby's augmentation of the ability to perceive cyberspace activity in certain bloodlines of dogs and horses, an epigenetic modification using nanotech.

"About time you listened, Tine," Gabie's digi said. *"Thought I might need to force an appearance if you weren't going to invite me."* He glanced toward the headstones. *"Any particular reason for talking here?"*

"Contemplation of my mortality," Justine said, tapping one foot against the grass.

Gabie laughed. *"You're still a young thing."*

"I'm older than you were when you died." And right now, she felt every damned one of her seventy-seven years. "Six years makes a big difference at this age. What's so damned urgent, Gabie?"

Her brother's digi—he was repeatedly explicit that this wasn't *him*, but a simulation—joined her on the bench.

"I've a couple of things to talk about," he said.

Justine sighed. "God, don't tell me I have to fix something yet *again*, Gabie. I am sick to death of always fixing things. Will it ever fucking end?"

A pause. Then, *"Unfortunately, Tine, fixing things is what you've always done best, especially in your middle age and beyond. The Family would be much worse off if you hadn't been there."*

"I'm *tired*, Gabie. Really tired. I'm going to die one of these days. Someone else needs to figure out how to fix things for the Family."

"I understand." He rubbed his chin, a habit from life which meant he had deep concerns. *"This should be simple compared to some of the things you've done—and you're the only one who can do it."*

"Oh?"

"Part of it, anyway. They're interrelated." A pause, and his image flickered—a sign of digi data gathering. *"Mike's really struggling right now. Problematically so."*

Oh God. She wasn't wrong to be feeling nervous about Mike if Gabie was concerned, too.

"I'm—worried," she admitted. "He hasn't shaken off that depression that plagued him during their time away. JoAnn hasn't said anything to me about it. I hope she would ask for help if he went too far down that road." Justine leaned her head back and slumped slightly on the bench. "But I have *that feeling*, you know?"

Gabie nodded. *"Exactly. Same for me. He's just—off. Sometimes he reminds me of Philip. It's—"* he fumbled for a word, raising his hands. *"A residual. Or something."*

"I thought we'd gotten rid of those pieces of Daddy-poo's programming in him," Justine grumbled. Even now she couldn't help referring to their father with sarcastic-toned endearments. A coping strategy to hide the deep hatred she felt for him.

Gabie shook his head. *"It's questions he's been asking. Things he wants to know. Archives he wants to check out that I don't think are a good idea for him to investigate on his own until he feels better."*

"Such as?" She had a good idea what Gabie was talking about. Their father's records.

"Choices our father made during my exile."

Justine exhaled. "That's what I was afraid of." Philip left biometrically sealed records that were only accessible to Mike as his clone. She shivered at what might be in those files. "So what are you asking of me?"

"Things happened in the Family when I was exiled, especially Philip's organizing those damn cult groups as part of his political aims. I know what's in the written records. But there was a lot more to those thirty years than what's been recorded. I want to understand what happened. And Brandon and Lily would like to know more about the history as well."

Brandon. Lily. The other Martiniere digis in existence, along with Ruby.

"Don't the files tell you enough?" She studied her pale, age-spotted hands. Even the best cosmetic regime hadn't kept the ravages away. "Donna-gran maintained pretty extensive records, along with the other Family heads."

Gabie grimaced. *"The files contain facts but not personal accounts. We need your perspective, Tine. What you knew. What you experienced. Not only would it distract Mike, get his mind away from picking at those damned files before he's emotionally ready to deal with them, but—it would be helpful for us digis. It would give us more data, help us become more complete. Lily in particular."*

Data. From what Justine had seen of digis since she become aware of their presence, data was one of the currencies of the digi world. The more information acquired, the more solid the digi's manifestation. There was a whole digital clone culture around the acquisition of data.

They must be getting this information about the details of digital clone operation from somewhere.

So how many more digis are out there besides the four I know?

A serious future concern. A reason to keep Mike sane. *He* seemed to function well as both digi and fizi—physical clone.

Justine sighed. Digital clones. Physical clones. Once science-fictional, now a reality.

I'm too damn old for this.

But she had become the fixer for the Martinieres, and it sounded like she still had a role to play.

"You want me to tell stories to Mike?"

"Yes." Gabie looked up. *"And here comes JoAnn."* His voice softened.

JoAnn Swait, Mike's wife, was the youngest daughter of Gabie and Ruby's late business partner Jeff. Mike and Jo had been close to each other from childhood, both obsessed with programming, nanotechnology, and robotics. Both families had been *thrilled* when Mike and JoAnn became a couple. Not just for business purposes, but because the pair had been *just right* together.

Gabie got up. She felt a faint whisper as his lips brushed her cheek. *"Anything you can do, Tine. Anything. I'm serious."*

"I'll do my best, Gabie."

A pang flowed through her as Gabie disappeared. She didn't know why he had left—unless it was to give her and JoAnn some semblance of privacy.

"Hey." JoAnn walked toward Justine. "You doing all right?"

"Just had a chat with Gabe."

She didn't use her nickname for him around the kids.

JoAnn heaved a heavy sigh as she joined Justine on the bench. Mike's wife was tall, elegant, and graceful. Her tightly curled dark hair was shorter than usual, legacy of the four weeks she and Mike had spent on the run pursuing Brandon's killers. A faint scar on her cheek showed pale in contrast to Jo's brown skin—another relic of that desperate quest for vengeance.

"About Mike." No question in JoAnn's voice.

"We're both worried about him. There's something off. Ever since…." Her voice trailed off. Mike had overclocked his cyborg heart and lungs when he rescued Lily and Brandon's digis from Philip's last toxic remnants.

JoAnn shook her head. "Mike's just not bouncing back. I don't know if I'm expecting too much, too soon, or if something else is going on."

"What do the doctors think?"

"Dr. Pramula says that the cyborg systems have partially recovered, though she's worried about the durability of Mike's heart. Dr. Sheri thinks it's a psychological effect, says that Mike went through a similar depression when recovering from cancer, and before his heart and lungs were replaced."

Oh God. A return to those years.

Justine remembered that era far too well. Sixteen-year-old Mike collapsing from a heart attack when he and Ruby were feeding horses in the field during a December blizzard. Followed by the discovery that he had cancer. Both direct effects of being cloned from an old man —Philip had been seventy-nine when the cells used for Mike's cloning had been harvested. Mike was his last successful clone, crafted in hopes that Philip could migrate his digital clone into Mike's body. If Philip didn't kill Mike in the process of using him as a blood donor.

Daddy-fucking-dearest was a couple of years older than I am when he created Mike.

And while she had, knock on wood, avoided the cardiac and cancer issues that plagued her father, Mike had all of them because, as he liked to say at times, *I'm a young man in an old man's body.*

"That's bad, isn't it?" JoAnn asked. "I can see it from your expression. That was when he shoved me away, so I don't know much about that era."

"Jo, he went to a really dark place. Gabe was the only one who could talk Mike out of some very bitter thoughts. He self-mutilated. Lashed out." She spread her hands. "I couldn't blame him. A teenager going through a heart attack. Cancer. Damn near died from heart failure before we could build his heart and lung replacements. And then the arms. Losing the ability to ride horses really broke him. It was a really grim three years, capped by Gabe's death. A damn good thing Mike had his dogs. If it hadn't been for Striker—" That dog had saved Mike, as far as Justine was concerned, Striker and his son Smudgie. "And his need to take care of Ruby after Gabe died."

JoAnn shuddered. "Mike was downright nasty at Gabe's funeral. Outside of screaming his head off from pain, I didn't see any of that depression during his leg cyborging, and that was a horrible process."

"Because he had you."

"I did see the self-mutilation and depression while we were on the run," JoAnn said, her voice low, her expression troubled. "But I thought he would get better once he was home."

"It's only been a couple of weeks since you came back," Justine said. "The damn kid thinks he needs to get back up and rolling—and he never really had time to mourn Brandon's death before leaping right into avenging him."

"True."

"Gabe suggested that I talk about the Family's history during the thirty years he was in exile. He thinks it will be good for Mike. Keep him distracted."

JoAnn took Justine's hand. "I sure as hell hope it works, because I'm starting to get scared."

And *that* worried Justine even more. JoAnn and Mike's relationship was as close as the one between Gabie and Ruby, perhaps even closer. She tightened her hand on JoAnn's.

"Then maybe it's time I went inside and we got started, you suppose?"

JoAnn's smile was her reward. "Mind if I listen in?"

"Not at all. Help me up, please." Her hips didn't always want to cooperate, especially after a long drive, and the damn bench sometimes made things worse.

But the hips were obliging enough that Justine used JoAnn's arm instead of her walker for support as they walked to the old ranch house. JoAnn carried the walker in her free hand.

Ron kept muttering about automating the folding and carrying process. One of these days she hoped her great-nephew could find the time to do it.

"Think you can make it up the steps?" JoAnn asked. "Or should we go to the front ramp instead?"

Justine set her jaw firmly. "I can make it." She wasn't that damn feeble. Yet. "Might take me longer than when I was younger, though."

JoAnn chuckled.

They slowly ascended the steps, progressed through the enclosed back porch, and into the kitchen that held so many fond memories of times at the Double R. The ancient green and chrome Formica table that was at least twice Justine's age, her favorite place to work when staying at the Double R. Memories of late nights drinking with Gabie at that table because both of them suffered from insomnia. Gabie and Ruby cooking together.

Now Ron leaned against the sink, gazing into a glass of water, scowling. He raised his head as Justine and JoAnn came in.

"He's really in a mood today," he growled.

"Yeah," JoAnn agreed. "Mike woke up hurting and pissed."

"I had to duck out for a few minutes because his tones...." Ron's voice trailed off and he shook his head. While he wasn't programmed to respond to Martiniere mind control vocals, he was still sensitive to them.

"Then I guess it's my turn to deal with him." Justine tightened her lips. Damn it, she was getting too old for this stuff.

"Want me to come with you?" JoAnn asked.

"Give me a few minutes," she growled. "If I need to, I'll call Ruby's digi up."

That softened everyone's expressions, because Ruby even in digi was formidable in her handling of grumpy Martiniere men.

Justine heaved a sigh, and clenched her walker. She rolled it down the hallway from the kitchen to Mike's office.

She rapped on the door. "It's me," she said, then opened it.

Mike lay far too still in a hospital bed that took the place of his desk, which was now shoved against a wall to make room for the bed. Justine hesitated, eyes on him, uneasy until she saw his chest slightly rise and fall as he breathed. Still alive.

He stared out the window at the winter horse pasture which also served as a summer hay field. Fresh-cut hay lay in long windrows, drying. He didn't turn his head as Justine entered, but kept gazing at something outside, scowling, his hand on old Smudgie's head. The heeler snuggled close to him, ears half-flattened in worry. Smudgie's young daughter Spot, still a puppy, huddled on Mike's other side, mirroring her sire's expression.

Even Smudgie and Spot see it.

"Hey," she said, settling in the chair by the bed.

She winced as Mike turned that glower on her. It wasn't as impressive as Gabie's *fight-you-to-the-death* glare, but it was still pretty damn intense. Today, Mike looked like Daddy-damn-dearest in his later years; skin tight against his bones, short black hair disheveled, face devoid of color except for dark circles under those piercing ice-blue eyes, lips drawn tight in disapproval.

"What the hell has you emulating Daddy-poo *today*?"

Mike slapped the light quilt covering his legs—his own move, not Philip's. Smudgie recoiled and flattened his ears, whining as he eyed Mike. Spot whimpered and nuzzled one of Mike's hands.

Good. At least that *got a reaction out of him.*

"God damn it, Justine. A perfectly lovely day outside and I'm *stuck* in this fucking bed. I thought I'd be done with this damn stuff once my leg cyborging was finished. But here I am once again, damn it."

"At least you have the prospect of getting better."

"Do I? Really?"

She lost her patience. "More than I ever will due to my *actual* biological age, damn it, so *stop fucking whining.*" Justine snapped the last three words, pushing the control tones *hard,* using the additional authority invested in her as the Matriarch.

Mike flinched. He looked down at Smudgie and caressed the old dog's head.

"Smudgie, boy, I'm sorry," he said softly. The dog licked his hand, raising his head to meet Mike's eyes. Justine kept silent, watching the interaction between man and dog as Mike scratched Smudgie around his ears. Spot shoved between them, rolling on her back. That brought a laugh from Mike, as well as an easing of his facial muscles, and Justine relaxed. A little bit.

Thank God for Mike's ties to his dogs and horses.

Would her father have been different if he had possessed similar connections? Or had Philip been capable of caring about anyone other than himself? He never owned pets, and barely tolerated Grandmother Donna encouraging her and Gabie to ride horses. Gabie was the one to intervene when Justine's half-brother Joey tortured and damn near killed her cat, not Philip. Daddy-fucking-dearest got angry at Gabie, not Joey. And the way Philip had treated Renate, the mother of her and Joey…Justine shuddered.

At last Mike rested his hand on Smudgie's cheek. Smudgie licked Mike's palm, then settled his nose in it. Spot nuzzled the back of Mike's other hand.

Mike sighed. "I feel like I did before my heart and lungs were cyborged, Justine. That weak. That exhausted. That much pain.

Honestly? I'm scared. What if I never get better? What if the last five years were the best I'll ever get?"

"What does Dr. Pramula say?"

Mike rolled his eyes. "Heart replacement is very likely. If she does that, she wants to upgrade and replace my lungs. I'm—" he blew hard. "Not looking forward to that. Or the recovery time. And there's still so much to be done. Get things in order for Ron to serve as the Martiniere in case my cyborg systems fail. Finish dealing with those hidden and Loyal indentureds created by my fucking *progenitor*." He snapped the last word, a fleeting control pitch echoing in her head, but not tugging at her. Just a shared angry resonance. "I just—damn it, trying to root that stuff out is a nightmare. I need to do so many things and I don't have the energy to do it."

"Then delegate."

"Most of it can't be."

"Mike, fretting, snapping, and snarling isn't going to speed up your recovery one damn bit."

"And Gabe keeps arguing with me, saying I'm not ready to look at some of those new archives we discovered. Damn it, now's the best time for me to learn about these things!"

Smudgie nuzzled Mike's hand as his voice raised. Spot crawled onto Mike's chest, whimpering. Mike stopped. He stroked Spot reassuringly with his free hand.

"He's right, you know," Justine said.

"I feel fucking useless."

"There *is* another means for finding out some of these things," she said. "Gabe wants me to share what I went through."

Mike snorted. "You've been pretty damn evasive whenever I've asked you about the past."

Justine took her time to answer that, thinking through her answer.

"And maybe I was wrong to be that way," she said finally. "But it's part of my self-protection. Look. Gabe wants to know more about my perceptions of Family history. You could use that information as well."

"Well, it would be one way for me to start figuring these things out," Mike admitted. "If you're willing to do it."

"I'd sooner not revisit those days. But Gabe asked. JoAnn's interested as well. And the other digis want to know."

JoAnn joined them, bending over Mike to kiss his forehead and resting her left hand on his shoulder. He closed his eyes, face softening at her touch. Smudgie's stub tail waggled, and he oozed up higher for a pat from JoAnn. Spot yelped, vying with her sire for attention.

"I think it's a good idea, Mikey," JoAnn said softly, as she patted Smudgie and then Spot. "For all of us."

"I don't know if I'll tell stories in order," Justine said. She looked down at her hands. "Some parts will be harder than others."

"That's fine," Mike said. "Anything, right now."

"Gabie?" Justine took a deep breath. "Can one of you digis record and file these stories?"

Gabie and Brandon both shimmered into being.

"I'll handle that, Justine," Brandon said. He summoned a screen and began inputting.

"Entirely appropriate," Justine said.

Brandon had been a video producer before he became the Martiniere-in-waiting, then spent years after that crafting 'casts in opposition to the institution of indentured labor.

Lily and Ruby followed, as Ron entered the room.

"So where are you going to start, Tine?" Gabie asked.

"Let me think about it for a moment," Justine said. She leaned her head against the chair back, considering. Which memory to begin with? What might be the best introduction to her storytelling?

Ah. *That* one.

She opened her eyes and coughed. "Ron, could you get me a glass of water?"

"Sure." Ron sprang up. He returned with a pitcher of water and a folding side table, then went back for glasses. He filled one for Justine and set it on the table.

"Thank you, Ron." Justine took a sip. "All right. Here we go. I've decided that the best route is to start at the beginning. So. Let me tell you how I ended up marrying Donald Atwood. That lays the foundation for other actions."

She didn't miss how Gabie winced. Hell, she shrank a little inside just thinking about what happened before Donald got her away from Daddy-damn-dearest.

But *someone* had to tell this story if they were going to record Family history, and she doubted that Gabie had shared the whole nasty mess with anyone, except perhaps Ruby.

"It's not a pretty story," she added.

2 / DONALD

DECEMBER, 2026

"DAMN IT, GIRL, YOU *WILL* LISTEN TO ME!" PHILIP MARTINIERE GLOWERED at Justine as he blocked the exit from the Martiniere's penthouse apartment in the Hôtel Martiniere, the Parisian mansion belonging to the Martiniere family, currently the main residence of her uncle Gerard. Every high-level Martiniere heir came back to the Hôtel Martiniere at Christmas, no matter where they lived.

Maybe someday she wouldn't have to do that.

"No!" Justine whirled and ran. She just had to make it to one of the penthouse's junior suites. Lock the door and hold Daddy-damn-dearest plus her brother Joey at bay. Message her cousins Gabie and Serg for help.

Before Justine reached the door to the closest suite, Joey leapt across the couch and tackled her. She fought back—Serg and Gabie had taught her dirty fighting to defend herself—and managed to nail Joey in the crotch.

"*Dearest Especially!*" she gasped.

Joey froze at her use of the mind control words that locked him temporarily in place. Coded specifically to Justine's voice for her protection, so that when she used them, she could stop Joey in situations *just like this.*

She pushed him off of her. Scrambled to her feet, started to sprint—only to be caught up short by her father's fist grasping her shoulder-length brunette hair.

Justine screamed as Philip yanked her toward him, pain knifing through her scalp as he kept jerking on her.

"I *said*, you will *listen* to me, girl!" her father snarled. *"Fragrant Flower."*

His words that controlled Justine, programmed into her at twelve. Coupled with Philip's vocal tones, *those words* froze her in place. She shuddered, gasping for breath between shrieks as her scalp throbbed. Daddy-poo hadn't used the specific tones to make the words hold her for long, not like he would do to Gabie—

Joey staggered to his feet and punched her in the gut. It *hurt. Bad.* She screeched again. Joey hit her hard and pain knifed through her, stabbing when she caught her breath between cries.

Oh God. Oh God. Would anyone hear her?

"Enough, Joseph," Philip growled. He shook Justine by her hair and slapped her repeatedly, bringing tears to her eyes. Agony ripped through her scalp. Her face burned from his slaps. "Justine. You *will* marry Walter Braun. You *will* do what you are *told.*"

The code word lock faded. Justine yanked herself free. More pain tore through her scalp, something trickling down her face. She scrambled away. No one between her and the main penthouse door. If she could just get *out that door* before Daddy-damn-dearest used the words on her again....

"Fragrant Flower!" A harsher tone this time, locking her muscles. She fell. Justine fought the body lock, only able to move her fingers.

So close to the door. *So* damn close.

She took a deep breath. *"Help!"*

Philip approached her again, pulling an injector pen out of his pocket. If he nailed her with that, he would marry her off to Braun, long before she was capable of saying no.

And that fucker—three times her age, cold-handed, dead-eyed, reeking of decay—no! Not tied to that asshole.

I'll die first.

This Christmas season was full of Braun encounters at Family receptions. Pushing her into a corner and feeling her up. Prying soft fingers pinching her breasts, rubbing between her legs. Whispering obscenities into her ears as he drooled on her neck, threatening abuses he planned to inflict on her once she married him—*no!*

Justine burst into sobs mixed with screams, fighting against the lock as hard as she could to kick at her father.

But she couldn't get up. The lock held her flat. Feeble kicks were all she could do.

The penthouse door slammed open as her cousin Gabie burst in. He took quick stock, and slugged Philip hard, in the mouth, grabbing the injector and throwing it across the room. Pulled her to her feet.

"Tine. Run. *Now.* Find Serg. With Donna-gran." The alcohol on his breath—Gabie had been drinking, *hard.* At least it gave him some protection, anesthetized him somewhat once Daddy-damn-dearest turned on him.

"Gabie—" This was almost worse. Oh God, Daddy-poo would hurt Gabie *bad* this time. He was in a rage already, and for *Gabie* to come to her rescue—

Gabie shoved her toward the door. "Go!"

As she staggered to the doorway, Philip started to say, *"Fra—,"* cut off by a second blow from Gabie.

"Tine. *Go!"* Gabie bellowed, a general compulsion tone in his voice jerking her into a run.

"Broken Angel!" Philip shouted.

Gabie shrieked as his code words locked him down hard. She *should* have turned back to help her cousin, but the immediacy of his pitch lingered. Justine careened down the stairs as fast as possible, clutching at the heavy wooden railing to keep herself upright, bawling from shock and rage, gasping for breath even as pain knifed through her.

Donna-gran. Donna-gran. Donna-gran pounded through her head, the only focus that kept her from collapsing. Their only recourse for help now. Their grandmother, Matriarch of the Martinieres. Even

Daddy-damn-dear wouldn't dare cross Donna-gran. She would be safe there, and maybe Donna-gran could send help for Gabie—

Justine crashed into someone at the next floor's landing. Her uncle Gerard held her steady.

"My God. Justine. You are bleeding," he said in French.

"It's Daddy-poo," she gulped in English. The words in French evaded her. "Used my code words. Trying to make me marry Braun. Was going to inject me—Gabie got me free but *oh God Uncle Gerry he's gonna kill Gabie!*" She sobbed harder than ever.

Gerard glanced up, toward the penthouse door, his lips tightening at the faint sound of Gabie's cries.

"Go to your grandmother. I will see what I can do to help Gabriel."

"Thank you," she choked, stumbling down the hallway, legs about to give out. The door to Donna-gran's suite was locked. Justine pounded on it. What if Daddy-shithead-dearest overcame Uncle Gerry? Philip *was* the Martiniere, after all, and outranked everyone.

Except Donna-gran, at least within the Family. This was her only safe place in this damned fucking mansion.

Why doesn't someone open this damned door?

"What the—" Cousin Piotr muttered in Russian as he opened the door. Justine staggered through it, falling to her knees in the middle of the living area and collapsing on her belly in front of Donna-gran's wheelchair.

"Justine. My God." Cousin Serg, Piotr's son, knelt next to her, gently pulling her upright as she sobbed. He continued in French, his breath stinking of alcohol, just like Gabie's, probably for the same damn reason—to make things hurt less if Daddy-damn-dearest turned his wrath on him. "What the hell is going on?"

"Daddy-poo," she gasped through the tears that just kept coming, still unable to find words except in English. "Trying to force me to marry Walter Braun. Getting ready to inject me. Gabie stopped him so that I could get away but *oh God Daddy-damn-dearest is pissed and he's gonna kill Gabie!*" She gulped for breath. "Uncle Gerry's going up to the penthouse. Oh God. Oh God."

"Go help Gerard *now*," Donna-gran said. "Both of you. Bring Gabriel back here. Get Justine to the couch, then go. Quickly."

Serg helped Justine to the couch, patting her shoulder before turning away. The door slammed after him and Piotr. She leaned her head back, closing her eyes, still shaking with sobs that wracked her whole body, sending pain zigzagging throughout her. She was bleeding all over Donna-gran's nice white couch but it couldn't be helped.

"Tania!" Donna-gran called in French. "Bring water, cloths, and the medkit." Her hands gently probed Justine's aching head. She switched to English. "Mary, Mother of God. He nearly ripped a chunk of your scalp off. What the hell made him so angry?"

"Braun." The tears kept coming no matter how hard Justine tried to stop them, words and sobs escaping her at the same time. "He was at breakfast. Proposed to me in front of fucking Daddy and Joey. I said no, hell no, and Daddy-shithead-dearest sent him away. Then we started arguing because he demanded that I give Braun another hearing. I tried to leave and—this—happened."

"Fucker." Her grandmother's voice was hard. "Marrying a seventeen-year-old to the likes of Braun? What the hell was he thinking?"

"I don't know. I really don't know." Oh God, she *hurt.*

Rattling of a metal cart, probably the one that held Donna-gran's medical kit. It stopped next to Justine.

She heard the click of a semi-automatic pistol slide being cocked.

"Tania," Donna-gran said quietly, once again in French. "You will have to do the stitches. My hands are too shaky today, and...one of us needs to be armed. Just in case. Better that it's me."

"Oui, madame."

Donna-gran continued in English. "Fortunately, your scalp is not torn that bad. Tania knows what she is doing."

Justine opened her eyes as the indentured servant injected her scalp with a painkiller, then began to work.

"What am I going to do? How am I going to get back to the States?"

She had to get back to the US. Daddy-fucking-dearest couldn't force her to marry once they returned to Los Angeles. But he had a lot of influence in Europe as the Martiniere, which was probably why he was trying to force the issue now.

But how *could* she return? She had flown over with Daddy-poo and

Joey in the corporate jet that belonged to the Martiniere Group. Commercial flight wouldn't work. Daddy-damn-dearest's minions could intercept her easily. And she didn't have enough cash on hand to pay for even a coach seat to the US, much less LA. At seventeen, she didn't have access to her Family trust funds. Wouldn't have access until she was twenty-four.

Borrow from someone in the Family? Her only possibility—and that still didn't prevent Daddy-damn-dearest's minions from abducting her at one of the airports.

"You can stay with me in Quebec," Donna-gran said. "But that's not a long-term solution. At best it is a delaying action. Unless you live a completely cloistered life, Philip *will* get his hands on you at some point."

"I know," Justine whimpered. "Oh God, Donna-gran. And school. Graduating from high school."

"Hold still, please," Tania said as Justine sobbed harder.

"Maybe I should have leapt out of the window," she whispered, a desperate calculation she had considered before, in detail, estimating how much alcohol she needed to drink to make it hurt less. "Or jumped over the balcony rail from the top floor. For everyone to see. Can't be hushed up. He can't do those things to me if I'm dead." She inhaled, hiccuping and choking on her tears.

"*No,*" Donna-gran said. Her tones were light but firm. "That is not the answer, Justine. We *will* find a solution." She took Justine's hand firmly in hers. "Now. Stop crying. Calm yourself. Make Tania's job easier."

Justine gulped and closed her hand tight on Donna-gran's. Her grandmother's command tones soothed rather than agitated her, unlike her father's.

"There," Tania said at last, in French. "There will be a little scarring but under the hair line."

"You're sure?" Justine's voice quavered.

Donna-gran patted her shoulder. "Tania is a registered nurse, my dear. She went into indenture to pay for her schooling."

"All—all right." Justine sat up slowly. "Damn it. Why is he acting like this? It's the twenty-first century, after all!"

"Your father fancies himself as being the latest manifestation of our Medici and Borgia ancestors," Donna-gran said icily. "And he has enough money and power to force your marriage to Braun without experiencing any consequences, unfortunately."

Justine winced as she buried her head in her hands. *Truth.* She had heard her father's praise of the Medici and Borgia political methodology enough times in the past.

A slight tapping at the door.

"Tania, please get that." Donna-gran picked up the pistol and slid it under her embroidery. "Stand clear just in case."

Tania eased the door open. Justine gasped as Serg and Piotr guided Gabie into the living room. He sagged against their cousins, his arms across their shoulders, moaning softly. His white shirt was tattered and bloody. Gerard followed them, carrying a pistol that he tucked into a shoulder holster once he was inside and had locked the door behind him.

"Oh. My." Donna-gran eased her pistol from under her handwork, disarming it and then reloading it. "Take Gabriel into the spare bedroom, please. Tania, this looks like more work for you."

Justine covered her mouth as she got a glimpse of Gabie's back. Long, bloody weals marked it.

"Philip was whipping him under command word lock," Gerard said harshly, in French. "We had words. Justine, you need to take pictures of this."

Justine followed as Serg and Piotr guided Gabie to the bedroom and helped him lie down on his stomach. She forced her hands to remain steady as she used her phone to photograph Gabie's injuries.

Donna-gran rolled her wheelchair to join them as Serg and Piotr eased what remained of Gabie's shredded shirt off.

"Gerard. What are we going to do?" she asked in French.

Her uncle Gerard shrugged. "Mother, what *can* we do? He is *the Martiniere,* and we do not have the strength to challenge Philip and Joseph. Not politically, not financially."

A sharp intake of breath from Donna-gran. "This is *not* the seventeenth century, much as your older brother would like to pretend otherwise. Philip has abused both Justine and Gabriel under your roof. You have rights."

"I pushed my rights as far as I dared to keep Philip from beating Gabriel to death."

"He is trying to force Justine to marry that pig Braun. That set this off."

Gerard tightened his lips, shaking his head. "We can move Justine out of the Martiniere's penthouse and Gabriel in here with you. Gabriel is of age. He is not dependent upon Philip for his livelihood."

"Except for working in his Los Angeles labs," Gabie groaned in English.

"You have protections there," Donna-gran said in English. "Justine, dear. Please forward copies of those pictures to me, Piotr, and Gerard."

Justine did so with trembling hands. Then she sent copies to Gabie and Serg. Just in case.

"Gabriel at least has resources. But how do we protect Justine?" Donna-gran went back to French. "I will *not* support this proposed marriage to Walter Braun. I do not care what Philip's plans are for financial and business alliances. Braun is not acceptable."

"Philip is convinced that Justine will scandalize the Family if she is not married," Piotr growled.

"She is no different from any of her aunts!" Donna-gran snapped.

Gerard sighed. He fixed Justine with a steady gaze. "Justine, my dear," he said in English. "For your safety, I recommend you find a good man, of appropriate financial and social connections, and *marry him as soon as possible.*"

"Bu-bu-but I haven't even graduated from high school," she whimpered. God, it *hurt* to breathe.

"It is not right. But once you leave my household, you will be at risk from your father again, and—I cannot shelter you for long."

"I may know of someone safe for Justine," Serg said. "Gabe. How about Donald?"

"Atwood?" Gabie groaned, flinching as Tania worked on him.

"Yes. He's a bit of a playboy, but he has money."

"Decent programmer," Gabie muttered. Then he yelped.

"I'll talk to him," Serg said.

Someone pounded hard on the outer door.

Then Philip's voice, projecting. "Let me in. *Now.*"

Donna-gran growled and spun her wheelchair. "You kids stay in here with Gabriel. Gerard. Piotr. With me."

Justine slipped to the doorframe. Serg stopped her. "Don't. Donna-gran can manage this."

"I want to know what's happening," she whispered back. "Listen without going in. It's *my* future, damn it!"

Serg assessed her. Then he reached in his pocket and pulled out a small case. "Put these in your ears."

"What are they?"

"Filter plugs. They won't shut out the control tones entirely—Gabe won't wear them for that reason—Philip uses his strongest pitches on him and they don't work for that. But you, listening—"

"Thank you." Justine put them in her ears. Then she went into the hallway that led to the living room. She heard the faint *snick* of Donna-gran's pistol slide and felt sick. If Donna-gran got into trouble for killing Daddy-damn-dearest....

"Piotr, let him in." Donna-gran's voice was soft and snaky. Justine shuddered at that malignant pitch. Donna-gran had more weapons than that pistol.

The door slammed open. "Where are they?" Daddy-fucking-dearest roared.

"That is *quite enough,* Philip!" Donna-gran snapped in French, the words heavy-laden with command codes. "You will behave in a civil manner or else *leave my suite.*"

"So you've chosen sides, *Mother.*"

"You are violating the hospitality of your brother's house."

"I am the Martiniere. My word rules within the Family!"

"And *I* am the Matriarch." Those words, laden with command tones, sent a shiver down Justine's spine, even though they weren't directed at her. "You have crossed a line. Beating Gabriel."

"Look at me. Look at what he did to me! He hit me!" Daddy-fucking-dearest screamed.

"To protect Justine," Donna-gran said, voice level and cold.

Her father laughed mockingly. "I suppose Gabriel's jumping into her bed! She's a slut, just like her mother!"

Rage flooded through Justine. Her fucking father would believe *that* about her? Gabie was her *cousin.* Her protector from Philip's rages. More like a brother than her own brother. No, she would never, *ever* think of Gabie in *that* way.

"*Philip. Crowned Pretension,*" Donna-gran snarled.

Oh, *that* sent an even deeper vibration through Justine's bones, even though it wasn't directed at her.

Coughing. Then, in a choked voice. "I have my rights, Mother."

"To do what? You abuse Gerard's hospitality, not to speak of your nephew and *your daughter.*"

Bitter laugh from her father. "So Gerry is hiding behind your skirts."

"No," Gerard said firmly. "I have overlooked your lashing out at other Family members because you *are* the Martiniere, and I am trying to preserve the peace for the good of the Family and for the Martiniere Group. However, when my niece, *your daughter,* comes flying down the stairs with her head bleeding because you have beaten her; when I enter your penthouse to discover that you are brutalizing *our nephew,* then that is too far."

"Justine defied me. Gabriel hit me."

"And that justifies your behavior?" Donna-gran said, her voice hard. "Philip, I thought I raised you better than that."

"There will be no more beatings in *my house,*" Gerard snarled. "I cannot stop you from verbal discipline of Family members as the Martiniere, but that *will not extend* to beatings. You will not lay a hand on anyone staying in *my house.* That includes staff, indentured or not. And you are only welcome here at Christmas, because that is my sworn obligation to you as the Martiniere. Otherwise, find another place to stay when you are in France!"

Justine shuddered. Gerard was *pissed.* He normally didn't stand up to his elder brother like that.

Enough. She was safe, at least for now. Her scalp hurt bad, along with her gut where Joey had slugged her, that knifing pain every time she inhaled. And her muscles ached from being locked down, *twice.*

Justine tiptoed back down the hallway and into the bedroom, closing the door and slumping against it.

Serg looked up from helping Gabie drink something through a straw.

"What's happening?" he asked in English, the language the three of them typically used around each other. French with the elders, Russian with Piotr, Spanish with the Spanish cousins.

"Uncle Gerard is standing up to Daddy-fucking-dearest," Justine whispered. Somehow, she found the strength to stagger over by the bed. She collapsed on the floor and leaned against the bed before extracting the tone filters. "Donna-gran used her words on Daddy-poo and I got hit with the feedback. These helped. Thank you." She raised the hand holding the filters.

Serg nodded toward the nightstand. "Put them there. What's Gerard doing?"

"Uncle Gerry said no more beatings in this house. That Daddy-damn-dearest is only welcome here at Christmas and that's it." She gulped.

"About time," Gabie mumbled.

"It won't stop him from verbally disciplining people. Gerry said Daddy-poo is not to lay a hand on anyone, including staff."

"It's a start," Serg said grimly.

She laughed hysterically, rubbing her face. *Tears* again, damn it.

"Donna-gran pulled a gun on Daddy-damn-dearest and used his control words." Justine gasped for breath. "Oh God. Oh God."

Serg eyed her. "You need some of this, too. Just a second, Gabe." He set the glass and long straw on the nightstand, then went into the bathroom, returning with a glass full of a bubbling red drink. "One of my father's concoctions. Takes the edge off of the pain and relaxes you."

"Thank you." Justine gulped it.

Her eyelids grew heavy within a couple of minutes. The residual pain in her scalp and her assorted other aches were still there, but fuzzy, and easing into pinpricks instead of hammer blows. Justine crawled over to the bedroom sofa and climbed onto it. She used one back cushion as a pillow and curled herself around the other.

She was safe. For once.

LIGHT. A GROAN. JUSTINE OPENED HER EYES. STILL ON THE SOFA. AT SOME point someone had taken off her shoes and tossed a blanket over her.

Gabie sat on the edge of the bed, shirtless, leaning on his hands, shaking his head. He had changed—or been changed into—pajama pants. But his normally brown skin was sallow in the dim light of the bedside lamp, and he took short, shallow breaths.

She realized he had been calling her name.

"You okay, Gabie?" Justine sat up.

He exhaled. "Bad dreams. Getting up the strength to go to the bathroom. I'll be fine once I get there—it's just making it to the door. I was thinking about crawling. Thought I'd better wake you up instead of scaring you with the commotion if I fall down."

"Do you want help?"

Gabie inhaled. "You in any shape to do it? I'm gonna have to lean hard on you, and I can't stand any contact with my back."

"We can try."

"Thanks, Tine."

She sat next to Gabie. He put his arm around her shoulders.

"One-two-three, *up,*" she said softly, and stood.

"Auugggh!" Pain knifed through her as they both moaned, agony knifing through her gut. Gabie wrenched sideways, away from her, and for a moment they wobbled back and forth. Justine braced herself against his weight to keep them upright. Then his hand fumbled lower on her upper arm and he pulled himself back toward her. They wavered, then steadied. Gabie kept shaking his head.

"You gonna be able to do this?"

"Hurts like a son-of-a-bitch," he said, panting between words. "Oh God. Serg left more of that painkiller in the bathroom. One for each of us. Other reason to wake you. Need it. Both of us." He straightened, voice quavering. "All right. Let's do this."

They made their way, step by painful step, to the bathroom door. Gabie whimpered with each movement. He grabbed the doorframe with both hands, wincing as a moan escaped him, then reached for the counter.

"I've got it now, Tine. If you'll just wait—"

"Right here, Gabie."

She leaned against the wall as Gabie closed the door, breathing shallowly to channel her own pain. Waited. Groans. Sound of toilet flushing, then water running. She straightened up as the door opened, and moved back into place under Gabie's left arm. He leaned heavily on her, but seemed steadier as they went back to the bed.

Gabie sat and rested his weight on his hands again. "Tine. If you could bring me that glass of painkiller in the bathroom, I'd be obliged. I didn't want to drink it before I got back on the bed. The other one's for you."

"No problem." She hurried to the bathroom and got both glasses, one marked GABRIEL, the other, JUSTINE. After she set hers on the nightstand, she offered the other one to Gabie, keeping both hands available to steady it. He drank it slowly, then handed the glass back to her.

Then he exhaled sharply. "All right. Here goes. Back on the bed. Process hurts like a son-of-a-bitch."

"Want help?"

He shook his head. "No. I just have to move carefully." Gabie eased himself back onto his stomach, punctuated with grunts, groans, and expletives in a mixture of English, French, and Russian.

"Ah," he sighed when he was finally settled. "If you could flip the blanket over my legs, Tine, that would be helpful."

She carefully covered Gabie's legs, cringing at the sight of his back. Old scars mixed with new weals. Old scars from other times when Gabie had intervened to protect her from Daddy-damned-dearest's rages, when he had lived with them after his own family had died in a plane crash.

"I'm sorry, Gabie. So sorry."

"For what? You didn't do this to me."

"But if you hadn't stepped in—"

Gabie sighed. "I was already on my way to the penthouse to get an old book for Donna-gran when I heard you scream, Tine. I *couldn't* just turn and go back downstairs. I paged Uncle Gerry, then hit the door."

She picked up her glass and sat on the floor next to the bed, resting her back against it, sipping the drink.

"Thank you, Gabie. Daddy-damn-dearest was going to inject me with something."

"Psychotropic. Meant to bend you to his will. Serg picked up the injector when he and Piotr supervised moving our things out of the penthouse."

"Do you know where my stuff is? I'd really like to change out of these slacks."

"I'm afraid I don't. I'm—in and out when it comes to what's going on," he said.

Silence. She drank the rest of the painkiller.

"I don't understand why Philip is so determined to marry you off," Gabie said. "Damn it, you're only seventeen. You haven't graduated from high school yet. What the *hell* is he thinking?"

She turned her head to look at him. "He doesn't want me disgracing the Family."

Gabie snorted. "Donna-gran's right. That's bullshit."

"It gets worse. You didn't hear what my fucking father said. Daddy-fucking-dearest called me a slut. Just like my mother." Justine choked a little on those words. Her mother Renate might have been a suicidal drunk, but she was most *definitely* not a slut. "And he suggested that you and I were hopping into bed together."

"*What?*" Gabie raised his head. "Fucking hell. Damn him. Damn him to hell." He choked. "You're as close to me as my sister would be if she were still alive, damn it. You *are* my sister, as far as I'm concerned. Oh, that motherfucker. What the hell does he think we are?"

"Donna-gran hit Daddy-fucking-dearest with his control words in the strongest damn tone I've ever heard from her after he said that. It just barely made my fucking father choke." Justine took a deep breath."

"Aw, *fuck*." Gabie sighed. "Tine, Uncle Gerry's right. We need to get you hooked up fast with someone safe, who can protect you. I'm really sorry. You deserve better."

"But who's both safe and powerful?" Her voice trembled. Some old man like Braun?

Well, she possibly could end up being a rich widow in her own right. That had its advantages.

Another exhale. "Donald Atwood is the best person that Serg and I could think of. Financial management heir. He's a programming wizard."

"That doesn't sound—too awful."

"He's twenty-six, Tine. Couple of years older than me. Mannerly, careful. But he loves a lot of women. Oh, does he love women. He'd be honest with you, though, if he started straying. He isn't a shit or a perv. And he'll stand up to Philip on your behalf. He's done a lot of financial investigative and programming work with Piotr and Serg. They know him better than I do. He would be open to keeping things contractual, and I'm pretty damn confident that he will do right by you."

"How soon can I talk to him?" They were on a schedule, after all. And contractual—after what had happened to her mother, love didn't appeal to Justine. As long as a marriage protected her until she could access her Family funds independently—that was all she needed.

"Serg said Donald could come by in the afternoon. If you're agreeable."

"I am." She blinked, her eyelids heavy. "Getting tired."

"So am I. Go ahead and turn out the light, if you don't need it to get to the sofa."

"All right." She rose. Before she flicked off the light, she kissed the back of her cousin's head. "Thank you, Gabie. Thank you for saving me."

"You're welcome," he murmured.

She found her way back to the sofa and curled up on it again.

Thankfully, sleep came quickly.

GABIE PRESIDED OVER HER FIRST MEETING WITH DONALD ATWOOD THE following afternoon, acting as the Family's representative. He straddled a straight-backed chair as he and Justine waited in Donna-gran's living room, leaning on the chair's back, wearing pajama pants and a soft, light shirt that he left unbuttoned. Serg and Donald entered, and Gabie straightened up but did not rise.

"Gabe. I heard what happened. Are you doing all right?" Donald's concern sounded real, not feigned, as he bowed politely to Gabie.

Justine studied Donald. Athletic build, medium height. Neatly styled short blond hair with bright blue eyes. He wore a dark blue double-breasted suit, elegantly fitted to his lean frame, light blue shirt, and a golden tie with matching pocket square. Fine dark blue Italian loafers on his feet.

Easy on the eyes. She could live with *this*, so much better than Walter Braun with sagging jowls, wispy white scattered hair, and soft but prying and persistent hands.

"I've been better." Gabie inclined his head. "Serg told you the situation?"

Donald's jaw tightened. "Yes. I—I don't have words. Or at least polite words."

"Considering I call my father Daddy-fucking-dearest at times, I don't think you need to be concerned about *being polite*," Justine said.

Donald's brows raised and the slightest smile twitched the corners of his lips. "You must be Justine. I'm Donald." He bowed to her, deeper than to Gabie.

She rose and curtseyed, then extended her hand. "Considering the circumstances, I think we can cut through the bullshit. I am C-19 safe."

"As am I." Donald took her hand, and kissed it. "These circumstances are fucking barbaric, and under the normal scheme of things I wouldn't even think of courting you, Justine. Not because there's anything wrong with you—it's just that you're so young. Nine years is a big difference at our ages."

"My fucking father is trying to force me to marry a man in his eighties, Donald. Nine years is nothing in comparison." His hand was firm, hard, and *warm* in hers, unlike Braun's soft, sweaty, clammy hands. She might be able to tolerate these hands on her body.

That slight smile twitched bigger. "You have me there, Justine. Shall we talk?"

"Absolutely."

He kept hold of her hand as they sat on Donna-gran's couch, still faintly pink where she had bled on it, even after a thorough cleaning this morning.

"All right. Do we flirt, or do we get down to business?" he asked.

Not at all what she had expected. "Business first. Gabie tells me you like women. Many women." She drew a shuddering breath. "I'm not sure, but I think I'm asexual."

"No beating around the bush, then. I like your directness, Justine. And yes. I enjoy many women. You're—not my usual choice because of your age. I promise discretion."

"Discretion is good."

Was it bad that she felt relief instead of—what? Jealousy? What was she supposed to feel?

"Agreed." He took a deep breath. "I won't force myself on you, but we should plan to consummate the marriage promptly. After that— wait until you're eighteen."

"Avoid that ground for forced annulment?" she asked, keeping her voice calm, though her stomach plummeted at the thought of sex with *anyone.*

"Precisely. Though it may not be a necessity. I won't know until I get some advice." His hand relaxed slightly. "Other details. When is your birthday?"

"I'll be eighteen in March."

"Have you completed high school?"

"Not yet."

"What are your plans for finishing?" Donald eyed her. "I assume you want to do that. From what Serg and Gabe have told me, you're a smart, ambitious woman."

Smart, ambitious woman.

She liked that. Braun had told her to shut her mouth one time too many, and he poo-pooed the need for her to finish school.

"Complete the last semester of high school. After that—college. Study business and management."

"I'd suggest accounting as a major, management as a minor, if that works for you," Donald said. "Can you finish your high school remotely? We shouldn't go back to the US until you turn eighteen."

"Yes, I started the transfer process to a remote program this morning. And I agree about not going back to the US."

It felt so strange to be discussing marriage in these terms.

"College applications?"

"Family tradition is the University of Paris," Gabie said. "Not a good idea. Too close to the Family."

"We'll talk that over, Justine," Donald said. "I will pay for it, of course. Wherever you want to go."

"Thank you." He had to have some sort of flaw. But what? His love for women—many women?

She could live with that. And it wasn't like she would be tied to him forever.

"How long do you think we should agree to remain married? With an option to reconsider and extend, if necessary."

"At least until I'm old enough to collect my funds at age twenty-four."

"Perhaps a year past that, to be safe. Seven years?"

"Seven years," she echoed. "All right."

"Then let's discuss prenuptial agreements," Donald said. "Besides you, who should I message mine to?"

"Gabie and Serg are my representatives," she said. "They'll handle running it through the lawyers."

"And Serg knows who my attorneys are." Donald nodded. "I'll support you until you come into your funds. We'll negotiate after that." He exhaled. "I'll ask you to keep my business arrangements confidential—I expect that you want the same."

"Yes." The Family attorneys would know how to phrase that part. "And property divisions?"

"What's yours is yours, what's mine is mine, and we'll split ownership of property obtained after our marriage fifty-fifty." Donald paused. "You get a personal allowance for clothing and other needs to match the one I assign myself—actually, more to start with, since you'll need appropriate things as my wife. I assume you don't have access to anything other than what you brought here for the holiday. Clothing. Jewelry. Other items."

"That's—generous." Braun was a notorious penny-pincher.

Donald shrugged. "I prefer to enjoy my life, and I don't see any reason why you shouldn't as well. You shouldn't be penalized for marrying young to escape that asshole father of yours."

"Thank you," she whispered, blinking hard as tears formed. "Are you for real?"

Donald smiled. "Darling, marriage to an upper-level Martiniere heir enhances my prestige in financial circles. I hadn't planned to marry for a while, because the wrong marriage could bring about disaster. You're helping me as much as I'm helping you. And—I hope that whatever becomes of us in the long run, we can continue to have a beneficial relationship. Is that too pragmatic? Not romantic enough?"

"This isn't about romance," she said.

"I understand. Shall we set a date, my dear?"

"As quickly as we can finalize the arrangements."

"Engagement ring. What do you prefer for a stone? Diamond? Ruby? Emerald?"

"A star sapphire," she said. "Blue, or lavender. Set in silver or platinum. I'll give you my size."

"A blue or lavender star sapphire set in silver or platinum. That can be done quickly. I'll bring it tomorrow." He delicately stroked her face. "Justine, I will do my damnedest to keep this abuse from happening to you again. No matter what happens between us in the long run." He shook his head and his voice hardened. "Your son-of-a-bitch of a father. This is so fucking *wrong*. I should be romancing you several years from now, after you've finished college. Courting you. Not treating this as a business transaction."

More tears came to her eyes. "Thank you, Donald."

"May I kiss you?"

"We're engaged now, I guess. So—yes."

His lips brushed against hers. She waited for that spark, the heat that other girls giggled about which would make her want to go further.

Nothing.

But he was gentle. He appeared to be mindful. He didn't slobber and paw at her like Braun.

He would get her away from Daddy-fucking-dearest.

3 / INTERLUDE ONE

July, 2086

JUSTINE BLINKED BACK TEARS. SHE HAD FORGOTTEN HOW IT FELT TO BE that desperate young woman. Walled those emotions away for *years*, keeping them at a distance while working with young women in difficult circumstances, instead of letting herself feel that pain. Told herself that it was *their* pain, not hers.

This story brought it all back.

Mike pushed himself up. He pulled a wad of tissues from a box on his nightstand and handed them to her. "Justine. God. I'm so fucking sorry for what my progenitor did to you." He winced. "And every time I revert, I must remind you—God. I'm sorry."

Justine wiped her eyes, shaking her head. "Mikey. It wasn't *you*. It was *him*."

Gabie's digi stirred. *"She's glossing over a lot of what happened. It was much worse. Tine's face was bruised for days after—"* He shook his head. *"Gerard extracted me from the penthouse at gunpoint. Even then, it was touchy until Serg and Piotr showed up. I'm surprised that Gerard didn't challenge Philip to be the Martiniere right then and there—but he was always cautious. I don't think he really wanted the job."*

JoAnn hugged Justine. "Oh God. That was awful."

"It got better," Justine said. She exhaled. "All the same, one difficult tale at a time, all right?"

Mike leaned over and took her free hand. "I'm sorry," he repeated.

Justine gulped. "Mikey. Watching you grow up to be so different from Daddy-damned-dearest was the best thing for me. It helped exorcise any notion I had that I might go down the same path—you and Gabe both did that for me. There was something sick and twisted about him."

"Mental illness runs in the Martinieres," Gabie said. *"I struggled with anger for years."*

Lily's digi stirred. *"Is that why Philip was able to possess me?"* Her lower lip trembled, and Ruby reached out to her granddaughter, taking her into her arms.

"We thought that your mother's exposure to indenture hormone-based mind control conditioning had warped your cognitive processes," Brandon said to his daughter. *"We didn't know that Philip's digi existed and had targeted you."*

Justine blinked back more tears. It was painful observing the vast difference between the saneness of Lily's digi and what she had been when alive. All the *might have beens.*

"It wasn't just the Martinieres," Ruby said. *"My family, the Barkleys. My father. I saw it in cousins. You got hit with a double genetic whammy, Lily-hon, because psychosis ran in my family as well."*

"Am I at risk?" Ron asked, his voice quavering.

"No," Mike said firmly.

"No," Ruby and Brandon echoed.

Brandon continued. *"It's one reason why you saw a counselor regularly from a young age, Ronnie. Between what we were going through with Lily, and what we knew about the Martiniere and Barkley heritage—I wanted to be certain."*

"We wanted to be certain," Gabe said.

"It manifested as depression and self-mutilation in me," Mike said. He swallowed hard. "But like you, Ron, I went through counseling early on, because I had a ton of issues. Still do." He coughed. "I hate to break this up, but I'm getting tired. Aunt Justine. Thank you."

Aunt Justine. Not daughter. She smiled at Mike, thankful that he deliberately chose to claim their adoptive rather than their biological relationship.

"I've had enough, too," she said. "But I'll share more, later on. If this one wasn't too much."

"It was intense," Mike said. "But thank you."

The digis faded away. Justine rose, shaky, and kissed Mike's forehead.

"I hope this didn't take too much out of you," he said. "But I am grateful for whatever you feel like sharing. Thank you."

"You're welcome."

All the same, Justine leaned heavily on Ron as they returned to the truck for the trek back to Moondance. And they were barely out of the driveway when she fell asleep.

———

ANNOYINGLY, THAT NIGHT WAS A WAKEFUL ONE. JUSTINE WASN'T CERTAIN if it was due to her normal insomnia or if telling *that story* kept her from sleeping. She tried to read, but had problems engaging with the story. A video?

But as Justine considered her options, she realized that another, less-intrusive digi presence hovered nearby.

"Ruby?" she said tentatively.

Ruby's form shimmered into firmness. *"Just keeping an eye on you. You looked pretty tired after that story—it was hideous."*

"It's probably the worst one I'll tell," Justine sighed. "I—can't tell what Daddy-damn-dear did to Gabie before—I just can't. That was the last time he beat Gabie."

"There was one other time after that," Ruby said. *"When Philip demanded that Gabe divorce me, at the end of our first marriage. Gabe never told me the full story, but I saw the aftereffect."* She shuddered. *"I'm surprised he walked away alive. I saw him the morning after. Hideous. Broken ribs. Internal bleeding."*

"Our father was a fucking psychopath," Justine said bitterly.

"You're all right, though?" Ruby stroked Justine's cheek. Justine

closed her eyes, savoring the contact. Her sister-in-law's digital touch was a faint whisper of a caress.

"I'll be fine," she said. "I had forgotten how angry Donald was when he saw what Daddy-poo had done to me and Gabie."

"*I never understood the relationship between you and Donald,*" Ruby said. "*Did you love each other?*"

"In our own ways, yes," Justine said. "Donald definitely loved my mind and we shared many goals—except that he enjoyed sex. Not as often as he implied in public, because of physical reasons, but when he had sex, he wanted it to be special. I—I don't know if I am truly asexual, or if I just shut down from any physical input because of things that happened to me as a child and teenager." She paused. "Donald and I founded the Rescue Angel together. He fervently believed in it."

And now she knew what the next tale she told Mike would be.

———

Two days later, Mike waited for them in a hospital recliner on the Double R's spacious front porch. The location provided a view of the occasional high clouds skittering from the south over the Thunder Mountains, now free of snow. It was sheltered from heavy sun until late afternoon, allowing them to stay outside and enjoy the typical early-afternoon breeze that began cooling things off.

Ron guided Justine up the ramp and settled her in one of the chairs next to Mike, angled so she also saw the mountains. She assessed the situation as she settled in. Smudgie and Spot rose from their places by Mike and came to her, hind ends wiggling, begging for pats. Mike grinned at her and them. The pallor that marked his face the other day had faded. No dark circles under his eyes today.

"Pain better?" she asked.

"It's a good day," he said. "Still can't make it up the stairs, but—" he paused as JoAnn came out the front door, carrying a pitcher of lemonade and glasses. "I can at least walk to the porch without passing out."

"Yesterday's video consult with Dr. Pramula was encouraging," JoAnn said as she filled the glasses. "Cautious, but it's possible that

Mike might just need upgrades to his heart and lung hardware, not go through full replacement. Still surgery, but replacement of components rather than everything. Fewer possibilities for rejection."

"That *is* good news," Justine said. JoAnn's expression seemed less worried than before. And the eagerness of the dogs for her pats—though Smudgie now veered off to Ron—was also a good sign. "The story I had in mind for today is probably one of the lighter ones, to go along with it."

"Nothing could be more depressing than that last story," Ron said, shivering. "I still cringe when I think about my relationship to *that man.*"

Gabie, followed by the other digis, shimmered into place.

"You should understand what lurks within the Family, Ron," he said. *"I dealt with a lot of rage. That's a facet of Philip in me."* He smiled at Ruby. *"Your great-grandmother helped me overcome that during the last thirteen years of my life."*

"Don't kid yourself. Your second wife laid much of the foundation for our healing," Ruby said tartly. *"If we had continued in the same vein as we had during our first marriage—"*

"We would have gotten there," Gabie said.

"In any case, that's another story," Brandon said. He nodded to Justine. *"Last recording came out well, Aunt Justine. So what's the topic for today?"*

"I'm going to tell how Donald and I laid the foundations for our later political and social justice work," Justine said. "Ruby said something to me about not understanding the relationship that Donald and I had. It was certainly—not a typical marriage, or a typical divorce."

She sighed, remembering her ex-husband. Partner. More partner than spouse, but without Donald's presence, above and beyond rescuing her from Daddy-damn-dearest, she doubted that she could have done as much over the years as she had.

As *they* had.

4 / FOUNDATIONS

"TINE. TINE." GABIE RESTED HIS HAND ON HER SHOULDER, SHAKING HER gently.

Justine startled up. "What's going on?"

Gabie's face was grim and he was fully dressed, wearing his favorite black and gold morning dress suit with gold cravat and gold-laced black brocade waistcoat. "Donald's waiting. We need to get you married, *now*."

"But my things—" Her plans were based on having another day to prepare.

"Need to leave what isn't already packed. Late last night, Donna-gran got wind of a scheme by Philip to keep us from leaving. Gerard and Piotr have our escape set up. Serg's implementing it."

She nodded. "My clothing—"

"In the bathroom. Cousin Kendra loaned you a wedding outfit."

"All right." She sometimes borrowed Kendra's clothing, so it would fit. Justine slid off the sofa—no other place for her to sleep in Donna-gran's suite, and she wasn't about to let Gabie insist on being a gentleman when he hurt so bad.

A garment bag hung from the door. Justine unzipped it and pulled out two jackets, a strapless beaded white and gold bodice, and white slacks. Matching shoes were in a side bag, with socks and underwear tucked in a side pocket. One jacket was floor-length with a train—Justine remembered admiring this outfit at Kendra's wedding last summer. The other was shorter. Both had notes pinned to them.

LEAVE THIS ONE WITH SECURITY AFTER YOU'RE MARRIED, the note pinned to the floor-length jacket read.

GOOD LUCK. OUR THOUGHTS, PRAYERS, AND GOOD WISHES GO WITH YOU AND DONALD. STAY SAFE, AND CONGRATULATIONS ON GETTING AWAY, the note pinned to the shorter, heavier jacket read.

Justine blinked back wetness.

I owe you, Kendra.

Cousin Christopher's sister, from Britain. Just older enough that Justine didn't know her well. She admired Kendra—her cousin was outspoken, an economic analyst at a London brokerage firm, married to a psychologist. Justine wanted to be like Kendra someday.

Justine dressed, and carefully applied her makeup. No jewelry handy except the diamond studs she left by the makeup bag last night. The only other gem available was the lavender star sapphire engagement ring that Donald slid on her finger yesterday afternoon. He found just what she had envisioned—a lavender star sapphire surrounded by small diamonds and pearls, set in platinum. With a matching wedding ring.

She wondered if Gabie played a role in finding this ring. It *was* the sort of thing he was good at locating.

Makeup finished, Justine carefully placed the bag and the long coat back in the garment bag, reminding herself to grab the makeup when she sent the long coat back.

Gabie leaned on a cane as she came out. She carried the garment bag over one of her shoulders. He nodded at the sight of her, half-smiling as he offered his arm.

"Cousin Arthur and Gerard are keeping Philip distracted," he said. "We've got a short time to get out of here without interference. Let's go."

"All right."

The house was silent and dark as they descended the stairs. Gabie's hand quivered in hers, revealing the effort he exerted to move normally and stay upright. He leaned on Justine as much as he did the cane, and she breathed shallowly because of the sharp pain in her ribs.

Piotr waited for them at the door. He helped Justine juggle her overcoat and garment bag. He started to help Gabie with his overcoat. Gabie waved him off.

"You will be warm enough, Gabriel?"

"I can't tolerate any more weight on my back." Gabie winced. "I'd rather be cold. That hurts less."

Piotr's lips tightened. "Take care. Both of you." He kissed Justine on both cheeks, then patted Gabie's forearm before opening the door.

Donald and Serg waited just outside in the gray dawn. Three black SUVs idled in the courtyard.

"My dear," Donald said, taking the garment bag, then offering his arm.

Justine took it, trembling, her focus suddenly on *this man who was going to be her husband.* His overcoat obscured what he was wearing. Donald helped her into the middle SUV, then handed off her garment bag to waiting security before joining her.

Serg settled Gabie in the front seat, then headed for the first SUV. The vehicles glided away from the door, courtyard gates opening slowly. Justine shivered. Was she really escaping Daddy-damn-dearest? They had to get past those gates first.

Donald's arm delicately tightened around her shoulders. "Just a little while, and you're safe." He felt steady, comforting. But how hard would he fight for her?

Several streets away, they passed a fleet of dark gray SUVs going the opposite direction. Justine inhaled sharply, recognizing the plates. Walter Braun's. The one time she consented to go out to dinner with him, she rode in his vehicle. A mistake. She spent the whole drive fighting him off. No way would she forget *that* SUV.

"Close," Gabie snapped. "Closer than I'd like." He pulled out his phone. "Serg. You saw them?"

"I did," Serg's voice echoed from the speaker. "Philip advanced the agenda."

"The agenda?" Justine repeated.

Gabie turned in his seat, wincing at the movement. "Philip intended to break down Donna-gran's door this morning, hand you off to Braun, and do—who knows what to me." He grabbed the back of the seat to hold himself steady.

"Is Donna-gran safe?" Justine asked.

"She already left the house," Gabie said. "Once you're married, she's taking me to her estate in Quebec so I can recover."

"Oh God," Justine whispered. If it wasn't for the ache in her ribs, she would lean against Donald.

Donald patted her shoulder. "Here. We rushed you out, but I have a present for you. I was going to give it to you later, but...you need jewelry for your wedding."

He reached inside his coat and produced a box. Justine took it, easing the lid open.

A diamond, pearl and lavender star sapphire necklace, set in platinum, with matching earrings.

"From me and Gabe," Donald said. "He found it; I paid for it. I didn't anticipate having to leave so quickly that you wouldn't be able to wear appropriate jewelry of your own choice, but I wanted you to have jewelry to match your ring."

"Thank you. Thank both of you."

Gabie smirked at her.

She glanced at Donald. "Could you—would you put them on me?"

"I would be delighted." Donald carefully fastened the necklace, then removed her studs, putting them in the box before slipping on her earrings.

"Thank you," she whispered.

"They look good on you," Gabie said. "A better match than I thought."

"Oh Gabie," she murmured, overcome.

THERE WERE TWO CEREMONIES, WHICH WAS TYPICAL IN FRANCE—FIRST THE official, legal one, and then the ceremony in front of a priest, in a chapel and not one of the huge, echoing, Gothic churches. Neither

Justine nor Donald took off their overcoats for the legal ceremony. But the religious ceremony—she slipped on the long jacket with train. Donald removed his overcoat to reveal an elegant dark blue morning coat with lighter blue cravat and waistcoat similar to Gabie's.

Gabie gave her away for the second ceremony as Serg took pictures. And Donna-gran was present, waiting for them in the chapel. For some reason this ceremony felt closer to the real one, even though Justine didn't wear a veil.

And then she repacked the long jacket, grabbed her makeup before handing the garment bag to security, donned short jacket and overcoat.

They raced to the airstrip where two corporate jets waited.

"Good luck, my dear," Donna-gran said, kissing Justine's cheek. "I'm glad you're safe now. Come visit after your birthday."

"Thank you," she whispered.

She tapped her fingers on her seat's arm nervously during takeoff, until Donald—*her husband*—gently wrapped his hand around hers. They didn't speak until the pilot announced that they were now in international airspace.

Donald exhaled. "We're clear."

"Now what?"

"Things are not as dire as I first feared. Piotr and your uncle Gerard have informed your father of our marriage by now," Donald said. "We are staying in a villa on a Caribbean island—Solitaire—a very exclusive resort, with tight security. We will be there for a few months, while *we* decide where home will be. We have connectivity for your school and my—hopefully *our*—work. My mother is there, to provide whatever other support we need." He smiled faintly. "Philip Martiniere will not tangle with her."

"I have no idea who your mother is," Justine said.

"Barbara Atwood is a majority shareholder in the bank that holds the largest line of credit for PJM Corp, your father's personal corporation, under her maiden name of Barbara Knowles." Donald's eyes creased, as if he were grinning, but he didn't smile. "She's the majority Solitaire shareholder—makes it her winter home. The biggest challenges were getting you safely out of the house, then us married and off the ground. Finding a safe place to hide was a lesser priority. I couldn't promise you anything, because I couldn't confirm the arrangements until last night."

"Oh my God. Really?" She stared at Donald.

His mother was Barbara Knowles.

"Really." A smirk finally matched his eyes.

She broke into half-laughter, half-sobs, unable to stop as she realized just *who it was* that she had married.

Donald Atwood was more than just Gabie and Serg's friend.

Barbara Knowles was at least three times as wealthy as Walter Braun. Widowed shortly after Donald's birth, never remarried. Connected to the British royal family by marriage. Distant cousins, but still—royal beyond Philip's wildest dreams. The Atwood family was highly secretive, more so than the Martinieres.

She had actually married up, despite Donald's claim that marriage to an upper-level Martiniere heir would enhance his status.

Donald eased the seat arm up and gently held her while she sobbed with relief.

"It's over now, Justine. You're safe. He can't touch you. He can't force you to marry that man."

She raised her head. "And us?" Her voice shook. "We need to consummate—"

"Mother's support means we don't have to rush. You need to heal first. Physically and mentally. Make sure you don't have internal injuries. Your grandmother's servant suggested that you be checked over by a doctor, because she fears you're hurt worse than any of us realize. We'll do that once we arrive."

"But—" Joey had always made noises about *male desires.* Another reason why Gabie and Serg taught her self-defense. She constantly kept her rooms locked and alarmed whenever staying in the same house as Joey. When he got drunk—and Daddy-damn-dearest, for that matter—she shied away from the memories of *that* night.

Thank God both Gabie and Serg had been at the house that time.

"I don't want our first time to be hurried, rushed, and painful," Donald said. "Inflicting pain and being forceful isn't something I enjoy. You said you thought you might be asexual—well, then, no need to make the experience any worse than it has to be, hmm? If at all. Your choice."

"Are you for real?" she gulped, breaking into a fresh spate of sobs.

Donald held her until she was cried out. Then he gently raised her chin with his index finger, so that he gazed steadily into her eyes.

"I look forward to getting to know *you*, Justine Solange Martiniere-Atwood. We're committed to spending seven years together. I would much rather start on a pleasant footing. When and if you are ever ready—then we'll make love. But we don't have to do it for the sake of holding off your father. Fortunately."

"Call me Barbie," Donald's mother said after she hugged Donald, then took Justine's hand. Barbie scowled, and glanced at Donald. "Oh my God, Don. Those bruises and stitches look worse than the pictures you sent. *He* did this to her?"

"Both him and Joseph," Donald said, his voice hard. "And Donna's indentured nurse fears there may be internal injuries. We've had no time to check with a doctor. Justine didn't dare step outside Donna's suite until we were on the way to get married."

Justine blinked under Barbie's scrutiny. Even though Donald had encouraged her to rest, she still was achy and stiff. Her head throbbed and she hurt all over.

Worry tightened Donald's voice. "Justine's pain medication was supposed to last longer, but she had to hit it hard. We ran out during the flight."

Barbie shook her head. "I'll call a doctor. Let's get her to the villa. You take care of the luggage and the house setup; I'll take care of your wife."

Donald kissed Justine's forehead. "You're all right going with my mother? I need to code the security systems."

"I think I'd better get used to it," Justine said, unable to stifle a nervous quaver.

"Oh, honey," Barbie said. "I went to school with your mother. What *that man*—" she spat out the words, "did to Renate was unconscionable. Don didn't have to say anything more than *Mother, I'm marrying Philip Martiniere's daughter to get her out of a bad situation.* I couldn't help Renate, but I can certainly help Renate's daughter."

Justine gulped and fought back tears, overwhelmed.

"Looking at you is like looking at Renate," Barbie choked. "Oh honey. I failed my best friend from school years. Anything I can do to help her daughter. *Anything.*"

Justine shivered and exhaled hard. She let Barbie guide her to a waiting SUV.

Safe at last.

She wondered if Gabie and Serg knew this about Donald.

THE NEXT WEEK PASSED IN A BLUR, THANKS TO PAIN MEDICATION AND allowing herself to disengage, rest, and heal in the sunny quiet of the villa. Donald and Barbie guarded Justine, along with a full contingent of hired, not indentured, staff. She slept in her own bedroom, adjoining Donald's, with a connecting door. After the first night, when she woke him while screaming during a nightmare of Philip chasing her around the Hôtel Martiniere with a bullwhip, they left the door open between their rooms.

It seemed to help.

All the same, she spent several nights shaking and quivering in Donald's lap after waking from nightmares.

"Some wife I am," she said on that last horrific night. "We haven't even slept together."

"I knew what I was getting into," Donald said. "It's all right. It really is." He sighed. "My mother has talked about your mother. She wondered if you were safe, ever since your mother died. When Serg approached me about your situation, I couldn't turn him down. I—" he hesitated, then weakly chuckled. "I couldn't reject the possibility of being a knight in shining armor. Blame that on how my mother raised me, I suppose. And yes—a bit of pragmatism. Marrying a high-level Martiniere heir, even for a short time, adds to my prestige. My choice to marry you was utterly pragmatic and in some ways, selfish."

"I can respect pragmatism," she said. "I'm my father's daughter in that aspect."

"And I'm my mother's son," he said.

Justine wondered what he meant by that.

January, 2027

She found out soon enough what Donald meant by *I'm my mother's son*. Barbie and Donald preferred to work outside, by the pool, with occasional swim breaks. Justine easily fell into the routine. It helped her unwind, though the slightest raised voice, the hint of anger in a vocal tone, any unaccounted-for thump or slam nearby startled her and set her heart racing, disrupted her focus.

But she could dive into the pool and swim a couple of laps until the tension ebbed. Donald often joined her, encouraging her to sit on the pool's edge for a few minutes afterward before racing back to her schoolwork. Sometimes Barbie sat with them as well.

"Is it getting better?" Barbie asked one afternoon, two weeks after their arrival, as they sat on the edge of the pool. "You don't seem quite so jumpy, but you're still losing weight from all the swimming."

Justine swallowed hard. Today was difficult, one of *those* days. A backfire on the street nearest the villa. A dropped, shattered dish in the kitchen. Unknown voices in the distance. All startling her up, on her feet and ready to run before she thought about it. The rhythmic swish of Donald's swimming soothed her, but—

"No more nightmares," she said. "But I just keep feeling like Daddy-damn-dearest is lurking around."

Barbie patted her hand. "PTSD, honey. Are you ready for counseling yet?"

Justine shook her head. "I want to—keep trying on my own." Philip's scornful comments about *counseling* echoed through her thoughts. Going into counseling meant he had won. "I just have to keep working on things. Find something to do besides schoolwork. I'm already way ahead in my classes and my teachers want me to slow down." If she kept up this pace, she would graduate just before her birthday.

And then what?

"Work isn't going to heal you, dear."

"No, but it keeps my mind busy. Then I won't think about things." She gulped. "Talking to someone—" she shook her head. "I can't. Not more than I've already done with you and Donald."

Barbie was quiet for a few moments, swirling her feet in the water. "How triggering would it be for you to handle data about women who have gone through similar experiences? I've seen what you're doing in stats for your classes. You're capable of working at a much higher level."

"I—could try it. Don't know how I'd react."

"You're good at stats."

"Gabie coached me a lot in the summers," she said. "I was interested, so he walked me through spreadsheets and data analysis. I seem to have a knack for it."

Barbie nodded. "All right. I'll send you the files. I need a fundraising presentation slide deck. It will take you less time to crunch the numbers and make pretty charts than it would me."

"Fundraising presentation?"

"I'm the founder of a nonprofit called Real Lives for Women. RLW."

"Oh." Justine had heard about RLW—their primary mission was helping women escape abusive situations and gain reproductive freedom. "So that's what Donald meant about being his mother's son."

"Don has been helpful in many ways," Barbie said. "Including work on our fundraisers."

"I see," Justine said, focusing on the water and the tiny waves made by swirling her feet. She summoned the courage to look back up. "Am I one of your projects?"

"Heavens, no," Barbie said. "You're my son's wife. If he hadn't married you—then probably yes. But Don chose to marry you—and Justine, given the degree to which he has dated women over the years, that says a lot. You're not the first woman of our social class he's helped out of a tight spot. But you're the one he married."

"But why? I mean, we've got an agreement." She swallowed hard. What *had* Donald told his mother about their marriage?

"I know. A commitment to seven years, then divorce. All the same —my son saw something in you, just from what your cousins have told him, just from what he was able to research before meeting you— and what he saw when you met." Barbie smiled. "When he talked to me that night before you married, it wasn't about rescuing my old friend's daughter. Don talked about you being beautiful, brave, and brilliant. That something shone through you that called to him. Something true, strong, and honorable. A woman whose mind and spirit he respected. Don admires bravery in others. He felt yours was above and beyond the norm."

"Oh."

Barbie patted her hand again. "What I heard was a man who was falling in love, Justine. Yes, you're the daughter of my good friend. But you make me realize that Philip Martiniere made *one* good thing, and that was you. Thanks to my dear friend Renate."

Justine burst into tears at that. Barbie hugged her.

Hands suddenly on her legs, but Justine recognized the touch as Donald, and safe. She smiled weakly at him.

"Is everything all right?" he asked, peering at her, worried.

"Justine is helping me with the RLW slide deck presentation," Barbie said. "And—I talked about our conversation the night before your marriage."

Donald nodded. "You're all right?" he asked Justine.

She gazed at him. He cared for her. He *honestly* cared for her. She wasn't just a rescue project—something she had started to wonder over the past week.

He took her hands. "I meant what I told my mother that night, and even more so since we've been married." Donald gently pulled at her and she slid into his arms. "You are amazing, Justine."

Justine gulped. "But—" She didn't want to say more with his mother around. Especially about sex.

"My dear, this isn't about sex," Donald murmured into her ear, as if he read her mind. He pulled back. "Come on. Let's go sit in the spa."

Once they reached the shallows, they walked hand-in-hand to the spa. Donald switched it on, and they settled in. He pulled her close.

"Listen," he said quietly. "Your being asexual is not as big an issue as you think. These scars on my abdomen?" He pointed to a four-inch scar that ran down from his belly button. "I have Crohn's Disease. I had a big chunk of both my small intestine and my colon removed when I was a teenager. Not so much that I need an ostomy bag, but enough to affect my libido. The area in my gut that produces the most neurotransmitters, which affects arousal—is gone."

"Oh," she said, her voice very small.

"Not completely gone. But I don't have a high sex drive, though I have a great sensual appreciation for women," he said. He leaned his forehead against hers. "Especially my lovely wife. I enjoy the dating. The company. Flirting. Physical contact, often without sexual arousal." He inhaled deeply. "I have a confession to make."

"What's that?"

"I'm falling madly in love with you. And I am scared to death that I will become a barrier to what you can accomplish. That you will outgrow me. That you are a falcon I'm training and will someday launch."

"Really?"

"The degree to which you've unfolded in these last two weeks— yes." He paused. "I love you, Justine Martiniere-Atwood. I love you more every day."

"I love you," she whispered back. "I'm amazed, but yes."

"Done with the worries about sex?" he asked.

"I'll try to be," she answered.

FEBRUARY, 2027

. . .

Justine had rough moments while crunching the data for Barbie, though not as much as she feared. Even so, she could only work in twenty-minute increments before things became far too real, and she had to take a break. Swim a couple of laps in the pool. Try the tempting snacks that Barbie laid out for her in the kitchen. Walk around the villa.

While the sunlight helped banish the memories from the Hôtel Martiniere, it didn't do a damn thing for the memories from Los Angeles. However, neither Barbie nor Donald preferred the gilded and dark wooden décor that her father found attractive. They favored postmodern minimalist Scandinavian-style décor in white and chrome, with colorful accents. Walking around inside the villa helped Justine separate from the immediacy of her own memories, because it was *so different.*

Reading the files also helped put her own experiences into perspective.

She was fortunate. While her family and class had put her in this position in the first place, it had also been the means of her rescue.

At first, Justine felt guilty. What made her so special?

A quiet inquiry from Donald one evening was enough for her to spill it out. He let her blubber, holding her while she sobbed.

"How did I get so lucky when so many women without my privilege aren't?" she finally wailed.

"Hey. Justine." Donald's voice was steady but quiet, not wavering, no tones. Calming—that had become what *Donald* meant to her.

She sniffled. "Uh-huh?"

Donald pushed a strand of hair out of her eyes. "What happened to you is not about class or privilege. This kind of abuse happens across all economic sectors. Not every woman with economic and class privilege can escape abuse. You are one of the fortunate ones who got away. No blame."

Her mother was an example of *one who couldn't escape,* until Renate killed herself. Justine shivered. She had been so close to taking that option herself—something she could now admit.

That was another night when she didn't sleep well.

Donald kindled an outside fire, wrapped her in a blanket, and held her in his lap all night. They talked in fits and starts between naps and stirring the fire, until the first light of dawn glowed over the ocean.

By then, she felt truly married.

Even though they hadn't made love yet.

"I WANT TO DO MORE FOR RLW," JUSTINE TOLD BARBIE AND DONALD over dinner the day she finished the slide deck work, just before Barbie left for a week of fundraising pitches. "I don't know what. I'm not ready to tell my own story. But I want to help."

Donald grinned.

"I hoped you would say that," Barbie said. "You have a touch for organizing and coordinating data—" her voice trailed off and she nodded at Donald. "You've wanted someone trustworthy to work on the resource lists and coordinate transports so we can expand our outreach, Don. You've married the person who can do it."

Donald reached out to rest his hand on Justine's. "We'll start tomorrow."

HER FIRST CLUE ABOUT THE SERIOUSNESS OF THIS WORK WAS THAT THEY met in Donald's office, under the highest security, and not by the pool.

"What we're doing has illegal components to it," Donald said.

Justine nodded. She had already assumed that, given the security. "Indentureds and contraception?"

"Some of it." Donald paused. "This is in direct conflict with some of the Martiniere Group operations, dear. Is that going to be a problem?"

She shrugged. "Only as much as it affects my eventual ability to collect my funds. I'd prefer not to harm Gabie, Serg, or innocent Family members. My father and brother, though—" She bared her teeth. "They're fair game. So, what is it? Indentured labor pools? Research?"

"Both. We're seeing forced pregnancies amongst indentured workers," Donald said. "Possible genetic research, perhaps cloning attempts, though the technology is not that advanced. Application of eugenic measures. Coerced mind control programming." He sighed, leaning back in his chair. "The connections amongst divisions are buried deep. Some are Martiniere Group, some are not."

"The Family mind control programming I've undergone might limit what I can do," Justine said.

"That shouldn't affect your work," Donald said. "You'll be identifying resources for indentured women who are being abused, and coordinating transportation."

"What sort of resources?"

"Escape from abusive contracts. Access to abortion and contraception. We have provider lists. But they change regularly based on local enforcement. We have transport, but again, that changes depending on the local situations. The volume and the changes are such that I need someone who can follow and track our clients on a daily basis. I can't keep up with it without making it my full-time job—and I can't afford to do that."

She raised her brows. "We're not living *that* high a life."

Donald had shared the details of their personal finances with her from the very beginning, relaxing when he realized that Justine knew her way around budgeting, didn't spend wildly, and didn't need to be taught financial management. One didn't exist as a high-level Martiniere heir, especially as one of Philip's dependents, without that ability. The allowance she got from Donald was twice what she was used to having—not that he spent foolishly, either.

"I'd rather save drawing on my inheritance for when I get sick. Sooner or later, it will happen. It always does. At some point I'll want to retire for health's sake, but—until that time, I'm going to work as much as I can."

His solemn expression yanked at her. Even though he fit in generous breaks, Donald often worked from early morning until almost bedtime, adding up to at least twelve hours throughout the day. Longer than her father or brother ever did. More like a typical workday for Gabie or Serg.

Justine impulsively went to Donald, hugging him.

For once, it was him clinging to her, not her to him.

EVEN WITH HER NEW TASKS, JUSTINE WRAPPED UP HER HIGH SCHOOL coursework within a few weeks. She was confirming the paperwork needed to issue her diploma and begin college applications when she heard a familiar voice talking to Donald, approaching the pool.

Gabie?

She pressed send on the paperwork as Donald and Gabie entered the pool area. Justine shot up, rushing to meet them. Gabie was dressed more formally than Donald, who preferred to go around the villa in long, baggy swim trunks and not much else. Gabie wore chinos and an unbuttoned, short-sleeved, tropical print shirt over a pale green t-shirt.

"Gabie," she said as Donald wrapped his arm around her.

"Yep," Gabie said, smiling. "Donald told me you were finished with high school. I thought you might want to see at least one Family member on this occasion."

Justine surveyed Gabie. His face was pallid and thin, like he had been sick.

"Are you all right?" she asked.

Gabie winced. "My back got infected. Better now, but I'm going to have a lot more scarring, unfortunately."

"I'd give you a hug but I'm afraid of hurting you. I'm so sorry, Gabie. My fault."

His smile widened. "Tine, you look great. You don't need to apologize. Seeing you happy and relaxed, safe, makes it all worthwhile."

"How's Donna-gran?" Justine asked.

"She's—holding on," Gabe said. "But she faces more surgeries. If you feel safe, plan for one last Family Christmas. I don't know how much longer she can survive."

"Oh. And Serg?"

"Things got rough after we left the house," Gabe said. "Piotr took the blame for allowing it to happen, for Gerard's sake. It's caused a split between him and Serg—he thinks Piotr has been twisted by Philip."

"That's not good news."

"Agreed." Gabie sighed. "I have a limited amount of time, and could spend all of it talking about the situation within the Family. Tine, just be wary when you go back into the world. Even with Donald and Barbie at your side. Philip hates RLW, and I don't know why he stays as clear of it as he does."

Gabie doesn't know about Barbie.

That was—interesting.

<hr>

THE MEETING WAS AN EYE-OPENER. GABIE BRIEFED DONALD ABOUT MIND control programming activities and genetic research forcibly imposed on indentured workers in the Martiniere Group labs. Justine didn't react but plugged in Gabie's data in her files, organizing and securing them.

How long had Gabie been doing this?

Gabie exhaled once he was done. "This is the last briefing, Don. I need to go silent to protect investigations in progress."

"The Feds?" Donald asked.

"Yes." Gabie swallowed. "They've approached me, and I'm going to say yes—after I return to LA."

"I placed a few hints here and there, hoping someone would talk to you. Good luck, Gabriel."

"Yeah. One of their other informants dropped enough information that they finally came to me." Gabie turned to Justine and took her hands. "Tine. This is the last that we'll see each other, outside of the next Family Christmas—maybe. Sooner or later, I'm going to disappear. Either it'll be because I went into witness protection, or because Philip killed me." He squeezed her hands. "Once I co-operate with this investigation, I don't dare implicate you in any way in what I'm doing. We'll have to be at arm's length, even at Family Christmas."

"I understand, Gabie." She sniffled. "But if my fucking father and brother kill you—I will make them pay."

"You and Serg both."

"And me," Donald added, resting his hands on Justine's shoulders.

Gabie half-smiled at that. "Thanks. Both of you. I can't stay. I have to get back to Cousin Kendra's yacht. Only a short window of time, but —I wanted to get this last report to you, Don, and say—not goodbye, but farewell for now, Tine. Hopefully we'll have that next Family Christmas. It all depends on how the case unfolds."

Justine shuddered at the haunted look in Gabie's eyes. She'd never, ever seen him like this before.

"Gabie. If I'm careful—one last hug? Please?"

He nodded.

She let him wrap his arms around her before delicately extending her own to place light fingertips on his back.

God. She could *feel* those damn scars radiating heat. He was still sick.

Gabie kissed her forehead. "Stay safe, Tine. I'm so glad to see you free from *them*." He bowed to Donald. "Don. Thank you. For every-thing." He exhaled. "I'll see myself out. Best not to expose Tine to outside scrutiny, at least for another month. I suspect I'm being watched, even here."

"You picked my door codes when I let you in, didn't you?" Donald's tone was half-joking, half-tense.

For a brief moment, a flash of the devil-may-care Gabie she once knew lit his face. "Did you expect anything else from me, Don? I always want a back door. Don't worry, I'll erase my traces after I go out." Then the solemn expression returned. "Best you reset them, anyway. Yeah, your door codes are tougher than most, and I'm a better hacker than the typical one, but still—"

"Standard procedure," Donald said. "I regularly reset them after visitors."

Gabie bowed to them. "Stay safe, and be careful."

Donald draped his arm around Justine's shoulders as they watched Gabie walk away, slow, holding his upper body tight.

"Your cousin is one hell of a crazy, brave man," Donald finally sighed. "Thank God I've never had to make that choice."

"You married me."

"True." Donald ducked his head in acknowledgement, then squeezed her. "But what I have gained was well worth any risks I have taken, my dear."

Justine smiled at that.

But her heart broke for Gabie. Donald was right. Crazy and brave, that was Gabie. Had always been Gabie.

And Gabie was facing this alone.

At least she had Donald and Barbie.

5 / INTERLUDE TWO

July, *2086*

"Before you ask," Gabie said, "the answer is no. I did not know about the connection between Barbara Knowles and Donald Atwood back then. The Atwood and Knowles families are secretive, more than the Family ever has been, and much smaller so they could hide things more easily. I always wondered about certain aspects of his life, but Don continually had an explanation. Philip would have known about the ties from the beginning, which explains why he was so hands-off once Donald married you, Tine."

Justine sniffled. Damn it, once again, memories made her cry. "I almost think Donald had you beat for secrecy, Gabie."

Ruby's digi snorted. *"That would take some doing,"* she said, a wry tone in her voice. *"Then again, if he kept secrets from Gabe, that says a lot."*

"Donald was very good at secrets," Justine said. Mike handed her tissues as the dogs crowded around her legs. "Womanizing was his best one. The Crohn's Disease and its impact on his libido? Very real. And I helped him cover it up, along with Coral, Francie, and Meg. They were actually medical staff, not his lovers."

"He fooled me," Gabie said, shaking his head.

"We had to create a rationale for divorce later on—but we'll get to that," Justine sighed.

"So Don called me a crazy, brave man." Gabie's digi half-smiled. *"He was one to speak."*

"Yes, he was." Justine smiled fondly, even with the tears running down her cheeks. God, she was getting soft these days.

"I thought I had a tough time of it," Mike said. "But Justine. Wow."

"Did I face further challenges? Absolutely." She shivered. "But I never, ever, was as helpless as I was before I married Donald. For that I owe him—and Barbie—a huge debt."

"Why did Philip want to marry you to Braun so badly?" JoAnn asked. "I know that politics had swung conservative again at that point. But forcing you into marriage? That's medieval!"

"Well, Daddy-poo had a long-range plan to become, if not an actual king, a plutocrat. A strongman. He honestly believed that he was entitled to rule because of our descent from the Medicis and Borgias."

"Did he ever." Lily's digi startled Justine. *"Unfortunately, I remember too much of what was in his head when he possessed me. Who knows what he would have done if his possession of Mike had succeeded?"*

"Either one of us would have eventually served his purpose," Mike said. "I owe you, Lily, for keeping his focus off of me. I just wish you hadn't suffered so much."

Lily shivered. *"What he would have tried to create in you would have been terrifying. A full resurrection, with nothing left of you. At least some pieces of me could resist. Sometimes."*

Justine exhaled and bent over the dogs while Mike and Lily's digi talked—finally. She wasn't going to interfere in that much-needed healing conversation between Mike and Lily.

Besides, it kept her from answering JoAnn's question.

Philip had not been above attempting to sell his rebellious daughter into indenture. She still didn't know what Braun had held over Daddy-damned-dearest, but she had been the payment for *something.* Braun's own words implied that.

ANOTHER RESTLESS NIGHT, THINKING ABOUT JOANN'S QUESTION. THE answer was so close that Justine could almost feel it.

Gabie was nearby again, more distant than before, probably wanting to talk but not so much as to intrude—especially if she might be undressing.

"I'm decent, Gabie," she said, chuckling.

"Being polite," Gabie said, appearing as an outline. *"One of the rules you learn quickly after becoming a digi—sometimes you really don't want to sneak up on the living."*

"Well, I'm awake. So. Do *you* know why Daddy-poo wanted to foist me off on Braun? Donald and I speculated that Daddy-dear owed something to Braun that he couldn't pay with cash, or that Braun had something on him."

Gabie's outline shifted uneasily. *"Tine, do you really want to know?"*

"Why not?"

A sigh. *"All right. I didn't learn this until much later, after Ruby and I remarried and I had the opportunity to talk to Remy Trask, Ruby's lawyer."*

"I remember Remy." Remy had been a rodeo princess along with Ruby, was one of her good friends for many years. Plus, Remy had worked for the Department of Justice in Los Angeles, most particularly on *US vs Martiniere Group.*

US vs Martiniere Group. Gabie's testimony in that case caused his thirty-year exile, to evade Philip's wrath. That Gabie survived everything he had endured was a testimony to his persistence.

"Remember that information I was giving Don when we met on Solitaire? It came from Braun, through a third party. None of us knew that at the time. Braun blackmailed Philip."

Justine shuddered. "Braun told me what my fate would be as his wife. Essentially a concubine, under lifetime indenture." She huffed. "So. Hand me over and Daddy-damned-dearest went free? No testimony from Braun?"

Gabie nodded. *"Trask described the information that started the original investigation—and told me the source. When we escaped, when you married Donald, then Braun ratted Philip out. It's more complicated than that, but—"*

"It's enough." Justine shook her head, chuckling wryly. "And when I ended up with Donald, I'm certain that was Daddy-dearest's worst fucking nightmare."

"Absolutely." Gabie's form grew more solid. *"Something else, Tine. Have you thought about becoming a digi when you die?"*

"I thought you weren't going to recruit new digis."

His expression tightened. *"Other digis exist. We could be facing some big problems."*

"And you need me to be a fixer."

"Your skills are strong, especially when you put on digigloves and work with deep programming. You could easily make a difference for the future. Not just Ron, but his kids. Grandkids. Others."

"I'll consider it, Gabie."

She needed to think long and hard about this prospect. Was it such a good idea for the children of Philip Martiniere to go digi? Especially someone with her history?

That thought created a stronger-than-ever longing for Donald. If only she could talk this over with him! However, unlike with Gabie and Ruby, she had never experienced any sense of Donald's presence lurking around her after his death.

Just an emptiness stretching into forever.

She didn't even have his grave to meditate over. The Atwood and Knowles families had claimed him, and—she wasn't his wife any longer.

August, 2086

ONE STEP FORWARD, THREE STEPS BACK.

Two days later, Mike was in worse shape than before. Back in his hospital bed, dogs lying next to him. No energy to get angry about his condition. Dark circles under his eyes, traces of blue around his nose and lips, even with an oxygen cannula. Face nearly as pale as the sheets he lay on.

Like he had been during his late teens.

"Hey," Mike said tiredly. "Change of plans. Have to transfer authority." Mike gulped for breath. "Back to you and Ron."

"Went bad last night," JoAnn said, frowning. "Lung programming failure. Not catastrophic, but—it advances surgery dates."

"Maybe we shouldn't tire you out," Justine said.

Mike shook his head, but even that looked tired. "Honestly, Justine. Even the prospect. Of a gloomy story. Brightens up my day." He wheezed after he finally completed the sentence. "Swear. Then story."

After they transferred the Martiniere's authority to sixteen-year-old Ron, within his role as the Martiniere-in-waiting and with Justine's approval as the Matriarch, Mike looked exhausted. But he eyed Justine with barely-concealed eagerness.

She decided against the story she originally intended to tell today. That one could wait. Perhaps an earlier story, one with horses.

Yes. Distract Mike with a story about horses. Mike and horses, an attraction that happened the moment Mike first saw them.

"Donald and I owned a vineyard near Eugene, Oregon," she said. "We had to go to ground after *US vs Martiniere Group*. I settled on a degree program at the University of Oregon, and the event trainer I had ridden with in Los Angeles had moved to the Corvallis area. We thought that living like rich heirs with money to burn on a struggling vineyard might just be the thing to keep Philip from looking too closely at the work we were doing for Real Lives for Women."

"So that's how we both ended up in the Willamette Valley around the same time," Gabie said. *"Me, chasing Ruby. You, playing a role."* He chuckled.

Justine noticed that Mike's eyes lit up even more, and a faint smile touched his lips.

"Oh, it was quite the experience," she said.

Pangs of regret washed through her as she remembered.

She had truly loved life at Mist Knoll.

6 / OF GRAPEVINES AND EVENT
HORSES

MARCH, 2028

"WE BETTER PLAN ON DOING SOMETHING DIFFERENT FOR YOUR birthday," Donald said, sitting on the pool's edge while Justine swam.

They were back on Solitaire Island. Testing relocation to New York and London had proved unsatisfying. Wintering on Solitaire seemed best, for now.

"What were you thinking of?" She treaded water near Donald. He had been moody lately.

There were several possibilities for his worries. Real Lives for Women. Where they were going to live—and where she would finish college. Political futures.

Justine's current studies, besides online coursework, incorporated more and more of the secretive political activities that Barbie and Donald sponsored. Learning to cover her organizing activities for their indentured reproductive rights programs under the guise of fundraising for Real Lives for Women. Developing a general pro-reproductive rights program for non-indentured women. Helping people transitioning to their true gender.

RLW covered a *lot* of activities. Oh, everything explicitly tied to it was above board. But it also provided excuses for Justine's interest in local conditions.

Barbie also taught Justine the mastery of skills she had started to acquire in her father's household. The art of dissembling. Putting on a catty, snarky face at gatherings that hid her goals, and allowed her to overhear important conversations. Flitting around like a butterfly, gathering media attention to distract from covert actions. How to make it look like she was eating and drinking at society functions while not risking a drink or bite due to potential contaminants.

That part came as second nature to Justine, raised in a Martiniere household. One summer, Donna-gran taught Gabie and Serg the ins and outs of dealing with neurotoxins and psychotropics that might adulterate food and drink, especially within the Family. Seven-year-old Justine paid careful attention to Donna-gran's lectures, even when Joey scoffed at the three of them.

Barbie taught Justine the high-society, female nuances of those precautions, lessons she *hadn't* learned because of her mother's death. Guarding her drink. Subtle modes of tamper detection worn as finger-nail polish. Projecting as someone who was habitually bulimic, to cover times when she might have ingested something problematic by mistake and needed to puke it up fast.

And Justine was eternally grateful to her mother-in-law for those lessons.

"Did you hear me?" Donald asked. "You had that faraway look."

Justine startled. "Sorry. What did you have in mind?"

"Want to go vineyard shopping in Oregon?"

Hmm. She swam over to the edge and climbed out, settling next to Donald. "What's brought this on? What trends are you seeing?"

Her husband didn't normally suggest something this big out of the blue—which meant Donald had spent some time considering it before bringing the idea to her.

She hadn't heard anything through her connections about vine-yards being a good investment of late, which might mean either Donald had gotten a tip…or a vineyard was a cover for something else.

"It's been a year since Gabe told us about being approached by the Feds," Donald said. "That, combined with Serg popping up to intensify your physical training, and what he's *not* saying—and undercurrents at Family Christmas."

Justine nodded. She and Donald stayed off-site during Family Christmas, in a nondescript but well-guarded condo, only appearing for formal functions.

Gabie was drunk the entire time. Not the fun-loving, plastered Gabie mode, but the carefully-controlled, play-acting, and viciously sardonic version of her cousin Gabriel who was too much like Daddy-damn-dearest. They exchanged formalities, nothing more. Philip was icily cold toward Justine and Donald. Justine made sure that she was never, ever, alone with her father or her brother.

And then she and Donald scampered back to Solitaire to celebrate their anniversary, followed by Serg moving in a week later.

"I think it's a good idea to lay low for a while," Donald continued. "Someplace out of the way, obscure, and easily defended. There's a visiting professor at the University of Oregon who intrigues me. You might want to take his classes, too."

"I've been curious about the programming courses at Oregon," Justine said. "As well as agribot courses at Oregon State. I just didn't think you'd want to live there, even temporarily. The Willamette Valley *is* wet in the wintertime."

London had been a particular disaster for them, not just the social scene but the weather—another reason to flee to the island.

"Eh, we can always cut out to Bend for sunshine," Donald said. "But. Eugene-Corvallis area. Spend five years pumping money into restoring the vineyard while you get your degree. Not somewhere your father or brother will show up casually. Pretend to be rich heirs playing back-to-the-land." He smiled at her. "A former Olympic eventer has opened a training stable near Corvallis, near one of the vineyards I want to look at. Now is a good time for you to develop a serious interest in showjumping and eventing."

"Wait. You've been talking to Donna-gran." Her grandmother had blocked Philip's objections about Justine riding and showing horses. Then Donna-gran developed cardiac problems, when Justine turned fifteen. That ended Justine's horse life.

Donald beamed at her. "Donna-gran showed me videos of you

riding in shows. I think you should go for it. And Lora Smith is in the perfect location."

Justine shook her head. "Lora Smith's in *Oregon*?" That was even more fascinating. She had ridden with Lora in Los Angeles. For Lora to move someplace like Oregon was surprising.

"I thought you would like that idea," Donald said. "The other piece is that I have a couple of clients who are also considering relocation to the southern Willamette Valley. There appears to be a rising trend of younger, more affluent couples moving into the area. With rising temperatures, the timing's right to rehabilitate some of the older vineyards to reflect those changes."

"So, it's a good base for us in several ways," Justine said thoughtfully.

"We aren't the only ones looking for places to lay low comfortably," Donald said. "And. Your father's been pushing me to add Martiniere security to my own."

Justine tensed. "Vygotsky, or House?"

"House," Donald said. "It's obviously about monitoring us. He approached me about it at Christmas, and I put him off with Mother's wish to only have our own security on Solitaire." He stroked Justine's cheek. "But we need to leave soon. I'd prefer not to consider hurricane season management, and the tropical heat doesn't agree with you much past your birthday."

"How do we handle Daddy-damn-dear's demands?"

"That's where the vineyard design becomes useful," Donald said. "We can justify using Martiniere security for the vineyard and the stables. A mix for when you go riding off-site. But the house? Our own people. I've already run through a plan with Serg—who will be joining us for a while, and that should keep your father's people straight. And, hopefully, after a while, I can convince your father to pull his security."

"Why wasn't I part of this discussion?"

"Oh, he had a number of rationales," Donald said.

"I bet." She shook her head.

"He's a sexist asshole. However, I had been considering rural property in the United States, ever since London didn't work. The security cost, timing, and training aspects of setting up in urban or suburban locations bothered me. I also needed time to think about probable locales, amenities and so on. When your father started pushing me to accept Martiniere security, I realized that this was a good way for us to transition from Mother's forces to our own." Donald chuckled. "I have no problems shifting those expenses to him." Then his expression grew solemn. "We need to develop your personal security staff, who are loyal to you and you alone. Even if we don't divorce in six years, it's time to start building that team. You need to have *Justine Martiniere-Atwood's* security, not mine or Philip's."

Before Justine could say anything more, Serg entered the pool area.

"The Feds have filed a criminal case against Philip's PJM Corp subdivision of the Martiniere Group, in Los Angeles. Charges of illegal, coerced mind control programming on indentured workers against their will." Serg took a deep breath. "Trial date's set for July. Feds are moving fast—" He glanced at Justine before continuing. "Rumor has it that Gabe is their star witness."

"That *is* a fast track," Donald said.

"They've been building a case for a while," Serg said. "From what Gabe last said to me."

"Sounds like we'd better buy that vineyard very soon, then," Justine said.

"Absolutely," Donald said. "I'd like to be in our new home before the trial starts."

June, 2028

THEY SETTLED INTO MIST KNOLL BY JUNE. THE HOUSE SAT ON A KNOLL overlooking the valley floor, vineyard between it and the barns near the road. It faced east so they had a view of the Cascades, including the Three Sisters, Broken Top, Mount Jefferson, and on a really clear day, Mount Hood. The house wasn't as modern as the island villa, but it was bright and well-lit, with an indoor pool, workout/training room, and—essential for work—secure basement facilities easily converted into a shooting range and secret offices. The vineyard had been sadly neglected in past years, but still produced decent grapes. It just needed attention.

Best of all for Justine's purposes, the property came with an indoor arena and small stable.

"You're committed to competing?" Lora asked Justine midway through that first assessment ride, between flatwork and jumping. "Because you need to be spending a lot of time in the saddle to catch up. You have that skill—had it when you were younger. You just need the hours to regain it."

"I don't have Daddy-dear's irrational fears about me getting hurt by horses to consider anymore," Justine said. She rubbed the neck of the dark bay lesson horse she was riding—a gelding named Mitch. Donald cruised the stable alleyways while Justine did her trial ride.

"And your husband?"

"It's a risk, like anything else in life," Donald said, coming back to the arena. "I don't ride at Justine's level, but I can handle a steady horse. I've been thinking about getting a Walker or some other gaited horse to ride around the property. I trust you to guide Justine safely." He scratched Mitch's nose. "I'm assuming that perhaps we shouldn't be horse shopping for Justine just yet? Or do we want to start quiet, work our way up to a more competitive horse or horses?"

"Your flatwork's decent, Justine, but you need hours in the saddle," Lora said. "I'd suggest focusing on jumping. That's your strength."

"Perhaps I should lease for a while," Justine said. "This boy's good, but I'll want more of a challenge soon enough."

"I regularly have young horses in training so there'll always be a choice to consider when you're ready to buy," Lora said. "Until then— Mitch is available for lease, but he's old enough that you should only ride him every other day. I have another lease prospect that you can alternate him with. She's hotter, but within your skill set. Especially if you're coming over for lessons regularly."

Justine ended up leasing Mitch and a chestnut mare, Katy. Lora found a black Morgan named Strider for Donald. While Justine schooled daily in the arena, she and Donald also took the time to hack out on their land.

Their land.

So many things seemed possible during that bright golden summer.

JULY, 2028

"JUSTINE?" HER FATHER'S VOICE SOUNDED STRANGE OVER THE PHONE.

"Yes, Daddy-dear." Justine scowled—she was working on plans for the Northeast RLW regional convention. She had expected this to be a call about the facility.

Donald swam over to the edge, raising his brows.

"Are you planning to attend the trial?" her father asked.

"No, Daddy-dearest, I am *not* planning to come to the trial," she said in the sweetest, most poisonous tone she had learned from Barbie. "Donald and I are still scrambling to get things organized with the vineyard."

A momentary silence. "Isn't that what subordinates are for—organizing things?"

"And who was it that said startups need to be hands-on, during more than one dinner table conversation while I was growing up?"

He snorted, just like Mitch would when feeling grumpy about jumping.

She continued before her father spoke. "This vineyard needs a lot of attention. And we intend to expand its offerings. That requires us to stay here, supervise the construction of the tasting room, network, and plan for events. Not go off attending trials, since we're not going to be witnesses."

Donald rolled his eyes and pushed off to resume swimming.

"The Atwood money isn't so big that you can blow off a threat to the Group this easily," her father said. "Especially with what your husband's spending on that vineyard."

"My husband forbids me from going to the trial," Justine said, smirking. Donald hesitated before executing a flip turn, side-stroking back toward her. She grinned at him.

Take that, Daddy-damn-dearest!

It wasn't often that she could turn Philip's sexism back on him like this.

"And you'd obey him over *your Martiniere*."

Oh, *those tones*. But her father's management of mind control pitches wasn't very effective over the phone.

"Technically, Daddy-poo, according to *your church*, that's the line of authority, and all that," she said airily. "Once I'm married, I'm under my husband's authority as superior to that of my father's, correct? Donald is right here, if you want to talk to him about it."

"Put him on," Philip growled.

Justine handed the phone to Donald.

"What?" he said. Listened. "No. Absolutely not, Philip. Not only do we have schedule conflicts, but I've been advised to tighten my security here."

A pause. "Who gave me that advice? Brent Colfax, head of the security detail you sent us. Uh-huh. Uh-huh."

Another pause. "My advisors are universally telling me to stay the hell out of LA right now, Philip, including Colfax. Especially since I'm married to a Martiniere. If it's not safe for *me*, it's not safe for *my wife*. I have to trust these people."

Yet another break in the conversation. "Understood. But it's my job as her husband to take care of your daughter in the best manner I see fit—and right now, given the political tensions, staying right here is best. My mother would love for us to visit her in Connecticut—but she's telling me the same thing. Stay put. Uh-huh. Uh-huh."

He rolled his eyes. "Certainly. Here she is." He handed the phone back.

"All right," her father grumbled. "I guess you have to obey your husband."

"It *is* how you brought me up, Daddy-dearest." More sweetness with thinly veiled sharpness underneath. "I am just following his advice. As you taught me."

You don't have to know that obedience was absolutely not *a part of my wedding vows.*

A heavy sigh. "All right, Justine."

He hung up.

Justine let loose the laugh she had been suppressing. Then she set down the phone, dived into the pool, twisted down to touch the bottom, and shot back up, smirking at Donald as they both treaded water.

"So?"

Justine laughed again. "I never, *ever*, thought that I could hang Daddy-damn-dearest by his own ideology. Never."

Donald chortled with her. "It was so worth it to hear Philip Martiniere fumble for justifications. So damn worth it." He pulled Justine to him, frog-kicking them to the shallow end where they could both stand, kissed her, then held her close.

Justine heaved a happy sigh as she leaned her head against Donald's damp chest. Sexual arousal still didn't happen for her. But having Donald hold her like this, kiss her—that was enjoyable.

And it was absolutely delightful to be married to a man who thought so much like her about the things they agreed were important.

They watched one day of the trial—Philip finagled a subscription for the hard-to-access televised full version, and sent the link out to the entire Family. Justine conceded that much, tuning in the day of Gabie's testimony.

At first everything went smoothly. Gabie was in his cool, detached mode—*so like Daddy-damned-dearest in that*—and answered questions smoothly. His face was thinner than she remembered, drawn down tight.

Then it happened. Defense counsel Rolland McKenzie started to say Gabie's control words. Gabie swayed, paling, grabbing at the sides of the witness box. He swallowed hard. The judge asked if he was all right.

"No, I'm not," Gabie answered. His body jerked and spasmed

immediately after he spoke, doubling over as he gagged and drooled, dry heaving, falling out of the witness box.

Justine screamed, then burst into tears, hands flying to her mouth in horror.

No. Oh no.

Someone had managed to get a psychotropic to her cousin. She whimpered as Gabie collapsed next to the jury box, body spasming, flopping like a fish out of water, shrieking in pain.

Psychotropic with nanos that augmented his reaction.

Something every high-level Martiniere heir dreaded.

Donald grabbed her, burying her head in his chest so she wouldn't see anything else as he switched off the feed.

Her worst nightmare. *Her worst fucking nightmare.*

His face was set and stiff when she cried herself out and straightened up.

"Can your father or one of his surrogates do that to you?" he asked. "Like what just happened to Gabe?"

"If he gets a psychotropic with nano augmentation to me—yes," she whispered.

"*Fucker,*" Donald snarled, angrier than she had ever heard him. "I swear. I will move heaven and earth to keep your father from hurting you like that. I will help you do whatever is necessary to stop him doing that to others." He shuddered. "I thought things were bad enough. What he did to you and Gabe before. But this. That man has to be stopped."

"Thank you," she whispered. "Thank you."

August, 2028

Her damned father won that round. Verdict of not guilty.

Serg was grim when he arrived at the vineyard the day after the verdict.

"Philip's in a rage even though he won. Gabe's safely gone," he said. "Protect yourselves. Stay on the property for the next couple of weeks."

"Where does Vygotsky Security stand?" Donald asked. "Not you, your father."

"What Philip did to Gabe on the stand through McKenzie—that pissed off my father and forced him solidly into our camp," Serg said. "Piotr's not ready to move against Philip—hell, I can't even talk him into tracking Gabe down because I have a bad feeling about the witness protection program's security. Gabe was betrayed by one of them in the first place. But Dad is concerned about Philip's goals, and is ready to organize resistance within the Family. Including hardening security, creating weapons caches, and secure sites for Family members to escape to." He eyed Justine. "Are you in with us? Because this has to be a long-range plan. We can't move that quickly, if we're going to do it correctly. Give it five years for things to settle down, and then we'll make Gabe the Martiniere instead of Philip."

"Whatever it takes," Justine said.

"I'm with her," Donald added.

"Good," Serg said.

BY THE NEXT DAY, SOMETHING *BIG* HAD HAPPENED WITHIN THE MARTINIERE Group. When Justine logged in to the private network that hosted the highly secret indentured chats, looking for coded help requests, the buzz choked the channels.

—*Programming's changed.*

—*Bekah ran for it. No more compulsions.*

—*Mind control in Lab 59 is GONE.*

She sat back in her chair, wondering, after ten minutes of reading messages like that. What the hell?

Maybe Donald knew. She went to his office.

"The chats are just wild this afternoon," she said. "Reports of programming changes. Mind control disappearing."

Donald flashed her a tight-lipped grin. "I know. I've been watching."

"What is it?" She joined him. "Did you do this?"

"Not entirely." He patted his lap. "Sit down. Watch."

The big screen in front of them displayed a map with green targets that first turned golden, then red. Justine recognized the locations as Martiniere sites working with indentureds.

"So you had something to do with it—"

"Programming advice only. Gabe did the rest of it, triggered to a not-guilty verdict." Donald's grin spread. "It doesn't completely defang the indentured mind control program. But it's wiped out records of the last ten years of your father's mind control research on indentureds."

"Holy fucking shit," Justine whispered. "Oh God. Daddy-fucking-dearest is going to kill Gabie for this. More than for his testimony."

"I'm working on something similar to protect you, my dear. If we end up divorcing—or something happens to me—should Philip come after you, you'll have the power to kill his databases. Take the entire Martiniere Group down. If anyone snoops into your files, it will take their systems down as well."

"Donald—" She shivered at the thought of that much power.

"I promised to protect you, no matter what," Donald said. "Watching Gabe's worm strip that mind control program from the files gave me ideas. You won't want to activate it except as a last resort. It's a self-defense mechanism that will leave the Group in shambles. But it *will* be a viable threat to your father, especially after this incident."

Justine shuddered again, unsure if it was the thought of the power or of the circumstances that might lead her to such an action that sent chills through her.

She turned her head to kiss Donald.

He responded eagerly.

That led to one of their rare lovemaking sessions, right there in his office.

VERDICT-FUELED RAGE WAS A DISASTER FOR THE MARTINIERE GROUP. Rebellion at the labs and labor pool compounds led to riots.

"It would have been easier if the verdict had gone against the Group," Donald said as they watched a news clip about a firebombing at one of the Group labs.

Justine nodded. "Follow that with the effects of the worm...." Her voice trailed off. She was very glad she and Donald were not in a major urban area.

"The Group will recover," Donald added. "The indentured divisions will take longer, but they'll bounce back. I looked at your funds today and talked to Mom about what she was seeing. Yes, your net worth has taken a dip. To be expected. But not as bad as it would have been before we moved your accounts."

"I'm glad you moved my shares out of the indentured programs," she said. Once she'd turned eighteen and her marriage had been confirmed with the Martiniere Family Trust administrators, Donald could manage her Family trust fund investments. She couldn't authorize sales or withdrawals against her shares—that was still limited to age twenty-four. But shortly after her eighteenth birthday, Donald shifted her Family shares from Philip's programs to Gerard's, Arthur's, and several other European Family members whose divisions focused on agricultural and robotic technology.

And then there was Serg's weapons tech sideline at Vygotsky Security. She and Donald both held shares in Vygotsky Armaments, from Atwood funds, not her Martiniere Family Trust shares.

Unrest is coming as a result of the creation of the indenture system, Donald said in March, 2027. *Can't be avoided. And in the long run, we may well benefit from this investment in Vygotsky Armaments. I'd sooner finance Serg's weapons than indentured labor pools.*

Justine agreed with that assessment.

September, 2028

They opened the tasting room with a flair on Labor Day weekend, with a catered reception, concert, and more. D & J Fine Wines marketed not only Mist Knoll products, but select wines and premium food items. The combination of the Martiniere and Atwood names brought attention from local society as well as connoisseurs from as far away as Seattle and San Francisco.

Barbie flitted in and helped Justine choreograph the events, bringing with her a group of fellow socialites that Justine knew from New York and Solitaire Island.

And that collection included three women whose names had been linked with Donald in the past. Coral Fuentes. Francine Meidenhoff. Margaret Salisbury.

She recognized the names, of course, when Donald told her.

"I need to introduce you to Coral, Francie, and Meg," he said.

"They've been your past girlfriends, right?" She'd run across their names in the society news reports around Barbie and past stories about Donald.

"It's—complicated," Donald said. "It's not a coincidence that they're medical professionals, and older than me."

"So—" She eyed him. "Tell me more."

"Coral's a doctor in general practice. Francie's a nurse practitioner. Meg's a RN. They're associated with Mom socially, have been for some years. And they're not visible in general practice."

"A boutique medical practice?"

Donald nodded. "With the pregnancy issues you've been having—I asked Mom to bring them, to meet you. We may want them around later on."

She exhaled. Heavy nausea. Spotting. Something didn't feel right. Donald's concern made sense. She hoped that her only connection with Coral, Francie, and Meg would be social—but was pregnancy supposed to be like this?

Maybe this was what being pregnant felt like for her.

It still didn't feel right.

<hr>

November, 2028

•   •   •

H*YDATIDIFORM MOLE*, HER OB/GYN CALLED IT. A MASSIVE GROWTH OF placental tissue with no embryonic development. Severe enough that Justine needed a hysterectomy, because placental tissue had grown into her uterine walls and couldn't be removed by any other means.

Thankfully it wasn't cancerous. But surgical complications kept Justine in the hospital for a week.

Donald frantically stayed by her side as much as the hospital would permit. Justine worried about Donald fretting himself into a Crohn's flare.

"Go home. Rest," she kept telling him.

He refused—until three days in, when Justine woke to see Coral sitting by her bedside.

"Where's Donald?" she asked, still fuzzy.

Coral rolled her eyes. "Barbie and Meg took him home. He finally told Barbie what happened, and the two of us were available to fly out with Barbie immediately. Francie will be here in a couple of days."

"Good." Justine exhaled. "I'm afraid he's going to make himself sick worrying over me. But I couldn't get him to go home or take care of himself."

"We figured as much," Coral said. "You were right to be concerned. He's having problems. His gut's rebelling."

Justine sniffled. "Oh God. I know it's the right thing, but now that he's not here, I miss him."

"Honey," Coral said, her voice soothing and reassuring. "You've been through an awful lot." She wrapped her hand around Justine's. "Both of you. This is a major blow."

"It's not like we were really desperate to have kids," Justine blubbered. "We were open to the prospect but just left things to happen or not—and then—this—"

"This is a major blow," Coral repeated. "Even if you weren't really eager to have kids of your own, it's still pretty damn final. Especially at *your* age."

At that, Justine completely broke down.

She didn't know what felt worse—the loss of the option to have her own children, or the fact that her body had betrayed her. Children always seemed to be something for a far-off future, but she assumed that sooner or later, she would have a child with Donald, especially after being so close during the past year.

I'm fucking nineteen—almost twenty—years old. This could have killed me in another era. What is my body going to do to me next?

Justine wasn't sure she liked facing her mortality like this.

However, given her money and class, she was one of the lucky ones—and she knew it.

Once again. When would her luck run out?

<hr>

Justine was grateful for the presence of the other women when she went home. Donald still battled a flare. Barbie, Coral, Francie, and Meg helped them manage their businesses, supervised their recoveries, and provided company. Sometimes that included a cuddle pile in Donald's bed with Coral, Francie, and Meg. Not sexual, just comfort. She learned more about the complexities of Donald's past with the others.

But most of all, she was just glad that Coral, Francie, and Meg were there, along with Barbie, to help with everyday things. They spent Christmas at Mist Knoll, because Justine couldn't face dealing with the Family. The women's presence made the holiday more cheerful, and simplified recovery management for her and Donald.

Serg and his father Piotr came by for New Year's, after Barbie and the others left. Cousin Kendra and her husband Scott joined them on New Year's Day.

Kendra hugged Justine when she returned the borrowed wedding outfit.

"I'm glad it worked for you," she said. "I thought it brought me good luck."

"Except for—this—" Justine gestured at her abdomen, "—things have been going well."

"I'm sorry."

"We hadn't really been certain about having children or not. This—kind of took care of things."

Kendra hugged Justine again, before they settled into the armchair seats in the small basement conference room to have a short Family briefing.

Piotr stood up. "Kendra and Justine. Since neither of you were at Family Christmas, you need to be briefed," he said. "Joseph tried to have Gabriel killed before Thanksgiving, and spent Christmas bragging about how he almost made Gabriel pay for his actions. He got laughed at for his pretensions, of course, because it didn't work."

"Is Gabe all right?" Kendra asked.

"Yes, Gabriel is fine. Sergei and I salvaged the situation. Gabriel is on his own, with a new identity, and no ties to the witness protection program."

"Is that a good thing?" Justine asked cautiously.

"Yes," Serg said. "They had him working as an investment advisor, in Arizona. In that capacity, he sent out recommendations to his clients to divest from Martiniere Group-connected indentured labor pool clients, and provided a detailed list of Group associates. That, combined with the worm, made him a target."

"Philip suspects that the worm was Gabe's work?" Donald asked.

"Gabe left noticeable traces," Serg said. "I suspect it was on purpose." He winced. "Philip had several after-dinner rants about Gabe over Christmas."

"Only about Gabie?" Justine asked.

She could have laughed at Serg's expression, but didn't.

"He did express regrets about your condition," Serg said.

Justine snorted. Philip had sent a bug-ridden bouquet after her surgery. Donald scanned it in the hospital, made a face at the number of listening devices laden in the bouquet—and somehow, accidentally-on-purpose, it was left behind.

"He probably regrets that we didn't bring his bugs home," she said.

That brought a faint smile to Piotr's lips. "Dealing with Gabriel is Philip's major focus at the moment," he said. "Which provides some opportunities—and at the same time, requires caution."

"Where does that leave our plans?" Kendra asked.

"I have been working with Donna to devise further mind control defenses for high-level heirs," Piotr said. "Kendra, Justine, I want to install them in you."

"I'll gladly cooperate," Kendra said.

"Agreed," Justine said. The horror of what happened to Gabie at the trial still lingered.

"*Good,*" Donald said, holding her tightly.

———

MARCH, *2029*

HER BIRTHDAY CELEBRATION WAS SUBDUED THAT YEAR. DONALD'S CROHN'S flare lingered through the spring. Justine spent most of her time managing their businesses and studying. Coral, Francie, and Meg returned, and took turns helping her with Donald.

"I'm a wreck," he sighed during one of his bad bedridden days. "I don't know why you're still here."

She stroked his cheek and hugged him carefully. "Because I love you. Because I owe you so much for getting me away from Daddy-damn-dearest. Because you need me right now."

"You're outgrowing me," he said, a sad note in his voice. "I already see it. You're becoming bolder and stronger. By the time seven years is up, my falcon will be soaring on her own."

"Let's deal with that when it comes," she said.

She didn't really want to think about what would happen in a few more years.

But that bright golden happiness of their first summer at Mist Knoll had faded.

———

APRIL, *2029*

JUSTINE RESUMED RIDING LESSONS IN APRIL. IT WAS TIME FOR HER TO GET serious if she wanted to be visible as a showjumper.

She started out on Donald's Strider, to get herself back in shape and to tune him up so Donald could ride once he felt better. Mitch and Katy returned as lease horses. Lora's resident stable manager, Ruby, was going home for the summer, to help her grandparents on their Northeastern Oregon ranch, the Double R. Lora had summer helpers but was glad to see Justine take on the two horses.

Ruby puzzled Justine. The redhead was working her way through an agricultural robotics degree at Oregon State without taking out loans. Ruby had the ability to excel in showjumping. But she focused on rodeo instead. Why wouldn't she want to aim for showjumping honors, which would bring her more funding?

But damn, the woman could sit a bucking horse. Justine watched Ruby ride through several explosions on her palomino mare. *She* couldn't ride a horse like Sunshine, who would blow up without warning, and buck as high and hard as a rodeo bronc.

Ruby made it look easy.

Justine knew better.

Summer, 2029

By summer, Donald resumed swimming and riding.

They didn't do much outside riding that year. A dry summer brought more wildfires than usual, smoke choking the southern portion of the Willamette Valley. Justine and Donald fretted over the impact the smoke might have on that year's grape harvest, but there wasn't much they could do about it.

At least none of the fires came close enough that they needed to worry about evacuation. They provided refuge for some of their local friends and their horses. But it was a hot, smoky-gray, brown summer. Nothing at all like the bright golden one of the year before.

Justine usually wasn't superstitious. But she wondered what omens lurked within the thick smoke that strangled the Valley that summer.

7 / INTERLUDE THREE

August, 2086

"So that's where the Mist Knoll wine collection at both Moondance and the Double R comes from?" JoAnn asked.

"Yes. I still hold a portion of the winery ownership," Justine said. "Get a shipment every year of the latest vintages." She was not going to cry about this story. She was *not*.

Was her entire life just a succession of sad stories? Justine shook her head, not wanting to think about that.

"It's not a bad line of wines," Mike said. He still looked tired, but his face wasn't as tight with pain as it had been. So the stories *were* working as a distraction.

"Fascinating to hear what that worm looked like from the inside," Gabie said. *"I had no idea. By that point I was Daniel Garcia, investment advisor. It wasn't until years later that I learned how much of a blow it had been to Philip's research and long-term political goals. It exceeded my expectations."*

"You blew Daddy-poo's research out of the water for several years," Justine said.

She swallowed hard as her throat tightened. The memory of that worm was inexorably linked to the results of the lovemaking that followed watching it in action. She was not going to cry after this story.

She was *not*. That hysterectomy had probably been the best thing ever, because it discouraged any dynastic notions Philip might have entertained involving her.

Mike eyed Justine. Then he shoved the box of tissues toward her. "You can cry, you know. I see it in your face."

She shook her head. "Those tears have all been shed—years ago."

Even as she said it, she knew she was lying.

As they headed for the truck, Deontae Swait, JoAnn's brother arrived, to help JoAnn and Mike through Mike's surgery.

"Good to see you, D," Justine said. "How's the husband?"

"Quincy's doing well," Deontae said, grinning. He jerked his head toward the house. "How are they holding up?"

"Back and forth," Justine said. "I'll breathe easier when the surgery's done."

"So will I," D said.

ONCE AGAIN, JUSTINE HAD A RESTLESS NIGHT. IT WASN'T JUST remembering the hysterectomy. It was the loss of a dream that she and Donald shared during the early years at Mist Knoll. Gabie had finally managed to create a peaceful life with his beloved Ruby for thirteen years. Why didn't she and Donald have that opportunity?

Because you resisted it. Because you feared marriage by then.

An unfamiliar digi presence hovered nearby. Justine sat up, cautious. Gabie's warning about the existence of other digis came back to her.

"Who's there?" She kept her voice steady.

Mike's form shimmered into visibility.

Dread clutched at her.

Fuck. No. Mike can't be dead, can he?

"Mike. What the *hell?*" No, no, *no.*

If Mike's digi was wandering, that was *so* not a good thing. It took an act of will for him to send it out—unless he was *dying* and the bonds between digi and body were fading.

"Did Philip have anything to do with your miscarriages?" Mike's digital voice was a bare whisper.

"Of course not! Mike, what the hell are you doing here? Get back to your body!"

Ruby popped up. *"Michael Marcus Martiniere, get back to your body! NOW!"*

"lost," Mike whimpered faintly. *"so lost."*

Fuck! He is *dying!*

"Gabie!" Justine bellowed. Ruby needed backup, and fast. Maybe getting Mike's digi back to his body wouldn't stop whatever was going on, but—

Brandon and Gabie's forms shimmered into shape, followed by Lily. Gabie and Brandon wrapped their arms around Mike. The three of them faded out.

"What the *hell* is going on here?" Justine demanded. "Ruby, is Mike…?" Her voice trailed off.

"They're trying to resuscitate him right now," Ruby said grimly.

Lily cocked her head to the side, as if she were listening to something they couldn't hear. *"They got him back in body. Grandpa and Daddy are with him."*

A knock on her door. "Who's there?"

Ron burst in, light spilling in from the hallway behind him. "Aunt Justine. Are you all right? I heard you yell."

"There's problems with Mike," Justine said, sinking back against the headboard. "He showed up here in digi."

Ron's face grayed. "No. God no!"

"He's still alive," Ruby said. *"But he's getting flighted to Portland for surgery."*

"Aw, fuck," Justine sighed.

"Should we plan on going to Portland?" Ron asked.

Justine shook her head. "Not until we hear from JoAnn—"

Her comm chimed. *"Deontae Swait,"* the identifier said.

Oh God. This had to be bad, if D was calling instead of JoAnn.

Deontae looked shaken as his comm projection solidified.

"D," Justine said. "Mike showed up here in digi. How bad is it?"

D frowned. "Heart and lungs both stopped. Complete failure of the cyborg cardiovascular programming systems. If it hadn't been for Gabe and Brandon's digis—" He blew hard, running his fingers through his short dreadlocks, black streaked with gray. "They're manually operating the cyborg programming. That's keeping Mike alive. Thank God for programming-savvy digis."

"Do we know how this happened, D?" Justine took a deep breath to slow her racing heart, calm herself and keep from reacting further. Dear God, Ron didn't need *her* to fall apart. She had to keep it together for his sake.

"Mike's systems got hacked," D said. "They were already in bad shape, otherwise it wouldn't have happened."

"That piece of Philip we yanked out of Mike?" Lily asked.

D shook his head. "No. It's something else."

A chill ran through Justine. "A digi that isn't one we know?" she asked.

Oh God, Gabie's right. There's a threat.

"Very possibly," D said. "MedicFlight just took off with Mike and Jo. I'm holding things down here, making sure everything is in order. I'm driving to Portland tomorrow."

"Should we go with you?" Justine asked.

"No. Jo needs someone with her but we shouldn't swarm them right now." D grimaced. "I'm afraid it'd be a lot of disruptions for you two and not much benefit. If things look bad, I'll send for you."

"We'll sit tight, then," Justine said. "Keep us posted."

"I will," D said. "Meanwhile—you and Ron stay safe."

Justine exhaled as D disconnected. "All right. Situation run-through. Ruby, Lily, how vulnerable are we here? No cyborg parts, but then again—" her voice trailed off. Lily hadn't been cyborged, but Philip had possessed her all the same.

"That's why we're here," Ruby said. *"Gabe wants me and Lily on watch. Especially for you, Justine, because you're acting as regent for the underaged Martiniere. A potential target."*

"Fuck. Let's talk defenses." Justine leaned her head against the headboard. "Resource allocation. Who goes with Ron, and who with me?"

"I'll sleep in here, on the floor," Ron said. "Get the air mattress and sleeping bag from the camp gear. That'll make things simpler."

"You sure about that?" Justine asked.

"As long as you don't mind. Probably makes sense for us to be in the same room for security's sake. And—" Ron paused. "It'll keep me from worrying about *you*."

"Don't bother with the air mattress," Justine said. "Sleeping bag on the bed at most."

"Eh, I'll go with the floor," Ron said. "I don't want to disturb you, Aunt Justine." He left.

Justine sighed. She switched on her reading light, and reached for the hard copy book she had been reading—an Ivan Doig from the Double R's collection.

Might as well read until Ron got settled. Hopefully she wouldn't wake Ron with a nightmare. She propped herself up with pillows and turning onto her side.

Ruby sat on the edge of the bed. *"Before Ron comes back—I'm really sorry about what happened to you. Did you and Donald ever catch a break?"*

God, even as a digi Ruby would come up with penetrating questions that made it seem as if she were mind reading.

Justine put the book aside. "On Solitaire, before the hurricanes and ocean levels rising took it out. That first summer at Mist Knoll. Maybe a few moments after that, and then those years after Gabie became the Martiniere."

"I'm sorry." Ruby rested a hand on Justine's shoulder. Lighter than a live human touch would be, but sufficiently solid to provide a form of reassuring contact.

"Considering how we got together in the first place, it's surprising we had even *those* moments." Justine blinked back tears. She was *not* going to cry.

"Do you ever feel Donald nearby? Gabe and I keep looking and looking for him in digital world, but we can't find anything. Maybe he's hanging around you."

Too much after today's story. Justine burst into tears. "No. Not at all. Nothing. Never."

"That was stupid of me. I'm sorry." Ruby's form flowed next to her,

placing pressure on Justine so that it felt like she was being held. A second, lighter, cool touch brushed against Justine's back—Lily?

"Oh no. Did something happen?" Ron asked as he returned.

"I just said something stupid," Ruby said. *"Connected to today's story. We don't have any news yet."*

"I see." Ron's voice sounded so much like Gabie in an unsure moment. "You all right, Aunt Justine?"

Justine nodded furiously, struggling with tears. Ron patted her shoulder gingerly—an odd sensation since he touched her in the same place that Lily was holding. The contrast between living and digi —*warm, firm*—made Justine gulp.

"If you want to talk, I'm here," Ron said, sounding awkward.

Justine shook her head. She closed her eyes as Ruby placed more pressure on her grasp, and listened to Ron wrestling the self-inflating mattress pad out of its bag, then the rustles as he pulled his sleeping bag out of its stuff sack, before crawling into it.

At last, her tears subsided. She opened her eyes. Ron curled on his side, facing away from her, breathing in a rhythmic sleep pattern.

"You all right?" Ruby whispered.

"As much as I'll ever be," Justine murmured. She pushed herself up to put the book back on her nightstand and switch off the light. Darkness revealed a faint glow from both Ruby and Lily.

"Go ahead and sleep. We'll hold you," Ruby said, stroking Justine's forehead. The contact felt soothing and suddenly Justine felt as if she could actually manage to rest.

"Uh-huh," Justine mumbled.

Ruby kept stroking her forehead. The repetition eased Justine into drowsiness—though she had to wonder if Ruby was doing *something* to make her feel better.

So many things we don't know about these digis.

JUSTINE WOKE AT HER USUAL TIME. THE COMBINED PRESENCE OF RUBY AND Lily reminded her of the cuddle piles that she, Coral, Francie, and Meg used to do with Donald when he had a difficult night. As she opened her eyes, the odd sensation of looking through Ruby's outline startled her. Before it became more solid, she saw that Brandon's digi was curled around a sleeping Ron.

I wonder how Mike's surgery went?

Once again, Ruby seemed to read her mind. She slid closer.

"Bran just got back. Surgery went well. Gabe's staying with Mike right now. He and Bran will switch off watching over him." A pause. *"There is some concern about cognitive function, so that's why Gabe's standing first watch. Mike was oxygen-deprived just long enough for it to be a worry."*

"Oh, fuck no," Justine groaned.

"Gabe thinks it will be just fine," Ruby continued. *"And there's things that he can do to fix any damage that the rest of us can't."*

"Still...." Justine murmured. She sighed, and pushed herself up. Grabbed her walker and headed for the bathroom before going to the kitchen.

Justine sat down heavily and collected coffee, English muffin, and peaches from their containers. Warmers and preserver zipped back into their storage compartments.

Ruby shook her head. *"Never will get used to stuff like that."*

"Says the digital clone," Justine said dryly, sipping her coffee before taking a delicate nibble of those wonderful, wonderful peaches. A rarity these days. She wondered where Paula had found them. "You're a fine one to talk."

Mmm. She held the last bite of that first slice in her mouth for a moment, letting it linger as she savored it, remembering how she and Donald went to the farmer's market in Corvallis for fresh peaches when they lived at Mist Knoll.

Then she sipped her black coffee. Real coffee, not fake. She was willing to pay the high prices for *real coffee.*

Lily joined them.

"You know," Ruby said. *"I had a pregnancy go into hydatidiform mole, too, when Gabe and I divorced."* She focused on her clasped hands. *"Brandon and I were down sick with that mutated flu when it happened. I wanted to think it was just a miscarriage, but—didn't have a hysterectomy. It wasn't that severe."*

Justine stopped chewing her English muffin. "I didn't know that."

But it made sense. That flu variant had gone through swine and horses before it hit humans. Ruby and her horses—*shit.*

"Yeah." Silence. Then Ruby looked up. *"And I was lucky because Dr. Sheri refused to report miscarriages to the damned abortion police."*

Justine stifled a shiver. After his initial sympathy, Daddy-fucking-dearest was downright vicious about her need for a hysterectomy—and shortly after that, he started campaigning to create the abortion police. God. He *would* have reported Ruby, if he had known. Just to make Gabie even more miserable.

"Did Gabie know you were pregnant?"

"Yes." Ruby winced. *"Once I got sick, I knew something was wrong above and beyond having the flu. And then I felt horribly sick, and it wasn't the flu."*

Justine nodded. "I remember a constant feeling that something was wrong." She exhaled. "Then, later, when Daddy-poo started pushing the abortion police, I knew that I had to act. Donald and I started up the Rescue Angel organization and we expanded our options."

Lily shook her head. *"I fell for Philip's ideology."*

"Did Philip really believe it?" Ruby asked.

"It was about control of women's bodies," Lily said slowly. *"Ever since Gabe's mother Angelica chose Philip's older brother Saul over him, Philip didn't trust women. Any woman."*

"Not surprised," Justine sighed. "He drove my mother to suicide." She shook her head. "I don't know what she saw in him. I don't know if Daddy-poo even loved her."

"In his own way, he cared for Renate," Lily said. *"Submissive. Respectful of him. But he didn't respect her. He didn't understand what Renate was capable of doing. She was just supposed to be his shadow and servant, not much better than an indentured concubine."*

Silence hung over them, broken by Ron coming into the kitchen, Brandon's digi trailing behind.

"News about Mike from Grandpa," Ron said as he went to a cupboard and pulled out a jar holding his favorite granola mix.

"Recent, or what Lily and Ruby know?" Justine asked.

"Just now," Brandon said. *"Dad sent me a message. Mike's awake post-*

surgery. Tired, of course. No cognitive impact from oxygen deprivation, fortunately."

"Good," Justine said, sighing with relief.

"But," Brandon said, raising his index finger. *"It's not perfect. Mike had a small stroke that affects his left side, primarily his brain-cyborging interface. Dad and Dr. Pramula are mucking around in his brain to reset things and create more defenses so that Mike's cyborging can't be hacked again."*

"You digis can do that?" Justine asked, a chill sending goosebumps up her arms. "You can hack our brains?"

"Mainly through the cyborg interfaces," Brandon said. *"And Dad's the best one to do this, because he knows the old Martiniere mind control programming protocols. They found some back doors that can be traced to Philip's initial programming of Mike, not something that Dr. Pramula would know to create defenses against."*

"Could those old programming protocols be used against those of us who *have* been programmed in the past?" Justine asked.

Brandon shrugged. *"That's a question for Dad. I don't know enough about the mind control programs to say one way or the other."*

Ron methodically mixed yogurt with his granola. "I need to know about these programs, as the future Martiniere. Despite what you and Grandpa did to eliminate indenture and the mind control processes, Dad, that mind control programming keeps popping back up."

"Talk to your grandfather about those details," Ruby said. *"Unless—Justine, what do you know about those programs?"*

"Not as much as Gabe will. Do we know anything about the attacker?" Justine leaned back in her chair.

"I don't think it's connected to Philip," Lily said. *"I know how he feels in digital. I didn't sense that around Mike."*

"So it's a matter of waiting," Justine said. "All right. Ron. The Martiniere Group isn't going to run itself, and now that we know Mike's going to be all right—at least cognitively—we better not leave him a mess."

"Meet you in the office," Ron said.

"We'll let you know when we hear something," Ruby said. *"Meanwhile,*

I need some downtime, and Bran, you probably do as well. Lily, you can take watch? Just in case?"

"Yes," Lily said.

SEVERAL HOURS LATER, JUSTINE AND RON HAD FINISHED WHAT THEY could do as substitutes for Mike. Justine decided to sit on the deck outside of Moondance's great room to read and take a break. The sunshades would keep the deck cool for another couple of hours. And after last night's excitement, she was *tired*, damn it.

As she settled into a lounge chair, Justine wondered how the process was going with Mike. No news was good news—maybe.

The prickling sensation that was Gabie snooping around alerted her. "Gabie. What's the news?"

He appeared, looking less solid than usual as he dropped into another lounge chair. *"God, what a fucking mess. Our damn father. Back doors upon back doors in Mike's brain. Some of them possibly created as part of the cloning process."*

That was *so* not a good situation.

Justine flinched. "Is Mike compromised?"

"No," Gabie said. *"But it took damn near everything I ever knew about mind control programming to make the resets work."* He shook his head. *"It's sad. Our father was a cognitive programming genius. He could have used that programming to help people with emotional and cognitive problems. Could have created designs that would have made a difference in recovery from strokes and other health problems."*

"Was this his doing?"

Gabie rubbed his face—a common gesture of his from life. *"Definitely not. But what I saw worries me. It's not Martiniere, though it has a Martiniere foundation. It's someone who has built on the Martiniere structures."*

"A former employee? A Family member gone rogue?"

"I wish it were as simple as that," Gabie said. *"Whoever's doing this knows the Electric Born methods. Not Zingter-tied, at least."*

"But you said it's not connected to our father." Damn it. Electric

Born. The religious cult their damn father had created. And unlike Gabie, she wasn't quick to rule out Zingter. Walter Braun's company had been involved with indentured programming, including the use of Electric Born methods.

"Not him. But definitely a branch of the Electric Born. I thought I'd taken care of all of those Heaven's Reach fanatics years ago."

Justine gulped. Of all the fanatics who had participated in the Electric Born, the collective of communes called Heaven's Reach had been the most extreme.

"You're telling me that fucking Heaven's Reach still exists?" Ruby appeared, scowling. *"I thought that nightmare was gone. I thought we finally put an end to them!"*

"Rubes, I'm sorry. I was wrong. There were still other survivors we didn't know about. Five of them. One of whom was our inside informant."

"Doug Gates? He's turned on us?"

"No," Gabie said. *"The people who tortured Gates. Including the original informant. Samuel Hawkins."*

"Was Hawkins manipulated?" Ruby continued to scowl at Gabie, hands on her hips.

He shook his head. *"No. My guess is that he sought to eliminate the Heaven's Reach leadership in order to depose his father and other competitors for control of the commune, plus go off in a different direction from what Philip was doing. That's why he betrayed them to Alvarez Armory. He talked a good game—and after Rafe was killed and I finished the job, there was no one to follow up and monitor what Hawkins was doing, beyond what Justine and Donald did."*

"How dangerous is Hawkins?"

"If he's like his father, then he's making all sorts of followers. I would not put it past him to indoctrinate willing victims to build their digi foundation, then kill themselves so they're fully digital."

"Fuck," Justine sighed. *"So that's why you want me to build a foundation to go digi when I die. And why you're looking for a possible Donald digi."*

"Ruby told me what you said about not feeling Donald's presence. I dug a little bit further. Donald took measures to prevent himself from being forced

into becoming a digi unless very specific procedures were implemented. It dates from after my death."

"What sort of measures?" Damn it, Donald must have been incredibly secretive about this project. Then again, while Gabie's ascendance and Philip's death allowed Justine and Donald to publicly reconcile—it hadn't been a remarriage. A lot had happened to both of them, and most important—she and Donald weren't Ruby and Gabie.

"Every damn digital record involving Donald that can be used to make a digi is either nuked beyond recovery, or it's locked down and keyed to you only, Tine."

"So I have to die for Donald to become a digi?"

"No. He created the base algorithm, but it's locked down hard and I don't know if it's complete. I may have to tweak the programming once he's activated." Gabie rubbed his face again. *"The two of you together in digi would be powerful. I—I'm afraid there's a lot more of them out there than I realized twenty-four hours ago. I hope I'm wrong."*

"What about Donald's files that are keyed to me? Can I access them now?"

"Yes. But I don't want you fiddling with them by yourself. Me or Lily by your side—Lily's getting very good at dealing with these files—and physical non-digi support for you. Digigloves for you as well."

Ruby appeared. *"Go take your break, Gabe. You're going transparent. I'll keep watch. Bran's with Mike?"*

"Yes. Thanks, Rubes," Gabie said. He faded out.

Justine sighed. "The more I hear, the more I dread this form of cyberwar. What's stopping digis from becoming more numerous than living people?"

God, she could just imagine what it could be like—in all the negative ways. Grandparents hovering over children and grandchildren, second-guessing their real-life choices and taking offense whenever their descendants took off on their own paths.

"I don't know," Ruby said. *"We need to devise some sort of control and policing mechanism—but I haven't the faintest idea what that would be."*

Justine shook her head. One thing after another. And if she went digi—an eternity of fixing things stretched out ahead of her.

Was that what she really wanted?

Not by myself.

THINGS WERE QUIET FOR THE NEXT TWO DAYS, WITH STEADY REPORTS OF Mike's improvement. Deontae returned to the Double R and covered for Mike and JoAnn. Justine worked in the basement office at Moondance. It was so different from the offices she and Donald once had at Mist Knoll—Moondance's design allowed for natural light to come in through a shielded sliding glass door and a small balcony. The great deck overhead protected the office from outside eavesdropping.

Gabie's second wife Rachel, the original Moondance's architect, had possessed a certain design flair. Justine appreciated it more each day—and the appreciation added another regret, that she had never known Rachel as her sister-in-law.

Her comm chimed. *"Mike Martiniere."*

Justine startled and flipped it on. "Mike!"

He grinned at her. No more dark circles under his eyes, and instead of bone-pale skin, his cheeks had a faint pinkish tinge.

"Good to see you, too, Justine," he said.

"You look a *lot* better."

"I *feel* better." He stretched. "I suspect I've had problems with the function of my heart and lungs for longer than we thought. Last spring's cyborg upgrades were hard on those systems, and, well—" He shrugged. "Dr. Pramula agrees. She's also unsure about how far back those heart-lung problems go. They may be a sign of tampering."

"Everything's all right now?"

Mike nodded. "Full replacement, and both Gabe and Brandon checked the programming. The other piece is that there were triggers set in my cloning to counter certain cyborg techniques. They've been defused."

"Well, we've been keeping up with things, but there are some matters I'd sure like to get you briefed on as soon as possible," Justine said.

"Maybe tomorrow," Mike said. "Another week locked up in the hospital because of testing and physical therapy. I don't have much strength. Meanwhile, I'm bored. Think you might have a short-ish story that isn't going to make you cry?"

Justine snorted. "From *my* life? Michael, who on earth are you kidding? We're getting close to the divorce. Founding of the Rescue Angel." She pursed her lips thoughtfully. "I can skim over several years. Why don't you give me a few minutes to get back upstairs? You round up the digis. Sound good?"

"Anything that isn't about cyborging, cloning, or hospitals sounds great right now," Mike said.

"All right. I'll call back when I get settled."

"Sounds good."

Justine exhaled and reached for her walker.

It was amazing how Mike's improved health brightened her outlook about the future.

Maybe life with all these damn digis wouldn't be so bad after all.

8 / IS THIS THE FUTURE WE WANT?

THE FIRST TIME JUSTINE THOUGHT SHE SPOTTED GABIE WAS AT FRESH FOOD Now, the new upscale supermarket in Corvallis. She ducked in on her way back from Lora's. Their cook Samy had heard a rumor about fresh fish suddenly becoming available, and messaged Justine on her way home from the barn.

—*Might even be salmon,* Samy added. —*I don't know and I can't leave what I'm doing. You'll be all right with that?*

—*For the possibility of salmon, you bet.*

Justine grinned at that thought. Samy was a Coral find, a young widowed immigrant mother searching for a means to get out of New York City without going into indentured debt. It took a while for Justine and Donald to get Samy used to their informal manners, but now…Samy was comfortable asking Justine or Donald to pick up something on their way home.

"What are you doing?" Brent Colfax, the security guard with her, asked as Justine turned off of her usual route. Driving herself was a major point of contention with the Martiniere security team that answered to her father. Most of them eventually unbent and relaxed about it—but not Colfax. Perhaps it was because he was the head of that team, or perhaps he was just that tight-assed.

Justine thought it was the latter. She had encountered enough security team heads like Colfax while living in her father's house. Colfax didn't even like it when she rode one of her horses around the vineyard without Donald.

Motherfucker's like having Daddy-fucking-dearest hanging around. Constantly. At least she could give him orders he *had* to obey, unless there was specifically a security crisis.

"Samy thinks that there may be salmon available," Justine said as she parked her sporty two-seater in the lot. "I'm going to check."

Colfax grumbled, but didn't object. He followed two steps behind her, like always.

A good thing. Justine caught a glimpse of a familiar silhouette loading a bag into the back seat of a nondescript brown sedan.

It took every ounce of will she possessed not to react, to turn her head away as if she hadn't noticed. Much as she wanted to run up and give Gabie a hug, if Colfax saw him, he *would* rat Gabie out to Daddy-damn-dearest.

———

"You're awfully quiet," Donald said that evening. "Something wrong at the stable? In classes?"

"No," Justine said. "I—think I saw Gabie getting into a car at Fresh Food Now."

Donald raised his brows. "Now that *is* interesting, because I thought I saw him yesterday, by one of those ag worker residential motels. Driving a small brown sedan?"

"Yes."

"Fuck," Donald sighed. "We need to be careful with Colfax and his crew."

"It was just *so hard*. I wanted to run over and hug him, thank him for getting me away from Daddy-fucking-dearest. For bringing you into my life."

He reached over and tucked a strand of her brunette hair out of her face. "Someday, my dear. Someday. Meanwhile, I talked to Mom. It's time to finish the transition from your father's partial security to exclusively ours. She's hearing political things that make me very worried."

"Political things?"

"Proposals for a national anti-abortion police force," Donald said. "Your father is bankrolling the organization promoting it. Mom wasn't certain about that aspect until last week. Now…she is."

"And having Daddy-poo's security on site makes us a risk for Real Lives for Women and—the other work," Justine said.

"Exactly. Family Christmas is a good time to make the transition. We'll take Colfax and his people to Paris. All of them, no one left at Mist Knoll. While we're gone, Mom will supervise a complete sweep of the property, then set up our new security systems. Then we leave Colfax et al in Paris, and she meets us with our new external security at the airport. Sound good?"

"Sounds *marvelous*." Justine was *so* tired of dealing with Colfax and his team.

* * *

December, 2029

ANOTHER GABIE SIGHTING, NEAR THE END OF THE COLLEGE TERM. COLFAX with her again, *of course, damn it*. This one was in a crowded bar. A girls' night out with wine and food industry friends, except, of course, for Colfax trailing along—Daddy-poo didn't believe in running female security. And why did it have to be *him* and not one of the nicer security men who tagged along behind her every time….

Justine distracted Colfax by asking him to get her a non-alcoholic drink when she spotted Gabie entering the bar—with *Ruby* from the barn, of all people. From the way they leaned into each other, plus Gabie's rare, relaxed grin at Ruby, the two of them were a couple.

Oh God. Ruby was glowing as she worked around the barn. Justine had overheard Ruby asking Lora whether it was all right for Ruby's new boyfriend to spend weeknights in her barn apartment, back in October.

Gabie must be the boyfriend. *Shit.* This made things very complicated. So far, she hadn't spotted him or that little brown car there, but—

Fortunately, Gabie looked around the bar. His face tightened into wariness and he and Ruby left, before Colfax returned with her drink.

Justine checked the drink discreetly, as she always did. Safe, but she still didn't trust Colfax.

They'd be leaving for Family Christmas in a few days. She would be *done* with him.

Meanwhile Gabie should be warned. His appearance made Colfax's insistence that he be the one to cover her off-site even more suspicious. Did Colfax or Daddy-fucking-dearest suspect that Gabie was in the area?

"I saw Gabie again," she told Donald after they went to bed. "In the bar. With Ruby from the barn. I think he's her boyfriend."

"You should warn him about Colfax and your security."

"How the hell can I get away without Colfax breathing down my neck? I can't leave the place without him. Even when it's not his shift."

"You're certain it was Gabe with Ruby?"

"Positive."

"How long do you think it's been going on?"

When had Ruby started acting like she was in a serious relationship?

"First part of November, and he's not around on weekends," she decided. That was when Ruby started being more friendly on Sunday afternoons, watching the clock, offering to take over tack cleaning so that Justine—and her entourage—would leave sooner. All polite, of course, offered in a tone of *I bet you want to get home to Donald sooner.* And the occasional glare at Colfax, getting snippy about him being in the way.

Yeah. How much did Ruby know about Gabie?

Donald rolled on his back and crossed his hands behind his head, studying the ceiling.

"He's aware that you're around, but is still dating Ruby and trying to avoid you. For nearly two months. Crud. From what I know about Gabe, that means serious interest in her."

"He was pretty skittish about getting involved with any of the women he dated years ago," Justine said. "Then again, they were all high-society types more interested in snagging a high-level Martiniere heir than any genuine interest in Gabie. Or Daddy-damned-dearest delegated Gabie to make up for something stupid that Joey did to a high-society daughter. The *polite* Martiniere heir, not the ass."

"Let's see. It's Thursday, which means—Gabe might be at the stable early tomorrow morning. I'll have Twyla from our security distract Colfax long enough for you to slip out."

"He'll notice if my car's gone."

"Hmm. Twyla to distract, Shanice to drive you to the barn and drop you off so that Colfax isn't alerted right away. Sound like a plan?"

"It's worth a try."

FORTUNATELY, THE NEXT MORNING WAS COOL AND FOGGY, BUT NOT RAINY. Justine and Shanice slipped out the back way from Mist Knoll, Justine disguised as a farmworker. They parked in a wildlife viewing area near the barn. Shanice gave Justine a radio plug to stick in her ear.

"I'll send a warning if I see someone coming," she said. "Yell for help if you need it. I won't listen in otherwise."

"Thanks."

She could trust Shanice. Justine slipped out of the coveralls over her workout suit. She jogged down the driveway on the grass, not on the gravel—that would alert the horses in the barn.

Nickers started up before she reached the barn. Justine swore softly, until she saw the lean, lanky figure studying the little brown car. That was what had set the horses off. Not her.

"Gabie." Her voice quavered as he rose from checking under the car for any sort of sabotage.

He froze, his body instinctively coiling to attack. Then he exhaled, releasing that tension, and straightened, turning to face her. His eyes were cold and hard as he glared at Justine and she shivered, suddenly reminded of her father.

Gabie had lost a lot of weight. His face was leaner than she remembered, with a new scar.

"I thought that was you," Justine said, trying to smile. This wasn't a Gabie that she could run up to and hug. This was a predator in defensive mode.

He sighed, and sagged against the car, that dangerous glower *so like Daddy-poo* fading from his face.

"All right, Tine. Just do me a favor. Don't have your minions kill me where Ruby will find out. You owe me that much."

Aw, fuck. She was now categorized as *someone I can't trust.*

"Gabie, *really.* Why do you think I'm here this early?" She glanced around, to ensure that Colfax wasn't sneaking up on her. "I don't have much time. Ducked away from Daddy-poo's guards, but they'll figure it out soon enough. Luckily, I have a habit of slipping out to jog by myself first thing in the morning. Pisses them off." A lie, but it served her purpose. He relaxed—slightly.

"How did you find out?"

"Caught a glimpse of you in Corvallis with Ruby."

"Shit. And I thought I was being careful."

"So far it's been just me," she said. And Donald, but she wouldn't mention that.

"Yeah, but if you've made me, then it won't be long before your entourage figures it out as well. Damn it."

"I'm sorry. But I thought I'd better warn you." She glanced around again. Why the hell did she feel like Colfax was watching? "Look. Don't get too spooked. We're heading for Family Christmas on Monday. That gives you time to tell Ruby."

He clenched his fists, then opened them, clearly wounded by the thought of the impending separation from his love. "Thanks for the warning."

God, she hated seeing her cousin like this. Especially since he obviously cared about Ruby. There had to be a way around this mess. Somehow.

"Gabie. If you want to come back, there are ways. Daddy-dearest does not have a lock on the Family. Even if he *is* the Martiniere, you still have allies."

Cousin Kendra would help shelter Gabie and Ruby. So would Barbie.

She had no idea how Ruby would fit within the Family, but from what she had seen around the barn, the redhead could hold her own against Daddy-damned-dearest.

"So did my father. And now he's dead." His face set in hard lines.

No. It wasn't going to be this easy, damn it.

"I'm just saying it's an option." She sighed. "Donald's getting sick of Daddy-poo and his controlling behavior. I'm transitioning from Martiniere security to Atwood security over Christmas. It will be different when I come back. But you best lay low this weekend." Let him know that he wasn't *completely* cut off from Ruby.

A weary expression softened his face. "I'll be working my ass off."

"Manual labor, I suppose."

"Yep."

"It's a waste of your talents."

"But at least I'm my own person and not dead. Which is what your father really wants." He heaved a heavy sigh and shook his head. "I have to get to work, Tine. Is Joey part of your entourage?"

"God, *no!* He still hates horses. Just like Daddy-dearest. He's still in Los Angeles." She paused. "Gabie. Be careful. If I could figure out your pattern...."

"I appreciate it, Tine." His voice was softer. She thought about running up to Gabie and hugging him. Something held her back. She watched him drive away.

Justine wearily picked up a jog and returned to her car.

"Colfax is having an absolute *meltdown*," Shanice said. "Did it work?"

"Yes," Justine said, finding it hard to keep regret out of her voice. "It worked."

Damn it, Gabie, I wish you wouldn't do this all by yourself. I wish you'd join with us to fight Daddy-damned-dearest. Let us help you.

But Gabie had to do it his own way; that had always been the case with him. Stubborn buttheaded Martiniere man.

Would she ever see her cousin again?

FAMILY CHRISTMAS WAS *HELL* THAT YEAR. DONALD FINALLY EXPLODED AT her father, when Daddy-damned-dearest berated them at Christmas Day breakfast about their termination of any vestiges of Martiniere security. They stormed out of the house with Serg, Philip bellowing angrily after them from the doorway.

The minute the gates of the Hôtel Martiniere closed behind them, Donald changed their charter reservation.

"We don't need to stop at the condo before we leave Paris," Donald said after he hung up. "I found an immediate charter booking so we don't need hotel reservations anywhere. No need to switch planes or stop other than to refuel. I'm sorry, dear, but Colfax and his men have access to our things at the condo. I don't trust a damn thing there right now."

"That's all right," she said, quivering because in spite of the blocks that Piotr had installed, the resonances of Daddy-fucking-dearest's tones impacted her, *hard.* And without Donna-gran present to moderate his temper....

"Did the blocks work?" Serg asked.

"I still get hit by the resonances. I know he was trying to compel me to do something, but I have absolutely no idea what it was."

"Good," Serg said.

Donald put his arm around her as he talked to his mother, letting her know of their arrival—with Serg. Once he finished, he kissed her temple and held her close.

It was reminiscent of their wedding day—and she suddenly realized that it *was* their anniversary.

Neither of them remembered it—or so she thought. They left both

Christmas and anniversary presents back home because Donald *had* anticipated this likelihood.

Donald gave her a jade and pearl earring and necklace set as they flew home.

"For Christmas and our third anniversary," he said. "Three wonderful years."

"In spite of my fucking father?"

He delicately kissed her lips. "Yes. I bought them at Cartier and carried them on me at all times. I thought something like this might happen, and I didn't want to risk leaving them behind."

"Thank you," she whispered.

Three years completed; four more years of their agreement.

If they chose to stick to it.

JANUARY, *2030*

GABIE'S LITTLE BROWN CAR WAS AT THE BARN. NO SIGN OF RUBY OR HER truck. Had Gabie persuaded Ruby to join him on the run?

Ruby reappeared after New Year's. The car disappeared.

No explanations, and Justine didn't pry. Gabie had made his choice clear.

MAY, *2030*

MIDTERM PRIMARY ELECTIONS WERE BRUTAL AS FAR AS REAL LIVES FOR Women and their shadow activities were concerned. The Real Truthers party debuted as a splinter Republican committee, running on an even more repressive platform than they promoted throughout the 2020s. But the Democratic party also showed signs of shattering.

"It's a mess," Barbie sighed. "We might be able to salvage the general election. The Truthers are solidifying their grip on the Republicans. The Rs might have lost another presidential election, but—they won't lose 2032. We need to be ready, because if they get their majorities in state Houses and in the Congress, they'll recriminalize contraception. They're almost there already."

Justine shuddered. "And then what?"

Barbie fixed her with a steady look. "We work on legalization of contraception and abortion, once more. We also need to watch movement toward expanding indenture. It was already difficult for indentured workers to earn their way free when your cousin testified against the Martiniere Group. But the proposals I've heard—will make it damn near impossible for anyone, especially a woman or trans person, to get free from indenture, once they've gone under contract. Any marginalized person is at risk of lifetime indenture."

"Daddy-fucking-dearest's work," Justine snarled.

Barbie nodded.

June, 2030

Horses were a welcome distraction from politics, college coursework, and business, especially now that Justine owned a high-level showjumper. The more she worked with Glory, the chestnut Selle Français mare she bought from Lora, the more Justine treasured her. The big mare enjoyed jumping, would even take herself over a course if turned loose in the arena when fences were set up.

Glory provided interesting challenges. If she got bored in a paddock or turnout field, she jumped the fence to go wherever she wanted. More than once, Justine found Glory in a different pen than her own, because the chestnut mare decided to go visiting.

The powerful mare needed careful guidance over any sort of difficult course, because she muscled through complicated fences rather than be precise, and sent rails flying. Justine and Lora drilled down on schooling Justine's eye for takeoff spots rather than allowing Glory to pick and choose her own. They also dedicated the spring to honing Justine's skill in rating Glory's speed.

They spent the summer and fall traveling to big horse shows, both Lora and Justine riding. Lora showed a string of young horses for their owners. Justine leased two of the young horses to ease the load on Lora when their owners couldn't ride. Part of keeping her amateur status. Ruby wasn't available, because she quit after her graduation from Oregon State in June.

"Ruby's shooting for Miss Rodeo Oregon this summer," Lora said when Justine asked why Ruby hadn't joined them on the circuit.

"Rodeo over showjumping?" Justine munched on a faux roast beef sandwich as they sat on tack trunks outside of the stalls at the latest show. "That's sad. She could go far in eventing and jumping. She's good."

Lora shrugged. "She's tied down to the family ranch for the fore-seeable future. Aging grandparents, no parents, and even with hired help, Ruby can't tour the show circuit like you can. Miss Rodeo Oregon lets her travel around the state, occasionally outside...though she might be gunning for Miss Rodeo America. I don't know how she's planning to cover things at the ranch if she wins that title, but I'm sure she'll find a way."

"Ah. That's ambitious."

"We've talked about it. She figures that rodeo titles will help with promotion of her ag robotics work."

"Choosing rodeo does make sense, from a marketing point of view," Justine conceded.

Still, the thought was tempting to hire Ruby and finance her rise in showjumping and eventing. Donna-gran might be interested in funding Ruby's showjumping career.

On the other hand, if Ruby was still seeing Gabie, it would only attract Daddy-damned-dearest's attention not only to them but to Justine's undercover organizing work. Traveling to horse shows provided a good cover for her to travel around the country and meet with local cells.

And then there was Donald. An ever-growing worry throughout the summer. He sent her flowers every time she won, even on horses besides Glory. Messaged pictures of the new display featuring her and Glory in the tasting room at the vineyard, adding her cups and ribbons to it when she shipped them home. Boasted of the painting of her and Glory he had commissioned. He *sounded* happy and proud of her during their nightly calls.

But. This summer, either Coral, Francie, or Meg stayed with him. Something new. Oh, she was glad they were with him. They gave her private reports on his health, and it was another bad Crohn's summer.

Donald mentioned a possible need for surgery during one call in August.

"No, honey, not this summer," he said when she pushed for more information. "You stay on the circuit. It's not happening that fast."

Should she go home to be with Donald? How sick *was* he? That worry kept her up that night, sending her to Glory's stall for consolation, crying into the big mare's neck as worry tightened her gut.

"Your presence isn't going to make a lot of difference right now, and Don's enjoying news of your success," Coral bluntly told Justine when she called the next day. "We'll let you know if you need to come home."

The mess on the political scene didn't help, either. The evidence of growing structural problems showed up as Justine and Lora traveled through the Southwest, then to the Midwest and East Coast. Higher poverty visible from the interstate highways—more rundown and abandoned places. More indentured labor. Infrastructure falling apart —Justine lost count of the times they needed to divert off of the interstate because of bridge collapses. Desperation in the voices of the women she secretly met with, grateful for even the tiniest bit of help Justine could provide.

Justine developed the habit of bringing extra food to those gatherings.

More security joined Shanice and Twyla, openly armed, guarding truck and trailer when they stopped for gas, food, and water. Shanice and Twyla carried weapons all the time now, even around the horses.

"We have to be ready," Barbie kept saying during their clandestine organizing meetings. "Organizations in place, ready to go live should we lose. And even if we win or hold our losses down, we need to keep building. One defeat won't be sufficient to shut down our opponents. We have to keep fighting, over and over again."

It seemed to be an endless cycle of organizing, gaining and losing, regrouping and organizing further.

And yet Justine felt like they might be making some difference.

Even if it felt like she was bailing out a sinking ship.

November, 2030

DESPITE THEIR HARD WORK, THEIR WORST FEARS CAME TRUE. THE TRUTHER faction dominated the Republican slate on Election Day. They earned a majority in the House but not the Senate—missed that just barely. The Southwest and the South elected Truther governors and legislators. Justine watched in horror, along with Twyla and Shanice.

It was the overwhelming victory that the Republicans had claimed they would win in 2020—ten years later.

"Well, we know what our work is going to be," Barbie said when Justine called her, in tears because the losses were just so devastating. "They won't get everything at once. Even with this victory. We must make them fight for every rollback they want to implement."

"It seems like a lot of work," Justine said.

"Every generation has to fight this battle. Right now, we're the ones with the money and privilege to organize, with fewer personal consequences than most people. It's up to us to lead the charge."

"I hadn't thought of it that way," Justine said.

But it made sense.

HER FATHER APPEARED AT JUSTINE'S LAST BIG SHOW OF THE SEASON, JUST before Thanksgiving.

Justine and Glory won a silver cup as well as a big multicolored ribbon. She rode back to the stall row after a victory lap of the arena, feet hanging out of her stirrups, Glory ambling along on a long rein. Shanice carried the ribbon; Lora the cup.

Glory stopped short. Justine looked down the alleyway. Her father stood outside of the tack stall with Twyla, looking uncomfortable.

"Step back and let me take care of this," Justine said quietly to Shanice and Lora. "That's my father. Philip Martiniere."

She gathered her reins and rode Glory up to Daddy-damned-dearest, a faint thrill going through her as his eyes widened at their approach. Glory was a soft touch of a mare, a pushover who would slobber over anyone who scratched her forehead and fed her treats. Since her father was afraid of horses, he wouldn't know the difference between gentle Glory and a stud horse who'd paw him as soon as look at him. Philip would just see a large animal that could hurt him.

Justine intended to take advantage of that position of power.

"Justine," he said, looking up at her.

"Daddy-dearest."

Glory extended her nose toward Philip, seeking a treat or pat. He backed up a step.

"You're—uh—doing pretty well at this. Quite the accomplishments this year."

"Thank you."

"Can we talk?"

"Go ahead."

He looked uncomfortable. "I—uh—thought you might get off the horse."

"Glory has to walk to cool off and unwind. Shall we go to the warmup arena?"

Truthfully not necessary, but there was no way in hell Justine was getting off Glory while her father was here.

"All right," he sighed, and fell in at her stirrup, keeping the horse at arm's length. They proceeded down the alleyway to the warmup, fortunately mostly empty. Justine let Glory take the reins through her fingers as she stretched her neck, almost to the buckle holding them together.

"You look good," he said awkwardly.

"Thank you." *What the hell does he want?* And why had Daddy-damned-dearest chosen to approach her at the show, of all places? "You'd better move closer to us," she said as they entered the warmup arena.

Philip grimaced but obeyed. "Justine. I know you're busy with your husband's business and all. But I wondered if you would be interested in working for the Group."

What the hell is he up to?

"You've got to be kidding."

His lips tightened. "I need—help."

With what? Politics? He doesn't need me for that. And he has to know that I'm on the opposite side. Donald and I haven't exactly been hiding our political preferences. Unless—he wants to neutralize me.

"Doing what?" Her mouth went dry.

"Logistics."

"You can hire people for that."

"Do you *have* to make it this hard, damn it?" Philip winced and looked away. "Look, Justine. I'm sorry. Is that what you want to hear from me?"

"It's a start."

Sorry for what? And just saying sorry isn't going to get you a big break.

"I've heard good things about your fundraising efforts even though the cause is—not the most appealing. The logistics work you've been doing for the winery and your husband's businesses. The fact is—I need someone in the Family to manage certain things. Can we at least discuss the possibility?"

"Right here?"

"No." A horse and rider galloped by them and Philip shivered. "Over dinner, at a place of your choice."

"Donald will be there."

"Of course."

"Let me talk to him and get back to you. We're not planning to be at Family Christmas, so it'll have to be before you leave for Paris."

"That would be fine." Philip glanced around nervously. "I'll let you go now."

She took mercy on her father and escorted him to the gate, then continued walking Glory for a couple more circuits.

"Did you want clear water in order to hydrate, no sparkling?" Shanice asked when Justine rode back to the stalls.

"I'm thirsty enough to drink anything," Justine said, finishing the code phrase for *everything's fine, no issues.* She dismounted. Lora brought Glory's halter to Justine and she slipped off the bridle, haltered the big mare, and fastened her in the cross-ties.

"Twyla was here when he came up. He was never here unsupervised," Shanice said.

"He didn't touch me."

"Good."

That dealt with, Justine finished caring for Glory, questions spinning in her head the whole time.

What the hell does Daddy-fucking-dearest want?

She called Donald once she and Lora settled for the night into the living quarters trailer near their barn row. She cranked the security screens as high as they could go.

After chatting about the show and her travel timing, Justine took a deep breath.

"I have complications, Donald." *Complications* was their code word for political issues.

"Oh?"

"Daddy-fucking-dearest wants to talk."

"About what?"

"He wants me to do logistics work for him."

Silence. Then. "What the fuck is going on?"

"I have no damn idea. I'm scared. Really scared."

"You can handle it. You're good at politics."

"But why the hell is he asking *me* to work with him? He's got Joey. All his sycophants. Why me?" She sighed. "He wants to discuss it over a dinner. I told him not without you there. That we would talk and I'd get back to him."

"Let's look at schedules when you get home. Should I send out feelers to our adjuncts?" Meaning Serg and Kendra, of course.

"Discreetly, but...yes."

JUSTINE FRETTED ABOUT WHAT PHILIP MIGHT WANT FROM HER ALL THE WAY home. Glory came to Mist Knoll with her—down time after a competitive season.

Donald met them at the stable and helped Justine settle Glory into her big stall. He sat down several times to catch his breath as they worked.

He had lost a lot of weight, too.

No one told me he was this bad!

And that was after Coral had *promised* to call her if necessary. Donald didn't have much weight to lose in the first place.

Damn it, I should call Daddy-poo and tell him I have a husband to take care of.

One way to dodge whatever it was that Daddy-damned-dearest was scheming.

Shanice and Twyla took a crawler up to the house with her luggage. Justine eyed the downpour outside, focusing on Glory as the big mare wandered around the oversized double stall. Glory stopped, pawed the sawdust and straw mix, then rolled. She rose and shook herself before nosing heartily into the pile of hay in one corner.

All good there.

Glory was a good traveler but the storm made Justine worry about colic. Not likely now. She turned her attention to her husband.

"Are you sure you want to walk up to the house?" No crawler waiting for them.

He shook his head. "I wouldn't make it. My crawler's down at the tasting room."

"Let me get it."

"No need." He pulled out his phone. "Serg? Yes. She's here and the horse is settled. All right. See you in a few."

"What's going on?"

Donald guided her over to one of her tack trunks and they sat. "Gerard, Kendra, and Piotr are here with Serg. Very hush-hush. We've spent the past day securing the stable. No one will expect us to talk in here."

"Uncle Gerard's *here*?" More serious than she thought.

"Came in dressed as a farmworker, no less."

"Wow." She leaned against Donald. *Something* was happening. Meanwhile, her husband— "Hon. You've lost a lot of weight. Why didn't one of the ladies call me?"

He hugged her. "You were doing so well. I didn't want to be a distraction."

"I should have been here, nonetheless." Yes, Coral had already told her what he was now saying. But damn it, she *was* Donald's wife. Didn't she need to act like it?

"Why? So you'd fret and worry over me? If things had gotten bad enough, they would have called. I've been enjoying your success vicariously, darling. Watching the live feeds from your shows has been the best thing for me. I would have watched you in person except that I knew the minute you set eyes on me, you'd want to stop." Donald shook his head. "I didn't want to take that away from you. And I was right. You're blossoming." He smiled. "My falcon is starting to show her strength."

"I still should have known," she said.

"Your nursemaiding me has not been a feature of our relationship in the past, and it is not going to be one in the future," he said firmly. "That's not who you are. That's not who *we* are." His jaw set and she knew it was pointless to argue further. "Besides, that's not what I want or need from you, dear one. You are my falcon. Watching you fly makes me happy."

How could she argue with that? Justine sighed. "What's going on with you? Now that I'm here."

"Surgery. It's a matter of timing—the doctors want me to gain weight first. It'll be easier to do over the holiday season." He exhaled. "And no. We are not using my health as an excuse to bail out on whatever it is your father wants from you. There's a lot in play. But you'll hear the details when Gerard gets here."

The big barn door slid open. Gerard, Kendra, Piotr, and Serg came in, Barbie trailing after the Family members. Serg closed the door after them and activated a protective shield. Glory raised her head from her hay and snorted as Justine felt the shield tingle through her.

"Uncle Gerry, I can't believe you came all the way from France on such short notice." Justine hugged him. He *did* look the part of a farmworker in dirty coveralls and a well-worn cap, dirt smudged on his face.

"Eh, I needed to brief you in person."

"What *did* Donald tell you?" Justine eyed the others. This was major. Uncle Gerry. Kendra—who, despite being female, was a powerful cousin in the Family.

"That Philip approached you about a logistics position," Serg said. He glanced at the others before continuing. "Given recent events in the Family and in the Group, I had to report it to Gerard, because—"

Gerard broke in. "The Board has told Philip that Joseph is not an acceptable candidate for the Martiniere-in-waiting. Philip will not propose a permanent substitute, but argues that Joseph can be rehabilitated. The Board wants someone reliable to step in that role, the Martiniere-in-waiting in all but name, and promptly. Someone who is not in Philip's back pocket."

"There's no way on earth that my father would ever put me in that position," Justine said.

"The position must be filled. Officially or unofficially," Gerard said. "And again, not an ally of Philip's. The Board has made that clear to him. If Gabriel were available—then it would be him. Without Gabriel —you are the oldest, most likely prospect that your father will accept."

"Why not Kendra?"

"He doesn't trust me. And I'm a woman," Kendra said.

"So am I."

"But you're his daughter," Kendra said. "That makes things different."

Justine shook her head, stunned by what she was hearing.

Martiniere-in-waiting. The heir not just to the Family but the Group. But the Salic Law structures of both Family and Group excluded women from attaining that role.

"My fucking father would never give me the title," she said. "You know that as well as I do. His ideology, coupled with Family rules, won't allow it."

"The position would not carry the title." Gerard sat on the other tack trunk.

"Who would I be holding it for? I'm certainly not having my own children, thanks to my surgery. A son of Joey? Someone else?" A sudden thought occurred to her. "Or does Daddy-poo have a previously unacknowledged child hidden away?"

Gerard shrugged, lifting his hands. "We have no idea. Gabriel is still alive. If we can persuade him to return—"

"Uncle Gerry, I *tried* a year ago. Gabie is convinced he doesn't have enough support to pull it off," Justine said. "And as for my father, why would he be so damn stupid as to put *me* in that powerful a position within the Group and the Family? He knows I hate his guts. Doesn't he?"

Piotr laughed, a bitter tone in his voice. "He has convinced himself that Gabriel corrupted you. That marriage has modulated your views."

Justine snorted.

"He holds you up as an example to the women of the Family," Kendra said. "You obey your husband. You're doing well showing your horse. But you're still feminine, and you're helping your husband with his business."

"Dear God. He's really painting me as that much of an angel?" Justine shook her head again as Donald chuckled, followed by Gerard and the others. "And not a word about my political organizing."

Piotr grimaced. "The follies of youth, he calls it."

"He needs you to put a veneer of respectability on his actions. Just as he has used Gabriel to cover up the wrongs that Joseph did when they were younger," Gerard said. "This gives us an opportunity to place an insider to monitor his actions."

"That assumes he will trust me with anything significant."

"Oh, he will probably not do that," Piotr said.

"Most definitely not," Kendra muttered.

"But you will be in position to observe and learn his plans," Gerard said.

"A spy," Justine said.

"Exactly," Piotr said.

"And you think he'd trust me? That he honestly believes I'll be loyal to him?"

"His hand is forced by the Board," Gerard said. "You are the one likely candidate that he feels he can control."

Justine took Donald's hand. "What happens when he discovers that he *can't* control me? You know damn good and well he won't hold back from attacking me if he thinks that will get him what he wants."

Barbie shifted her feet. "Because you are married to the man who has a controlling interest in his bank."

Donald squeezed her hand. "Mom and I made the switch this summer."

"Philip will not physically attack the adult daughter who has been confirmed in her position by the Board of the Martiniere Group," said Gerard. "Especially when she is married to the man who—as Barbara says—controls the line of credit that belongs to his personal division."

Justine took a deep breath. "I would have the backing of the Board?"

"Absolutely," Gerard said.

"And complete support from Vygotsky Security," Piotr said.

"All right. I'll talk to him. If we can get through the initial agreements without killing each other—I will serve, at the Board's pleasure."

What have I done? she thought, even as she said it.

But—she was a high-level Martiniere heir. And the Family had made a request of her.

She could not turn it down.

JUSTINE MOVED THROUGH THE REST OF THE DAY IN A STUNNED DAZE, UNTIL she was in bed with Donald. She couldn't stop quivering. It didn't feel like she was coming down sick, or chilled. More like fatigued muscles going into spasms—except it not like that, either.

Donald kissed her forehead. "Sweet one, talk to me."

Tears blurred her eyes. "I'm only twenty-one, and God help me, the Family has tied this around my neck."

"Almost twenty-two," Donald murmured. "It's just talking to your father. Not actually accepting the position. You could turn it down."

"No." She pulled back. "You *don't understand.* The Family is *commanding* me to accept this position with Daddy-poo! Gerard and

Piotr for the elders; Kendra and Serg for my generation. And my fucking father wants it, as well." She burst into sobs. "What if it's a trap? What if I'm a sacrifice in the Family political games?"

"Sh. Sh," he crooned as she sobbed, stroking her back.

When her tears slowed, Donald kissed her eyes. Her cheeks. Then her lips.

"Mother and I considered this to be a possibility in August," he said, leaning his forehead against hers. "That's why we transferred control of her interest to me. Justine, I will fucking ruin him if he even *hints* at hurting you. Not just financially. I have the programming nearly completed for the worm that can completely destroy the Martiniere databases."

She half-hiccuped, half-laughed. "Dear God, Donald, what the hell is going on that you and Barbie saw this coming in August?"

"Joey really messed things up. Transferred to Philip's *political organization*." Donald's lip curled. "The polite euphemism for your father's hired heavies."

"Messed up how?"

"Joey trashed your father's indentured research division."

Justine flinched. "I won't have a damned thing to do with that division."

"No, Philip's appointed a replacement. Albert Morris." Donald flopped onto his back. Justine curled into his side. "Joey completely wrecked the indentured research corporate financials, and left the organizational structure in shambles."

"That doesn't just happen for an organization of the Group's size. Even at the division level. Or is my brother not just incompetent, but *spectacularly incompetent*?"

"Oh, I think Joey is quite talented in his incompetence." Donald chuckled. "But yes. Mom got word of the situation, and checked things out."

"But I'm young, and I hate Daddy-fucking-dearest's guts. Why would he—and the Board—turn to me?"

"Your age means that both sides think you can be manipulated." Another, longer pause. "They don't know you very well."

"What about us?" she whispered. "Because if the Family drags me into this...."

Donald shut his eyes tightly for a moment, then reopened them, sorrow furrowing his brows.

"You are my brave, beautiful, fierce falcon, Justine." He kissed her forehead. "I always feared that I would lose you to your family." He drew a deep, shuddering, breath. "I have said that you would outfly me. That I would watch you soar, and not be able to keep up."

"I don't want to lose you." She sniffled. "You're the best thing that has happened to me."

"You won't. No matter what happens legally," he whispered into her ear. "Even when we divorce—and I don't see any way around that now—I will be your strongest advocate, your most devout supporter. As long as I live, I hold the power to keep your father at bay—and I will make my best effort to guard your back."

"Oh, Donald." Tears rolled down her cheeks.

"We have a few short years left together, and I plan to build as many defenses for you as I can in that time. Hush." He kissed her again. "Fly, my falcon, fly. For all of us. Please."

Justine shivered.

The pleading tones in his voice, along with his words, were more convincing than the Family's desire to set her as a watchdog on her father.

But the cost. Dear God, the cost.

Was this really the future she wanted? That they wanted?

Can't I just live my life with my husband?

Justine already knew the answer, even as that plaintive thought occurred to her.

She was a Martiniere, not just an ordinary Martiniere but a high-level heir. Her life was not her own; had never been her own.

Damn it, Gabie. If only you were here to fix things.

She hoped to hell that her cousin had found some peace with Ruby, and, if not, with some other woman. It was the one thing that made her sacrifice worthwhile. He had sacrificed himself for her often enough —*those scars on his back*—

It was time for her to start paying back not just Gabie, but Serg,

Kendra, Piotr, and the others within the Family who had won her this position.

And Barbie and Donald as well.

The cost, however. The price she would pay.

With any luck, it would be worth it, and they could destroy her father.

9 / INTERLUDE FOUR

August, 2086

"This explains a lot," Mike said. "I wondered about the appearance of Justine Martiniere-Atwood's signatures and routings at about that time in the Group databases. And then, when it was just Justine Martiniere—"

"That would be after the divorce."

"So you did take the position," Gabie said.

She shook a finger at him. "Ah-ah-ah. No spoilers. And I made him grovel pretty damn hard first."

Uneasiness rose within her. Something was wrong. Gabie had *known* this. She briefed him about it several months after he became the Martiniere.

Mike pulled up a screen, frowning at it. "Justine, what was Glory's show name?"

Aw, fuck. If anyone still alive in the Family could find those records, it would be Mike.

But maybe it was time to disclose that part, too.

Justine sighed. "Gloriana JMA."

Mike's jaw dropped. "Oh. *Oh.* My God, Justine, you turned down trying out for the Olympic showjumping team?"

"I didn't have a choice. Too many commitments even before I got that proposition from Daddy-damned-dearest, and Glory was developing soundness problems." She let herself smile. "She did turn out to be a good broodmare."

"I'll say she did," Mike said.

Ruby's digi sidled behind Mike to look over his shoulder. *"Oh. Wow. So that's what became of Glory."*

"Once I sold her to be a broodmare I didn't want to look too often," Justine said. "But she produced several champions."

She closed her eyes for a moment. That choice had been *hard*. But much as she wanted to keep Glory as a personal riding horse and broodmare, it just wasn't possible. Not with her growing responsibilities to the Group, to Rescue Angel, and to the developing resistance against Philip within the Family.

"I'll say," Mike snorted. "Dam to a prominent sire? Actually, *two* prominent sires since one of her sons was known for his daughters? I may not know the Selle Français bloodlines like I do Quarter Horses, but all of this—is impressive."

"Yeah. I visited her a few times. Her foals were gorgeous."

But even those few times were painful. The big blaze-faced chestnut mare kept giving her *that look*. That she remembered the shows and the competition, and were they going to do the fun stuff again someday?

A picture sent to her just before Glory died at the age of twenty-five, in 2058, showed the big mare with that look of eagles in her eyes, even though her body showed her age, with a broodmare's sagging paunch and white hairs spreading across her face.

Oh Glory. If only you'd lasted a couple more years—I might have been able to move you to the Double R.

"And that is probably enough for today," JoAnn said.

"Aw, darling, it was fun to hear about Aunt Justine's showjumping career."

"I know." She smiled at him. "But you're looking tired." JoAnn glanced up. "We'll be back at the ranch in a week, as long as everything goes smoothly. If it works for you to tell stories by comm, then when Mike gets bored with the hospital again—"

"Certainly."

The screen faded and she realized that Ron and Lily were with her.

"You look tired after that one, Aunt Justine," Ron said.

She sighed. "I *am* tired."

At least she might sleep, instead of her thoughts roiling over the emotions evoked by the telling of today's story.

Yeah. Right. And she'd believe that one when it happened to her.

After all, she *had* started to edge into the major complexities of the Group that had formed her into the weapon she became.

Fly, my falcon, fly. For all of us. Please.

Donald's words echoed clearly in her memories.

ANOTHER RESTLESS NIGHT. JUSTINE WONDERED WHICH DIGI WAS WATCHING over her, because she sensed someone's presence. Ron was back in his own room so probably not Gabie or Brandon—one would be with Mike, the other with Ron.

It was probably Lily or Ruby. But it didn't feel like them, either.

Justine shivered. "Donald?" she whispered, a faint breath of hope that perhaps *now* he would unlock the algorithm and appear as a digi.

Nothing.

Justine sighed. Exhaled, and turned over, not wanting to talk to any other digi right now.

Donald. Glory. Kendra. So many things lost from that brief era when anything was possible—even a berth on the Olympic showjumping team.

But, as always, her fucking father altered the course of her life.

"I SURVIVED MY FIRST TREADMILL TEST WITH THIS CYBORG EQUIPMENT," Mike said when he called two days later. "Always a relief when you've got a fake heart and lungs."

"So young an age to have to think about this," she said. He was only thirty-one, soon to be thirty-two.

Mike shrugged. "I'm a young man in an old man's body. The age of my body at a cellular level is much older than my actual biological age. But I don't want to dwell on my mortality. I'm suspecting your next story may be about the dinner with Philip, and what happened after that?"

"Do you want the dinner or the work?"

"The work I'll find in the files later. I want to know who and what you were then. What you observed. That dinner and other personal touches that won't be in the files."

"All right," she said. "But I'll warn you. This isn't a happy story."

"Are any of them?"

She had to think about that.

"Not really," she said finally.

10 / DEALING WITH THE DEVIL

DECEMBER, 2030

JUSTINE COMMUNICATED DINNER ARRANGEMENTS TO PHILIP'S EXECUTIVE assistant, Raven Deschamps. An apt name for the dark-haired, dark-eyed man. When she was younger, Raven had intimidated her with his dour presence. But she didn't live in the same household with him anymore, didn't see him on a daily basis, and if this position with her father came through—while she would have to deal with Raven regularly, he would *have* to respect her.

Then she made reservations for herself and Donald at the hotel affiliated with the restaurant. This way, all they had to do was take the elevator down to the restaurant. Easier on him. The suite had two bedrooms, allowing Coral and Francie to come along for medical support.

This allowed them to show up early at the bar to await her father. Upstage Philip at his own game, because he usually tried to be the first one at any meeting like this,.

They arrived in mid-afternoon and settled in. Soon, it was time to go downstairs. Justine eyed Donald. He cut a fine figure in his bespoke dark blue Italian suit with the light blue shirt, gold tie and matching pocket square. It hid his weight loss.

God, her husband was gorgeous. Especially since Coral had given him a shot to bolster his energy, before she and Francie headed off for their own adventures in downtown Portland. He appeared energetic and strong, almost like he had been their first year together.

So why did he need that shot? Did Donald just have Crohn's going on—or were they were hiding something more from her?

Damn the man. He wouldn't always tell her about his health problems.

"An early anniversary present," he said, producing a jewelry box.

She opened the box to reveal a stylized falcon brooch, small and subtle, tiny diamonds outlining feather details and black onyx eyes. "It's beautiful."

"It also has listening and recording capabilities," Donald said. "Tap the eyes, and that activates the transmitter. Tap the tail to turn a recording on or off."

"Oh, Donald." She smiled at him.

"Only the best for my falcon. I *told* you I intended to give you tools to protect yourself. This is the first."

"Will you pin it on me?" The famed Martiniere emeralds had a brooch that possessed similar capabilities. But the emerald set— earrings, necklace, and brooch—had disappeared when Gabie's parents died in that plane crash.

He smiled as he pinned it on her skirt suit jacket, dark blue like his. "Happily." Then he offered her his arm.

Once they settled in the bar, Justine left instructions with the host to have Philip meet them there before they went to the private view room she had reserved. Donald reached across the table and took her hand.

"Once your father shows up, I'm likely to be a bit handsy," he said, a wry smile flitting across his face. "He'll understand that body language. Marking you as my possession. But it's going to be more blatant than you expect from me."

"Thanks for the warning."

"I didn't want you to hit me if I patted your behind," Donald said.

"Good idea." She *had* reacted several times during their first few months together. Donald didn't grope but he had moments when he wanted physical contact for reassurance. Sometimes that included touching her legs, butt, or chest.

"No matter what happens, going forward, I'm here. We're a team." He closed his hand on hers and raised it to his lips, just as Philip entered the bar and looked around—ten minutes early, of course. It didn't appear that he had been outside—not damp, shoes dry—so he was probably staying at the hotel as well.

"Daddy-damned-dearest just walked into the bar."

Donald's response was a smirk as he kissed her hand again, while Philip headed over to them. "I will follow your lead. Will stay quiet and out of the way unless he says something that pisses me off. This is your battle."

"Justine." Philip bowed slightly.

"Father." Not the time for sarcastic insults. That would come later, if necessary. She had other tools now. Justine inclined her head regally.

"Donald." He turned to face her husband, giving him a smaller bow.

Donald bowed to Philip, marginally less deep than the one Philip gave him. "Philip."

Justine signaled the host. "Our room is ready."

She was glad of Donald's earlier warning as he rested his hand on her butt and squeezed it before sliding up to encircle her waist as they followed the host, Philip behind them. She used the cover Donald provided to rest her hand over her brooch and press the tail.

After placing an order for drinks and appetizers, silence fell in the room. Philip fixed Justine with a steady gaze. She met it, not looking away.

I'm not the same little girl who escaped you, Daddy-damned-dearest. You'd better figure that out now.

"I'm surprised you aren't wearing a *fragrant*—"

"*Lucifer,*" she countered. To her satisfaction, his priming word didn't freeze her at all—and the blocking word Piotr had given her paused him.

Her father raised his brows once he could move. "That's a very powerful use of tones, Justine."

"Did you think I would meet with you without having some appropriate tools?"

"Point taken. So."

"You need an assistant. Raven is not sufficient?"

He scowled. "Raven is not Family, Justine. And I need someone reliable to assist with general operations of the Martiniere Group. External Affairs Division."

"Joey isn't an option?"

Philip snorted as their server entered the room. He didn't speak until the woman left.

"I assume you've already spoken to Piotr and have some idea of what is happening within the Family."

"Yes."

He's identified Piotr and not Gerard as the head of the opposition. Interesting.

"Then you know that the Board does not find Joseph to be an acceptable candidate for the title of Martiniere-in-waiting. Personally, I've not found it important to have that position filled." Philip rolled his eyes. "But the Board insists these days."

"You're putting me up to be the Martiniere-in-waiting?" Her stomach dropped. This. Was. Un-fucking-believable.

No. *Daddy-fucking-dearest* would not do that.

Her father's double take was priceless. "What? You seriously think I'd place a woman in that position? Even the submissive woman you've become?"

Donald's lips thinned. Was he angry or was he stifling a laugh at the characterization of her as *submissive*?

She shrugged, playing the diffident, empty-minded social butterfly that Barbie had taught her to switch on when needed.

"I don't know, Daddy-dear. I had thought you might have reconsidered some of your past stances. People *do* change, after all."

She weighted her tones carefully, studying his response.

A quick scowl in reply to her sardonic pitches. Equally fast assessment of Donald's matching glower. And, finally, of her. Justine made herself *relax, damn it,* lean against the chair's back, sip her drink, and face her father's glare with a faint smile.

Philip exhaled and dropped his eyes, looking for his drink. His hand didn't fumble, but when he looked back up, he nodded to himself.

"My dearest darling daughter," he said, using sarcastic tones that resonated within her, but not as deeply as they would have before Piotr had installed the block. "I assure you that I have not changed *that* much, so check your ambitions. Nor do I anticipate this position to last for very long. Five, perhaps ten years."

"And then what?"

Not that long. What the hell does he have in mind?

"The Board will have calmed." He shrugged. "Since you don't seem to have any problems with contractual arrangements, as evidenced by your prenuptials—"

"Excuse me?" Donald interrupted, frowning. "What do you mean by that?"

Justine resisted the urge to exchange worried glances with Donald. It wasn't surprising that Daddy-damned-dearest had gained access to their prenuptial agreements. They knew it was a possibility.

"Your prenuptials." A smirk twitched her father's lips. "Marriage for a set period of time is *so* convenient, isn't it? You don't have to make it work forever."

"Oh, Daddy-dear, I don't think you want to count on that." She dialed her pitch up to full sarcasm. "It is a contract, open to mediation and discussion. You did notice that modification clause in both the prenups, I assume? Nothing was set in stone. Just laying the groundwork for a separation and divorce with minimal financial impact after seven years, if we decided to go that route." She took a deep breath. "After Walter Braun, I wanted a means of control. An escape route. Just like I assume that any contract you and I negotiate will be open to discussion and mediation. And there *will* be contracts. I will not step into a position with the Group without one."

Another period of matched glares between Justine and her father.

"You *have* grown up," her father finally conceded.

Donald cleared his throat. "I consult with Justine regularly about financials. And contract negotiations."

Philip's gaze switched to Donald. "And?"

"Even at seventeen, when we were first married, my dear love had a terrifyingly intuitive grasp of financial functions that people two and three times her age lack." Donald reached out and took Justine's hand. "My mother concurs."

The momentary startle on Philip's face was priceless.

"You can consult with Barbie about Justine's capabilities, if you wish," Donald continued, his voice hardening. "The restrictions on women in Martiniere Group leadership roles are outmoded and old-fashioned, but it is not my family, nor is it my business, other than how it affects Justine." He raised her hand to his lips and kissed it.

Philip laughed harshly. "And you'd happily get your hands into the management of the Group any way you can, eh, *Atwood*? Even through your wife?"

"I meant what I said, *Martiniere*." Donald paused. "Justine's safety and health are my primary concerns. This is Justine's work, not mine."

"You're here."

"At her request. I think such a request is wise, considering past circumstances."

Philip snorted.

"I will have my final say, and then I'll be quiet. I would advise you not to underestimate your daughter's skills. She *is* your daughter, Philip, in many more ways than you realize. However, I will *not* sit by and listen to *my wife* being disparaged." He coughed, and Justine cast a wary eye at him. *Was* he all right? "I may not have been your first choice for her spouse. But trust me, I know the value of *my Justine*, and it angers me that you are so blind to it because of her gender."

A tense silence. Philip finally inclined his head at Donald.

"Acknowledged," her father said.

Donald squeezed her hand, then let go.

"Now," Justine said. "If you two are finished measuring dicks, can we cut to the chase? It's all very entertaining. But." She pushed as much disdain as she could into her next words. "I'd like to get some real work done."

Philip winced. Donald half-smiled.

"Do you have to be so crude?" her father growled.

"I've held enough negotiations with building contractors and other testosterone-intense men as part of managing the winery to call it as I see it. So. You mentioned a contract. You've talked vaguely about what my duties will be. Let's stick to that, all right? Pretend I'm Albert Morris, and we'll go from there."

"You don't look much like Morris," her father grumbled.

But for the first time in her life, she saw something like respect in his expression when he looked at her.

It was *almost* worth everything she had gone through to get to this point with him.

———

THE CONTRACT THEY HAMMERED OUT WAS NUANCED AND MULTIFACETED. By the end of the evening Justine was grateful not just for the University of Oregon's business and law classes, but her winery experience and the work with Donald and Barbie.

Philip initially balked at the compensation rate she demanded.

"You're not hiring your daughter," she said calmly. "You're hiring me as an outside consultant, by the terms of this contract. You need to pay me what I am worth."

"Damn it, girl, you drive a hard bargain."

"Where do you think I learned it? Your dinner-table negotiation lectures might have gone over Joey's head. Not mine." Her voice sharpened. "Speaking of my brother—I will *not* work with him, nor will I work with the indentured labor and research divisions."

"Those are Morris's concerns."

"Excellent. I mean it about Joey. I will not take responsibility for his actions. He is not to pester me. Is that understood?"

"He *is* your brother."

"This contract is with *you*, Philip Martiniere. My reporting lines of authority are delineated in the contract. Joey does not fit in there."

———

AT LAST, THEY WERE DONE.

"You're not coming for Family Christmas?" her father said as he stood up.

"We have other plans," Justine said. "However, I will be in communication with the Board once they have approved this contract. And I will review it carefully for any changes before my final signature."

For a moment her father's features softened again and he shook his head. "If only you had been born a man."

"But I wasn't." She didn't let herself react further. That was what he wanted.

Was that disappointment that flashed across his face?

"More's the pity." He bowed to Justine and Donald, and left.

Once he was safely clear, Justine tapped off the brooch's recording and sank against the back of her chair, shivering, the enormity of what she had done sinking in.

She had successfully negotiated a contract with Daddy-fucking-dearest.

Would wonders ever cease?

"You did it," Donald said. "You pulled it off, my dear one."

"Did I really?" Doubt began to creep over her.

"Yes. And it was wonderful to see," he said. He picked up her hand and kissed it. "It's marvelous watching my falcon soar."

She let herself relax against Donald. The heat of his body worried her.

Was she doing the right thing?

Once they returned to their suite, Justine called Serg while Donald went into the bedroom to change. Coral and Francie were still out.

"It's done. Contract signed and I personally submitted it to the Board for their approval. I will be the First Secretary, Martiniere Group External Affairs."

"Congratulations."

"Thank you," she said, tired now that the adrenaline rush was easing off. The implications of what she had just committed herself to sank in. "Five-year term."

Longer than the rest of my marriage will be, most likely. A grim reality.

"We'll talk at Family Christmas?"

"I won't be there. I don't intend to establish a precedent and...." Her voice caught. "I want a quiet Christmas with Donald. He has surgery after the first of the year. I do *not* want this made known to your father, to the Board, or to Daddy-fucking-dearest. Let them think what they please, until it's necessary for *me* to tell them."

Serg was silent for a moment. "I'm sorry, Justine."

"It will be all right," she said. "I just—"

"I'll let Dad, Kendra, and Gerard know that the deal has been made."

"Thank you."

They discussed the logistics of using Vygotsky Security to create appropriate security that the Board and Philip would approve of—and networks that would be satisfactory to Donald. After Justine ended the call, she went to the bedroom to change and talk to Donald.

She halted abruptly in the doorway. Donald had stripped off his outer clothing and hung up his suit, but he was asleep, on top of the covers.

Justine leaned against the doorframe, blinking back tears.

This was the catch with Donald. The flaw. His pride about his health, and always wanting to appear strong in front of her.

He was so damned right that she would someday outfly him. Sooner or later his health would ground him—and he was so *damned fucking noble* that he would insist on divorce so that he wouldn't encumber her.

Doubts surged back. Was she doing the right thing?

If she were a good wife, she would have brought Donald's health up to her father. To Piotr, Serg, and Gerard. She would not have signed that contract, but would have devoted herself to Donald.

But she was a Martiniere. The opportunity to have even the limited power her father offered her was—tempting. It was the pathway to stopping Philip.

First Secretary, Martiniere Group External Affairs. Albert Morris was her equivalent, only *Internal Affairs.* She would get the access codes tomorrow morning so she could start learning her position.

To be honest with herself, however, it was the power she craved.

Female or not, she was a Martiniere. And Martinieres desired power.

Justine gulped, and eased the door closed before collapsing on the couch to cry.

When she couldn't sob any longer, she sat up and stared out the window into the darkness.

No more tears, she vowed.

Bringing down her father was supposed to have been Gabie's job, especially since most of the Family leadership not in Philip's pocket already considered him to be the Martiniere-in-waiting. But. Her cousin was brave and bold, not suicidal, and if her father got his hands on Gabie now—it would mean Gabie's death. Gabie had done what he could to bring down Philip. And he had gotten her free from her father.

Now it was her turn, to use the Family and its structures against her father, as only she could. She was Philip's daughter. The ultimate insider. Her job to end the danger her father presented, even if it took the rest of her life to do it.

The suite door opened. Coral and Francie slipped in, whispering— and Coral paused when she saw Justine, one quick moment before Francie. She strode across the room and sat next to Justine.

"Is everything all right?" she asked.

Justine shuddered. "Donald barely had the strength to make it through dinner and the negotiations. He collapsed while I called Serg —he's in bed. Asleep by the time I was done. It wasn't that long a call. At least he stripped down to underwear before...before. And hung up his suit."

"I was afraid of that," Coral said.

"I signed the contract. I start work with my father in January. January 5th." She exhaled. "Coral, he won't tell me how bad things are. Keeps avoiding telling me the details. This seems worse than before and I get the feeling that this is more than just Crohn's. Is this—" she choked, despite her vow of *no more tears*. "Is this a surgery that will result in ostomy?"

Coral stayed silent, frowning.

"I don't care what you've promised him," Justine said. "The situation has changed. I need to know. Now that I'm—what I am—I have extensive responsibilities. But I want to do right by my husband."

Coral sighed. "It's not definite, but—there will be at least a temporary ostomy."

"Thank you." The result Donald dreaded most of all. "I'll provide you with access to my schedule. Please use it, so I can be there for important medical affairs."

"Justine, you know we'll take care of him, you don't need to—"

"I have to hand him over to the three of you soon enough. Stopping my father before he does something even more horrendous must be my priority, more than being a wife," she said. "Please indulge me. Let me be Donald's wife for what time is left for us to be together. Now. What else is wrong?"

Coral hesitated. Francie came back from their room and sat on Justine's other side.

"We need to tell her," she said. "I know what Don says, but—she's right."

Coral exhaled through her teeth. "There may be cancer. You would think by now we would have decent tests, but it's unclear until they get the inflamed portion of his intestines out of him. The blood work is obscure. He hasn't wanted you to know that. He's had several false positives before, and didn't want to worry you."

Justine groaned and buried her head in her hands.

Damn you, Donald. Damn your pride. Damn your desire to conceal your illnesses.

More tears. Francie and Coral held Justine.

Her last night of freedom. The last night she could afford to cry.

Tomorrow, she became First Secretary of the Martiniere Group, External Affairs.

But tonight, she could allow herself to be only Justine Martiniere-Atwood, wife of Donald Atwood, who had just learned a hard thing about her husband's health.

Francie got up. She returned with a tumbler of whisky.

Justine took it. She normally sipped her drinks, but this one she tossed down fast, like Gabie and Serg used to do when anesthetizing themselves at Family Christmas.

"Come on." Coral eased her up. The two women guided Justine to the bedroom. At the door, she straightened up.

"I've got this," she said.

"Do you want us to join you two? A cuddle pile?"

Justine shook her head, staring at Donald's still, sleeping body.

"I want to be—just us tonight," she gulped.

She closed the door and went into the bathroom to change. Carefully removed her new brooch, studying it. It was beautiful and she loved it, especially because it was not just gorgeous but functional—like so many of the things Donald appreciated.

Including herself.

Oh, Donald.

Her heart ached. She hadn't anticipated growing to love Donald like this.

She could walk away from that contract she just signed, but it would be in contradiction to everything she had fought for and claimed to hold dear since she left her father's house.

She couldn't do that. Gabie had sacrificed himself for her. So had Gerard. Donna-gran. Serg. Kendra.

Justine owed them.

SOMETIME DURING THE NIGHT, DONALD WRAPPED HIMSELF AROUND HER. Justine woke in his arms, his leg thrown over hers. Rain pounded on the windows. Another gray Western Oregon December day.

She lay still. Their fourth anniversary would be coming up at the end of the month. Three more years. Bad enough that she had spent a large chunk of the summer and the fall competing, away from him. Her new position meant divorce was coming, and oh, that was going to hurt.

No more tears, she reminded herself.

Donald stirred, sliding his leg off of her. He rolled her to face him. She gazed into the blue eyes of this man she had learned to love and cherish over the past four years, the man who had rescued her from her father and had never taken advantage of her, who had helped her prepare to confront Philip.

"How's my First Secretary of the Martiniere Group, External Affairs, doing this morning?" he asked. "I'm sorry I fell asleep so quickly. I had so many wonderful things I wanted to say because I am so damn proud of you, beloved."

"Feeling—overwhelmed at the moment," she admitted. A pause, then she continued. "I know about the cancer possibility."

"I didn't want you to worry," he said. "Then—your father approaching you—I didn't want to hold you back."

Justine closed her eyes for a moment, then opened them again. "Please. Don't hide things like this from me. Especially now." She exhaled. "I pushed Coral. She will have a link to my schedule. I want to be here in-person as much as I can." She gulped. "I am your wife. I want to be your wife—as long as possible."

He kissed her. "I will tell you what's going on, as long as I determine that it won't distract you."

"You may not be in the best position to judge."

"Trust me, Justine. Please."

Justine couldn't fight with the pleading tone in his voice. He *needed* that trust from her. She shivered and closed her eyes as he pressed his forehead against hers.

If only they could stay like this forever.

A COURIER KNOWN TO JUSTINE FROM HER DAYS IN HER FATHER'S HOUSE appeared at the hotel suite's door just after breakfast. She signed for the computer and set it up on the table next to the window. A little experimentation revealed that it was personalized to her biometrics. Donald's careful hands-off explorations revealed several monitoring apps and one bug. But the computer also came with a security case to protect its data. That went both ways.

"I'm still going to isolate it from the Mist Knoll networks and our traveling networks," Donald said. "You talked to Serg?"

Justine nodded absent-mindedly, forming her plan.

—*Video call to Raven Deschamps* was her first message. Justine sighed and hit the link. The *recording* button flashed at her and she hit *accept*.

From now on, *any call* she made to someone from the Martiniere Group would be recorded.

"Hello, Justine," Raven said, his voice warmer than usual. "Congratulations."

"Thank you, but it still needs to be confirmed by the Board."

Raven rolled his eyes. "As if they'll say no. A majority lobbied for you to take this position."

"True. So. What's the agenda?"

"First, we need to discuss your security."

"I already am well-provided for, thank you."

"Atwood security is a potential security breach for the Martiniere Group."

"I don't have Atwood security. I have my own. Separate from Donald's, which is Atwood. Shanice L'Étoile is my security chief. Let me send you her contact information. Serg Vygotsky certified her, and she worked with Brent Colfax."

"*Of course*, she's Vygotsky-certified," Raven muttered. "All right. I'll let Philip know. Access links are in your messages. I just sent them. We can get you up to speed in several ways—let you spend time with the files, then do briefings with the relevant people. Or do it division by division."

"I'm not fond of letting things pile up. I'd much rather read up on each division, then talk to people."

He nodded. "How do you want to prioritize your divisions? I can message the heads, have them expecting the contact."

"Let me look at the overviews today and come back with a plan for you tomorrow."

"All right."

"I'm also authorizing Dr. Coral Fuentes for schedule access, highest priority."

Raven's brows shot up. "Your husband's ex-girlfriend?"

"She manages his social life these days. There will be situations that require my presence. Coral doesn't need to see my confidential sched-ule; she just needs to be able to add things." Justine paused. "Raven, I'm not giving up my role as Donald's wife."

"All right."

They spoke for another fifteen minutes before Justine signed off. She pulled up her access links and began to read, taking careful notes.

At some point Donald rested a hand on her shoulder and she star-tled. She had worked the entire morning and well into the afternoon without eating.

"You're not going to get it all figured out the first day," he said. "Time to play."

"I'm sorry." She stood. "We *were* going to do something fun, weren't we?"

"Don't be sorry," he said. "I've been sitting on the couch watching you work. You've become even more terrifyingly competent. But it's time to take a break. "I downloaded the recording from your brooch and reset it. I'll show you how to do that."

"It worked?"

"Like a charm. The recording is clear." Donald grinned.

"Good."

At least he looked less frail than he did yesterday.

11 / INTERLUDE FIVE

"Did Donald have cancer?" Mike asked.

"Yes," Justine said. "It was the primary reason behind his retirement and our divorce." She blinked. *Not* going to cry, damn it.

Nor did she want to look at that unreadable expression on Gabie's face. Of all of them, he knew the most about living with a spouse who had cancer. He talked to Justine about Rachel's experience a couple of times when he was still alive, usually on the anniversary of Rachel's death. Ruby was his dearest love. But Rachel had also earned his love, and her years of cancer haunted him. She could just imagine his reaction to her disclosure about Donald.

"I don't understand," Lily said. *"I know how Philip thought about women. Why did he comply with the Board? It doesn't fit what I saw of him."*

"I no longer had a uterus," Justine said. "Therefore, I was not tied down by biology. And he thought he could control me, a weak woman, more than any other possible candidate from the Family."

Lily nodded. *"All right. Now I understand."*

Mike sighed. "God, my progenitor was an ass."

"We can all agree on that," Justine said.

Mike turned his head. "What, Jo? All right," he said, in answer to something Justine couldn't hear. He looked back. "Looks like they're hauling me off for more testing. Thanks for the story, Justine."

"You're welcome," she said.

The call switched off. She leaned back in the lounge chair on the deck, waiting. Gabie's presence buzzed across her skin. He didn't ask for permission but manifested in one of the deck chairs.

Justine didn't look at him. "Go ahead, Gabie. Yell at me for abandoning Donald."

"Tine. That's not the issue—it's pretty clear that Donald felt his health was handicapping you. No. That's not what's bothering me. Why didn't you tell me about Donald's cancer when I talked about Rachel? I would have understood."

"Because Donald was still alive, and I didn't have his permission to share. I—Gabie, I respected his wishes. No matter what they were, just as he respected mine."

"A complicated man."

Now she dared glance at her brother's digi. Gabie looked like he did before he handed over the title of Martiniere to Brandon. They could almost be reenacting one of those nights during his short tenure as the Martiniere, when neither of them could sleep, and they spent long hours talking in the kitchen of the Double R.

Except that it was midday and they were at Moondance. Gabie was dead, a digital clone of the man who had been her brother, and she was —well, today she didn't feel like death was near. But it would claim her, sooner rather than later.

Gabie smiled sadly at her.

"Yes," she agreed. "Donald was a complex person. He loved me dearly—and I loved him too." She swallowed hard. "But after Barbie died, right before we started divorce proceedings, I realized that it was selfish to hold onto him. He would have stayed if I had asked, but it would have killed him so damn quickly. That—plain and simple—is why we divorced." Justine closed her eyes tightly and shook her head.

"I'm sorry, Tine. I'm really sorry."

She gulped. "I had two years left on that contract with our fucking father when Donald and I divorced, and I was negotiating a two-year extension for my position as First Secretary. Cousin Arthur was colluding with Gerard's son David to dump Philip, and Piotr was deep in that mess along with Kendra. Donald would have been at even greater risk if we had stayed married, and with his health—" a tear threatened to break free and she dashed it away. "It was safer for both of us. He couldn't be used against me, especially since we playacted a nastier break than it really was."

"So our fucking father forced you into a divorce, just like he did with me," Gabie said, a glower tightening his expression. *"Just not directly."*

That yanked at Justine, and she buried her head in her hands, gulping, tears wanting to come. She forced herself to control her breathing. Long. Slow. Calm.

Her breathing steadied and the risk of tears faded away. She raised her head.

"It was the hardest damn thing I ever did in my life, Gabie. That divorce ripped me apart in so many ways—and I had to wear that casual, blithe, social butterfly face the whole fucking time. We had to protect Rescue Angel as my position as First Secretary became more political, and I just couldn't risk him. I couldn't. Donald was my last refuge, my final protection." She shuddered.

"Philip's reason for forcing my divorce was that it would destroy me even more than the most painful death he could concoct," Gabie said. *"He must have practiced on you."*

"Probably. Holy crap, that whole situation with you and Ruby was awful. We saw Daddy-damned-dearest's hand in it the whole time. I survived Arthur's attempted coup; kept my position as First Secretary and protected Arthur, Piotr, and Serg. Then I learned that Daddy-poo was creating an indentured army. I went to Donald with that discovery, because I didn't know how far I could trust Serg and Piotr."

"That bad."

"They were compromised and who knew *what* they were doing to survive. This would have been 2037. And you—you had disappeared completely."

Gabie rubbed his face. *"2037 was when I started rebuilding myself after the divorce. Craig Yellowhawk wanted me to inherit Moondance. His sister and her family weren't interested in keeping it for themselves, but they wanted the ranch to go to someone of Craig's choice. I was his caregiver and we had been friends for years."*

"Yeah." She exhaled shakily. "2037 was the year I was grateful as hell for Donald insisting that I maintain my own security. But it kicked off seven years of dancing on the edge, not able to network with Serg until 2044."

"June of 2044, by any chance?"

"Roughly."

"Another coup attempt. I know that much. Serg sent me an Aunt Marguerite tippling with the Bourbon message through Rafe Alvarez. That Joey was being an ass."

"I didn't know about that message. That was all Serg, not any of us." Marguerite. Bourbon. Code words based on centuries-deep Martiniere family history involving their Medici ancestors. It indicated a wish for immediate action—preferably by the lead Martiniere heir, which would have been—Gabie. "I wasn't part of it. Did you respond?"

"It was the wrong timing and the connection with Joey—Philip was my primary target, not your brother. Ass though Joey was."

Justine shivered. "I'm glad you didn't," she said.

"I had too much at risk. Bran was eleven and had already been targeted once, along with Ruby. I started working with Rafe Alvarez as a part-time mercenary in his Alvarez Armory organization, focusing on stopping Philip's takeovers of small water districts and municipalities across the West. I couldn't do a damn thing otherwise. My hands were tied, with no likelihood of even being able to say my own name thanks to mind control."

"The timing sucked for me, too. I wasn't quite ready."

"How much of this are you gonna tell Mike?"

"I don't know," she said. "I still need to think about it further."

"And there's the danger we face now, that damn near killed Mike. I investigated further. Traced the attack on Mike back to Samuel Hawkins and Heaven's Reach. Definite. He's not as good at making digis as our father was, but...."

"But Hawkins is capable of doing just that," Justine said.

"Yes."

"Damn it." She rubbed her forehead. "How soon do you want to try to resurrect Donald—if it's at all possible?"

"I want Mike and Deontae on this as well," Gabie said. *"Lily, Mike, Deontae—Ruby and Brandon for your support. And the newest in digigloves for you to wear. D has ordered them but they won't be available for a few days."*

"More time before we try it, then."

Why Deontae?

JoAnn's brother didn't have a digi construct, not like Mike, for whom being a digital clone was tied to his being a physical clone. And while Deontae was a wizard with digigloves, it wasn't the same thing as having a construct.

Wait. Mike would have JoAnn as a support. Deontae for her, then. That made sense.

"Maybe less time than we thought before we try it. Mike's improving quickly. But every little thing you can share with us about Donald in these stories—without exceeding your comfort level—will help us make his digi stronger. The more data the better."

Damn. She had hoped to drift away from telling the parts about Donald. That still choked her up. Would he really *want* to be resurrected as a digi?

If he felt it would keep you safe, yes.

"Which means more stories about events right up to the divorce," she sighed.

"I'm sorry, but...yes."

She leaned back in the lounge chair. "All right, then," she conceded. "But I have to think about what I can and can't tell." Even though Donald was dead, there were some stories that were only his to reveal.

"Fair enough."

⸻

Justine dreamed about Donald that night. He was living with the ladies on Nameless, the island in British Columbia that he had retreated to after their divorce.

But the layout was identical to the now nonexistent villa on Solitaire, except for Nameless's flora outside a transparent dome. A Pacific storm howled outside the bubble. Inside, however, fan palms, date palms, and several other varieties that she loved from the Solitaire era grew around a pool surrounded by tropical foliage.

Justine fought through a choked, humid passageway, vines snaring her arms and legs. When she looked up, she saw the rain-streaked dome overhead and the wind-whipped conifers outside, glimpsed the pool ahead. But blurring kept her from viewing the people around the pool other than as outlines. Something wrong with her eyes, or a shield effect?

Finally, she reached the pool area. A translucent barrier kept her from proceeding further. Shield effect. That was interfering with her vision.

She sighed and turned to retrace her steps.

"Justine." Donald's voice, loving, achingly familiar.

She whirled. He stood on the other side of the barrier, wearing swim trunks, face unlined with age and worry—the young man she had first grown to love as she struggled with her PTSD. Not the old man she held as he died.

"Donald." She choked on his name, gulping.

He passed through the barrier. *"Shh. Shh. Soon, love, soon."* His arms wrapped around Justine.

Then it faded. Justine opened her eyes to the darkness of her suite at Moondance, the pale yellow glow of a nightlight by the bathroom door casting shadows. She rolled to her side, blinking. Was that the very faint outline of a digi standing by the slider window?

"Donald?" she whispered.

She blinked.

If that was a digi's outline, it was now gone.

But when she closed her eyes, she could almost feel Donald's arms around her.

Digi, memory, or—delusion?

Justine couldn't decide.

It took another three days before Mike called back. This time he sat upright in a chair by the window of his hospital room. Justine lounged on Moondance's deck, enjoying the morning before it got too hot and stifling to be outside.

"I'm eager to hear about what it was like to be First Secretary so young," Mike said.

Brandon snorted. *"Me as well."*

"You youngsters," Gabie snarked.

Justine exhaled. "It wasn't as easy as you think, gentlemen."

On the other hand, both Brandon and Mike had become the Martiniere at a young age. They might appreciate this tale. And Ron might learn from it, should he have to step up to the title of Martiniere soon.

12 / FIRST SECRETARY OF THE MARTINIERE GROUP, EXTERNAL AFFAIRS

"YOU READY FOR THIS?" SHANICE ASKED JUSTINE AS THEIR FLEET OF SUVs pulled up in front of the Martiniere Group's suburban Los Angeles headquarters.

"As ready as I'll ever be," she answered.

Justine waited as Shanice stepped out of the SUV, scanned the area, then nodded to her. She eased out of the vehicle along with Twyla and Robert, and stepped away after activating her falcon pin's recording application. Shanice and Twyla fell in at Justine's sides while Robert followed, the remaining three members of Justine's security force exiting their SUV and forming around that core.

She kept her eyes on Raven Deschamps and the man next to him, Albert Morris, waiting in the lobby, flanked by a line of Martiniere security—not Vygotsky but the squad assigned to headquarters, primarily loyal to her father. Morris didn't fit the pattern of her father's usual sycophants—fat, face flushing and sweaty, with bright blond hair. Well, the hair fit. But the outright obesity, given her father's obsession with physical condition? Either Morris was damned good at what he did, or the real power in Internal Affairs lay elsewhere.

Justine intended to find that out, as soon as possible.

Meanwhile, she had consulted with Kendra about the latest fashions for Los Angeles corporate leadership. Something edgy but not provocative. For this first day, Justine settled on a black and silver sleeveless tunic top with diagonal cross-body paintbrush stripes, a knee-length gray jacket with three-quarter sleeves, black slacks, low square heels with black and silver diagonal stripes that matched her tunic, and elbow-length gray gloves. Black, silver, and gray would be her signature colors within the Group.

Branding, always branding.

Raven's lips twitched upward as she halted in front of him. "Justine. It is truly a pleasure to welcome you to Martiniere Group headquarters." He bowed to her, almost as low as he would to her father.

She bowed in return, not as deep. "It is my pleasure to be here, Raven."

"May I introduce Albert Morris? Albert, this is Justine Martiniere-Atwood, your External Affairs counterpart."

Justine inclined her head slightly as Morris extended a hand. "Pleased to meet you, Mr. Morris. However, I do not shake hands."

Hadn't he been briefed on her preferences, or was this a power play? Morris was tagged in the files that Kendra had sent her as a *toucher.* Was he one of *those* men, who disregarded women's preferences?

"I am pleased to meet you, Justine."

"Ms. Martiniere-Atwood," she corrected. That fit the profile of one of her father's followers, right down to disrespect for women.

Well, *she* was establishing boundaries promptly.

He flushed even more. "Can't we be casual, given our positions? And my preference is to shake hands." He kept holding his hand out.

Justine crossed her arms. "In my world, business informality is earned," she icily informed Morris. "I do not physically contact my co-workers."

Especially here.

He raised his brows. "We appear to be at an impasse."

"Are we? I am a Martiniere. You are not. No impasse exists, because you are not part of the Family."

Was it her imagination, or did Raven smirk just a little at that?

"I see. So you intend to throw around your connection to the Old Man."

"My *father* has certainly changed if he encourages such informality," Justine said, projecting a command tone. Morris twitched. "And the Martiniere Group is still a *Family*-held company, not a *public* one."

Not her imagination. Raven *definitely* smirked at that jab.

Judging by his reaction, Morris had at least mild mind control programming installed. So unless Morris was more competent than he appeared, the real power in Internal Affairs was elsewhere.

Was a similar subordinate in her organization? Probably.

Morris dropped his hand. "Have it your way, *Ms.* Martiniere-Atwood."

"Thank you for remembering my name, Mr. Morris. Raven, I understand that the Board wishes to meet with me?" She smiled brightly at Morris. Another knife twist in his ample gut. He flinched.

"Right this way," Raven said, turning.

Morris tried to walk next to her, but Shanice and Twyla cut him off. The rest of her security fell in close, so that Morris and his security had to follow her. Justine carried her head high, not looking to either side as they marched through the lobby and into an elevator. Raven tapped in a code while Justine's security surrounded her.

Raven turned away from the control panel with an even bigger smirk. Justine swayed as the elevator rose.

Fast ones in this building.

"I'm afraid that didn't quite go the way that *dear Albert* imagined," he said.

Another mark in the column that says Morris isn't the one really in charge of Internal Affairs. Raven wouldn't dare snark if Morris had any real power.

What's Raven's game? He's been much more friendly to me than usual. Kissing up to a new source of power within the Group and the Family?

"Dear *Albert* is going to learn that I don't play," she said.

An appreciative brow raise from Raven. "My. Justine, you have certainly—" he paused. "Become *interesting*, these days."

"I serve to entertain," she said, in a sardonic tone that could have come from Gabie at his sharpest.

"So I see," he said as the elevator door opened.

Their elevator had beaten Morris's, Justine noticed as she followed Raven into the boardroom. Elevators with adjustable speed, controlled by the code that Raven had tapped in?

Add that to the list of *things she needed to learn about headquarters.*

Twyla followed Justine into the boardroom, to serve as her assistant. Philip sat at the head of the long conference table, two empty chairs on each side, with a second chair behind each empty chair for an assistant. Raven gestured to the empty chair at her father's left hand. Justine nodded and followed him.

Sinister—left—side.

What did Daddy-damned-dearest mean by seating her there? He intended some sort of message by that.

Probably an allusion to my being female.

Her father's twisted religious ideology contained an element about Eve sitting at the left hand of God. She needed to be watchful in case Daddy-damned-dearest had ulterior motives for this placement— which he did, no doubt about it. She just didn't quite understand *why*—yet.

Philip nodded at her. Justine returned the gesture and sat. Twyla handed Justine her computer cube and she activated her screens. Then she relaxed against the back of her chair as Morris entered the boardroom.

"Sorry," he muttered as he made his way to his seat, hunching his shoulders slightly as the other Board members stared at him. "Elevator issues."

Point to her. She'd gotten here first. She needed to keep doing that.

Morris dropped into his chair with a big *oomph* and fumbled with the computer cube that his aide handed to him.

Justine eyed Morris's assistant. Ash-blond hair. Broad shoulders. Suntanned pale skin. Chunky, but the build of a muscular, big-framed man, not the obesity of his nominal boss. He moved with grace and control. Clearly did some form of training and conditioning.

The possible *real* power in Internal Affairs. He matched the other phenotype her father preferred amongst his sycophants. All muscle, hiding brains.

She needed to get his name.

Philip called the meeting to order. After being sworn in as First Secretary, Justine settled, waiting for her turn on the agenda. Fortunately, she had studied presentation skills with Barbie and Donald as well as in her college classes. Unfortunately, she inherited a mess from Joey and hadn't had the authority to institute the needed changes in time for this meeting. Her presentation covered general references but she saved the details for later, when she would be meeting with her own division heads. No need to leak that information in advance.

"You're somewhat vague on your proposed action plan, Justine," Uncle Gerard's younger son Vincent finally pointed out.

"I'm not going to make disclosures before I talk to my own people," Justine retorted. God, Vincent was younger than Gabie and he was already at Board meetings. She had thought that David, Vincent's older brother, would be acting as Gerard's assistant.

Why is Vincent here and not David? Did it have something to do with David's rebellion?

Vincent opened his mouth to say more but a grunt from Gerard silenced him.

At last the meeting was over. Justine handed her computer cube to Twyla.

"Justine." Her father spoke directly to her, for the first time outside of the formalities during the meeting. "Can we meet around—four-thirty, fiveish, today?"

She checked her calendar. The meeting with her subordinates was scheduled for two pm. Hopefully it would be *done* by then.

It will *be done by then.*

She was the boss. She could make it happen.

"Certainly," she said. "Closer to five than four-thirty, I think."

"Then I'll see you in my office."

"Until then." She turned and started to march out of the boardroom, only to be intercepted by several Family members.

"Good to see you, Justine." Cousin Christopher, Kendra's brother. An ally.

Justine chatted with Chris, asking about his children, then Kendra and her husband (*as if she hadn't already spoken to Kendra a day ago, something Chris definitely knew. Appearances*).

"Good job," Uncle Gerard said, echoed by cousins Arthur and Paul.

She exchanged pleasantries with the three older men. They were important allies.

Piotr smiled at her but didn't say anything.

Morris stomped out of the boardroom, no one speaking to him.

At last she was able to leave. Raven joined her. "Let me show you to your office suite."

They got back into the elevator, continuing higher until they reached the top floor. *Same floor as Daddy-poo,* she thought. Then scowled. Odds were very good that Joey's office was on this floor as well.

Another reason for this not to be my primary office location.

Working remotely was not a new thing for Martiniere Group leadership, especially given their far-flung divisions. She had been most adamant during negotiations that she was *not* relocating to LA.

Chicago—perhaps, in a few years, should she actually have to divorce Donald. Closer to some operations she wanted to keep an eye on, and central to the Real Lives for Women networks that Barbie had expanded.

She admired the plaque on her door before entering the suite. And, once again, she was on Daddy-damn-dearest's left side as she faced the door—he was on her right side. Her suite consisted of an outer office, a meeting room, and her main office. Not a corner office—that was her father's. Where did Joey fall in the scheme of things? One of the other corners? And where was Morris?

Well, she would learn that soon enough.

A young man rose from behind the reception desk—one of the slender, long-faced blonds more common in her father's employ than Morris's stocky assistant. "Ms. Martiniere-Atwood. I'm Eliot McNaughton, your executive assistant." He bowed to her, not extending a hand. Good. At least *he* read her preference file.

"I do not need an executive assistant," she said to him. "I already have one." She gestured toward Twyla. "Ms. Norton is prepared and ready to serve."

I didn't expect this. Which mean he was probably her father's man behind the scenes. On the other hand, if he was competent—she needed to check his records.

A faint frown broke McNaughton's otherwise expressionless face. "You'll require someone who has worked inside the Group for many years to serve in this role. I have been the executive assistant to the First Secretary of External Affairs for five years."

If McNaughton was competent, then a lateral transfer to another division was definitely possible. If she could win him over, she might have a direct line to the problems with External Affairs.

Five years in the position. Yes, I want to cultivate him.

"By this afternoon, there will be other positions opening up. I'll look at your resume and consider you for reassignment. Fair enough?"

He nodded. "There are accesses that will need to be transferred from me to your assistant," he said. But his displeasure still showed in a faint scowl.

No. This man, while knowledgeable, wasn't the hidden power in her organization. Oh, he had some organizational strength, undoubtedly. But her father's real puppet wouldn't be so open in his facial expressions—unless McNaughton had gotten sloppy while working with Joey.

Now *that* was entirely possible.

"You and Twyla need to make this happen."

McNaughton nodded. "We better go to HR," he said to Twyla.

"All right," Twyla said.

Justine looked around the outer office. Dear God, it was the same dark and gloomy gilt stuff that her father preferred.

Her personal office was better. A wall of tinted windows behind the desk—she intended to move that desk so that its back was to a solid wall and not windows, preferably the one shared with her conference room. She could switch out some of the paintings—something she planned to do, anyway—and send a bunch of the fripperies to storage. Strip it down to bare bones.

"Satisfactory?" Raven asked.

"It'll do for the amount of time I plan to be here," she said. "As I told my father, I'm not relocating to LA. I will be here one week a month, other days here and there. This office is good enough for that."

"Very well." Raven bowed to her and left. Once he was gone, Shanice and her security went over the offices. Justine didn't settle in her chair until the surfaces passed a quick contact test for toxins, and the bugs had been identified.

Then she exhaled, as the others retreated.

Time to work. She grinned and cracked her knuckles, then pulled off her gloves.

Let's see how deep I can dig into the files since I'm on site.

Some archives were protected from off-site download. Those had to be her priority this week, so she could peruse them at her leisure later.

———

THE MEETING WITH HER SUBORDINATES ENDED UP BEING SHORT AND SWEET. But disappointing, because the two division leaders Justine intended to quiz down hard before dismissing them resigned before the meeting.

After the meeting ended, Justine reviewed potential replacements. She recommended her choices to Twyla and Shanice for further investigation, and found a slot for McNaughton. Then called him into her office.

"I need someone knowledgeable to work with Bart Abluour in North American biologics marketing," she said.

"I didn't realize that Abluour was the head of that division."

"He will be, shortly. I'm putting you in place now, so that you're already established once he gets final approval from my father."

Brief surprise flitted across McNaughton's face. "What is my role?"

"You're his head of media production. But you will also report to me—and, by the way, that assignment *is* confidential. I also want you to review your body language and vocal tone control training."

"You know about that?"

"I *am* Philip's daughter. A high-level Martiniere heir. You're damn right I know about the control training." She used a faint command tone, enough that he snapped stiffly upright, at full attention. "Your face reveals too much about what you're thinking and how you're reacting. Either you never got the *good* training, or you've gotten sloppy. Fix it if you want to stay in External Affairs."

McNaughton nodded, keeping his face unreactive. *Good.* "So you don't trust Abluour?"

"I don't trust *any* of you until you've proven yourselves. But your record says you're competent, and you have the required experience. You're wasted as an executive assistant. Time for you to move up."

"Thank you. What am I to report to you?"

"Rossings messed up the division badly and the marketing is pathetic. I don't know if the problems come from the top or lower down. I want better production values on everything from slide decks to social media to traditional video. *Everything* that goes out of the North American biologics marketing division needs to be revamped and rebranded. Take a hard look at our competitors. We're in the Dark Ages." She pointed an index finger at him. "I know what does and doesn't look good in today's agriculture market, and the costs are outrageous for the poor media quality the Group is releasing. Find out what's going on. Let me know if Abluour is doing his job or if he's padding accounts. Rossings was padding accounts."

"You discovered that, then." A faint impressed note in his voice. "Joseph either didn't pick up on my hints or he didn't care. Rossings was gross in his corruption."

"It didn't take rocket science. Do not make the mistake of thinking I'm like Joey. I'm twelve credits away from a dual degree in accounting and management from the University of Oregon, plus several years of practical experience working with Atwood Investments and Mist Knoll winery. What does Joey have in comparison? Dropped out of—how many universities now?"

"Four."

"I'm not Joey, and the sooner everyone in External Affairs realizes that...."

"You're most definitely not like your brother," McNaughton said. "And it's not just because you're a woman."

"A good thing that you have recognized this reality." She smiled at McNaughton. "Congratulations, Mr. McNaughton. Serve me well, and this won't be your first promotion while working for me. Understood?"

"Completely."

"Then you better go about getting up to speed on your new position."

"Thank you." He rose, bowing deeper to her than when he first entered.

"Oh," she said.

He stopped short of the door. "Yes, Ms. Martiniere-Atwood?"

"What is the name of Morris's assistant? The big man who looks like he should be security instead of an executive assistant?"

"Greg Hallock." McNaughton returned, leaning on the back of a chair.

Worth a gamble to ask the question. "So, is Hallock the one who's really in charge of Internal Affairs instead of Morris?"

McNaughton burst out laughing. "Oh, Ms. Martiniere-Atwood. I am going to *enjoy* working with you. Your brother never figured that out—and the answer is yes. Everything goes through Morris, but the real power is Hallock."

"I thought so." His tone confirmed her suspicions. "Does he have more power than you did as his equivalent in External Affairs?"

The expression on McNaughton's face was priceless, even though it swiftly returned to non-responsive.

He's learning.

McNaughton sat back down. "Yes. Joseph—*Joey*—wanted control."

"Do you like Hallock?"

"The fucker's crossed me one time too many."

Aha. A correct guess. Justine folded her hands together.

"Here's a confidential side job for you, Mr. McNaughton." Oh, he liked that, leaning forward eagerly. But damn it, he still needed to work on that body control. "I want a report on Hallock by the end of the week. I want to know *everything* about Hallock. Strengths. Weaknesses. Vulnerabilities."

"What's our goal?"

"I intend to screw him over before he does it to me," she said.

McNaughton smirked. "I will enjoy watching that happen, Ms. Martiniere-Atwood."

"Subtlety will be the name of the game. Remember what I said about reviewing your body and vocal control training. I don't want Hallock to know what hit him when I make my move."

McNaughton nodded.

"All right—Eliot," she said. "We should be on a first name basis."

"All right, Justine."

"And one last thing, Eliot. This side project is absolutely confidential." She weighted her tones. "I am the only one with whom you'll talk about our plans for Hallock. Understand?"

His eyes gleamed. "Absolutely, Justine." He rose and bowed lower than before.

Justine leaned back in her chair.

Wonder how quickly Daddy-damned-dearest will hear about this?

McNaughton was sufficiently conscientious to make a final report to her father.

What he did after that—would be telling. But pointing him at Hallock would keep McNaughton's focus elsewhere.

She glanced at the clock. Four-fifteen. Another meeting ahead with a promising underling she planned to jump up to a higher level, and then time to meet with her father. Four-forty-five was her goal.

It would be *interesting* to hear what her father had to say.

———

Four-forty-five. Adequate time for rumors to swirl toward her father about her first-day actions. Just enough into their meeting window that he would be nervous, wondering if she was going to delay or cancel their meeting. She wanted him guessing, trying to figure out *just how far will Justine push things?* Justine pulled her gloves back on, checked her appearance in the mirror behind her door, then stepped out.

"Twyla, please let Raven know that I'm ready to meet with my father." Justine paused as she stood by Twyla's desk. "Why don't you come with me? If Raven is with him, then I want you there as well."

"All right." Twyla messaged Raven and spoke softly to him. "He will not be in the meeting," she told Justine.

"All the same, I'd prefer to have you waiting with Raven in the outer office."

"Understood." Twyla rose gracefully. She wore silver and black, like the rest of Justine's security detail, except that instead of slacks she wore a skirt and her black hair was unconfined, flaring in tight curls.

More style choices. Shanice and the other Black women in Justine's security kept their hair short or restrained. But Twyla, even though she was officially security, looked more like a traditional assistant than security.

Justine pitied anyone who might underestimate Twyla as a result of her innocuous appearance. Would that include Raven? Hard to say. Raven was canny.

Raven opened the door to Philip's office as they entered the outer office. He bowed low to Justine.

"You didn't need to come over, Twyla," he said.

Twyla shrugged. "Justine might have a request and it's better if I'm here." She smiled at Raven. "And I thought I might learn a bit more about the *unwritten* office procedures from you, if you don't mind."

"Not at all," Raven said as Justine went into her father's office, closing the door after her. She continued to the waiting chair. Her father rose and bowed to her. She bowed back, then sat.

"So," he said. "It appears you've made an impression on your first day."

"The resignations?" Justine steepled her fingers. "It was a little disappointing. I had hopes of making examples of a couple of them. Charpentier and Rossings, to be specific."

"Examples?" Her father's posture almost mirrored her own. "Are you *certain* you want to start out that way?"

"Charpentier and Rossings resigned before I did anything. A good thing, because they screwed up, badly. They *don't* need to be employed by the Martiniere Group. How the hell did they reach that level of authority? Looks like they've been getting swapped around between divisions. Rossings is padding his personal income, and there's a lot of fuzziness around Charpentier, who may have been doing the same thing."

His brows rose. "Pretty bold statement for your first day on the job."

"You gave me the position, Daddy-darling. I intend to be more than a figurehead. Besides, I've run into my fair share of problematic men in charge."

His snort was almost identical to hers. "*Men*, of course."

"Oh, there's always a few women who fall into the same classification," Justine said. "But specifically for the Group—considering I'm the highest-placed woman in the Group, the middle management levels are predominantly male, and the workers are mainly female, it's an excellent assumption that the problem children are men."

"Not that you're necessarily much of a woman these days."

"Oh?"

Don't react, don't react, don't react.

Justine forced herself to do nothing more than raise her brows and touch her lips with her gloved index fingers.

A brief flare of disappointment tightened his lips. "After all, you did have a hysterectomy. I suppose you've kept your ovaries?" He leaned forward slightly and licked his lips.

"That," she said slowly, inserting a dry tone into her voice, "is between me, my husband, and my gynecologist. Now. Did you have any *other* business, *father?*"

He leaned back. Was that a disappointed expression? "A check-in was my intention. But it appears that you've had a productive and informative first workday."

"It has been."

A faint smile twitched his lips. "And good job in identifying Charpentier and Rossings as the primary problems with your divisions. McNaughton was impressed, and he's quite pleased about being promoted. I suppose that's one way you intend to co-opt my watchdogs."

If McNaughton said anything to Daddy-dear about Hallock, he's not showing his hand.

But probably not. From McNaughton's reaction, he hated Hallock enough to help bring the man down.

"He's of more use to me where I put him. McNaughton has talent, but he's damn sloppy about controlling tones and body language around me." She scowled at her father. "I'm conducting a thorough audit of External Affairs. Those two were just the most obvious problems. I can't stand shoddiness like I'm seeing in the numbers. You and the Board gave me this job. I'm going to do it the way it should be done."

Philip surveyed her again, and she his face softened slightly.

"Ah. It is definitely too bad that you were born female, because you would make a fine Martiniere-in-waiting. But that's neither here nor there. A good first day, daughter. I'm glad to see that not all of my offspring run toward the less competent side of things. I'll see you tomorrow."

"Thank you." She rose and bowed before leaving her father's office.

Joey must have really screwed things up.

She *wasn't* going to think about what her father said about her potential to be a Martiniere-in-waiting. No way in hell that it would happen, not with Philip Martiniere in charge of the Family and the Group.

Damn it. She'd concede the position to Gabie—but no one else. Even if she had to put up a puppet to serve as the Martiniere because it was denied to her as a woman.

Justine's mouth quirked wryly.

Didn't take long for the ambition bug to bite now, did it? One complement from Daddy-damned-dearest and I'm as power-hungry as any of my kin.

All the same—if she couldn't be her father's replacement as the Martiniere, then she was going to ensure that whoever did was someone who met her approval.

Which explicitly ruled out her brother Joey.

ONE WEEK IN LA, BEFORE SHE COULD RETURN TO THE PORTLAND CONDO where Donald was waiting, in preparation for Monday's surgery. Justine put in long hours to ensure she had done everything that required face-to-face contact before she went to Portland.

Finally, it was Friday. Justine got on the shuttle to Portland.

Several things about this flight bothered her. First, only Shanice and Twyla could fly with her, not the rest of her security. Secondly, she noticed how they muttered about the security screening. Yeah, it was an executive shuttle. But when her security didn't like the conditions, she listened to them. Unfortunately, they'd had the same opinions about a different shuttle company when they'd flown to LA.

Justine skimmed through costs of private charter aircraft as they flew. She didn't want to continue traveling on executive shuttles over which she had no influence or control, remembering what had happened to Gabie's parents and sister on one such flight. She was at risk and wanted—no, *needed*—more control over her transportation, especially as she continued working within the Group. Reduce the likelihood of being a target as she angered more established figures who had been doing shady things within the Group. Or Philip's shadowy minions who had been doing dirty work for the Group.

Charters aren't going to work, she decided. Not for what it would cost. For her purposes, buying or leasing a plane made more sense. Which meant—a greater upfront investment if she was going to maintain her own airplane and crews.

Something to discuss with Donald—but not until after his surgery.

Donald had purchased the Portland condo in his own name, not theirs, specifically to deal with medical needs. Justine hadn't been here before. It was one of two penthouse apartments at the top of a building in the Pearl District—the other was also his, for their security and other support.

"Leaving you two alone tonight, at least until you go to bed," Meg said. "He has an emergency button if there's any problems."

"Thank you." Just how many people were crammed into the other condo so that she and Donald could have some privacy? "You'll be all right?"

"Just fine." Meg smiled at her. "We have more space than you. Two more bedrooms. And not everyone is staying all night."

Justine nodded. Security would come into their condo after she signaled that she and Donald had retreated to their bedroom. That provided more space for the others.

"See you tomorrow, then," she said to Meg, grabbing the handle of her roller bag and going inside.

A reading lamp illuminated the otherwise darkened main living and dining area of the condo. Donald slept in a recliner near the corner windows, reading glasses on his face, tablet flat on his lap, wearing t-shirt and pajama pants that outlined his sparse frame. Justine winced—he looked worse than he had just a few days ago. Her heart wrenched. She crossed the room to kiss his forehead.

Donald's eyes popped open, and he pulled off his glasses, moving them and the tablet to a side table. Then he smiled at her.

"There you are. Sorry to have fallen asleep."

"It's all right." She perched on the recliner's arm. "I'm two hours later than I had planned."

"I've missed you." He wrapped his arms around her, sitting up to kiss her. "I'd pull you into my lap, but everything hurts right now."

"I'm sorry. Let me get out of traveling clothes and into something comfortable, then I'll be back."

"Eh, I need to move around, anyway. Help me up and we'll talk while you unpack and change. Security screens are at highest levels, so we can talk freely."

Donald leaned on her as they walked to the bedroom. At least it didn't *feel* like he had lost any weight. She helped him lie down, then turned to her suitcase.

"So," he said, lying on his side, watching her. "Tell me *everything* that you couldn't say over the phone."

Justine laughed. Then she proceeded to do so while unpacking. When she was done, she kicked off her shoes, then collapsed on the bed.

"I need to change," she said. "But even on the shuttle I was working. I think this is the first time I've really stopped since last Sunday."

"Come cuddle," he said.

"Skin-to-skin?" She studied him, acutely aware that she was still analyzing body movement and vocal tones, assessing even her beloved husband as a potential threat.

Ugh. Thank God she wasn't *staying* in LA, much less working full-time in Headquarters. That hyperawareness would ease after a day or so—she hoped.

"If—you wouldn't mind, and aren't too tired," he said. "At least your top."

"Absolutely no problem, dear." Justine pulled off her shirt and then her bra. Donald awkwardly sat up and took off his t-shirt. As she lay back down, he settled on his side next to her, resting his head on her chest with his arms around her.

He sighed. "I'm so glad you're here. It's been a rough week. Getting ready for surgery. Thinking about you. Thinking about—the future."

"I'm sorry." She ran her fingers through his hair and stroked his cheek.

He closed his eyes. "I'm afraid because this pain feels so different. I'm glad to have you comfort me. But damn, I'm being so weak. I'm so sorry about this timing."

"It's all right," she whispered back.

For once he wasn't hiding his illness. But damn, that it took something this bad for him to do it—*damn* his stubbornness.

Almost as stubborn as a Martiniere man. Almost.

CANCER. CONFIRMED.

Chemo followed surgery for Donald.

Justine shouldered more of the Real Lives for Women work as Barbie's health faltered. When Donald recovered, she shifted those responsibilities back to him.

It wasn't until nearly Christmas that she could slow down and catch her breath—once more at Mist Knoll instead of Paris. Against Philip's objections, but Justine insisted that she and Donald needed the down time—she had finally disclosed that Donald had health problems.

That was the one argument Philip couldn't counter, not without looking like a hypocrite. She *was* prioritizing her husband, which fit right into Philip's ideology.

Christmas, then their anniversary.

"Fifth anniversary," Donald said as they sat in front of the big fireplace in their bedroom suite.

Justine shivered. "Soon to be my first anniversary as First Secretary."

Donald sighed. "Two more years together. I need to retire this year, darling. I can either work my ass off as an investment manager, or I can deal with the rising demand for the RLW secret support services and take over Mom's role as she becomes more frail. I can't do both anymore—and you have far too much to handle right now to manage RLW."

"Are you sure?" She knew he enjoyed his investment work.

"Unfortunately, yes. I need to choose one or the other—and the world has enough investment managers." He squeezed her. "Besides, I want to spend as much time as I can with you, darling. Before...." His voice trailed off.

"Yes," she said. "Before."

As they snuggled close, she sighed. Five short years.

It wasn't long enough. Even with two more years to go.

If only there was another way....

But there couldn't be, not with what was stirring within the Martiniere Group. Serg claimed to know where Gabie was. Justine sure as hell hoped he was right, because...if things came together, then within the next four years, Daddy-fucking-dearest would be banished. Imprisoned.

Something.

Gabie would become the Martiniere, and then....

Unfortunately, Gabie wouldn't become the Martiniere fast enough to prevent her divorce from Donald. Not unless things changed. Drastically.

13 / INTERLUDE SIX

August, 2086

"I DON'T UNDERSTAND WHY PHILIP WASN'T AWARE OF THE PROBLEMS IN *External Affairs,*" Lily said, frowning. "*Or was he not as competent as he liked to imagine himself being? I could believe that. I saw it in the moments he allowed me to be myself. Realized it when I died. But that was too late for me.*"

"*He overestimated his competence,*" Gabie said. "*The mess I inherited when I became the Martiniere—*" he shook his head.

"*I was still dealing with it as the Martiniere, right up to my death,*" Brandon said.

Justine startled. Her nephew's digi was much more silent than he had been in life.

Brandon's digi had been hijacked by Philip when Brandon was murdered. Philip forced Brandon's digi into one-year-old physical clones of his body over the course of three months, in an attempt to discover why he couldn't possess Mike's body.

Even for a nonliving, digital being, the experience was horrific, from what little Justine knew. Multiple forced meldings of Brandon's digi with physical clones led to suicidal toddlers who found ways to die rather than tolerate the older version of themselves crammed into their brain. Though Bran talked to Gabe and Ruby about what he had endured, none of the digis chose to share Brandon's experiences with living persons.

Too horrendous, Gabie said the one time that Justine pressed for more information. *It's a mercy for the sanity of Bran's digi that it occurred for so short a time.*

And Brandon was quieter—not brooding—but he was not the same as he had been while alive. Living Brandon had been a smartass, like both his parents.

The only time Justine saw the digital clone of her nephew smile was at his children. When Lily said or did something that was so different from what she had been in life. Or when Ron demonstrated his growing skills as the Martiniere-in-waiting.

"Daddy-fucking-dearest was not the legend he created for himself," Justine said. "If he had been, he would never have allowed the Board to force me on him. And even though he got rid of me as First Secretary after seven years, he still ended up taking me back as Director of Security. Gabriel, if you had said the word, I could have destroyed the Group. I was ready to do it."

"Nothing would have come of it," Gabie said. *"I was still significantly locked down and couldn't have taken power. Too bad, because maybe then Rafe Alvarez would be alive, and Heaven's Reach wouldn't have developed as far as it did."*

"Heaven's Reach," Ruby said slowly. *"That viper's nest. How do we defang it for real? I keep thinking we've eliminated it—and then it comes back."*

"I've been talking with Justine," Gabie said. *"As well as doing my own investigations. Hawkins has been Philip's surviving ally. He made those partial digis that helped Philip's digi trap both Lily and Brandon. Heaven's Reach is closely allied with Jeremy's division and Brandon's killers."*

He flicked up several file links. Justine quickly reached for them. She sorted through the connections, routing several to Ron.

"Taking care of this immediately," she said firmly. "Ron, I've preapproved several recommended actions for you. We'll cut them off from Group funding."

"You sure you want to act this soon?" Gabie asked.

Justine bared her teeth at her brother's digi. "Don't tell your sister how to do her job, Gabie. Thanks for the links. They fill in some missing gaps."

"All right," Mike said. "When I get approval from Dr. Pramula, I'm ready to do something about Heaven's Reach and Samuel Hawkins, once and for all."

"Are you sure, Mike?" JoAnn frowned worriedly at him.

He took her hand. "My heart and lungs are fully updated, hon. It's time."

"Our first action needs to be the creation or awakening of Donald's digi," Gabie said. *"I'm still not sure which it will be. Justine, do you have any sense of his presence?"*

"I'm not sure," she said. "But it might be like waking your digi. I have to say the right thing at the right time. I keep getting these sensations, but he's not answering me."

"There were conditions that affected how I could manifest, and I didn't have the time to program my algorithm properly before I died," Gabie said. *"I'll send you my file, Tine. That might be what you need."* He cocked his head and gave her that artless grin of his. *"You woke me to being a digi, after all. You might also be the key for Donald's digi."*

"I'll—try," she said.

"In the meantime, let's keep recording stories," Brandon said. *"I'm programming them so that Donald will be able to use them. If he didn't already provide his own files."*

"I tried to leave hints for Don before he died." Gabie frowned. *"But he was in pretty bad shape at the end. I don't know if he was able to create his own algorithm."* He sighed. *"But I was able to wake Ruby without her deliberately creating files, so—"*

"Meanwhile, I have a physical therapy appointment," Mike said. "It looks like I'll be able to go home in a couple of days. Let's have our next session at the Double R—I plan to focus on getting the heck out of this damn place before Labor Day."

"A laudable goal," Justine said.

SHE REVIEWED THE FILE GABIE SENT, WRYLY NOTICING THAT IT CONTAINED a link which would allow her to activate her own algorithm so that she would become a digi at her death. *Did* she want to do it?

Perhaps if they activated Donald.

Justine pulled on digigloves for better, deeper, accesses, and traced her way through the algorithm, thinking hard about Donald. His long, lean face, normally solemn, but the way a smile would light it up when he saw her. The pain it carried during their divorce.

The faint triumphant expression when she told him that Hallock was dead, at her hands.

Their joy at Gabie's defeat of Philip—and their ability to reunite publicly.

A favorite memory, one she *wouldn't* share with anyone else—

Shall we remarry, like Gabe and Ruby? Donald had asked Justine during those heady days after Philip's death and Gabie's ascension as the Martiniere.

On the one hand, she wanted to say *yes*, passionately and thoroughly.

On the other—Meg had died, Coral's health was faltering, and Francie needed Donald's presence to cope with daily life. He couldn't be away from Nameless Island for long.

While I'd love to, I'm afraid you still have obligations, she said. *Coral and Francie need you more than I do. They've been there for you when I couldn't. I can't take you away from them.*

True, Donald conceded.

And by the time Coral and Francie were no longer a concern, Donald was in failing health.

She was there for Donald at the end, shortly after Gabie's sudden death. With Donald as he died.

Recently-widowed Ruby was her bulwark during those times.

But even then, Justine hadn't shared everything with her sister-in-law—including just how close she was to her ex-husband. Ruby would have wanted to know why they didn't remarry…and that discussion wasn't one that Justine wanted to share.

AN EARLY FALL STORM LASHED THROUGH NORTHEASTERN OREGON THE night after Mike returned to the Double R—a typical pre-Labor Day cold front. Justine sat by the deck's slider door in her suite at Moon-dance, watching the downpour. Maybe this winter would be a proper wet and cold one.

She shivered, suddenly thinking about Donald.

"I'll never understand why you chose British Columbia instead of a tropical island, love," she said out loud. "I know the tropics were your preference. That you didn't like the gray and the wet."

Was it her imagination or did she feel a sudden sense of his *presence*?

"Donald. Please. If you're there. Please." Justine gulped. "I need to know. I need to have hope. Gabie says that digis aren't really who we were in life, even though we have the memories. But when I see him and Ruby together—oh God, Donnie. Please." She blinked back tears. "Your falcon is old and tired. I've fixed so many things for others. Please. If I have to spend an eternity as a digital clone fixing things—I want you there with me."

She waited, half-expecting to hear, feel, or see *something*.

But the sensation never grew stronger, never formed into a solid outline.

This was hardest of all. *Could* they resurrect Donald?

He wasn't responding to her plea. That didn't bode well. Live Donald would have rushed to console her.

If Donald *was* a digi, she wasn't sure she would like this permutation of him should this be a deliberate choice on his part.

<hr>

THE DAY AFTER THE STORM WAS BRIGHT AND CLEAR, SKIES THAT VIVID HARD blue which followed autumn storms in the high-elevation Thunder Valley, warm with a little bite of damp that warned of approaching winter. Mike sat on the Double R farmhouse's front porch, upright this time, in the swing, JoAnn sitting next to him.

Justine settled into the lounge chair.

"And now it's time to talk about the leadup to the divorce, and

Rescue Angel," she said. "I'm still amazed that Daddy-poo never figured out I was the primary person behind Rescue Angel. That he eventually handed off Vygotsky Security to me."

"Wait, what?" Gabie scowled at her.

She smirked at him even as her heart sank. Another memory that hadn't carried through to digi. "How do you think Serg and Piotr survived *two* coup attempts against my father? I protected them."

Mike chuckled. "Gabe, even though you're a digi, if you drop that jaw any further, you'll catch flies."

"I—just—" Gabie shook his head. *"Little sister, you were sneakier than I thought."*

"Not a surprise to me," Ruby said. She smiled at Justine. *"But then, we always had a lot to discuss when we had our Ladies Shooting Practices."*

Ruby still remembered. What was the difference between her and Gabie? File corruption, or memories not carried over?

Gabie shook his head again, half-smiling. *"Dear God, Philip never did realize who he should be watching out for, did he?"*

"In part because I played my role honestly," Justine said. "I sincerely wanted to clean up the problems in the Group, because they were part and parcel of the mess that Daddy-damn-dearest created as part of his long-term political ambitions." She cleared her throat. "So. The divorce. Rescue Angel. Donald and I spent a lot of time planning in those years, and the things we planned…weren't always what you might expect."

14 / TANGLED WEBS

"Got a moment?" Eliot McNaughton fell into step beside Justine as she entered headquarters.

"Always," Justine said. Cultivating McNaughton was worth the effort, because he kept her apprised of currents within the Group. Even better, sometimes Philip talked to McNaughton about things that concerned him, and Eliot reported them to Justine.

Once they were inside her inner office, Justine switched on her blockers. McNaughton waited until she nodded before he spoke.

"You're still affiliated with your mother-in-law's Real Lives for Women group, right?"

"Yes," Justine said, a chill gripping her gut. RLW faced some significant legal challenges. She couldn't definitely prove it, but she suspected that Philip was involved with them.

"Might be a good idea to back off on that connection. Philip is ranting. And one of my sources over in Legal passed me this." McNaughton flicked Justine a file. She opened it.

Expense list. Billing records. Work done for the Real Truthers, including...court filings. And funding for the organization's research section dedicated not just to ending contraception and abortion, but criminalizing it.

Done by the law firm that worked for Philip's personal corporation, PJM Corp.

All authorizations bearing her father's signature.

Is this information for real, or is it a trap?

Justine looked up at McNaughton.

"Thanks for the heads up, Eliot."

"Just *do something* with it, will you?" He shook his head. "It's not involving the Group, on the surface, at least. But I don't like this one bit."

She leaned back in her chair. "Neither do I."

Careful. Even though he's an apparent ally—don't say too much. Don't go too far. Daddy-damned-dearest could be using Eliot to lure you into saying something damning.

He gave her a quick smile. "Which is why I came to you. If you can get the information to the right people, maybe that will slow things down." He shook his head again. "I don't like shadowy politics. And Hallock is Philip's right-hand man in the political gaming."

"Figures."

Aha.

McNaughton's hatred of Hallock was legendary within the Group. Her father played the two men against each other. *She* thought that Hallock was the more skilled of the two men when it came to manipulation and dirty-dealing—Eliot possessed compunctions which Hallock lacked.

Those scruples also appeared to include support for women's rights. Not surprising—Eliot's ambitious younger sister encountered obstacles within the Group, until Justine brought her into External Affairs.

Even that was bothersome. External Affairs was becoming known as friendly to ambitious women within the Group, and obtaining Justine's patronage was a major goal for many of them.

But such a reputation was risky, given her father's stance on powerful women.

And now, this.

"Thank you, Eliot," she repeated.

"You're welcome," he said. He bowed and left.

Justine sighed and stared out the window. A hazy day today, with a rare prospect of rain that afternoon. Now what?

Donald was spending the week with her in LA. She could tell him about this tonight.

Cousin Kendra should know about this latest development as well. Kendra's latest project involved seeking out potential Group ties to the rise in anti-reproductive rights legislation worldwide. Philip was making noises about running for President of the US. His platform included demands for legislation to create a national-level police force to enforce the laws already on the books in some states, and drafting Federal legislation that outlawed abortion and many forms of contraception.

But.

She needed to be careful. This was exactly the sort of rumor that Philip would feed to Eliot. It needed to be confirmed before anyone acted upon this information. Much as she liked Eliot, he could be used as a weapon against her.

***

"If this is real, it's the smoking gun we've been looking for to prove Philip's collusion with this legislation," Donald said, after examining the records McNaughton had passed to her. "What do you think?"

"It's a possibility," Justine said. "But I have questions about this information's reliability. Eliot didn't tell me where he got it—just that it was a random source in Legal. I haven't asked for details before, and asking for sources wouldn't fit my pattern now."

"So far, he's been reliable," Donald agreed. "But that could also be a strategy to encourage you to develop blind faith in him."

"Exactly." She frowned, studying the projection. "And Eliot specifically suggested that I back off from RLW. Daddy-poo hasn't made that demand of me just yet. I wonder how long it will be until he does."

"You have that big fundraiser next week."

Justine grimaced. She was the headliner at a banquet that Barbie organized, and was putting off writing a speech for it, figuring that there would be time once she was done with her monthly marathon week at the Group.

"Now I wonder about the timing of this tip," she said. "I hate to cancel on your mother, but—I wonder if this is a warning through Eliot from Daddy-dearest?"

"You don't think Philip would be more direct?"

"External Affairs under my control does too well for him to throw his weight around too much," she said. "Oh, God, I don't know. It's entirely possible. I don't know what to do yet. We need to confirm this information." She paused. "I'll go ahead with the banquet, but that will be it for my aboveground work for RLW." She gestured at the projection. "Let's assume that this means we're facing further surveillance. It's time to take the next step. I have to go underground with my support."

"Agreed."

HER FATHER CALLED HER INTO HIS OFFICE THE NEXT MORNING. "I'M concerned about how some of your political activities reflect upon your position with the Group," he said.

"Oh? Such as?" A chill tightened her gut. Was this a coincidence, or had Donald's protective screens on their condo failed?

"That speech for Real Lives for Women that you're doing next week."

"It's my farewell speech," she said. "I've already discussed it with Barbie. And I intend for it to reflect well on the Group."

Well, she hadn't discussed it with Barbie *herself*—but she was positive that Donald had relayed the information about McNaughton's files to his mother by now.

"Reflect well on the Group? How?" Her father scowled at her.

"My visible connection to Real Lives for Women has allowed me to increase the number of women we've hired and retained for specialist positions since I became First Secretary. Look at the stats."

"True," Philip conceded.

"It's also helped reduce our labor complaints and lawsuits. Which means reduced expenses."

His scowl deepened. "Granted. But the way the political scene is going—"

Time for deflection. Justine gave Philip one of her social butterfly smiles.

"Daddy-dear, External Affairs is keeping me far too busy to be playing around with politics, so I'm backing out gracefully. I don't know how you can juggle managing the Group, the Family, and the Real Truthers. I don't seem to possess the same talent that you have for balancing politics and business."

Philip snorted but looked pleased with the compliment. "Perhaps it's a masculine thing. I am glad to hear that you plan to sever ties with Real Lives for Women. When it becomes illegal, that association *will* reflect poorly on the Group."

"You think that will really happen, Daddy-dear?"

Child-like voice, Justine, child-like voice! Play to his prejudices.

An even smugger expression crossed her father 's face at the tone of her voice and her lack of argument.

"Oh, yes, just not right away, Justine my dear. You need to discuss the matter with your husband, and have him speak to his mother. The risk inherent in such activities could be—problematic."

"I don't know that Donald has much influence with his mother," she said.

"He had best be cautious, then. And you may want to think very hard about that prenuptial agreement of yours. It will turn out to be a good thing for the Group if you can divorce Atwood easily, should it become necessary."

"It certainly seems that way." Justine exaggerated her check of the time. "I need to go. Urgent meeting with Logistics." She scowled, exaggerating her frown. "I still don't have the answers for why the biologics shipments to our Midwestern clients are delayed. We're almost past the spring application window."

"A Covid breakout in the indentured labor pool is what I've heard."

She shook her head. "Unless Hallock is lying to me, that shouldn't have this degree of impact." She was long past pretending that Albert Morris ran Internal Affairs. "We can't afford to be unreliable with these shipments. Our opposition is running too close, and given our investment in the processes, we can't afford to make many more mistakes. We'll lose those clients because they don't trust us. I don't blame them, after the way those shipments were mucked up under Joey's management. I've made too many promises that things have changed, so I have to perform."

Philip smiled indulgently. "Then you better go take care of those biologics shipments. I'll talk to Hallock."

"Thank you." Justine rose.

Dodged a bullet.

But still concerning.

"So it's out in the open now," Donald said.

"Yes," Justine said. "And I worry—has he been able to circumvent our security?"

"I'll reprogram things and run more frequent checks." He summoned his computer projection, quickly inputting several commands.

"Thank you."

"Damn it. He really *did* refer to our prenups in the context of making it easier for us to divorce?"

She nodded.

Donald leaned in close to whisper in her ear. "I suppose this means we need to choreograph the lead-up to our divorce?"

"He's certainly giving us appropriate grounds for it, isn't he?" she murmured.

"Well, we'll talk with Mom next week." Donald lowered his voice even more. "In the meantime, what do you think? Should we be creating the foundation for a big, dramatic split? Or just let it happen?"

She shivered. "I'd sooner just let it happen—but I'd prefer not to do it at all."

"I know what you mean." He paused, then spoke in his normal voice. "Security check doesn't find anything, but I've reset passwords and parameters."

"Then it must be nothing more than my upcoming speech."

"Very likely. And as for us—the more obvious and dramatic we can make our divorce, the safer you'll be in the Group. And we *need* you there."

"I know." She leaned her head against him. "But I don't have to like it, do I?"

"No. You don't. I don't like it either. Do we have an option?"

"I'm going to do my best to find one," she vowed.

"My brave, beautiful falcon," Donald murmured. "Please. Keep yourself safe. If something happens to you because of Real Lives for Women—I couldn't bear it."

"I'll do my best," she said, forcing a brave smile onto her lips. "After all, I *am* Philip Martiniere's daughter. I will not go down without a fight."

"That's what worries me," Donald said. "That's how I fear I'm going to lose you. Not to divorce. *Really* lose you, to death, because I can see your father setting you up to be killed." He hugged her. "Less than a year until you come into your full inheritance. That's when things go into play. I'm frightened for you, my love. The situation is going to change drastically."

"I can activate my private corporation, and move certain activities and investments to that structure."

"But working for reproductive rights will become more dangerous for you," Donald said.

She grinned at him. "One doesn't attain high goals without risk."

"It can't be helped," Barbie said after Justine explained the situation. "And Don is right. You're more valuable to us where you are in the Group than as a visible participant in RLW."

"I just hate that my position is the reason for my stepping down," Justine said. It was hard for her to look at her mother-in-law without wincing. Barbie's stroke left her features uneven and when she was tired, her words slurred.

"You are precious to both me and Don," Barbie said, patting Justine's hand. "You're already in a high-risk situation, but it's one that will reap benefits in the long run. Better for the cause that you survive to keep on fighting. We can't always pick our battlefields, but—the one you've been placed in by your family is crucial."

Justine took those words to heart.

SUMMER, 2032

JUSTINE AND DONALD SPENT THE SUMMER CREATING THE FOUNDATION FOR JSM Corporation, her private Family organization and holding company. She consulted with Kendra and David, Gerard's older son, to ensure that JSM's structures would fit within the Group's already established protocols, while remaining an independent entity.

"It's unusual for one of the Family women to set up their own holding company," David warned. "You'll draw additional scrutiny from Philip."

"It's unusual for a Family woman to hold my position within the Group," Justine said. "Private individual corporations are the norm for high-level heirs with Family responsibilities. While I'm not a candidate to be the Martiniere-in-waiting, my responsibilities are very similar. I already have a lot of attention from Daddy-damn-dearest because he's monitoring everything I do. Let him watch. I'm counting on it. Prove to him that a woman can fucking do the job."

"True," David conceded.

Kendra's analysis was equally cautious.

"You'll need to be careful about what goes into the corporation," she advised Justine. "Your focus is on security-based operations?"

"Donald and I are separating our interests in that area," Justine said. Security interests were an excellent cover for the underground version of Real Lives for Women. "Things are not going as smoothly as I would like between us as a result of my becoming First Secretary."

She hated not being open with Kendra, of all people, but—Kendra was still Family, with ambitions of her own.

"You realize that Philip is going to monitor your activities even more closely because of that emphasis?" Kendra asked, echoing David.

Justine fought back a sigh. *Of course* this would be the general reaction from Family members, especially her allies.

"I'm counting on it, Kendra. Let him look as hard as he wants. Serg and Piotr have a lock on certain aspects of security within the Group, but—there are things they *aren't* covering. I plan to be careful, but we can't depend on Serg and Piotr for everything."

"That's true."

"And there's a need within the Family for woman-friendly security applications," Justine added.

"Are you ever right on that aspect," Kendra said. "As you already know."

"I won't let anyone else be hurt like I was—if I can help it," Justine said.

ANOTHER SERVICE JUSTINE DEVELOPED AS PART OF JSM CORP WAS A private fleet of corporate jets, managed by her personal security. Three jets, services provided to Family women as a cover for their real purpose—safe transport for indentured women in trouble. Donald backed the investment costs, in the form of a loan that Justine would start paying back once she gained control of her Family inheritance in March of 2033.

"What's this all about?" Philip demanded at one of their meetings. "Secure travel for women?"

"Don't you think that the women of the Family deserve to have transportation that they can depend upon, without outsiders imposing on them?" Justine countered. "Daddy-dear, the executive shuttle services are a nightmare. Charter services are expensive for what you get. I'm providing an option for the women of the Family as well as other rich women, because I'm sick to death of the alternatives. A safer, more secure choice, with the luxury that Family women deserve."

Her father rubbed his chin thoughtfully. "I hadn't considered that possibility. But I'm surprised that you borrowed the start-up funds from Donald and not me."

She flashed another one of those false social butterfly smiles at him. "While things aren't going that well between me and Donald, I still intend to take advantage of being married to him and use *his* money, not the Family's, to set this up."

"That's a good idea," Philip said.

"Besides, it will be more palatable to certain Family members if you're not at all connected to JSM Corp." She held out the final lure. "The women will feel free to speak more freely as a result, and if I discover anything interesting—well, I'm not adverse to letting you know what's happening."

The wolfish grin Daddy-damned-dearest gave her in response was satisfying—but she was still nervous about all of this. Had she and Donald done enough to camouflage their real efforts?

October, 2032

Once JSM Corp was solid, just awaiting her twenty-fourth birthday for full implementation, it was time to proceed to the next step.

"There's going to be an ugly period ahead," Justine said bluntly to Coral, Francie, and Meg. "Donald and I will be roleplaying a nasty divorce, and you three will end up in the middle of it. I'm warning you now so that you can back out if you want."

"What kind of ugliness?" Meg asked—she was the most cautious of the trio.

"Examination of your connections to Donald, amongst other things," Justine said. "I'll claim that you are negatively impacting our relationship. All three of you. That Donald is more interested in you than me." She took a deep breath. "That I was forced into a relation-ship structure I didn't desire, and now that I've gained my inheritance, I want free from it."

All three women winced, along with Justine.

"Do you *really* feel that way?" Meg asked.

"Of course not! You know better than that. Your support is price-less." Justine shook her head. "It's an argument my father will under-stand, unfortunately. It's going to be horrible." She sighed. "I hate doing this. Hate it, hate it, hate it. But—if I don't, given what's happening on the political front, even worse things will happen."

"And Don's on board with this?" Francie asked, a skeptical tone in her voice.

"You can ask him—but yes. We're planning a slow escalation because of Barbie's health. She knows what is going on, but neither Donald nor I want to put her through the actual implementation."

Coral nodded. She regularly reviewed Barbie's medical reports as a second opinion for Donald—just as her equivalent with Barbie did the same for Donald, and Justine, when she needed it. Barbie might survive for six more months—but she was unlikely to live much longer than that.

"I think that's a good idea," Coral said. "Not until March?"

"Not until after my birthday, when I have full control of my inheri-tance," Justine said.

"Six months, then," Meg said.

"Pretty much, depending on what happens with Barbie," Justine said. "We will be working out the choreography with you." She exhaled. "I'm not looking forward to this at all. Donald's the only other person who knows the details. Just—whatever is said in public, please be aware that it's a part I'm playing. You know the stakes."

Coral's lips tightened. "The Real Truthers funded by that damned Electric Born cult. Abortion and contraception police, also backed by Electric Born. Your father in charge of it all."

"If my damned father gets even a fraction of the political power he's dreaming of, no woman is safe," Justine said. "And I'm going to stop him. Whatever it takes—" she gulped. "Even divorcing Donald."

November, 2032

HOME AT MIST KNOLL FOR THANKSGIVING, ALL TOO AWARE THAT THIS refuge was soon to go away.

"I wish we could find an excuse to avoid Family Christmas this year," she said as they curled up in front of the fireplace in their bedroom. "Just like I wish we could avoid the Inevitable."

The Inevitable. That was what they called the divorce. Neither of them wanted to be more explicit.

"Unless Mom dies."

She shivered. "I don't want to avoid Family Christmas *that* badly." Barbie's death meant that the Inevitable started creaking into high gear.

Donald ran his fingers through her hair. "I've been thinking about our choreography. Perhaps you should move up your prospective involvement with a lover sooner rather than later."

Justine scowled. "I'm not real thrilled about that."

"I know." He kissed her forehead. "I'm sorry. I'm thinking you need someone on the side who works to make you more reactive to me and the ladies. Someone who is visibly influencing you."

"So my response to you would be a projection of my own behavior because I'm looking outside of the relationship?" Justine considered this possibility. It could work.

Donald shrugged. "There would be legitimate reasons for you to have an affair. You've gained power in the Family. You have your inheritance, so you're free from me. Both your father and Joey have reputations for roving eyes—wouldn't be that unusual for you as well."

"But then there's an issue with the Electric Born morality and women," she pointed out. "I'd have to be careful who I choose. And I'd be in violation of my marriage vows if I took a lover—that could backfire with my father. He's tied in hard to that cult. Double standards."

"It wouldn't need to be a physical affair, to start with," Donald said. "That would also fit into the morality issue, since you wouldn't be cheating on the marriage physically. Those who would criticize a physical relationship wouldn't see anything wrong with you having an emotional affair—I've studied enough of their theology to figure that out. If anything, it would put you on a higher moral foundation than me."

"An emotional affair?" Justine pursed her lips thoughtfully. "A flirtation that leads to a deeper connection but not at all physical?"

That was doable.

"Something like that. You would appear to be virtuous, and the person involved with you—man or woman—would be seen as helping a wounded person."

"Hard to find someone who is safe," Justine said. "That's the problem. Has to be someone I'm already connected to, who isn't going to end up causing us more difficulties in the long run. Not someone involved with RLW. Outside links—I don't know anyone I'd trust in any of our political circles, and none of our winery connections will work. That leaves someone in the Group who isn't Family."

"How about Eliot? He's no longer a direct report to you."

She considered the possibility. Eliot paid about as much lip service to Philip's growing involvement as the guru of the Electric Born religious cult as she did. Their friendship was growing closer. It wouldn't take much more intimacy to take their relationship to a different level.

And Eliot was—for someone who worked for her father—a decent person, and not hard on the eyes. He wouldn't get all handsy and rush things. She suspected that he might even be willing to keep any relationship primarily emotional and not physical.

She—still had problems even thinking about hands other than Donald's on her body. Definitely *never* anyone like Walter Braun.

Though she could program Eliot—*no!* That would make her *just like* Daddy-damned-dearest.

Justine shuddered.

"It's not absolutely necessary," Donald said. "Justine, seriously, if it bothers you that much—this plan isn't set in stone. You don't *need* to take a lover."

"That's not it," she said, her voice low and faltering. "I just had this thought that I could program controls into Eliot. And I encouraged him to keep upgrading his mind control programming." She choked. "My God, Donald. What the hell am I turning into? A manipulator? I'm no fucking better than my damned father!"

"You stopped yourself from thinking about it. That's the difference between you and Philip."

"I'm afraid I'll lose that difference when we divorce," she whispered. "Without you to keep me honest, what will I turn into?"

Donald kissed her hands. "My dearest, you don't give yourself enough credit."

"Are you sure?"

"Trust yourself, my love. You are not your father. Not when it comes to this. You have scruples." He leaned forward and kissed her. "You won't program Eliot as part of a relationship. You don't operate that way. I trust you. Now you need to trust yourself."

She laughed, brokenly, and rested her head on his chest.

Donald gently raised her head so that she looked into his eyes.

"It's time for you to fly, my dearest falcon. Time for you to soar without me. I love you—and I am setting you free, to become who you really are."

***

MARCH, 2033

RESCUE ANGEL BECAME THE NAME FOR THEIR REPRODUCTIVE RIGHTS services, as more states passed anti-contraception laws to augment restrictive abortion laws. The security arm of JSM Corp vetted Rescue Angel organizers, through yet another shell corporation that carried no surface connections to Justine or Donald. A bigger version of their earlier work with Real Lives for Women.

Barbie died right after Justine's birthday in March. The gradual escalation of public arguments between Justine and Donald started at Barbie's funeral reception, with Coral and Justine sniping at each other until Donald stepped in. That led to a screaming argument between Justine and Donald that got a lot of publicity.

Justine worked at Group headquarters the week after, doing her best to project a shaken but determined façade, especially for the paparazzi that now haunted her. Officially, Donald went back to Mist Knoll with Coral, Francie, and Meg. Unofficially, they messaged nightly through Rescue Angel networks.

It was still hellish.

Eliot slipped in to see her toward the end of the day on Wednesday.

"No news," he said. "I just thought you might want to see a friendly face."

Justine let her chin wobble. "Thank you, Eliot. It's been a—difficult time."

"I imagine." He eyed her. "The gossip is spinning throughout the Group."

"The Old Man's little pet getting her comeuppance?"

"Some of that. Not so much within External Affairs. You've done too many good things for our people."

"Thank you, Eliot."

He cleared his throat. "Perhaps I'm being presumptuous, but would you like to have dinner tonight? Something off-site so you can vent freely, if needed?"

Is this Daddy-damned-dearest's idea? Is he using Eliot to trap me?

No, damn it. Eliot was a decent man, just like Donald. Most likely, Eliot was just trying to be a friend.

"Thank you." She let her voice quaver a little. "I appreciate that."

"Would you like me to drive?"

She smiled at him. "Actually, perhaps we should have my security drive us."

"I'll make reservations." He named a restaurant where they'd taken clients before—a known Martiniere Group haunt on the beach. "Leave in half-an-hour?"

"That would be good," she said. "Thank you, Eliot."

"See you soon."

Justine ran a security scan after he left.

Then she sent a message to Donald via their private networks.

Bait taken.

She added the name of the restaurant where they would be.

She fretted until she received an answer, just before she went to meet Eliot.

Good luck.

The code that meant Donald had leaked the information about dinner, as they had planned.

She took a deep breath. This was really happening. No turning back now.

———

Paparazzi drone cams and recorders waited at the back entrance of the Group's headquarters, held at bay by her own security drones. Multiple questions blared at Justine and Eliot as they strode to her waiting SUV. She ignored them all, plowing straight ahead, pretending that they didn't exist.

"Whew," Eliot said once they were settled in the back seat. "Is this normal?"

"Ever since the big fight at Barbie's funeral last week," Justine said grimly. She wasn't faking that reaction.

"I'm sorry, Justine."

She shrugged, tightening her lips. "I'm a high-level Martiniere heir working for the Group. A big public explosion in my personal life is considered to be news."

"Oh God, Justine." His voice *sounded* sympathetic.

She exhaled and buried her head in her hands.

"I can't take it anymore," she said. "I only married him to get away from my father—and now that I've gained control of my inheritance, I don't need Donald."

"It's that bad?"

She nodded. "Those three women—the things we did—all to entertain *him*."

"I had no idea."

The one thing Justine couldn't do while playing a role was force credible tears without a trigger. But she blinked hard, as if she *were* fighting them.

"I just—now that Barbie's gone—" Her voice trailed off.

Eliot raised his hand as if to touch her, then pulled it back. "I'm here." His voice quavered.

Nerves? His own efforts at concealing his motives?

"Thank you," she said, looking away from him.

They didn't speak further until they reached the restaurant.

"You can hide your face against me if you want while we go in so the cameras don't get a clear pic," Eliot offered. "I'll guide you."

"Thank you." She shuddered when his arm went around her shoulder to direct her as she turned her face against Eliot's chest. His touch was light, gentle—not Donald's, but not very different, either. He released her the moment they were inside.

Justine smiled weakly at him. "Thank you, Eliot."

"My pleasure." His hand twitched toward Justine, as if he sought to comfort her.

Then they were led to their table.

Now it begins.

15 / INTERLUDE SEVEN

August, 2086

"Aw, come on, Aunt Justine," Mike groaned. "Are you just going to leave us hanging like that? What happened with McNaughton? The Rescue Angel?"

Justine glanced at the sky. Dark clouds hung over the Thunder Mountains, hinting at an approaching squall. She *did* like watching a good storm come through the Thunders. Ruby had taught her to appreciate them.

"It *kept* getting interesting from that point," she admitted. "But that whole period was an era of chaos and misrule." Justine scowled at Gabie. "Meanwhile, *some of us* were living a quiet life, away from corporate scheming."

"2033," Gabie mused. "*Ruby and I got married in June because she was pregnant with Brandon. We built the first Double R labs. Brandon was born in December. I hustled day work around the County as well as working the Double R. Ruby took in bookkeeping. Serg got cash drops to me, irregularly — that saved our butts more than once.*"

"*Except for Gramps's death in January of 2034, those were two really good years, though,*" Ruby said. She smirked at Gabie. "*We had the ranch to ourselves. Were working our butts off, with a baby. Yeah, we were living tight, but it didn't feel like a hardship."*

"Ah, Rubes, as always, you're right." Gabie smirked back. *"The privacy to do things we couldn't any other year, that summer of 2034."* Gabie waggled his eyebrows at Ruby.

She laughed.

"I'm glad *somebody* has good memories of those years," Justine said, a sour note creeping into her voice. "For me, it was the beginning of a very difficult period."

"Don't think that we escaped, either," Gabie said. *"Winning the Superstar Innovator in the fall of 2034 changed things for us."*

Mike checked the time.

"You know, I'm not in any hurry to do anything today," he said. "If you want to get this section over and done with, I'm good."

Justine thought about it.

Why not? And she might have the opportunity to watch a good storm in the process.

"All right," she said. "As I said before, it was an era of chaos and misrule. Not just in my life, but within the Group. 2033 to 2039. Six very difficult years. But when they were done—the Rescue Angel was fully operating, and Donald and I had our systems coordinated so that we could still meet in secret."

16 / THE BEGINNING OF CHAOS
AND MISRULE

Március, 2033

Dinner with Eliot on Thursday and Friday that week as well. The paparazzi went ballistic, swarms of cams and recorders doubling each day. But each night, her SUV dropped him off at his home before she went to her condo. No kisses exchanged. Nothing more than Eliot's hand on her shoulder, guiding her as she hid her face from the cams while they walked from a building to her SUV, or her SUV to a building. Those were her rules, and Eliot didn't push them. Thankfully.

Her father dropped into her office late Friday afternoon.

"What's going on?" he asked. "Your face is plastered all over the gossip media."

Did it take you this long to figure that out, Daddy-damned-dearest? Or were you just waiting...and seeing?

Justine sighed. "Now that I have full access to my funds, and the impact of divorce on Barbie's health is no longer a consideration—I'm not accepting certain behavior in my marriage."

"It's true about the other women?"

Justine bit her lip and looked away from Philip. "Yes. When I go back to Mist Knoll tomorrow, I'm issuing ultimatums. I may need to exercise the option in our prenups. Or I may not. It all depends on who is more important—his harem, or me."

"I'm sorry." Daddy-damned-dearest's voice sounded triumphant and not sorry at all. "But you chose Atwood over Braun. What's your game with McNaughton?"

"With Eliot? Nothing serious. He's someone I can trust to give me a perspective on what's happening without assuming there's more going on than friendship. He's helping me figure things out before I see Donald this weekend."

"He's a good man," Philip conceded. "But just think. If you'd married Braun, you'd be a rich widow by now."

Justine snorted. "Daddy-dear, did you even *look* at the prenup that Braun wanted me to sign? I would have been nothing more than a concubine for him to whelp brats on. Barely better than an indentured courtesan. If I hadn't died from pregnancy complications like the one I *did* experience, I would have inherited very little."

To her surprise, Philip startled. "What do you mean? I didn't see anything like that in the prenup drafts he showed me."

"Then you saw something different from what I did. I kept a copy, along with a video of him explaining *exactly* what he wanted from me." She pulled up her display, selected the file, unlocked it, and flicked it to her father.

Philip paled, then reddened as he read through the contract and watched the video. A vein pulsed hard in his forehead by the time he was finished.

"I never knew this aspect," he growled. "That betraying—" He caught himself.

Rage stirred within her. He believed her—now. She recognized that tone.

But when she was seventeen and trying to tell Daddy-fucking-dearest what Braun's plans for her were? She couldn't get him to *look* at the prenups.

Settle. Calm. This isn't relevant right now.

Justine throttled her anger.

"Betraying?" she asked sweetly, instead.

He waved a hand. "Nothing that concerns you, Justine. What *are* your plans?"

"I'll be the judge of what does and doesn't concern me, especially if it concerns External Affairs," she said, so sweet-toned this time that her father side-eyed her.

"It doesn't concern External Affairs," he said. Too sharp. Too fast. Defensive. Enough that she *definitely* wanted to look into it. "What are your plans?" he repeated.

"For what?"

"Your future with your husband, and after."

"You're asking me now?" She shook her head. "If we can't reconcile this, I'll start the divorce process. It's not going to be pretty."

"You could do worse than Eliot—afterwards."

Justine shook her head again. "Daddy-dear, right now I have absolutely no interest in remarrying. I don't have children and I won't be able to have children. Frankly, I have little to no interest in a sexual partner."

"You'll be placing yourself back under my authority?"

"Daddy-poo, I have no further desire to come under any man's *authority*, as your church puts it. I am of legal age and have full control of my inheritance. I have my own businesses. Most of all, I do not subscribe to your ideology, and I see no need for a man's headship, as defined by your church. I am financially independent and I intend to continue being so. That is one area where Donald has been scrupulously fair. I respect him for that."

That vein in his forehead pulsed harder. "Justine—"

"Let me remind you. I'm neutered. Spayed, if you want to be more precise. I won't be bearing children out of wedlock—any children at all. I don't fall under your church's traditional biological definition of a woman anymore. Furthermore, *I don't belong to your church*, and never will."

Philip exhaled through his teeth. Silence hung between them.

"You're right," he finally conceded. "You are not the typical female in need of protection."

"Thank you, Daddy-dear." She checked the time. "And now, it's time for me to meet Eliot for dinner." She rose, her father joining her.

Justine stopped him at the door before they stepped into the outer office. "Another thing. I don't have a sex drive and I never have had one, even when I was a teenager. Stop treating me like I'm a bitch in perpetual heat."

Then she marched off without looking behind her to gauge his reaction, much as she wanted to do that.

It would spoil the effect. And besides, she could check the security cams later. If Daddy-damned-dearest's reaction was a good one, Shanice would save it for her.

"I HOPE I'VE BEEN ABLE TO HELP," ELIOT SAID OVER DINNER—VEGAN PHÔ that night.

"You've been more helpful than you could imagine," Justine said. "And you are much better company than any of my close family will be at the moment."

Eliot rolled his eyes. "Hallock got sick of Joey's blathering about you and me. He told Joey to shut the fuck up."

"Oh really?" Not that she blamed Hallock because Joey on one of those rampages was obnoxious, but—Hallock defending her? Defending Eliot?

"Really," Eliot said. "Joey's not exactly a favorite with Hallock, either."

She chuckled. "Does anyone truly like my brother? Don't answer that, I already know what you'll say. I've heard those whispers myself."

He laughed, smiling flirtatiously. "Perhaps his goons."

"Who haven't a single brain cell between them."

Eliot choked on his drink. He set it down carefully and wiped his lips. "Oh, Justine. Donald is an absolute fool to be looking at other women."

"Well, he's been doing more than that," she said acidly.

"Are you safe at Mist Knoll?" he asked.

"Donald's not violent. Never has been. At most there'll be yelling. I might have to put up with the women, but—" she shrugged. "If I don't like it, it's not as if I don't have options. Either at Mist Knoll itself, or renting someplace to stay."

"You could spend more time in LA," he suggested.

She frowned at that. "Why? I'd just as soon not be in the same town as Joey and my father for any longer than necessary. Maybe I'll get a condo in Chicago."

"You do have friends here," Eliot said. Was that a wistful note in his voice? "People who wouldn't mind seeing more of you."

Justine ate some noodles, thinking through her response. "I didn't think I had that many friends in LA," she finally said.

"More than you think."

His hand eased across the table, close to hers, not touching. She looked at it, then at Eliot. He smiled.

"I have to think about—everything," she said. "It's far too soon."

* * *

DONALD DIDN'T MEET HER AT THE EUGENE AIRPORT. JUSTINE EXPECTED this, but his absence caused a nagging ache deep inside. The grayness of the wet, cloudy day didn't help her mood. It was fully thirty degrees colder in Eugene than it had been in LA, and even the greening of the fields as security drove her to Mist Knoll didn't cheer her up. The tagalong media drones trailing her SUV hovered at the edge of her vision, making her keenly aware that privacy was now a rare thing.

All the same, Justine heaved a relieved sigh as they turned into Mist Knoll. Blockers meant the paparazzi couldn't send drones and mobile cams after her.

But they *could* zoom in on the house's exterior from outside the property line.

So no front-door greeting from Donald, either. She hadn't expected it, but she was still disappointed. Justine's shoulders slumped and she tapped open the lock, dragging her roller bag after her.

"Justine." Donald stood six feet from the door, out of visual range. He opened his arms. She secured the door, her fingers fumbling with the code as her vision blurred. Then she went to him. The tears that she couldn't force all week, even when it would have been helpful, broke free. She sobbed into Donald's chest as he murmured soothingly to her.

As her cries eased, he kissed her forehead.

"It's just us this weekend," he said. "I staged a very public argument in the tasting room, and all three of the ladies left. In reality, they're scouting for a new place. God, Justine, this is awful. Are you all right?"

She snuffled. "The paparazzi. Daddy-fucking-dearest. At least someone has the sense to keep Joey away from me, or else I'd kill him. He's gotten so bad that even Hallock told him to shut up, according to Eliot."

"Oh, honey. It's not too late to stop this charade."

Justine shook her head. "I've done too much this week. Gone too far. Dear God, Donald. I told Daddy-fucking-dearest last night to stop treating me like I was a bitch in perpetual heat. I—haven't looked at that recording, but Shanice tells me his expression was priceless as I walked away from him."

"Oh, Justine. Oh, my brave falcon. Come on. There's a fire in the fireplace. Let's just be together while we can."

She sniffled. Then disengaged to grab her bag's handle. Donald put his arm around her as they went to their suite.

"The ladies are looking for a new place?" she asked as they settled on the couch. "For the four of you?"

Donald nodded, then sighed. "A post-divorce residence, but also a transitional residence or two. Nothing right away. It will take a good six months to a year to locate the right spot. I started looking around and—there's more complications than I had anticipated. I'm glad I started the search now. Finding a place sufficiently isolated that also can be accessed quickly, if necessary, with connectivity, free from the legal constraints that the Real Truthers are building state-by-state, is becoming more of a challenge. Add in climate change factors and the options diminish significantly."

"Does this slow our timeline?"

"No. Still projecting that we go back and forth until next March. File for divorce then. By that point I should have inserted Donald's Little Divorce Present to the Martinieres into the Group's databases.

I'm taking my time with the coding. Your file accesses are helping but it needs to be done subtly, without anyone noticing."

"Donald's Little Divorce Present to the Martinieres?"

"A dead man's switch. You respond to prompts on an irregular basis. No response—it queries further, including checking with me. If you're out of contact for more than twenty-four hours after the initial query and I don't know where you are, it starts trashing databases, starting with PJM Corp." Donald glowered. "I intend to send messages to both your father and Joey warning them about it. The other piece— anyone poking into your personal files in the databases will get a warning, then their systems come under attack."

"Thank you."

"I want to keep you safe," he said. "Seriously, though, Justine. If you want to call this off, I have no problem with changing our plans. I really would prefer to stay married." He nuzzled her neck.

"Maybe if we had been able to have a child," she said wistfully. "But the Family—"

"I know," he sighed. "The Family. I knew from the beginning that your fucking family has its hooks into you. More than that, you're the key to stopping your father." He shivered. "I can't keep up with you in the corporate world. Trying to launch Rescue Angel, while managing Real Lives for Women has been plenty for me."

"Will the stress of playing these roles be too much for your health?" She frowned. "That would be enough reason to change plans."

"I can't do any more. But you can. Unless it becomes too much for you. I'll always have a place for you should that happen, my love."

"Thank you," she whispered. "Thank you, beloved."

TOGETHER AND BELOVED FOR THREE WEEKS. THEN BACK TO LA. A SECOND month where she and Donald were on the outs, and Eliot danced closer. Reunion with Donald.

The continuing tension affected her appetite and her nerves, and Justine was losing weight. Too much weight. But food just didn't sound good.

In July, Serg wanted to meet in Sedona, Arizona, and introduce her to a special man in his life. Justine decided that maybe it was time that she found a retreat that didn't involve Donald. Sedona banned any and all paparazzi, drones, and cams. The place bristled with blockers; a known refuge for celebrities, with ways to slip privately into town.

Donald was disappointed, of course. But it fit into their current pattern of escalating conflict. Time to create her own life.

She was having lunch in a lovely little cafe with Serg and his man, Rafe, when she spotted Eliot and another man in a neighboring bar patio. Arms around each other, occasional kisses. *Definitely* something going on there.

Hmm. Eliot has a secret life.

Serg and Rafe both noticed her sudden focus.

"What's up?" Serg asked.

"Eliot McNaughton is making out with a man in the patio next door," she said.

"McNaughton? Isn't he trying to seduce you?" Serg raised his brows.

"The very same," she said. They hadn't discussed the divorce strategy around Rafe. His family was prominent in banking and knew Donald. She also was more interested in talking business with Rafe— he ran his family's security subsidiary, Alvarez Armory. It helped to know about other operations besides Vygotsky Security, given the plans she and Donald had for developing their own security operation.

"McNaughton will have a problem with Philip if he learns about this," Rafe said.

"Only if Daddy-poo finds out about it, which is probably why Eliot's in Sedona." Justine scowled. "Eliot's far too useful to get on Daddy-damned-dearest's wrong side. I need to warn him."

"Want a picture?" Serg asked.

"Can you do it discreetly, without violating the rules?"

"*I* can," Rafe said.

"Then go ahead."

Serg leaned forward as Rafe slipped away. "This makes McNaughton useful for a number of other purposes."

"You bet." Justine wondered if *she* was providing cover for Eliot. It would be ironic if they were *both* using each other—she *had* wondered about that possibility.

"You gonna talk to him about it?"

Justine grinned at Serg. "Damn right. This opens up a lot of possibilities."

Rafe returned, flicking a file to her. She brought it up, scanning through the pix. Oh yes. She had something on Eliot now.

Part of her mourned, because now the best case was that he was bisexual and had someone else who really mattered to him. It closed off options.

Worst case, he was gay and acting out a role with her. Somewhere in between—he just wasn't into being true to anyone.

Don't be a hypocrite, Justine! she chided herself.

After all, *she* was role-playing with Eliot.

She didn't tell Donald about Eliot until she returned to LA, not trusting the security in her Sedona lodging. Serg didn't trust the comms, so she didn't either.

"This makes things even more interesting," Donald said.

"Absolutely," she agreed. "I'm staying over one more day to talk to him."

"And then back to Mist Knoll?" he asked, a longing note in his voice.

"Yes," she said, her heart aching.

Eliot's face went deadly pale when she showed him the pictures. "How—where?"

"I was having lunch with Serg and his new man in the café next door," she said.

Eliot buried his head in his hands. "Here I thought Nick and I were being so damned careful."

"Not careful *enough,* damn it! If those fucking cams had been following you to the Sedona exclusion zone—"

He flinched at the snap in her voice. "Justine. I'm sorry. Really. I suppose this is a second betrayal, after Donald—"

"Not really." She checked her shielding again. No. She wasn't going to risk it. "We'll go to dinner tonight, and then to my place. To talk, and make a plan."

Hope flared in his face, bringing back a flush of color to his cheeks and a softening of the tight muscles around his eyes. "You're not going to tell your father?"

"Fuck, no. You're not the only one with whom things are not as they seem."

And perhaps that was saying too much, *here.*

Eliot's eyes widened as he parsed what she had said, his mouth forming an "O". Then he nodded at her, a faint smile twitching his lips.

He understood. That was oddly relieving.

<hr>

To her relief, Eliot was as good at playacting over dinner as she was. They let the flirting become more intimate, to all appearances toying with boundaries. At the end of dinner, Eliot took her hand and kissed it, lingering. She forced a smile that she sure as hell hoped looked like a come-hither expression.

Silence reigned in the SUV until they reached her condo. Eliot took her hand, guiding her protectively, like he always did.

Once they were in her condo, Justine dropped the façade. They stood six feet apart in her living room, Eliot cringing away from her glower.

"All right. You're seeing Nicholas Reitman, have been for six months." She flicked the file with the info that Serg had collected for her over to Eliot. "He works in real estate. No conflict with the Martiniere Group, as near as I've been able to learn. But you know how my father will react if he finds out about your relationship."

Eliot exhaled. "Yes. He hates gays worse than women."

She crossed her arms. "What's your game, Eliot? Am I a high-visibility cover for your relationship, has my father put you on the assignment of *break Justine and Donald up,* or is it something else? He speaks very highly of you, by the way, and hints that you might be a better man for me than *my husband."*

Eliot tightened his lips and shook his head. "Justine—I—God. I need a drink."

She crossed the room to her bar and poured him a straight shot of good Scotch, a liberal serving. "Here." She kept her voice sharp and hard as she thrust the glass at him.

He tossed the drink back in one gulp. "All right. Some of it is genuine concern, and a little bit—cover." He exhaled. "I'm not reporting on you to your father. Or Joey. Or, God help me, Hallock." He paled at that. "God, if Hallock finds out—"

She eyed him, then poured herself a drink, waving the bottle at him. "Sit down, Eliot. Do you want more?"

"Um. Yeah."

She pointed to the couch. "Sit," she repeated, placed the bottle on the coffee table, and dropped into the loveseat across from Eliot. "How good a game can you play? What's your goal?"

"You're not mad that I'm—seeing someone? A man? While—" he waved his hands wildly. "Leading you on?"

Justine laughed. "Oh, Eliot." She let her voice sharpen. "I don't give a shit about what you and Nicholas are up to. I *do* give a shit about what will happen if my father finds out."

"You won't tell him?"

"If you help me, fuck no. It's none of his damned business." She waved a finger at him. "But if you betray me—"

Eliot poured himself more Scotch. "All right. What do I have to do?"

She contemplated him. This was risky as hell. She sighed and sipped her drink.

"I need you to continue doing what you have been doing. With me. In public. We will intensify our public intimacy. In private—you can tell Nicholas that you're safe with me. We may have sex but without commitment or obligation."

Eliot frowned, brows furrowing. "But—Justine, I don't understand."

She took a deep breath. "I need you to playact that you and I are lovers."

"So you're using me?" A touch of hurt in his voice.

"You're a nice man. And I appreciate who you are and what you do. But." She chose her next words carefully. "I have no interest in taking a serious lover for real. Any lover. Eliot, I'm ace."

"So this is payback to Donald for what he's done to you."

She shook her head. "Publicly—yes. Privately—it's complicated." Another deep, shuddering, breath. "Donald and I are playing a long game right now, and part of it requires that we divorce. Staying together risks what I'm doing in the Group, as well as what Donald's doing politically."

"The Real Lives for Women connection," Eliot said slowly, his face clearing. "Oh God. I see it now."

She nodded. "Exactly. Eliot, if you remain true to me, I'll do my damnedest to protect you—Donald and I both. I'm serious. We need to bring Hallock down, and hinder Daddy-fucking-dearest's political plans."

"And your goal?"

"If the Group were different, I'd be the Martiniere-in-waiting, if not the Martiniere myself by now." Another sip of her drink. "But. There's another candidate. My cousin. Gabriel. Son of the previous Martiniere. Now in hiding because he testified against what Daddy-fucking-dearest is doing to indentureds."

"You'd put Gabriel in charge?"

"I will do whatever it takes to stop my father's political goals," she said, letting her full anger show. "I can't be the Martiniere. So. Gabriel. He's a good and honest man, and his philosophy aligns with mine and Donald's."

Eliot flinched. Then he finished his second drink.

"I'm in, Justine. Not just because of Nick. Hallock—and your father —need to be stopped. I hoped that Gabriel's testimony would change things. There's a reason why I'm in External Affairs and not Internal—I can't support what's happening there, but—the Martiniere Group is a good employer. Especially working for you."

"Fair enough." She exhaled, suddenly tired with the relief that things seemed to be working out. "And we can create opportunities for you and Nicholas to be together. You cover for Donald; I'll cover for Nicholas."

"So where do we go from here?" Eliot asked. "And—thank you for being honest about being ace. I'm—bi. Honestly so. My relationships have been fifty-fifty, but Nick—I think he's the one for me."

"Congratulations," she said. "May you never have to face what I am right now. I love Donald deeply, but between Family politics and what he's doing for Real Lives for Women—" She didn't continue, but shivered.

Eliot got up and sat next to her. "You can lean on me if you're comfortable with that. Not just as role-playing."

"Thank you." She did slide closer to him, until their thighs touched, and he put his arm around her. Justine clasped her drink, not relaxing into him. "I'm very particular about touch, Eliot. Past trauma. But I do allow some people to put their hands on me. You are one of the few."

"I'm honored. And—I admire you and have ever since you became First Secretary." He paused, clearing his throat nervously. "If it wasn't for Nick—he caught my eye because I couldn't have you."

She laughed bitterly. "Hold on to Nick, Eliot. You're better off not being deeply involved with a Martiniere, especially a high-level heir like me. We use people, even those we love. *Especially* those we love. It's who we are."

"Let me enjoy having the best of both worlds while I can, okay? Don't worry about me." He squeezed her with a gentle pressure that eased quickly. "Now." His tone changed, became more business-like. "What happens next?"

"Escalating involvement, off and on, depending on the ebbs and flows of my choreography with Donald. Divorce filing in March, after three months of public fireworks." She buried her head in her hands. "I am not looking forward to those three months. It's been horrible so far."

"I will be there for you, Justine," he promised.

"Thank you." She raised her head. "As for tonight—I'll walk to the SUV with you, and we kiss. Give the impression that we've been making out, but nothing more than that."

"All right." He squeezed her again. "And maybe it's time for me to go."

Justine nodded. They walked hand in hand to the front door of her condo building. Eliot's kiss was delicate, sweet, and vaguely reminiscent of Donald in their early days together.

Transactional. I can handle transactional, she told herself.

***

DECEMBER, 2033

DECEMBER WAS A MONTH FROM HELL. SERG CONTACTED JUSTINE AND Donald to put together a bigger cash drop for Gabie.

"Things are tense," he said. "Joey keeps popping up wherever I go. I won't be able to get money to Gabe for some time after this in order to shake Joey off my tail, maybe even two years—and God, from the way Gabe looks, he needs the money. Bad."

Justine kicked in ten thousand dollars. They needed Gabie alive and well. He was probably still doing that damned manual labor in God-knows-where. Gabie had fantasized about being a cowboy. She hoped this hardship got it out of his system. Time for him to stop playing games and assume his responsibilities to the Family.

Both she and Donald were nervous as they went to Paris. Still keeping a separate residence—no way could she stand to be around the Family full time.

Serg brought Donna-gran and Piotr to their condo on the second night in Paris.

"Got something to show you all," he said, after raising additional security screens. He flicked up a picture.

Justine covered her mouth to contain her gasp. A bearded Gabie grinned proudly at them, cradling a newborn. The full, thick beard didn't quite hide the thinness of his face—he was clearly on short rations. And the newborn—even as a baby, its features clearly were those of a Martiniere, skin definitely tan. From Gabie's Hispanic mother, or from whoever the mother was?

Oh, that will so piss off Daddy-damned-dearest, the racist fuck that he is.

—*My son, Brandon Edward,* the caption read. —*Born December 12th, 2033, 6 pm Pacific Standard Time, in the United States.*

A son.

Gabie had a son.

Justine buried her head in her hands. This was good news, fit their long-range goals, but—*Gabie had a son,* and it hit her harder than she expected.

He succeeded where I failed.

Stupid thing to think.

At least Joey didn't show any desire to reproduce, so—a clear line of succession, if they could safely make Gabie the Martiniere. Oh, there were other high-level heirs with young children, but—Gabie's father Saul was her father's elder brother, *had* been the Martiniere before Philip. Gabie *should* be the Martiniere-in-waiting now, if not the Martiniere. This just hammered that reality home.

She shuddered, and Donald wrapped his arm around her, kissing her temple, quivering a little himself. Justine turned her head to meet his eyes, seeing the sadness in his face. The sorrow they shared.

Brandon's birth date was the same as the day she had undergone her hysterectomy five years ago.

Thank you, she mouthed.

He kissed her forehead.

"Do we know where Gabriel is?" Donna-gran asked. The strength in her voice didn't match her apparent feebleness.

What sort of role-play is Donna-gran pulling?

Not that her secretive grandmother would tell.

"I met him near Pendleton, Oregon," Serg said. "He got a call while we were there. His wife went into labor. From what I could overhear, he kept telling the person calling that his wife needed to go to the hospital, that he now had the money to pay the bill, and that he would be there shortly. So, close to Pendleton."

Donna-gran's lips tightened. "We need to send him more money."

"I already have," Piotr said. "The traditional twenty-five thousand dollars for the Martiniere-in-waiting's first son."

"Gabe closed out the PayMeCash app shortly after he received it, Father," Serg said. "Shut off all the links I have to him. He's running pretty skittish at the moment. Wherever he is in that region, things are pretty tough. If he's working in agriculture, they've been hit with a livestock virus that causes cows and sows to abort, and can cross over to humans. It's worst in a place called Thunder County."

"*Can* we find him quickly, if necessary?" Justine asked.

Serg nodded. "I have a pretty good idea of where he is."

"Good."

Gabie had a son.

That was a punch in the gut.

THE KNOWLEDGE OF GABIE'S SON RATCHETED UP THE TENSIONS OF FAMILY Christmas, adding realism to Justine's public arguments with Donald. Somehow, Daddy-damn-dearest got wind of the news about Gabie's son and he was more explosive than ever. But it wasn't just his rages and Joey's sulks that put Justine on edge; it was the memory of her hysterectomy that Brandon's birth had awakened.

As planned, her worst fight with Donald was the night of their anniversary. Realistic because they were both jangled, now that the Inevitable's gears were turning faster than ever. She still didn't know for certain where Donald was going to be living after March—security reasons, and she understood that. It still hurt. It added a note of finality to the Inevitable. The fucking divorce.

Justine flew to LA without talking to Donald, and took a sedative so she could keep from sobbing because that last damned argument had been so fucking convincing.

It's beyond playacting now, she thought. And that set off more tears, even with the sedative.

The sight of Eliot waiting for her at the airport was more welcome than she anticipated.

She took him to bed for her comfort that night, three months ahead of schedule.

———

THE NEXT THREE MONTHS WERE EVEN MORE HELLISH. NO DONALD. NO respite, except for Eliot. And even then, Justine tried to be mindful of Nick's claim on Eliot, remembering how thoughtful that Coral, Francie, and Meg had been of her.

Though they get him in the end.

She wasn't going to do that to Eliot and Nick. There *wouldn't* be anyone else in her life once this damned divorce was over. Just whatever role-play Eliot needed to keep his relationship with Nick hidden. She owed that to him.

She and Eliot fled to Sedona for Valentine's Day, and Nick met them undercover while she hid out in a separate room. Eliot only appeared in public with her.

Meanwhile, Daddy-damn-dearest pretended to hide his rejoicing at the demise of her marriage. Joey openly gloated, until Hallock administered the threatened beating.

For that, she sent Hallock her compliments and took him out to a tense lunch, the two of them feeling each other out for weaknesses.

She had no more frailties now that she was cutting Donald out of her personal life. Justine was becoming a finely honed instrument of vengeance, the hunting falcon that was still Donald's pet name for her.

Unfortunately, she had the impression that Hallock was just as hardened as she was, if not more so.

———

AFTER TWO MONTHS OF SNIPING AT EACH OTHER IN PUBLIC, DONALD SENT Justine a message via the Rescue Angel networks, on March 7th.

—*It's time. Donald's Little Divorce Present to the Martinieres is fully operational.*

The attached files contained instructions for activation and maintenance.

But one file was a simple message.

I MISS YOU. I HOPE MCNAUGHTON IS DOING RIGHT BY YOU. DESPITE ALL THAT'S BEEN SAID, I STILL LOVE YOU. I WISH—THERE ARE SO MANY THINGS I WISH. MOST OF ALL, THAT DECEMBER OF 2028 HADN'T HAPPENED, AND THAT WE HAD A LITTLE BOY OR GIRL TO CONSIDER. I AM STILL HERE IF YOU NEED ME.

That message gutted her, but Justine had no more tears left.

Her response was an image of a stooping peregrine, trailing broken hearts. She couldn't find words.

She filed for divorce the next day.

October, 2034

2034 WASN'T DONE WITH HER YET. THE DIVORCE SETTLED IN SEPTEMBER, after much drama.

"You are not going to believe this," Serg said, over dinner in October to celebrate her acquisition of the penthouse floor of a Chicago condo, using her share of the proceeds from the sale of Mist Knoll. Serg had one of the two apartments; she had the other. Justine felt better having a base other than Los Angeles.

"What?" She was short with her cousin. Nick was going through health problems and she was doing her best to cover for Eliot. She didn't have a lot of nerves to spare for yet another revelation.

"Have you been following a social media program called the AgInnovator?"

"No. What is it?"

"A new online game show that funds agricultural technology development. Including ag robotics and microbials."

Gabie's major and minor at the University of Paris. "No. Oh God, don't tell me he's that stupid—or desperate."

"Desperate is the better word." Serg flicked her a news story summarizing the AgInnovator results.

THE INAUGURAL AGSUPERSTAR WINNER IS RUBY BARKLEY, OF THE

Double R Ranch, in Lakeside, Oregon. She is married to Gabe Ramirez, with a son, Brandon, who will be one year old in December. They will use the funds to develop an agricultural nanobiobot intended to monitor field conditions and dispense soil and plant treatments, including microbials. The RubyBot is intended to be user-friendly and cultivated in onsite growboxes that a farmer or rancher can use for transport and distribution in fields without specialist knowledge.

Justine skimmed through the story. Reading between the lines, it was clear that Gabie and Ruby were living tight, living broke, and needed the money.

"Fuck," she whispered. "It *is* Gabie, damn it. And he's married to Ruby. Ah, fuck. That just gives my fucking father a target."

"What do we do?"

"I haven't the faintest idea."

She set up a personal meeting with Donald in Sedona to share the revelation about Gabie. Eliot covered for her.

Donald shook his head. "Let's hope that his visibility keeps him safe. Everything else is on track?"

"Cousin Arthur calls for a Group meeting in February. That starts the process."

"Are you holding out all right?"

"As well as can be expected. Eliot has a solid lead on some shady deals that Hallock's involved with. But the source is Joey. Could be a setup."

Donald frowned. "Don't risk yourself if your gut is telling you that, dear. Your instincts are good."

"God, Donald, I don't know what else to do!" She paced around the small room. "It goes down in February. We're so close. So damned close. If I could just get a handle on how to dump Hallock first—that would swing the odds in our favor." She wrapped her arms around herself, not daring to ask him to hold her.

"Another thing." Donald moved closer to her. "A warning to pass on to anyone you hold dear who uses this place as a refuge. It won't be safe for much longer."

"What the hell, Donald?" Her heart sank.

"Word spinning through the hacker networks." His face tightened. "Major political hack that will wreck all of the restrictions here. Not yet, but soon."

"Oh God." She shivered. "And Nick has health problems. I'm trying to be mindful of his needs and not hog Eliot, but covering for them is already hard. This will make it worse."

"The smart thing is for you to get visibly involved with Nick as well."

"That will *really* set Daddy-poo off."

Donald rolled his eyes. "Read this file, later because it's big." He flicked it to her. "Your father has his own little harem on the side. Starting with Mariah Meyers. He keeps it quiet because of what's happening with his political activity and the Electric Born, but— these aren't Joey's women. They're your father's. Joey's covering for him."

Twists upon twists. Ironic that Daddy-fucking-dearest was doing the same thing they were.

She tucked it away. "Thanks. But how does my getting involved with Nick make things better?"

A tired smile quirked his lips. "Why do you think Francie and Meg —or Coral, for that matter—use me for cover?"

Justine thought about it. "Oh. *Oh.*" It *was* an elegant solution.

Donald nodded. "And once you get that relationship established, come to Victoria, if you have a need."

"B.C.? But Victoria doesn't have blockers and barricades—"

"This is only for you, Serg, Eliot, and Nick."

She startled. Donald was still cagey about where he was living.

He nodded again. "My dear falcon. You look stressed and strained. Understandable. Don't run yourself into the ground. Our plans depend on you remaining healthy." He opened his arms.

Justine looked at Donald's chest. The temptation to fling herself against her newly divorced husband and find comfort in his arms overwhelmed her. So easy.

And it would break her heart all over again when she left this room by herself, to be alone again.

She shook her head. "Thank you. But I don't dare." Her voice cracked and she swallowed hard. She shuddered. "I—I will keep your offer in mind, Donald. But I can't let down my guard and take refuge in your arms anymore."

"I can no longer touch you?" Sorrow tinged his voice.

Justine buried her head in her hands. "I *want* you to touch me, so, so badly. To be in your arms. But I can't. Not—and do what has to be done." She raised her head. "Once we've succeeded—yes. Before then, I risk saying to hell with it all and walking away from a half-finished job. I can't live with that."

"All right." He sighed. "May I at least kiss your forehead?"

She bit her lip and nodded, closing her eyes and steeling herself as Donald's lips brushed against her. His citrusy scent, the warmth of his body, the memories of finding support and consolation there swarmed over her.

Justine almost broke down. Almost reached for him.

But she didn't.

Her eyes were dry when she opened them.

But there was wetness in Donald's eyes. Regret? Pity? Both?

"Fly, my falcon, fly," he said softly. "But remember you have a safe place. A refuge. We may not have a biological child—but our Rescue Angel child thrives."

"Thank you," she whispered. "Thank you."

And then she fled, because she was half a minute from yielding, and throwing it all away.

17 / INTERLUDE EIGHT

August, 2086

Justine choked, gasping for breath as that memory overwhelmed her. The agony of one of the worst days of her life, when she didn't dare touch the man she loved, because that contact would be enough for her to turn her back on her duty.

"Aunt Justine, are you all right?" Ron started toward her, but Mike was faster, kneeling next to her lounge chair.

"Hey, hey," he murmured, taking her into his arms, as thunder echoed from the mountains. "It's the past. Over and done. You're having an anxiety attack. I know what those are like. Breathe with me. Don't think about the memories. Breathe."

Justine gulped.

Anxiety attack? I never have those. Never, ever.

And yet, that memory was so *fucking vivid*. More so than any other of the memories she'd been sharing. Donald standing there, so close and yet so untouchable—*oh God*. That triggered yet another remembrance she didn't want to share.

Instead, she sagged against Mike and followed his soft-voiced coaching, laden with soothing tones.

Mike might be her father's clone, but he was nothing at all like

Daddy-fucking-dearest. Not in his scent, not in his touch, rarely in his expressions and voice. Mike always smelled of dogs and horses and hay, with a faint whiff of leather. And the steady, firm touch of his plaskin-covered cyborged fingers didn't vary in warmth. The pressure was *just right*, almost like Donald's. His glares and glowers were more like Gabie's than her father's. And his voice—except for the rare moments when he used his vocal tone programming, he tended to be soft-spoken.

Another hand brushed against her back, rubbing firmly. She startled.

"Just me," JoAnn said. "You're all right with that?"

"Yes," Justine gulped. "Yes."

"This storm's gonna be a good one," Mike said. "Look. You can see the flashes on the other side of the Chief. Soon it'll roll over the peaks and be in the valley, and we'll have a good natural light show. Think about that. Not the past."

She shuddered and drew a deep breath. Mike and JoAnn placed her between them on the porch swing, both putting an arm around her. Ron watched Justine with a worried expression on his face as he sat in the lounge chair. The digis were gone—they weren't active during thunderstorms unless there was an emergency. Too much electrical interference in the air.

Justine leaned against the wooden seat back and watched the flashes of light pass over the mountains, then crossing the valley. She calmed in Mike and JoAnn's soothing presence. They silently watched the storm, rocking in the swing, until the gray cloud wall bearing hail and heavy rain chased them inside.

MIKE INSISTED THAT JUSTINE AND RON SPEND THE NIGHT AT THE DOUBLE R. The storms were bad enough to cause problems over the Blues with the autodrive network, and while he didn't outright say he was concerned, both he and JoAnn scrutinized Justine with worried expressions throughout the evening.

In bed in her room at the Double R, Justine let herself think about the other remembrance that had been triggered by her story. The worst day ever.

Donald's dying.

"Can you cuddle?" Donald gasped that last morning, a pleading expression furrowing his brows and tightening his lips. They both knew his death was approaching. The dull look in his eyes. His fading in and out of coherence. Justine had thought Gabie's quick death was hard. But this stretching out of the process was equally awful.

She nodded, eased down the bed rail, and carefully crawled into the bed with him, lying on her back. Donald rested his head on her chest with a deep sigh, and she held him as close as she could. He was so lightweight anymore, skin and bones, heat radiating off of him.

"My falcon?" he whispered.

"Yes."

"Will you marry me again?"

She gulped at that. "I don't think there's enough time left to set it up."

"Not—legal. Not necessary. Just the words. The commitment. Before."

"I will." They both knew what he meant by Before. The final separation, now upon them.

Donald slid off of her chest to rest on his side. She turned to face him, heart aching to see the dullness of approaching death shadowing those once bright blue eyes.

"Will you take me to be your husband, Justine? To have and to hold, for richer or poorer, in sickness and in health, to love, honor, and cherish for eternity?"

His voice quavered on the last word. Eternity. Not 'until death do us part.' Eternity.

Justine shuddered at the implication.

Her voice choked before she could answer. "I do."

She swallowed hard. He wanted eternity. Neither of them were people of faith, but if her dying love wanted that promise from her—there was no one else for Justine, had never been.

"Will you take me to be your wife, Donald?" Another choke. "To have and to hold, for richer or poorer, in sickness and in health." Her voice broke on the word health. "To love, honor, and cherish." Another crack in her voice, and she

wasn't certain she could make it through the last two words without bursting into tears.

No. She couldn't do that. Justine summoned up every ounce of willpower she possessed so that she could say those final words without faltering.

"For eternity," she whispered.

"I do," he said, without hesitation. He tried to move his head to kiss her but couldn't stir more than a quarter-inch.

She moved to him. Lingered through what would be their last kiss, stroking his cheek, his forehead. Fought back the tears. No. She would be strong. She would be there for him. Tears could come once he was gone.

At last, Donald fell away from Justine. She turned onto her back and helped him rest his head on her chest once more, holding him tight.

Oh God. She should have remarried Donald long before he was on his deathbed. Her fault. Her failure. Her most grievous fault.

"Thank you," he murmured.

He was silent for a while, his breathing slower, but steadier than it had been, his eyes closed. Then he opened them.

"I still regret what happened with your pregnancies," he said. "Maybe if we had waited longer?"

"We don't know that for certain."

He coughed. "We saw it in the Rescue Angel. Childbearing too young."

Running the Rescue Angel exposed Justine and Donald to just about everything that could go wrong in reproductive medicine—including other women with hydatidiform mole. Worse cases than hers—some cancerous.

"True," she conceded.

"The Rescue Angel was our greatest offspring."

"That it was."

"I love you, my falcon. Now and into eternity."

Those were his last coherent words. Justine held him close, fighting back her tears when he became agitated and disoriented, shouting garbled phrases that didn't make sense. She whispered comforting words that she hoped Donald heard and understood.

He calmed. His breathing faltered, stuttered, time between breaths becoming longer.

And then it stopped. A long, final exhale with no following inhale, all the sensors blaring before the staff shut them off.

When Justine finally left Donald to the personnel ready to take his body away, Ruby rose from the bench where she had been waiting, just outside Donald's room. Justine went to her recently-widowed sister-in-law. They stood together, arms around each other, bereaved women who had lost their beloveds.

"Now it's just us," Ruby said.

The finality of Ruby's tone spurred tears. But Justine didn't tell Ruby about reciting those wedding vows with Donald. She just couldn't.

Justine shuddered. No, not a memory she would share with anyone.

GHOSTS FOLLOWED JUSTINE AS SHE ROLLED HER WALKER TO THE DOUBLE R's kitchen the next morning. Not digis but memories, faint shadows of years gone by.

After starting the coffeepot, she dropped into her usual chair at the green Formica and chrome table. Instead of snapping up her screens to review the news and her mail, she looked outside. No clouds. Bright blue sky, as blue as Donald's eyes had been, like it always seemed to be after a stormy Thunder County night. Storms at Moondance weren't as wild, and the sky wasn't that vivid brilliant blue afterward.

She rested her chin on her hands, still haunted by those shadows trailing her to the kitchen. Memories. Gabie and Ruby, flirting as they cooked. Mike, maturing from the scared five-year-old clone they rescued from Daddy-damn-dearest to become the Martiniere after Brandon's horrific death. Brandon and his wife Kris. Mike and JoAnn, with patterns of their own as they cooked. Ron's childhood. The Swaits.

And Donald.

He was nervous the first time she brought him to the Double R, right after Gabie revealed himself when he, Ruby, and Jeff Swait won the AgSuperhero. Neither she nor Donald were ready to drop the public façade of being estranged, but she convinced him that the Double R was a sanctuary.

She and Donald first made love again during that visit, after all those years apart.

Justine buried her head in her hands. This morning, those memories *hurt.*

Why had she been so resistant to remarrying Donald once it became safe? They could have had those final years together. She would have had the legal right to insist that he be buried *here,* with the rest of her beloved dead.

Footsteps startled her upright.

"Hey." Mike glided into the kitchen, followed by the heelers Smudgie and Spot, who headed for their dog beds tucked next to a wall. Spot gamboled toward Justine, but Mike snapped his fingers at her, coupled with a soft whistle. Spot halted, looked at him, then, after he pointed to the dog beds, settled on her bed with a heavy sigh.

"Hey," she said. "Good to see you up and walking."

"Pour you some coffee?" he asked.

"Oh God, yes. Thank you."

He poured two cups and brought them to the table. "It feels good to be up and moving without help or a cane. I can't ride a horse yet— maybe in a week."

"That's tough."

Unlike her father, Mike loved horses, had ever since he first came to the Double R. Mike was more dedicated to the ranch life than Gabie had been, defined by the horses and dogs that were so much a part of who he was.

Mike Martiniere. Dog handler. Scientist. Horseman. Rancher. The Martiniere.

Nothing at all like his progenitor. Gabie and Ruby made sure of that in their raising of Mike, nurturing him from a scared, defiant little clone with only biting and rage as a defense, to forming this confident man.

Mike surveyed her carefully. He fixed her with a stern look, and *that* gaze brought back memories of Daddy-damn-dearest. "How are *you* doing? I didn't expect you to end the story where you did."

She picked up her coffee to buy a moment as she sipped it, taking a couple of swallows before setting it down carefully.

"It's hard," she said. "Going through those days. That last—was one of the hardest days of my life."

"I can imagine." Mike took one of her hands. "Justine. I promise you. We *will* get Donald back as a digi. I know we can."

She gulped. "Are you sure? I've called and called him. There's nothing."

That wasn't quite true, but she still wasn't certain of that fleeting presence.

"It just takes the right link and the right codes, and those super-amped digigloves," Mike said. "I think we're close. We *have* to be close."

"I hope you're right," she whispered.

Mike's brows furrowed. "I *have* to be right," he said. "The *other* digis attacked Gabe last night."

"No. Oh no." Dread coursed through her gut, coffee sitting sour in her stomach.

"He's fine," Mike said. "Just recharging this morning. Gabe's the oldest digi out there besides Philip, and sneaky as hell, three times as canny as he was in life. And Ruby, Brandon, and Lily helped stop it."

She exhaled, relieved. "That's good."

"But we need Donald," Mike said grimly. "Because Hawkins has someone behind him who's almost as tricky as Gabe. Hallock is with Hawkins, Justine. We need all the firepower in digi that we can get— and that means Donald."

"Which means I need to figure out what Donald's key is."

God damn it, Hallock, you couldn't fucking stay dead.

Another argument for her to go digi, damn it.

The intense glower Mike directed at her was pure Gabie, not Philip. "You woke Gabe's digi, without digigloves."

"I did it through sheer desperation, Mike. You and JoAnn had been missing for days, and I had no other choice."

He sighed and his face softened. "Things may be just that desperate again, if we don't find a way to shut Hawkins and Hallock down."

"Damn it." She shuddered. "I'm missing a piece. I know it."

"Does telling the stories help?"

"I'm not sure."

"There's a lot of references to children in these latest memories. To the Rescue Angel as your child. Could that be a key?"

She inhaled sharply, recalling *that final memory*.

The Rescue Angel was our greatest offspring.

Part of Donald's last words.

It couldn't be that simple.

Could it?

"I need to think," she said.

"Those details are important," Mike said. "Even more than the organizing particulars behind the attempts to depose Philip. Maybe—if you can handle it—we need to hear more about what you and Donald were doing during those years." He squeezed her hand before releasing it and getting up to rummage in the refrigerator. "Jo and Ron will be down soon. I'd better get breakfast started."

Justine kept thinking about Mike's words as she pulled up her morning readings and skimmed through them.

Rescue Angel. Child.

Could the key to Donald's digi be as simple as that?

The Rescue Angel was our greatest offspring.

And Gabie *had* said that he tried to leave clues for Donald about going digi.

She stared into the distance, ignoring her displays as she considered the possibilities.

MIKE CONTINUED TO INSIST THAT JUSTINE AND RON REMAIN AT THE Double R, and sent security to Moondance to gather up the things they needed for an indefinite stay. Gabie appeared, to reinforce Mike's decision.

"You're safer here, Tine," he said. His digi form was less substantial than before, but determination set his jaw and his brows furrowed in the most intense form of his *The-Martiniere-Has-Spoken* glower. *"Both you and Ron. Digital security is stronger at the Double R, and it's easier for me and Ruby to protect you."*

"But couldn't Brandon and Lily guard us at Moondance?"

Gabie shook his head. *"Brandon's resonances are better here. Lily's the only one of us who is stronger at Moondance. Me, Ruby, Bran—the Double R is better."*

She yielded, because fighting Mike and Gabie together took just too much energy. Mike went back to work that day, closeting himself with Ron to review decisions Ron and Justine had made while filling in for him.

"You rest," he said firmly when Justine would have joined them. "Your job is to figure out the key to Donald's digi. No stories today. Maybe tomorrow. Deontae's coming back tonight, with those high-amp digigloves. We have to get them programmed to you before you can use them."

"The battle's going to be soon?" she asked.

Mike nodded. "That's why D's coming here. Now. *Rest.*" He used the barest command tone, a soft sneaky version that was hard for her to resist.

"Good," she said, instead of snapping at Mike's tone use like she usually would.

Restraining herself made sense, because Mike was right. She needed to rest. JoAnn's brother knew as much about digital clones as Mike did—perhaps more, since he had been constructing defenses against digis. Deontae's arrival with those *special* digigloves meant that it was almost time to open Donald's locked files.

An end to waiting and thumb-twiddling. She was ready for it to happen.

But first, she had to make sure *she* was ready.

JoAnn helped Justine settle into the hammock that had been Gabie's during his last summer alive, then Mike's while he recovered from cyborging. A steady, soft breeze ruffled the limbs of the Jeffreys pines overhead and rocked her. The heat of the day plus the murmur of the wind in the branches lulled her into napping as she thought about the past, searching her memories for further clues to what might activate Donald's digi—if he had, indeed, created one.

If not, they would need to make one for him. And things she might have forgotten would be crucial to the construction of Donald's algorithm.

At some point between drowsing and idly gazing at the mountains, Justine drifted into a vivid dream.

She danced with Donald in the Double R's living room. Gabie and Ruby, Brandon and Kris, the three couples waltzing while little Mikey watched them from a pile of pillows and blankets on the couch as a blizzard raged outside. Part of wintertime life at the Double R, after Gabie became the Martiniere.

Donald spun her and she ended up in his arms.

"Have you figured it out yet, my falcon?" he asked, his face transforming into the drawn, skeletal tightness it had been before he died.

"Figured what out?" she asked.

"My keywords, so you can wake my digi."

"Why aren't you answering my call?" she retorted. "Gabie did."

Donald shifted shapes again, back to a younger self. *"I've tried to answer you. I'm blocked. You have to break that block before you can access my algorithm. Yes, there is one."*

"How? What needs to happen to break it?"

The music ended and Donald bent to kiss her.

"Remember our vows. Remember our greatest enemy. Remember our greatest offspring. Don't delay, my love. Time grows short." He faded away.

Her eyes shot open, to see Deontae Swait walking up the hill from the airstrip.

Vows. Enemy. Offspring.

To love, honor, and cherish for eternity.

That part was easy. The vow she had made on his deathbed.

Rescue Angel. Offspring.

But their greatest enemy? Would that be her father? Or was it Hallock? She didn't dare get that one wrong.

Deontae swerved from a straight path to the farmhouse's back door and headed for her.

"How are you doing, Justine?" Today his hair was free from its usual covering, styled in short spiky dreadlocks with a hint of gray amongst the black.

"I'm still alive," she said tartly. "That's something at my age."

"Alive is good," D chuckled as he dragged a lawn chair over to sit by the hammock. "Mike says we're close to starting that access of Donald's files."

She tightened her lips. Should she tell D about this dream? He would be her support once things got underway, after all.

"I don't know if this is relevant," she said carefully. "Donald hasn't been answering when I call for him. However—once or twice, I've had a sense of his presence. He *might* have tried to pass on information to me while I was dreaming, and I just woke from one of *those* dreams."

"What did he tell you?" To her relief, D took her notion seriously, pressing his fingertips together as he studied her.

"He says he's blocked, and that I have to break it using keywords before we can access his algorithm. He gave me three clues. Vows. Enemy. Offspring."

D pursed his full lips before rolling them inward so tight that they nearly disappeared. "And do you know what he meant?"

"For two of them, yes. But our greatest enemy—would that be my father, or would that be Hallock?"

"Hallock," D said without hesitation. "Definitely Hallock."

Relief flooded through her because that felt *right*. "That fucker. He just won't stay dead. Like my damned father."

"He is an ambitious fuck, dead or alive," D said. "But he's not dead, Justine."

"*What?*"

D shook his head. "I don't know if we're dealing with a clone of Hallock or Hallock himself. But he's like Mike. Heavily cyborged—but alive, with a digital presence."

"How?" she asked.

D's lips tightened again. "Heaven's Reach got their hands on him. Swait Secure found out."

"God damn it." She exhaled.

Heaven's Reach. *Fucking Heaven's Reach.*

She would make sure that nothing remained of that damn toxic cult before she died, even if it killed her.

She could just imagine Ruby's rage at this disclosure, not to speak of Gabie's.

September, 2086

THEY MET IN MIKE'S OFFICE THE NEXT MORNING.

The digis' fury at Deontae's news was precisely what Justine expected. Ruby ranted and paced, swearing, while Gabie growled, brows furrowed tighter than ever. Brandon didn't say anything but watched his parents fume while Lily hovered nervously by him.

"You know, this isn't going to help anything," Brandon said finally. *"Mom, Dad, you think you've vented long enough?"*

He used a twist of a tone that caught Justine's attention. Her nephew hadn't been a tone user while alive—he wasn't programmed, nor had he been given the mind control training to use normal tones, much less something as subtle as that twist.

Nonetheless, it worked. Ruby halted and Gabie turned his *fight-you-to-the-death* glower on Brandon.

Brandon raised a hand. *"So Hallock lives, and Heaven's Reach is responsible. That doesn't eliminate the need to gather more data to help resurrect Donald's digi."*

"Justine, you mind sharing your dream?" Deontae raised his brows at her. She recognized the diversion technique—and the way Gabie was glaring, they'd have another ragefest happening soon if she didn't shift his attention, and *fast*.

She exhaled. "Not at all. Gabie, I think Donald reached me in a dream."

Gabie's focus shifted and his face softened. *"A dream?"*

Justine nodded, and repeated what Donald had said to her in the dream.

Gabie cocked his head. *"That could be. If he's blocked—that would explain a lot."*

"Knowing more about the personal history might help," Mike said. "How much contact did you have with Donald after the ending of your last story?"

"Quite a bit, actually," Justine said. "Especially after I discovered the truth behind the Electric Born. That would have been a couple of years after Cousin Arthur's attempted coup failed."

"What year?" Mike's eyes narrowed as he focused on her.

"Starting in 2037," she said. "Rescue Angel began direct interventions with Electric Born women in 2038, after Hallock got me kicked out of the Group. But we kept that knowledge to ourselves until 2039. Then in 2044, we tried once more to depose Daddy-poo."

"2044," Gabie muttered. *"Now that was a year. I started working with Rafe Alvarez and Alvarez Armory that year."*

"Think you could cover 2037 to 2044 without too much of a strain?" Mike asked, a demand underlying his soft voice as he continued to fix Justine with a steady, determined gaze.

She recognized the tone. Mike speaking as the Martiniere, politely commanding the Matriarch. But it was a command, nonetheless.

"I can try," she answered.

18 / ELECTRIC BORN

THE FAILURE OF COUSIN ARTHUR'S ATTEMPT TO DETHRONE DADDY-DAMN-dearest in 2035 sent Serg, Piotr, and Vygotsky Security underground. Justine didn't know where Serg and Piotr were, though she suspected that they turned to Donald for help. But their disappearance left her with no recourse when things blew up with Gabie.

Eliot and Nick comforted her as she watched the vids about Ruby and Gabie's marriage imploding, with growing shock. Justine had taken Donald's advice and started a relationship with Nick, albeit pretending a more volatile liaison than the one she had with Eliot. She and Nick argued publicly, and made up with even more fanfare. Before Daddy-poo could say anything critical about her having *two* men, Justine sent him some pictures from Donald's file about his collection of women. That shut Daddy-damn-dearest right up.

Making Gabie suffer was apparently a higher priority for her father than harassing Justine about her lovers. She realized what the hell was going on when Mariah Meyers was linked to Gabie as the Other Woman. *That* woman was Daddy-damned-dearest's number one concubine. He held a hidden indenture contract on Meyers. That was enough to make Justine suspicious about Meyers taking an independent interest in Gabie.

When social media and then regular media featured Ruby and Mariah Meyers fighting over Gabie in a Pendleton bar, that confirmed Justine's doubts.

This was Daddy-damn-dearest's doing. That *couldn't* be Gabie acting that awful on his own. Not the cousin who had taken beatings for her. Not the man who had gotten her out of Daddy-damned-dearest's clutches.

She gulped after *that* vid. "All right. I'm going to Oregon. I'm telling Ruby what's *really* happening. And then I'm going to shake some sense into my fucking cousin, and break whatever that bitch Meyers did. Daddy-poo used her to program him. I *know* it."

"Justine. *No*," Eliot said, worry heavy in his voice. He and Nick exchanged glances—the three of them were staying in Justine's LA condo while she spent her week in Los Angeles, before she returned to solitary life in Chicago.

"This divorce can't happen!" Justine turned on him. "Daddy-fucking-dearest is involved, up to his neck. Has to be, with Meyers in the mix."

"That's not a good idea," Eliot cautioned. "This reeks of a Hallock plot. For the love of God, Justine, *don't*."

"I'm *going*," she insisted. She pulled up her screens to summon one of her jets. It wouldn't be available to go to Northeastern Oregon until tomorrow afternoon, but by God, she was going to *do something*.

She owed it to Gabie. He had gotten her away from Daddy-damn-dearest. Now it was her turn to rescue him from her father's vengeance.

She didn't notice the worried looks that Nick and Eliot exchanged.

NICK INSISTED ON TRAVELING WITH HER AFTER NEITHER HE NOR ELIOT could persuade her out of talking to Ruby.

"I have clients who might be interested in Thunder Valley property," he said when they got into the SUV. "I want to see the place myself —and neither Eliot nor I think you should be doing this alone."

"Whatever." She flung herself against the SUV's seat as Shanice drove them to the airport.

Most of the time, she got along well enough with Eliot's lover. But his bossy and commanding traits led to arguments. Nick reminded Justine of some of her less-savory cousins, especially since he occasionally exhibited a casual sexism which Eliot lacked. But Nick would back down when she called him on it. He was smart, and cared for both her and Eliot.

But if he hadn't been Eliot's love, she wouldn't have Nick in her life. He wasn't her type. However. His command of martial arts and street fighting skills was better than Eliot's, and he helped her stay fit and trained. Especially important now that Serg was on the run. Nick prodded Eliot to practice fighting skills. Absolutely necessary for anyone around a Martiniere.

Justine drummed her fingers impatiently on the armrest, planning. First, she'd talk to Ruby and let her know what was *really* going on. Then she would find Gabie and do whatever it took to get his head straight. He had played cowboy long enough. Time for Gabie to remember his responsibilities to the Family. And then she would confront Daddy-fucking-dearest.

It was time for her to *act*, damn it.

Cousin Arthur's attempt to eliminate Daddy-damn-dearest hadn't worked. Once she got Gabie straightened out and back together with Ruby, then *they* would depose her father. The two of them, with help from Donald, Eliot, and Nick, would lead the charge.

They would *fix* the Family, once and for all.

Nick hung back as they approached her jet. She didn't think about it because he regularly supervised their luggage. Justine ran up the stairs to the main cabin, impatient to get things rolling. It wouldn't take that long to get to Thunder County. She was already speculating about how much time she would need to search through the Pendleton bars to find Gabie.

She stopped short inside the main cabin. Donald rose from his seat.

"What the hell are you doing here?" she demanded.

"Keeping you from doing something stupid," he said.

"What the *fuck*—" Oh, she knew what had happened. Nick and Donald were friends, had known each other from boarding school. "God damn it, Donald. Nick!" She whirled to confront Nick, who *wasn't there*, as the cringing attendant closed the cabin door and headed for the cockpit, a sheepish expression on his face. She spun back to face Donald. "Donald. What the hell?"

"I am *not* going to let you throw all your hard work away," Donald snapped.

"I'm not throwing anything away!"

"Like hell. Sit down, Justine, before you fall down." He dropped into a seat as the plane started moving.

Angry as she was at *all three of these goddamn men*, she still had enough sense to sit and buckle in. "So where the hell are you kidnapping me to?"

"We're going to take a little cruise in a secure setting while we talk about what exactly is going on," Donald said. "Because while your damned father *is* behind Mariah Meyers and her efforts to force Gabe and Ruby's divorce, the implementation is Hallock's design. And—" he pointed at her. "Your fucking father not only wants to destroy Gabe; he's anticipating that you will react exactly like *this*. You've already told him that you know Meyers is his toy. That gives him the excuse to use her against Gabe *and* you. He's handed the execution of his plans to Hallock, damn it, Justine."

"So who ratted me out? You damn fucking men. Always thinking I can't take care of myself!"

"Most of the time you *can* take care of yourself," Donald said. "But *this* is damned stupid, racing off to see Ruby and mixing it up with Meyers. It just makes you more visible and makes Ruby and Brandon a target. And Meyers—her involvement should inspire further caution in you. Not this recklessness."

"I suppose you all think I'm just being a hormonal woman," she growled. It was what Daddy-poo and Joey would say.

"Bullshit. I know better. You don't have the ovaries to mess with your hormones, so unless someone's been playing around with your medications, that is no fucking excuse." He scowled. "Come *on*,

Justine. I know what's happening." His voice softened. "This divorce stinks. It's too reminiscent of our own for my comfort, except that Gabe and Ruby aren't roleplaying. Not with Meyers involved. You are being set up because your father—and Hallock—are calculating that you will react and not think first. And I have proof that this is exactly what they are planning."

"All right, then," she growled, glaring at Donald. "Convince me."

<hr>

Two hours later she was calmer, if no less angry, her fury now pointed at Hallock and her father. Not that she didn't have enough left over for Donald, Nick, and Eliot.

Meddling men!

"I still don't like what the three of you did," she said as the plane touched back down in LA. "Too damn much like you're protecting the *little woman*. Fuck that shit!"

"Your boys were frantic about your behavior, Justine," he said. "I passed the information to Nick about Hallock's involvement in Gabe and Ruby's divorce. When you wouldn't listen to them, they contacted me. We all have too much at stake—and you've been running hard for a long time. You're vulnerable."

She snorted. "So you have them watching me."

"Is it any different from the communications you have with my ladies, for similar reasons? Or the backchannel you have into *my* security, should I show signs of doing something correspondingly stupid?"

Justine had to grant him that.

By the time she was back in the condo, her anger had cooled. Especially since Nick and Eliot had a special dinner prepared for her.

Didn't mean she liked what they had done behind her back—and she let them know it. While thoroughly enjoying the pampering that they gave her in apology.

<hr>

September, 2037

. . .

THEN THINGS BLEW UP, CENTERED AROUND A NEW RELIGIOUS CULT, THE Electric Born, who openly venerated Daddy-damn-dearest and Joey.

It was one thing for them to play the religious cult game—Justine parried Joey and Daddy-damned-dearest's proselytizing with pointed remarks about heresies and the Martiniere Catholic heritage. She even went so far as to officially annul her marriage to Donald. Made quarterly appearances at one of the social justice-oriented Los Angeles parishes, as well as donating to church-related social justice charities.

Electric Born affiliation became popular within Internal Affairs, especially within Hallock's divisions. Reports of workplace prayer sessions drifted back to Justine through Eliot's connections. Endorsements of human rights abuses sanctioned by Joey and Daddy-fucking-dearest. A greater focus on "being right with the Divine Philip and Joseph" than doing their assigned tasks amongst the Internal Affairs indentured labor pools.

Unfortunately, she lacked solid data about the degree of Electric Born influence within the Martiniere Group. Rumors, all rumors, damn it.

"We have to do something about the Electric Born," Eliot reported to Justine late in August. "It's infecting our divisions. Productivity is down this quarter and client complaints are up—including exclusive clients of Internal Affairs."

"I've tried to talk to my father and Hallock about the Electric Born problems," Justine said. "They won't listen because we don't have the data to show the effect on the Group. *They* claim the opposite effect." She waved a hand at Eliot's data projections. "We need *their* internal data. Numbers of Electric Born indentured, and whether it's connected to productivity decline. By division. *If* those records exist."

"They do."

"How do you know?" She arched an eyebrow at Eliot.

He swallowed. "Because I've been cultivating a middle-level manager in Internal Affairs who is as appalled by the influx of Electric Born into her division as we are."

"*Really.*"

"There's nothing to the relationship, Justine," Eliot blustered. "It's simply easier to gather data—"

Justine held up her hand to stop him. "I don't care about that, Eliot. How reliable is this person?"

"I have her access codes."

She raised both eyebrows at *that*. "They function?"

"Only at her workstation, during normal working hours."

Justine tightened her lips. One of Hallock's security mechanisms. "You've not tried them yourself?"

"She doesn't know I have them. And since access is limited to normal business hours—I can't sneak in there. It's keyed to her and her assistant—both women."

Justine leaned back in her chair, resting her chin on her steepled hands, thinking.

If she had that data, she could take it to the Board. This was potentially explosive enough to overthrow Daddy-fucking-dearest.

"All right," she said finally. "We'll do it on the Friday afternoon before Labor Day. You get—what's her name?"

"Candace McGovern."

"All right. You get Candace out of there. Give me the codes and Candace's biometrics. I have masking software. I'll download the files."

"Are you sure that's safe?"

Justine shrugged. "It's what is required. Better I do it than anyone else—I'm more likely to have an escape route if things go wrong."

Besides, she didn't want to trust this data to anyone else.

LATE DURING THE SLOW, DEAD FRIDAY AFTERNOON BEFORE THE LABOR DAY long weekend, Eliot flirted with Candace and kept her occupied. Justine, wearing experimental masking software and the gloves she always had on outside of her own office, slid into Candace's workstation and downloaded files.

The newest and greatest thing in her covert data systems management was a data chip implanted into the thumbnail of her non-dominant hand. Implantation hurt like hell but it was well worth it, especially given the extra precautions installed by the black-market data chip source recommended by Donald.

But. Using that chip required her to take off that glove. Justine didn't like removing her gloves in Group headquarters due to potential exposures to who the hell knew what. Internal Affairs had ongoing research into the use of contact neurotoxins and psychotropics. Easy enough for one of her opponents, especially Hallock, to apply them to a surface she might touch. Shanice scanned her office every time Justine entered it, but it was the only safe place in the damn building.

Besides the thumbnail chip, Justine had a backup chip implanted in her right elbow. An extra step for backing up data, but—she wasn't about to screw around. Her thumbnail chip could be fried or pulled, but unless someone knew about it, the elbow chip would go undetected. She just couldn't use it as a primary download site.

Justine skimmed some files before she downloaded them into both chips.

Fuck.

She gasped at what she saw. *Everything* was recorded in those damned files, including statements of purpose, long-range goals, and progress toward those goals. Not just membership in the Electric Born.

Crappy operational security.

The implications frightened her. The situation was worse than she had thought.

The Electric Born weren't just a little cult that allowed her father and brother to strut around as objects of adoration. They were the foundation for a mind-controlled indentured army loyal to Philip, with secondary loyalty to Joey.

She reviewed the rest of the records while they copied onto her chips, sickened at what she read. Horrific experimentation within the Electric Born indentureds. Persistent violations of every fucking damn regulation about human experimentation. Body modifications. Sexual slaving. Cyborging and extreme mind control programming. It made the abuses that Gabie testified about look like a kindergarten recess.

Every bit of it got backed up to her elbow chip.

Then she reached the files on the most secretive and experimental of the religious compounds—a chain of agricultural communes called Heaven's Reach, with headquarters in northern Idaho.

A text from Eliot alerted her.

—Silent security alarm's triggered! Masking software's failing! Get out of there!

—Take care of yourself and Candace! she sent back, still frantically trying to break the heavy defenses on the Heaven's Reach data. *—I'll be right behind.*

No answer, not that she expected there would be one.

Justine backed out of the files as quickly as possible, disconnected the link between thumbnail chip and elbow chip, toggled the elbow chip to its highest stealth setting, and set Candace's workstation to self-destruct. She pulled on her glove and hurried away.

Before she reached the elevators, the steady *tromp-tromp* of marching, armored, Martiniere security echoed down the hallway. Justine veered from the regular elevators, desperately punching in the stairwell code keyed to a careless person in Internal Affairs. She slammed the door shut behind her, hesitating for a moment. Upstairs, fifteen flights to her own office? Or downstairs for twenty flights, to get the hell out of the building?

Downstairs.

She might be able to finesse things if she were in her office, but if things went really bad...she didn't dare get trapped. Justine raced down the stairs as fast as she could, relying on the railing to keep her upright, grateful for her standard working choice of flats instead of heels as she ran.

Justine careened to an abrupt halt on the tenth floor as she heard that *tromp-tromp* of security marching up the stairs below her. She entered the code for the tenth floor, this time as herself.

Aw fuck. Betrayed. Is Candace a plant? What now?

Tenth floor was External Affairs. Her own turf.

Justine swung the door open—and Hallock stood there, with a contingent of Martiniere security, smirking at her.

"Going somewhere, Justine?"

Justine summoned every damn ounce of arrogance she could portray as Philip's daughter.

"Why, yes," she said. "I'm checking in with Maudie Kingston about Canadian marketing concerns."

"Taking the stairs. With no access codes showing from the thirty-fifth floor. And Kingston's left for the weekend. *Really*, Justine."

"Really." She kept her voice flat and calm. "I often use the stairs for exercise. Don't you?"

"Notice any issues on the twentieth floor?"

She shrugged. "Someone I didn't know was headed upstairs."

"Someone you didn't know," Hallock said mockingly. "*Really.*"

"It's your floor, not mine," she snapped. "I don't know everyone who works for you."

"Or perhaps you were poking around somewhere that you shouldn't have been, hmm?" Hallock sneered. He grasped her left forearm and yanked off her glove.

"Let go of me." She tried a tone on him.

Five against her, counting Hallock. Security carried stun sticks that could be jumped to kill levels. She *had* no choice but to fight as hard as she could.

His face twisted. "You shouldn't have done that."

"*Let go of me!*" she snapped in a harsher tone.

Hallock slapped her.

Her training kicked in automatically, and she fought back. Three of the security force swarmed Justine and forced her to her knees.

"*You fucking bitch,*" Hallock snarled, the impact of his tone lessened by his sniffing back blood from the hit she landed on his nose. He wrenched her left thumb back *hard*.

She bit her lip to keep from screaming, straining against her captors. If she couldn't manage to get free—she clucked to activate the self-destruct but *it didn't work.*

Agony knifed through her as the bone in her thumb broke.

Hallock laughed. "Good luck trying to prove anything from that data you downloaded. Your access triggered a data dump and no one will see it. Stupid bitch." He twisted her broken thumb harder and she gasped, panting. Disconnected from the agony, like she had learned to do when Daddy-damn-dearest beat her as a teen.

"Gimme the pliers," Hallock growled at the one security man who stood clear. "I'll tear off her thumbnail to get that chip. Or maybe even her whole thumb."

"Yes, sir," the man said.

He sounded like Serg.

The man brought out the pliers from his waist pack with one hand, and plunged an injector into Hallock with the other. Hallock's grip eased on Justine as the security crew let her go. She bent over her hand, gasping. God. It hurt. Worse, the self-destruct was partially enabled and it *burned*. But she couldn't give into her pain, not now—

"Come on, Tine, we've gotta go." Serg's voice, steady. He eyed the other three security staff. "You know what to do with him."

Somehow, with Serg's help, she rose to her feet and staggered into the elevator.

"I can get you out of here but that's it," Serg said. "Gotta protect my cover. Would have stopped Hallock sooner, but my recording block wouldn't last that long. I'm maxing it out as it is."

She nodded, panting and slumping against the elevator wall as she cradled her broken hand. "Just get me to Shanice."

"You better lay low for a bit. What the hell is so important that you'd take a risk like this?"

"You're better off not knowing," she whispered. "What are *you* doing, Serg?"

"You're better off not knowing," he repeated back to her.

At least Serg had been in the right place at the right time.

"Thank you," she whimpered.

She didn't dare ask about Eliot or Candace.

Eliot and Shanice waited for her in the SUV. "Oh God, Justine," Eliot gulped as he saw her hand, swollen to twice its normal size. Her thumbnail glowed bright red.

"Get me to Donald," she moaned, collapsing against the back of her seat. "Did Candace get free?"

"On her way to the Rescue Angel program," Shanice said, examining Justine's hand as the driver took off.

"Good. Eliot, get Nick to the fucking airport. Now. Bugout time." Justine panted against the pain. Shanice injected her with something. "We're not going back to the condo. We're headed for Donald."

At least she had enough forethought to have a jet waiting. Just in case.

As the warm fuzziness from the shot oozed through her, Justine sent the prerecorded help message to Donald.

—*Falcon bugs out.*

She was barely conscious by the time that Shanice and Eliot helped her onto the plane.

———

JUSTINE WOKE IN AN UNFAMILIAR ROOM, HER LEFT HAND IN A CAST. Donald sat by the bed, holding her right hand, face pale, hair uncharacteristically disheveled.

"Did he get my chip?" she murmured, still fuzzy, memories clouded. Nothing hurt. She must still be on painkillers.

"No. Coral extracted it while casting your hand because the chip was on the brink of exploding. My God, Justine."

She half-closed her eyes. "Did you look at the files? My backups in the elbow chip?"

"No, the thumb chip was trashed. I didn't know about the elbow chip. Just a minute. Which elbow?"

"My right one."

He was silent as he carefully accessed her elbow chip. She heaved a relieved sigh. The flashing lights of the display projection were bright enough to glare through her half-closed eyelids as he skimmed through the files.

"My God," he repeated, horror in his voice. "This is—fuck."

"Did anything about a group about Heaven's Reach make it onto the elbow chip?" She opened her eyes.

"Unfortunately, only a partial. My God," Donald said a third time. "I—God, Justine. This is worse than Gabe's testimony."

"Absolutely." She exhaled. No time to wallow in the shock of the information. "What's the situation? My status? Do I need to go underground like Gabie and Serg?"

What about Donald's Little Divorce Present?

Was it time to unleash it?

"You're still good. Nick and Eliot are safe in Los Angeles. The three of you have an alibi for Friday and Saturday," Donald said. "Hallock apparently disappeared and resurfaced after a major drinking binge with the three of you."

"*Good.*" She wondered how much he remembered. If Serg got Hallock to Piotr, there was a good chance his memory was wiped.

"The sedation shot Shanice gave you knocked you flat for thirty-six hours, much longer than we expected it to work. Coral's worried about the degree to which you've been running yourself ragged. What happened? How did you find out about this?"

She told him about the complaints from clients. Her suspicions. Her careful planning to break into the Internal Affairs files. Hallock's attack on her—Donald's nostrils flared wide and his lips thinned as she described it. Serg's timely intervention.

"What a fucking damned mess," he said when she finished. "Did you know that Serg was there?"

"Not a damned clue," she said. She inhaled sharply. "But God, I'm glad he was, along with some of Vygotsky Security. Hallock was ready to pull my thumbnail, and the damned chip's self-destruct mechanism malfunctioned."

"*Fuck.*" Donald's face set in hard lines. "I'm going to kill that fucker Hallock—"

"*No.* That son-of-a-bitch is *mine.*"

"After what he did to you—"

"He's *mine.*" She exhaled. "And I will make the asshole pay. *Myself.*" She gulped.

"The thumb is shattered, my falcon. Coral says you're edging into osteopenia. You'll need a surgeon to put it back together long-term because it's beyond her level of skill. The degree of force he exerted—it wasn't all osteopenia—*shit.*"

"What about my father? Does anyone suspect anything?"

"Eliot thinks not. Apparently Serg and his crew took care of it. Your father was off playing with Meyers in Europe. Fortunately."

"Good." God, that was lucky. But given what she had discovered— "What cover do we have for my disappearance from LA? Do we need to unleash the Present?"

"No. From all reports, you're in Chicago, recovering from one hell of a binge. You, Eliot, Nick, and Hallock took off for Seattle late Friday afternoon. The three of you left him in a downtown hotel and went your separate ways—except Hallock was more impaired." He coughed. "I set that up. Rescue Angel has been awfully damned busy over the last thirty-six hours, ever since you sent the emergency message."

She sighed. "Oh God. Thank you, Donald."

He stroked her cheek. "Fuck, Justine. I'd yell at you for being reckless, but given what I've read so far, we have one hell of a problem. What you discovered is well worth the risk. I want to recover whatever we can about Heaven's Reach—*safely*. No mucking with the files for you."

She groaned. "Those files are gone, according to Hallock. Data dump."

"They could be resurrected."

"If I can get access to them—"

"Hell, *no*. It's not worth the risk to you. We'll find another means." Donald kept stroking her cheek. "My God, Justine. I yelled at Eliot because you're down to skin and bone. I thought he and Nick were *taking care of you*. He said you haven't been eating, haven't been sleeping, and they're both worried about you. You need a break."

She drew a deep, sobbing breath. "And how the hell do I stop the Electric Born if I do that, Donald?"

"I don't think this is something you can do within the Group, my dear. Maybe it's time you think about an exit strategy."

"I have to try."

He growled. "If you say so. But if you insist, I'm going to make my own demands."

She laughed weakly. "Have you forgotten you're not my husband anymore?"

"I am your ally and your colleague in Rescue Angel and that's enough for me to issue some ultimatums," Donald said. "Your physical condition is a security risk. Look. You're covered for the remainder of the holiday weekend and the week after. Think about taking a break longer than that. Please."

"I'll try," she conceded. "Meanwhile, just where the hell am I? Chicago? Portland? Somewhere else?"

Donald's face relaxed and he chuckled. "You're in my secret island lair, Nameless, in the Haida Gwaii. My residence is granted under a special dispensation from the Haida, through Coral. The ladies work in the local medical clinics."

"Oh. Wow." She had expected Donald to seek out an island dwelling post-divorce, but she thought it would be a tropical island. Not in British Columbia.

"I'll take you out to look around tomorrow," Donald said. "But right now, Coral needs to talk to you."

CORAL DIDN'T MINCE ANY WORDS.

"You look like a woman twenty years older than your biological age, Justine. The stress is killing you. It's time to take a break."

And other firm but harsh details about Justine's current state of health.

Justine sat up after Coral left, pushing herself against the headboard, wincing as she put pressure on her left hand. She found the controls that opened the window blinds. Early evening, daylight lingering because they were so far north, and the window opened on a lovely little cove with big firs and cedars down to the edge of the rocky beach. She stared out the window at the intersection of water and trees.

Safe. For now. But how long could they keep Daddy-damned-dearest at bay? No matter what, she had to assume that she was now compromised.

Her days as First Secretary were *definitely* numbered. That would deal with Coral's concerns.

Someone tapped at her door.

"Come in."

Donald entered, his expression solemn.

"Don't say it," she sighed. "You talked to Coral. I just got the lecture."

"I already knew it before she talked to you," he said.

She made a face. "What the hell happened to medical confidentiality?"

"You never revoked my permissions to know about your medical condition—just as I never revoked yours for me." He sat on the bed and took her good hand.

"All right," she sighed. "Other topics. How did I get hurt?"

"Boating on Puget Sound," Donald said. "Your thumb got caught in a rope. A stupid but unfortunate mistake caused by being drunk and trying to fix something Hallock did while you four were sailing."

"Then why didn't Nick and Eliot go to Chicago with me?"

"Because you turned bitchy after it happened and told them to get the hell away." Donald paused. "One of the Rescue Angel agents has a close enough resemblance to you that she can play your double. That's who is in Chicago and who had the apparent injury in the Sound."

"You've really thought this through."

"Honey, from the moment you sent that emergency message, I've been on the run, putting the pieces together to cover for you. Serg gave me part of what I needed. The rest is all Rescue Angel."

She was now aware enough to notice the dark circles under his eyes.

"Looks like I'm not the only one who needs a break."

"*I* have this place," Donald said. "This—" he pointed to himself. "Is just from the last day or so."

She eyed him. He returned her gaze steadily. She couldn't deny the loving concern in his expression, as well as the fatigue. But there was also a non-verbal pleading that she recognized. Donald wouldn't ask, but—she knew him well enough to recognize that he wanted contact. Touch, to soothe and reassure himself as well as her. *Her* touch, not Coral or Francie or Meg.

And Donald had pushed himself harder than he should have for his current health, to save her. She was very damn lucky. This time.

It could have been much, much worse. She could be dead. Or a prisoner confined in one of those damned indenture labs—rumor had it that some disappeared Martinieres had met that fate. She held no illusions about what her father would do to her if he had the slightest justification.

Justine's skin crawled at the thought of what *might have been*, without Donald's help.

I'm fucking scared. I need it as much as him.

Justine sighed, yielding to mutual desires. "My hand hurts, and Hallock wrenched my arm pretty bad because it's aching as well. I—I need contact."

"You're sure? You've been pretty firm about physical contact between us being a hindrance to your role as First Secretary."

"This is a fucking bad setback. The information was worth it, but I think I've just blown my usefulness as First Secretary."

"Just getting access to that much data about that fucking Electric Born program has been a help," Donald said. He kicked off his shoes and eased onto the bed, taking her into his arms, careful not to jar her.

She settled into his chest with a sigh, and closed her eyes.

This could only be temporary. But for now….

January, 2038

It took four months for Daddy-fucking-dearest to strip Justine of her position. Ironically, he replaced her with Eliot.

"You'll have to stop seeing Nick in public," she warned Eliot.

Eliot nodded, tight-lipped. "We've already said our goodbyes."

"God, Eliot, is it worth it?"

"Maybe I can get information about Heaven's Reach. And Nick is doing his own investigations."

She had shared the data with both Nick and Eliot upon her return to LA, after spending the week recovering on Nameless Island. They both deserved to know.

"Be very careful," she cautioned.

"We intend to be," Eliot said. He leaned in to kiss her. "And we plan to continue visiting you in Chicago."

"You're safest cutting ties with me," she said.

He raised his brows. "Me, perhaps. Nick will be our relay."

"Stay safe. Both of you."

She sighed as he nodded and left. Despite everything, she had become fond of both Nick and Eliot. And she owed them one hell of a lot.

SEPTEMBER, 2039

HER TIME WAS HER OWN NOW. JUSTINE FOCUSED ON DEVELOPING HER security business as a cover for Rescue Angel activities, and rescuing indentured women from the Electric Born labs. She started working with Rafe Alvarez and Alvarez Armory, but didn't ask questions about Serg. Rafe stayed in Serg's Chicago condo when he came to town, easing that emptiness she felt whenever she realized that the apartment had been vacant for almost five years.

Then Serg knocked on her door, his face grim.

She greeted him with a big hug, no questions asked.

"I have bad news," he said. "Cousin Kendra's gone."

"Gone?" Her gut chilled and she stared at Serg. Kendra and her husband Scott, with their two adorable kids, had stopped in Chicago over Labor Day for a visit, before cruising on their yacht in the Caribbean. Justine had been worried about them, but there weren't any storms forecast.

More than that, Kendra and Scott were the only other Family members who knew about the purpose of the Electric Born, for safety's sake. Nick and Eliot reached a dead end when it came to checking the records on Heaven's Reach—*any* unauthorized investigation led to severe sanctions. Eliot barely avoided getting caught. Nick nearly lost his real estate license over using his channels to investigate. She told them *no more,* to keep themselves safe.

"Kendra and Scott's yacht came under attack by pirates," Serg said grimly. "By the time help arrived, it was too late. The boat was in shambles."

She drew a ragged breath. "I suppose we'll get ransom demands. I'll pay whatever it takes."

Serg shook his head. "They were tortured." He sighed, then snapped up a picture. "This brand was found on their bodies. Do you know anything about it?"

She stared at the charcoal-shaded cross of the Electric Born, with the red and black Martiniere trefoil superimposed over it. The mark of Heaven's Reach. Gulped. Looked at Serg.

"I think I'd better bring Donald into this." She paused. "Does this mean that Vygotsky Security has resurfaced?"

Serg nodded. "We've exhausted our purpose for remaining underground. Philip isn't focused on us anymore."

She supposed that was a minor blessing.

But her father—Joey—Hallock—*whoever*—would pay for this.

They would pay.

19 / INTERLUDE NINE

Sᴇᴘᴛᴇᴍʙᴇʀ, 2086

Jᴜsᴛɪɴᴇ's ᴠᴏɪᴄᴇ ᴛʀᴀɪʟᴇᴅ ᴏғғ.

Mike glanced sharply at her. "Only up to 2039."

"*Michael.*" JoAnn's tone was sharp, rebuking.

Mike sighed. "I get it, Jo. This story contained a *lot*. All the same, we're running short on time. And we're still only at 2039. A lot of space to cover, and it should happen today."

"I have to take a break," Justine said. "Not that much happened between 2039 and 2044. Donald and I kept digging for more information about Heaven's Reach, and creating our own network within the Electric Born. The next story will be about 2044, and I can do it this afternoon, *but I have to take a break first.*"

She didn't wait for Mike's response, but unfolded her walker and rolled it out of his office, heading *outside*. She needed time to think about what happened next and just how to approach the events of 2044 and after. Time to separate herself from the stories before she burst into more tears.

Why was she crying so much?

Justine shoved that thought away.

Focus.

The ten years between 2044 and 2054 were *huge*, but as far as the daily events and the contacts between her and Donald? Not significantly different from what happened in 2038 through 2039. Just a slow slog of rebuilding and preparation.

Footsteps behind her. Deontae joined Justine.

"I've got this," she said.

D opened the door for her. "You shouldn't be outside alone," he said.

"What's going on?" she asked. "The Double R is supposed to be secure."

"Bug alert right after you left Mike's office," D said. "Mike killed it, but we don't know yet if it's been transmitting or not. I've got shielding and a takedown zapper, just in case it called in a drone attack."

Justine didn't answer right away, considering her choices.

"How bad can it be?" she asked.

"Miniature weaponized drones," D said. "Possibly coming in swarms. It's something that has been popping up over the past few months, and it *is* tied to those Heaven's Reach fuckers."

"Do you have a zapper for me?"

He grinned and offered his arm. "But of course, Justine. Going to the cemetery?"

She laughed and slipped her arm into his, pushing the button on her walker so that it folded itself. Given the choice, she preferred an arm to that damned walker. Even if this new one was self-folding and could follow behind without her dragging it along. Ron had modified it for her over the last week.

"Does everyone know my patterns?"

"Pretty much." His face went tight and solemn. "We have to assume that those fuckers listening in know as well."

"I've gotten too predictable," she sighed. "I suppose it's a failing of age."

D shrugged. "On the other hand, you have experience and cunning on your side, lady. You've been through one hell of a lot. I reviewed Brandon's recordings last night. You were how old during that last tale —twenty-nine? Thirty?"

"Something like that."

"Damn, woman. You lived a lot in those years. Achieved a lot."

"Donald called me his falcon for a reason."

Oh, it felt good to not be leaning on that walker. Especially since she was on the arm of an attractive, middle-aged Black man, with his own husband. An unavailable man who wouldn't expect anything from light flirtation, while engaging in word play. Perfection.

Best of all, a fellow warrior, who *understood* the price she had paid.

"I was young and reckless during that era," she continued. "But that crook in my thumb? That was the legacy of that damned encounter with Hallock."

D nodded. Then he tensed, and snapped up a message.

"Mike says the damned bug transmitted."

"Fuck." She sighed. "Any idea how it got in?"

"Small enough that it could have slipped into the house during the last twenty-four hours, since Jo's last scan. She just launched Defender bots to patrol the immediate grounds around the house and tighten up security," D said. "She's activating the Guardian individual protection shield bots—take one the next time you go out. And I have screens up. If you're up for it, let's find out how far these fuckers are willing to go. Draw them out."

Justine grinned at D. "I may be an old lady of seventy-seven, but I am *always* game to take on idiots and assholes. Hallock's forgotten what I did to him. Time that I reminded him not to fuck around with a Martiniere."

D laughed.

They reached the cemetery gate. D helped her settle on the bench. "I'm prowling around the edges. I'll holler should we get some incoming." He slipped her a small, teardrop-shaped fob. "The zapper will tell you when it detects intruders, and how many. Closer the better for using it. You don't have to aim when it's time—it's self-directed. You just need to tell it if you want quarter, half, three-quarters, or full power. Full power gives you three shots, half six, three-quarters nine, and one quarter twelve shots." He showed her the settings on the fob.

"Oh, that's a *lovely* piece of tech."

Deontae grinned big, then turned solemn again. "Hopefully Jo's latest version of the Defenders will be enough to keep any drone swarms away. But if it isn't—"

"Then we get to play with our toys." Justine leaned back on the bench.

"Exactly. One more thing. Be mindful about using it around digis. It may interfere with them."

"I'll remember that."

"Good." D left the cemetery, pausing to attach a sensor to the gate.

Then he lined out in a big rolling stride that covered a lot of ground, a farmer's *gotta get there on foot without tiring myself out* pace. Something that Gabie had developed during his years in exile; something she had seen in Ruby, Brandon, Mike, D's father Jeff, and now Ron.

Justine leaned back. *Was* there anything about the years between 2039 and 2044 that might be useful to share? Surprising that none of the digis seemed to be around.

And then she sensed a presence. An unfamiliar digi. Donald?

No. Damn it.

Something about it felt hostile—a new sensation.

Could she call for help without that strange digi becoming aware? Who? Not Gabie. He was still recovering from that attack. Ruby? Probably with Gabie. Brandon? Most likely huddling with Mike and Jo as they wrestled with security.

Lily.

Her great-niece had helped stop the attack on Gabie.

Lily.

And Lily wasn't quite like the others. She was sneakier, thanks to those years directly under Daddy-fucking-dearest's influence.

Justine thought hard about her great-niece. About her own anger when she learned that Daddy-fucking-dearest had possessed Lily and distorted her life. As Lily developed her digi self, it was clear that she would have been a major asset to the Family and the Group during her life, if Philip had *only left her alone.*

So much lost, damn it. So fucking unfair.

Plus Lily had been a beautiful dancer, just like Gabie's mother Angelica.

Aha. A faint familiar thread of digi aura that was entirely different from that alien one. Justine focused on Lily's tombstone.

"Liliana Angelica Martiniere," she said out loud, as if musing. "Our little ballerina. So many regrets, my dear Lily. So many *sacrifices and dangers.*"

She stressed *sacrifices and dangers.* Lily's basic keywords.

Stronger sense of Lily's presence. *Good.*

"I wonder what you would have become," Justine continued. "What *programming* you would have done."

Programming.

Another one of Lily's keywords.

The *other's* aura grew more powerful. No. It wasn't Donald.

Hallock!

She was certain of that, now.

But her awareness of Lily's presence also strengthened.

"Most of all, I wonder if you would have shut down that fucking *programming* that killed your grandfather." Justine shook her head. "I have this hunch that you would have found Heaven's Reach, and *Greg fucking Hallock, I know the fuck you're there in digi!*" She yelled the last words.

Damn it, my digigloves are in the house.

Even though they were the plain ones and not the juiced-up ones that still needed to be programmed to her, if they were in her pocket, then she might have half a chance of holding Hallock off. Another screwup.

Can't make that damn mistake again!

D spun and ran toward Justine as Hallock manifested in front of her, smirking.

"*Ah, Justine. So overconfident in your ability to handle me.*"

"It worked in 2047, didn't it?" she retorted. "I'd sure as hell like to know how you survived, especially that early in the development of digital thought clones."

Come on, Lily, come on.

"*Philip's algorithm killed Gabe's body before he could write anything more than his half-assed digi algorithm. And my digi is going to kill your body.*"

"I'm seventy-seven years old, Hallock, and could keel over any day without your help. Why don't you come up with a threat that has some teeth to it?"

He moved closer. *"I can make this hurt, very, very bad."*

"And that might be enough to raise the digi of my ex-husband."

Lily—Ruby—someone—help!

Hallock laughed. *"Good luck with that. His digi is locked down hard. But I will take much pleasure in telling it that I made you suffer as you died. And you won't have a digi. I'll make sure of that."*

She laughed back at him, even as anger surged within her at his calling Donald *it*. "Do you really think you can do anything worse to me than I've already gone through? Dead is dead, digis or no digis."

There! She saw Lily's presence as the faintest of outlines. And Deontae was almost at the gate—no, he stopped. Whirled.

The fob in her hand buzzed. *"Invading drone swarms approaching Defender blockades."*

Hallock leered at her. *"No one can help you now, Justine."*

"I thought I killed you," she said, hoping to distract him as Lily eased closer. Hallock didn't seem to notice her.

"Not good enough. Especially thanks to Heaven's Reach."

As he reached for her, Ruby appeared behind Hallock. He whirled to face Ruby. Lily popped between Hallock and Justine. He didn't seem to notice Lily as he dove at Ruby, not until Lily ripped into him with teeth and fingernails, shredding away small pieces of Hallock's digi.

Hallock summoned a weapon, a sword of some sort. Lily wrested it from his grasp and threw it away, making it dissolve into a gray cloud. The shreds that Lily tore away kept reforming on Hallock, while the chunks he ripped from Ruby faded quickly, Ruby's digi becoming more translucent. Lily managed to avoid him. But she wasn't quick enough to keep him from hurting Ruby.

Would using the fob weaken Hallock, give them a chance—no! Not worth the risk! She might harm Ruby and Lily as well. Where were Brandon and Gabie? Fighting other digis? Had Mike needed to slip into digi world?

If only she had her digigloves. Then she might be able to wipe out those chunks of Hallock. If only she had picked up one of the Guardian shield generators before leaving the house. Then she would be protected. If only she and D had taken the time to program those supergloves. Then she would be even more effective in holding Hallock off herself, without risking those precious family digis.

Fucking "if onlies" are gonna kill you, Justine Solange Martiniere.

Ruby extruded a containment bubble—a particular skill of hers, but was it strong enough to hold Hallock?

Hallock backed away from Ruby, directly into Lily—who ripped off a whole arm this time. This, too, evaporated into a gray dust cloud. Ruby threw the containment when Lily ducked away—and missed. Hallock disappeared.

"Are you safe?" Justine yelled.

Lily gathered up Ruby and her shards. *"Going away. Recharging. Get into the house where you're safe!"*

The digis faded away as D finally reached Justine. Without hesitating, he swept her up in his arms and raced toward the house.

WELL. THE ATTACK PUT PAID TO ANY STORIES THAT AFTERNOON. AFTER debriefing with Mike, D, and JoAnn, Justine settled in the living room, tired but not yet willing to admit she needed a nap. The others busily added programming safeguards to the main house.

"We'll program those digigloves tomorrow morning," D said, before diving into manipulating algorithms. "Then you need to have them on you at all times."

Meanwhile, her regular digigloves were within reach.

No sign of Gabie and Ruby's digis. What did that mean? Gabie's projection was faint during this morning's storytelling. Neither he nor Ruby were part of the hackerfest now happening in Mike's office. Perhaps they were out on security patrol.

Or maybe Ruby's digi was injured worse than it seemed.

Justine closed her eyes.

No. Not Ruby!

She couldn't stand to lose this manifestation of her sister-in-law. Who knew what a recreation of Ruby's digi would be like—even if they could generate it? And what kind of shape was Gabie in if Ruby was very damaged? Even as a digi, he was *so* reliant on her for his well-being.

Gabie. Ruby. Where the fuck are you?

As if her thoughts summoned them, first Gabie and then Ruby appeared.

"Huh. Just as I was thinking about you," she said.

Ruby raised her brows at Gabie. *"I told you that Justine called us non-verbally when Hallock appeared."*

"Definite and powerful summons," Gabie said. *"Tine. Did you call us out loud?"*

"No," she said. "I just wondered where you two were, to myself. I don't *think* I'm so senile that I wouldn't know if I was speaking." She paused. "And I didn't say anything when Hallock appeared. Not right away. I felt Lily's presence before I even said her name."

"Mike is the only other living person who can call us without speaking. Everyone else needs to have us hanging around to summon by thought alone," Gabie said. *"Mike can do it because he already has a digi, thanks to his cyborging and cloning effects."*

"What the hell does that mean?" Justine asked.

He scrutinized her. *"I don't think you already have a digi. Unless Donald did it."*

"If he did, he never told me about it." She gulped. "And Hallock said that he had locked Donald's digi down hard. We'll need to do another rescue mission like we did for Brandon—but we don't have Lily as an insider this time."

"Perhaps," Gabie said. *"And perhaps Donald already has his insider."*

Justine shook her head. "No, Gabie. I don't have a digi."

"You have something." Gabie eyed her speculatively.

"I don't have a digi, Gabriel!" she snapped. Even *thinking* about that prospect sent ice shards prickling through her gut.

"But you have the ability to call us with your thoughts. And of all the living Family members—except Mike—you sense individual digi presences the fastest. You woke me. You knew that Hallock was approaching you in digi. Tine, only you and Mike can do that—and we know why Mike can."

"No. No." Donald hadn't, *wouldn't* do something to her like that. Not without telling her.

Which left—*no!*

Don't deny it, Justine. Your fucking father would have done it to you. Look at what he did to Mike.

She drew a deep, shuddering breath. If it were so, she needed to figure this out, and damned fucking soon.

"Did our fucking father manage to slip some programming into me?" she asked, her voice quavering. "Programming I wouldn't notice, but that would have left me vulnerable to his digi? Like he did to Mike?"

"It's entirely possible."

She tightened her lips and fought against the urge to hyperventilate, to slide into an irrational panic.

No more anxiety attacks.

"What does it take to find out?"

Gabie sighed. *"I can go into your mind with your permission, but it would be easier if you were sedated and had Mike monitoring you."*

"I can handle one hell of a lot of pain." She raised her chin.

"Tine, it's not an issue of pain. The process can be very disorienting. Vertigo. Hallucinations. It's better that you're not entirely present for this one."

"Then it's a distraction—"

"No. It's a necessity. I'll be right back." Gabie disappeared.

Justine buried her head in her hands. What the hell was she getting herself into?

Ruby nestled next to her, the light pressure of her presence comforting. *"What Gabe wants to do isn't a bad thing,"* she said.

Justine half-laughed, half-sobbed. "But it's fucking scary as hell, Ruby. How—when—where did my father get the opportunity to muck around in my brain?"

"Your father, or Hallock?"

"That's not much of a comfort, Ruby!" Justine snapped, as Mike entered the living room. He knelt in front of Justine.

"Gabe says that you might have some similar programming problems as mine."

"I don't know when or where it might have happened," she said.

"It's all right, Justine." Mike gently took her hands. "I'll be with you the whole time, both physically and in digi. It'll be fine."

She gulped, and looked deep into Mike's blue eyes, so much like Daddy-damned-dearest. Her father's clone. Not her father.

She could trust Mike.

She *had* to trust Mike.

JoAnn joined Mike, helping Justine into bed before Mike administered the short-term sedation shot. Mike held both of her hands as Justine lay in the bed, warmth and drowsiness washing over her.

"I'm here with you," he said, his digi presence warm, comforting. *"I'm watching over you."*

That reassuring aura eased her into unconsciousness.

It was dark when Justine woke, her head throbbing. Mike—physical, not digi—still held her hands. JoAnn was gone, along with Ruby. Justine blinked at him and Gabie's digi, thoughts still fuzzy, all except for one.

"Did *he* muck around in my brain?"

"No more than the usual programming one would expect from someone raised like we were," Gabie said. *"It's not outside programming, Tine. It's something about* you.*"*

"So what does that *mean*?" This was nuts, absolutely nuts.

"It's something you've developed in yourself," Gabie said. *"Through discipline or training, you've created the ability to perceive unmanifested digital entities on your own. Now if we can just learn how you did it...."*

Justine gulped. "Oh my *God*."

Mike squeezed her hands. "We'll figure it out. D and the others are almost done with the security upgrades. Tomorrow morning, bright and early, we'll program the digigloves and go from there. With your consent, I'll share my observations with D and JoAnn. One way or another, we'll get an answer."

She sighed. "My head hurts like a son-of-a-bitch."

Mike smiled wryly. "I know that feeling. I'll get you some aspirin."

"Thanks."

"Rest, Tine. A good night's sleep will make one hell of a difference." Gabie faded away as Mike retrieved the pill for her.

She lay awake in the darkness, thoughts still muddled, until the pain eased.

JUSTINE SNAPPED INTO SUDDEN QUICK AWARENESS, ALERTED TO A *PRESENCE* curled around her, hand resting on her breast just like Donald used to do when they cuddled. How long had it been there?

She forced herself not to react to the unfamiliar presence. Definitely not Hallock.

Donald?

She bit her lip before she could blurt out his name. That had sent the presence away before. Possibly tied to the programming Hallock had done to him. Perhaps she needed to do something else—yes.

Remember his keywords. Key phrases. Try that first.

"I take you, Donald, to be my husband," she whispered. "To have and to hold, for richer or poorer, in sickness and in health; to love, honor, and cherish for eternity."

The presence felt warmer and more *there*.

First key phrase. Yes! It's working!

"Our greatest enemy is Greg Hallock," she continued.

Lips brushed against her neck.

Donald, oh Donald.

"Our greatest offspring was the Rescue Angel," she finished.

The contact felt *real*, more solid than any touch from Ruby. The hands turned her over and she came face-to-face with a shadowy version of Donald.

"I take you, Justine, to be my wife. To have and to hold, for richer or poorer, in sickness and in health; to love, honor, and cherish for eternity."

The form grew more solid.

"Our greatest enemy is Greg Hallock." His lips brushed her forehead.

"Our greatest offspring was the Rescue Angel."

Donald. His digi was more solid than Ruby's or Gabie's.

"Donald," she whispered—*Donald, definitely Donald, oh God, Donald.* "Oh Donald. How did you get free from Hallock?"

"I'm not entirely there yet, my love." The digi's arms wrapped around her. Donald. Definitely Donald. *"But once you unlock those files, I will be. I've been hiding, waiting for a chance to slip out so that you can activate me. Doing this makes it easier for you to unlock those files and break that last block. It protected me from Hallock, in spite of what he told you, but it also kept me tied down."*

"How did you slip out?" She blinked back tears.

"Lily yanked off Hallock's cyborged arm. Despite it happening in digi, it was enough to interfere not only with his digi manifestation but with his cyborging. A phenomenon unique to cyborgs with digis, like him and Mike. I took advantage of that lapse to send this little portion of myself to you, hoping you remembered that dream."

She gulped. "It *was* you. Oh love, it *was* you."

"Yes. I could manage that much." Another kiss. *"I have to go. Hallock's in for repairs, but he'll wake soon. You can unlock my files, then I'll be completely free."* A third kiss. *"For eternity, my dearest love. For eternity. Or at least until our files degrade."*

"For eternity," she whispered back.

He smiled at her. *"Patience. Soon enough. Have faith. I'll see you soon."*

Donald's digi faded away. Justine broke into joyful tears. He was so close to being free. *So close.*

And he was a digi. If that was just a partial of him—dear *God,* he was strong. She refused to think about the implications of Hallock being able to contain Donald if he was so strong. Perhaps it was only because Donald hadn't been fully activated. Well. She just needed to unlock those files and he'd be complete.

We'll make you pay, Hallock.

Someone knocked at her door.

"Come in," she said, voice cracking.

Mike hesitated in the doorway, his figure outlined by the hallway light. "You all right, Justine? Monitor said you were awake and crying."

"Donald," she whispered. "I made contact with his digi. He's not completely free, but when I unlock the files—it'll be complete."

A big smile spread across Mike's face. He strode across the room to kneel by Justine. "That is *fantastic* news. But you're all right?"

She nodded. "Just—the knowing. Donald's a digi. And he's *strong*. Stronger than any other digi."

Mike hugged her. She leaned her head on him, sniffling.

Donald had made his own digi. Just like Gabie.

Oh God, what a relief that was. Just a few more steps to go.

Donald was a digi.

THIS TIME SHE RESTED IN THE PORCH LOUNGE CHAIR WHILE THE OTHERS SAT around her. Programming the super digigloves had taken a lot of energy from Justine—physical fatigue, not mental. Her thoughts raced as she considered the morning's events.

"It's been a long time since I've seen you smirk like that, Tine," Gabie said.

She laughed. "I'm just—happy."

"It is a relief," Mike said. "Donald present in digi form, and we just need to deactivate the locks on his files."

"That could be more challenging than we expect," Deontae cautioned. "Hallock's likely to have defensive measures on those files."

"But Donald being activated and ready to move makes a big difference," Lily said. *"Easier than releasing Dad. Donald hasn't been getting split up and stuffed into clones. He'll be on the inside working against Hallock. Much simpler, especially since you have those super digigloves."*

"Those digigloves aren't a magic tool," D said, scowling. "They'll suck a lot of energy out of you, Justine. You need to rest and build up your strength for tomorrow. Or the day after."

"Tomorrow," she said firmly. She wasn't going to leave Donald like this for any longer than she had to. "But for today—I may be tired out, but my brain is spinning. And I think we need to consider what I did to Hallock. He'll try to use that against us."

"You think you have the energy for that story?" Mike asked.

She grinned at him. Nephew. Father's clone. Mike.

"For this one? Oh, do I ever have the energy to tell you how I got rid of Greg Hallock—then, at least."

20 / VENGEANCE IS MINE

MARCH, 2044

A SHORT, SWEET STRAIN OF XYLOPHONE CHIMES ECHOED THROUGH Justine's Chicago condo. Paused. Repeated. Paused. Repeated.

Serg was back from whatever it was he was doing, and wanted to talk. Justine exhaled, checking the time. Ten o'clock. What the hell? Normally, Serg didn't contact her when he returned this late at night.

Something urgent.

She should answer. They set up this routine after she left the Group, as part of the integration of JSM Corp and Vygotsky Security, at least the aspects of Vygotsky under Serg's control.

Justine sighed and keyed in the jazzy acknowledgement chords. She *had* been comfortable in pajamas and bathrobe, planning to settle in bed with a book and detach from everything that had happened over the past week.

She was more than ready to schedule a secret visit to Donald after she officially celebrated her thirty-fifth birthday next week, just to get a break.

By now, they had established a comfortable routine for her to drop in at Nameless for a few days to a week every two months or so. Concealed identity, secretive in and out, varied and unpredictable patterns. The visits were important not just for her physical health but for her mental health. Coral approved, but she still kept a close eye on Justine's habits.

Coral would *definitely* not approve of late-night meetings like this. They created stress levels that led to manifestations of the worst of Justine's workaholic behaviors. Working late into the evening and on weekends. Bulimia. Insomnia. Heavy drinking.

Oh well. Coral wasn't here to disapprove. Justine pulled on slacks and a sweater.

—*I'm decent now,* she messaged him. —*Come on over.* Serg knew the code to her condo, just like she did his. She went into her living room and took a bottle of whisky and two shot glasses from her bar. A late evening meeting usually required alcohol.

"Hello, Justine."

Piotr's voice startled her as she finished pouring two drinks. She almost spilled the precious, expensive, getting-to-be-rare Scotch. Justine carefully set the bottle down on the bar, then whirled to face Piotr and Serg.

"Piotr. It's been years."

He nodded. "I have been staying underground. No need to give Philip a target."

Justine nodded and brought down a third glass. "I'll pour you a drink."

After pouring the third glass, she handed them their drinks, picked up hers, and sat in the big white armchair that was *hers* and no one else's. Shades of her father, but she really didn't care what others thought about her these days. She was only accountable to Donald— and Coral.

"So," she said, once she settled in her chair, put her feet up on the ottoman, and took a sip of whisky. "I'm assuming this isn't a social visit, Piotr."

Piotr eyed his drink, then took a big swallow. "What do you know about the Electric Born, Justine?" he asked in Russian.

Her lips tightened.

Damn it.

"Too much and not enough," she said, responding in Russian as well, then took a sip of whisky. "What's brought them to your attention?"

"You are aware that they are behind a separatist movement in the Southwest that is taking over small utility districts and small towns?"

"Yes." She thought about another sip and decided against it. Not yet. "It is part of a strategy that Daddy-fucking-dearest is using to make himself an oligarch."

"It is surprising that JSM Corp is not doing more about it," Piotr said cautiously.

She scowled and took that sip. "Has Serg told you about the events that led to Daddy-poo dumping me as First Secretary?"

"Just that you had a confrontation with Greg Hallock."

Justine extended her left hand, deciding to switch to English for *this* discussion. "See that crook in my thumb? Hallock did that to me."

No, she wasn't going to take another drink. Not yet.

Piotr pursed his lips. "Why?"

Oh, what the hell. She had to tell the whole damn story. Justine took a bigger swallow of her drink.

"Because I set off an alarm when copying confidential files about the Electric Born. I tried to download files about Heaven's Reach, the secret program within the secret program. Hallock caught me when I tried to escape. If it hadn't been for Serg's presence inside of Hallock's security, I'd be dead or in one of my fucking father's indenture labs as an experiment."

Piotr flinched.

Serg frowned. "I didn't know *that* was what you were doing," he said. "Hallock didn't give us any clues, and Donald didn't tell me what was at stake."

"For damned good reason. We're still trying to piece everything together." She tossed down the rest of her drink. "Short version, the Electric Born cult is a means for Daddy-fucking-dearest to establish a programmed, indenture-based, personal army. He hasn't gotten there yet, but not for lack of effort. Some of those indentureds ended up working for External Affairs clients, and they were problematic. I received complaints and relayed them to Hallock. He didn't act. I needed to find out what was going on—and the only way I could reach the data was through getting an insider's access code at their own workstation. Which I did." She shivered. "And then there's Heaven's Reach."

"I taught you how to break those accesses without risking yourself." Piotr scowled at her.

"Those means didn't work for accessing the Electric Born deep records," she said flatly. "What do you know about Heaven's Reach?"

No reaction from either man. Justine took a deep breath.

"If the true purpose of Electric Born is bad, Heaven's Reach—from what little I've been able to piece together—is purely hideous. Trying to break those accesses on the Heaven's Reach files set off the alarm." She exhaled and got up to pour herself another drink. "More, anyone?"

Serg shook his head.

Piotr eyed his drink. "No. But why break your thumb?"

She took her time, filling the glass as full as possible.

"I went in with a thumbnail chip and an elbow chip backup. Somehow, Hallock knew I had the thumbnail." Justine settled back into her chair. "I tried to trigger the chip's self-destruct when Hallock confronted me. It failed. Hallock broke my thumb and asked Serg for a pair of pilers to rip off my nail. He hit Hallock with a sedative instead." Another big swallow of her drink. "So that's what I know about the Electric Born. Believe me, however, Heaven's Reach is much, much worse. From what little I've been able to access, anyway. That information is very, *very* protected."

"You have known about this for seven years." Disapproval colored Piotr's voice. "And yet you have not shared this information with the Family."

She took another big swallow of whisky. "Much of it was destroyed in an automatic data dump triggered by my access. You and Serg were running under cover at the time. A potential risk. And—" she sighed. "Cousin Kendra knew."

Silence fell around them.

"Kendra knew," Serg finally said in a flat tone.

"She was the logistics person for Chris," Justine said. "I don't know if Chris knows. I doubt it."

Lie.

She and Donald had counted on Kendra telling her brother Chris about the Electric Born.

Piotr exhaled through his teeth. "Christopher knows. He sent me to you for more information. He's preparing another challenge to Philip."

Justine tossed down the rest of her drink. "All right." She clicked up two copies of her files and flicked them over to Serg and Piotr. "This is what Donald and I know."

She watched as Piotr and Serg flipped through the records. Piotr blanched at one point—she suspected he saw the incomplete Heaven's Reach files.

At last both Serg and Piotr closed the files.

"This is bad, Justine," Piotr said, his voice quavering slightly. "Even if Philip hasn't been able to achieve this yet—it is bad."

"Yes." She didn't flinch away from his accusing glare. "Gabie's last hack is why Daddy-damn-dearest hasn't reached his goals." Justine sipped from her drink. "Electric Born was too big for me to fight within the Group. Donald and I have prioritized Heaven's Reach in our research, because of their human weaponization programs."

"These pieces—" Piotr gestured.

"Destroyed beyond any accesses except directly from the Martiniere or Martiniere-in-waiting. That means Gabie."

"Gabriel is not an option," Piotr said harshly. "He cannot say his own name, much less the name of the Group. It will take either Donna or Philip to break that mind control lock. I tried."

"You saw Gabie recently?"

Serg nodded. "Last year. Electric Born tried to move in on his ex-wife in Thunder County, over a water rights fight. They crudely programmed Gabe's son as well."

"Gabie's kid is what—*ten years old*? God!" She shivered.

"Eleven, now," Serg said. "Gabe enlisted Rafe—he's remarried, to Rafe's sister—and Rafe brought me into the action." He shivered. "One of the men involved was part of Philip's security. Gabe damned near beat the man to death, because that man had assaulted Brandon. Gabe told the man—don't know his name—that if he wasn't needed to carry a message to Philip, that Gabe would have killed the man with his bare hands for harming Brandon. Gabe *would* have done it. Very deliberate and calculated. Almost like something Philip would do—if he had the guts to dirty his own hands."

"*Fuck.*" She hadn't seen that side of Gabie, but suspected it existed. The attack on his son must have been *bad*. Justine drained the glass. "What do you want from me, besides information on Electric Born?"

"Philip is suffering from lung cancer," Piotr said. "We need you to come back to the Group."

"Aw, *fuck.*" Justine smacked her head against the well-padded back of her chair. "You really think that Daddy-damned-dearest will go for that?"

"Raven Deschamps and Eliot McNaughton brought that very proposal to the Board, day before yesterday," Piotr said.

"And Hallock?" God, she wanted another drink.

Her family. Her fucking family.

Raven, for God's sake. If *Raven* brought that proposal to the Board, along with Eliot, there was an internal coup happening within the Group that had nothing to do with the Family—aimed at Hallock. For Raven and Eliot to make this move meant they wanted her to run point.

God.

"For the moment, he is overruled." Piotr stretched and rose, Serg following suit. "Be prepared to be approached in the next few days."

"So what role is Christopher playing in all this?" she asked, as Piotr headed for the door.

Though she already guessed. Chris wanted to overthrow her father.

Piotr turned. "With Gabriel out of the picture, Christopher is putting together a plan to oust Philip, with himself as the Martiniere."

"I'm out of it, too," she said. "So that's why Chris sent you to me. Not just for more information about Electric Born and Heaven's Reach."

"Yes. To give you warning so that the approach isn't a surprise."

She sighed. "Thank you, Piotr. I appreciate it."

Piotr bowed deeply to her, like he would do to the Martiniere or Martiniere-in-waiting. That sent a chill through her.

"We'll talk more in the morning. For now, good night."

"Yes. We'll talk."

Justine stayed seated until the door closed after Piotr and Serg.

Then she sighed again, and pulled up her comm to contact Donald.

—*The falcon game begins once more.*

THE SECURE COMM CHANNEL FROM DONALD CHIMED AS SHE FINISHED pouring herself that third, nearly-brimful, drink. Not surprising—his time zone was two hours behind hers, so it was earlier in the evening for him. She clicked it onto full video and returned to her chair, sipping on her drink.

"They're pulling you back into the Group." A statement, not a question.

She nodded. "I just got a visit from Serg *and* Piotr."

"Piotr's resurfaced?"

"Uh-huh. Apparently, Daddy-damned-dearest has cancer and will be undergoing chemo." A gulp of her drink. "Raven and Eliot recommended to the Board that I return to the Group—no idea what position. I can't see Eliot stepping down from External Affairs. Chris is planning his own coup attempt, but—I think Raven and Eliot see this as a chance to bring down Hallock. And Raven's involvement suggests endorsement of *that* process from Daddy-poo."

Donald raised his brows. "What's your estimate that Chris will succeed?"

She laughed bitterly. "Remote." She paused, staring into her drink. "Unless Daddy-damned-dearest dies in the process, and then it will be fucking chaos."

"Really?"

"Chris will not be the rallying factor that Gabie would be. And there's news of Gabie. He's out of the game. Piotr says that Gabie's subjected to a heavy mind control lock that even he can't break. Only Donna-gran or my father can touch it."

"Then you're right. Fucking chaos. What's your move, my falcon?"

She sighed. "Accept the position if there aren't too many restrictions. Do what I can to protect those dear to me when the storm hits.

Do my damnedest to bring down Hallock. With Raven and Eliot supporting me—it's a strong opportunity."

"And if your father goes down?"

"Get Gabie to Donna-gran to break the block, and make him the Martiniere before someone else steps up. Or—" She took another big drink. "Say *fuck it all*, fuck tradition based on that stupid Salic Law, and take up the title myself."

"You won't support Chris?"

"His claim isn't as strong as Cousin Arthur's was. No." She stared into her drink. "It will be either Gabie or me as the Martiniere if Daddy-fucking-dearest is removed. We're the only ones capable of managing the Group and the Family. Chris doesn't have the perspective needed to be much of a Martiniere. His anger at his sister's death is driving this and—while vengeance is a motivation I understand, Chris is too hot and angry to do it justice. I know vengeance well—but it is best served cold."

"I'm behind you, my falcon. I'll amp up our security and precautions. Are you going to stop your visits?"

"Fuck no. I'll need them more than ever."

"*Good*. Keep me posted about what's happening."

"I will."

They chatted further before signing off. Justine sipped on her final drink of the day, brooding.

Back to the Group, damn it.

She wondered who would approach her first.

THE MESSAGE ARRIVED THE NEXT DAY.

—*Justine. Is it possible to schedule a lunch with you soon? PJM.*

Daddy-fucking-dearest himself. Which…made things interesting.

She considered the options before responding.

—*Brunch tomorrow in Los Angeles. I'll send you the reservation after I make it. JSM.*

It was tempting to call Eliot, but she chose not to do that. In and out, a one-day trip. Once she knew the score, then it was time to contact Eliot.

JUSTINE WAS SIPPING A MIMOSA WHEN HER FATHER ENTERED THE PRIVATE outdoor venue she booked for their meeting. He looked better than she anticipated—pale, yes, but he was always pale. Not as thin as she expected, based on her experience with Donald's cancer.

"Daddy-dearest." She set down her drink and rose to kiss his cheek.

Might as well play the game.

"Justine." To her surprise, he reciprocated.

They settled in their chairs. Philip ordered a coffee and a vegan omelette.

"I didn't realize you were going vegan," she said, after the server left.

Philip grimaced. "I have lung cancer and cardiac issues, Justine. Trying a diet as well as chemo."

"I'm sorry to hear it." She kept her tone neutral.

A scowl. "Perhaps." He waited as the server deposited the coffee in front of him and refilled Justine's mimosa. "But that's why I wanted to talk to you."

"I had wondered," she said. "So how are you handling the Group and the Family? Chemo is rough."

"That's what I'm here to talk to you about." He sighed. "Raven and McNaughton think that bringing you back into the Group is the best option, and they've taken a proposal to the Board."

"That's interesting, considering why you dumped me from External Affairs."

"Yeah." Silence, then he continued. "I depended on Hallock's reports for that action. Now I find that Hallock has become a problem."

She shrugged. "Then get rid of him."

"It's not that simple, Justine."

Justine side-eyed him. "You're the Martiniere. How could getting rid of a problematic non-Family employee be difficult?"

No answer. Philip looked down at his coffee, wincing.

She quickly put the pieces together. There was only one thing that could stop her father from dumping Hallock.

"Oh my God," she said. "He's blackmailing you?"

Hallock could hold many things over her father. And Hallock was in a position to know the worst.

Philip flinched. "*Blackmail* is a harsh word, Justine. However. Hallock knows too much, and if I fire him—it could be a problem for the Family and the Group. Even if I had the energy to deal with it."

"So you want me to take care of Hallock. Get him out of the Group." Dear God, there had to be a catch of some sort. But what?

A faint smile touched her father's lips. "I've been following your development of JSM Corp's security subdivision. I have—concerns— about handing this job over to Piotr and Sergei."

I just bet you do.

"Why?"

"Past behavior. Past alliances. I want you in the Group as Director of Security, equal to McNaughton and Hallock. A permanent position."

Now that is interesting.

"Where does Vygotsky Security and main Martiniere security fit into this chain of command?"

"Both report to you." Her father fell silent as the server brought their food, then continued. "I want all security out from under Internal Affairs. I believe that Hallock is campaigning to take control of the Group and make it a publicly-held corporation."

"Like he could ever pull that off."

"You know I have enemies amongst the Family. Some of them could easily ally with Hallock. Removing security from his control will slow his efforts." Her father took a bite of his omelette and frowned. "Damn it, my taste is off. Anyway. I know there's no love lost between us, but—I also know that you hate Hallock's guts."

She cocked her head sideways. "And the catch?"

Philip choked on his coffee. Surprisingly he didn't manage to spew any of it.

"Oh, Justine. If only you had been born a man. No. Director of Security is yours, as long as you don't directly knife me in the back." His lips tightened. "I can count on you for one thing. Of all my opponents, excepting Gabriel, you're the one who won't destroy the Group in the process of unseating me."

You might be surprised, Daddy-damned-dearest.

"And Joey?"

Philip took one more bite of his omelette, then carefully wiped his lips. "Your brother is a major fuckup. A useful tool, and nothing more than that." Another sip of coffee. "You can't become the Martiniere. But I can trust you to ensure that whoever does follow me won't destroy everything."

As if you haven't done enough to wreck the Group yourself, not to speak of the Family.

"All right." She sipped on her mimosa, no longer hungry. "It won't be a fast process. Hallock's screwed me over once. Getting rid of him will require time and careful planning. Several years."

"That's why I want you to do it. He's nailed you before. When you strike, you'll succeed." Her father gave her a thin-lipped, brief smile. "I *have* been keeping track of you, dearest darling daughter."

She took a deep breath, ignoring the sarcasm. "Who's the designated replacement for Hallock?"

"Raven."

That made sense. "Are there any restrictions or limitations on this position you're offering me?"

"Electric Born. I retain control of them, and everything associated with them." Philip scowled. "That's where I let Joey play. Keeping him sequestered and supervised. Under no circumstances are you to interfere with that operation."

She could mess this whole thing up by raising a fuss about Electric Born and Heaven's Reach. Or she could compartmentalize Joey and keep him in that part of Internal Affairs. Like their father had clearly decided to do.

I need to be sneaky about that.

There was no way in hell she was going to let Electric Born and

Heaven's Reach run rampant. But. Director of Security. She could do *so damned much* in that role.

He fidgeted at her silence. "So will you do it?"

"Yes," she said.

"Thank you." He coughed into his napkin, then put it down. "Raven and McNaughton will be in touch with you." He rose and bowed to her.

Justine wryly noted that he left her with the bill.

Figures.

She also saw blood on the napkin. Was her father was sicker than she thought?

That—might significantly complicate things. And it explained why Daddy-damned-dearest had decided to turn to her. Maybe.

MAY, 2044

SLIDING INTO HER NEW ROLE IN THE GROUP WAS MUCH SIMPLER THE second time around. Knowing the upper-level organization helped.

Twyla continued as Justine's assistant. Justine established her main office on the tenth floor in Group headquarters, keeping a bare-bones top floor office for appearances sake. Then she spent six straight weeks in Los Angeles, including shopping for a beach compound, because she wanted to review *everything* to do with in-house Martiniere security herself.

Training protocols. Conditioning protocols. Weapons protocols. As far as she was concerned, it was time to enact uniform standards of competence; something that hadn't happened under Albert Morris or Hallock.

She put Piotr and Serg in charge of training. Vygotsky standards were higher than the in-house teams. Piotr handled training and conditioning; Serg weaponry. Nor did Justine exclude herself or her security from training and conditioning sessions.

Set the example.

It wasn't a problem with the Vygotsky staff—but the in-house security needed to learn that their new Director was as tough as they were, if not tougher.

Justine ran several loudmouths into the ground during early morning conditioning runs. Serg and his senior staff brought her in for fight demonstrations. That provided opportunities for her to dispense with even more testosterone-poisoned blowhards—and she noticed that both Daddy-fucking-dearest *and* Joey often dropped in to watch when she was challenged during sparring matches.

She ended up being the teacher, not the student, in those matches. More than once, she glimpsed Daddy-damn-dearest grinning as she defeated someone.

After a couple of weeks, once the challenges from the in-house braggarts diminished, Hallock himself decided to take her on.

Her father wasn't present for that match, but Joey was.

Opportunity.

Justine's form-fitting protective gloves contained nano programming dispensers, and she injected herself with a full dose of anti-nano preventatives.

Hallock tried to use his size against her. But she was quicker and more agile. She took him down three times, the last time dumping him on his belly and cuffing his hands behind him as a cover so she could jab his wrist to dispense the nanos. He made it easy by fighting the cuffs and chafing his wrists.

Justine finished by kneeling on his back.

"Enough?" she asked.

"Enough," he growled.

She uncuffed him and stood back. He tried one more attack. Her hard blow to his chin didn't knock him out, but he rolled to hands and knees, shaking his head.

"That's enough," Serg said firmly, as Justine flexed her hands, waiting for a new attack, biting her lip at the pain in her left thumb.

Damn! Had she managed to break it *again*? Why had she even bothered to have it fixed if it kept breaking?

Hallock rose slowly and bowed to her, then left the gym without a word, his sycophants following after him.

"You've made a bad enemy," Serg muttered to her.

She laughed despite the throbbing in her hand. "We were already enemies, Serg. Hallock would happily see me either dead or in an indenture lab. Perhaps now he'll have learned a little caution."

"For your sake, I hope you're right. What about your hand?"

Justine shrugged. "It'll be taken care of." At least it was Friday. She had a quick trip to British Columbia already planned. Coral could patch it up.

Serg shook his head and turned to the next set of fighters. Justine grabbed a towel and left the gym, heading for the showers. Leave early today. Discuss programming possibilities with Donald, now that Hallock's nanos were in place. Plan a visit to Donna-gran to pick her brain. Everything was on track for her schemes.

Joey fell in stride next to her.

"You're getting faster than ever, little sister," he said.

"You'd better remember that," she answered, choking at the alcohol on his breath. Sure, it was three in the afternoon on a Friday, but was her damn brother drinking on the job? Probably.

"Oh, I will." He smirked at her before she went into the locker room.

Shanice taped Justine's hand before they left for Donald's.

Despite the lecture she received from Coral, the victory was worth it.

And she and Donald devised a programming strategy. It would take time to establish the protocols, especially given the degree of stealth she needed to discreetly program Hallock. But he would *never* be able to do something like break her thumb again, if she could help it.

AFTER THAT WEEKEND WITH DONALD, JUSTINE MOVED ON TO THE NEXT step—meeting with Raven and Eliot. She invited them to Chicago for the weekend—not to stay in her condo, but in a timeshare two floors below her penthouse. They met in her condo.

"Congratulations, Justine." Eliot kissed her cheek.

"Congratulations." Raven bowed to her.

She waved them over to the table in the living area that doubled as a dinner and meeting place. "Thank you. Coffee? Tea? I've brewed a pot of Lapsang Souchong."

"I've missed our times drinking tea," Eliot said. "Tea for me."

"Tea as well," Raven said.

"So. You two are responsible for my new position in the Group. Thank you very much. But I also assume you have your reasons."

Eliot half-smiled. "It seems that there is an *interesting* alliance against a potential threat to the Group."

"That doesn't involve the Family," Justine said dryly. "Yes. My father was most explicit that—*issues*—affect his ability to terminate Hallock's employment."

"Most explicitly, your father's involvement with the Electric Born," Raven said.

She schooled herself not to react, only arching one brow. "What part? Where they venerate him as next to God, or—other activities tied to his schemes?"

Raven's expression became more solemn. "If Hallock goes public with what he knows—it's not just a threat to Philip but to the Group."

She leaned back in her chair and steepled her fingers. "Hallock gives an opening to elements within the Family that will be problematic for the Group's long-term survival should they manage to dispose of my father. I've heard my cousin Christopher speak about what he would do if he were the Martiniere. I do not agree with him. There are too many dependents within the Family at risk if the Group is taken public."

"You're dedicated to the Group's survival as it is?" Eliot asked.

"Yes. Hallock is a significant threat to the Group's future. Do you really want to see him hold my father's position? What he would do with that power, especially with the Group as a publicly-held corporation—"

It wouldn't happen—she would become the Martiniere herself first. Neither of them needed to know that. Internal Family business.

Both men relaxed.

"Then we're on the same page," Eliot said.

"Yes. So. Let's plan."

By the end of the weekend, they had a strategy. It wasn't going to happen fast—she set a target date of June, 2047, for eliminating Hallock.

Part of that involved things she didn't talk about, like Donald. Dealing with the threat posed by Chris and other renegades within the Family. Their plans depended on no significant changes in the status quo. Which was a reckless assumption.

Three years was a long time to enact a strategy.

But it was what it would take in order to do things correctly—and even then, things could blow up in her face.

She wanted to minimize those possibilities.

January, 2047

Things simmered along for the next two-and-a-half years. Her father's health swung back and forth. Justine defused Chris's rebellion and protected the leaders, but there were other festering currents within the Family.

Donna-gran remained closed-mouthed about sharing technical mind control information with Justine. She had to research her own strategies.

But there were possibilities for implementing them. Raven, as her father's representative, brought the four of them together for private quarterly meetings, in an attempt to mitigate the ongoing battles between Eliot and Hallock. Justine remained outwardly neutral, waiting for her chance to discreetly program Hallock. But Hallock watched her warily and didn't let down his guard.

Which was as she expected. Part of the reason for the three-year-timeline. Meanwhile, she built up her networks both inside and outside the Group.

Opportunity finally arose at their gathering in January of 2047. Hallock came in late; tired, and less watchful than usual—they met in a house located on a sandspit on the Oregon coast, miles away from any airstrip. He drank recklessly and passed out in the living room. Justine, Raven, and Eliot retreated to their separate rooms. She changed into pajamas and waited for an hour. Then she slipped into the living room, ostensibly on her way to the kitchen to fix herself a drink to deal with insomnia.

Hallock snored in his chair, his feet up. Justine cautiously approached him. Delicately placed her spread fingertips on his temples.

"Cold Dish," she murmured, lightly pressing a keyword sequence to activate the nanos she'd injected two and a half years earlier. His eyes snapped open and he stopped snoring, but he didn't move as she finished the programming.

Crude. There were better ways, but they required either psychotropic administration (she wasn't playing with those chemicals), more frequent physical contacts (she wasn't going to do that), or sexual contact (another thing she was *not* going to do). Her grandmother had divulged *that* much.

When she was finished, she stepped back, then continued to the kitchen. Hallock's gaze followed her.

She poured a drink and switched off the kitchen light, leaning against the counter. There was just enough illumination from the outside security lamp for her to see dim shapes, and she was in a dark corner. Justine nursed her drink. Damn, she did not know enough about this process. Had she done it correctly?

It was taking him far too long to start snoring again.

Footsteps.

Hallock was trying to sneak into the kitchen, but she had grown up around Gabie, the king of stealth, and had honed her awareness since then. Justine watched the doorway. As she spotted his burly shape, she fumbled behind her for a knife from the butcher block holder. Damn it, where was the fucking thing? She *thought* she was standing next to the block.

"Oh no you don't, *bitch*," Hallock snarled.

Justine slid away from the corner as he charged toward her, faster than she expected. She threw the remainder of her drink in his face. It didn't slow him down. He slammed her against the refrigerator and she saw momentary bright flashes—a hard hit.

"*Cold Dish*," she gasped. It paused him for the barest of moments.

Then Justine buckled down to the serious business of fighting for her life, because it was clear something had gone wrong, and Hallock intended to kill her.

Throwing what she could at Hallock when they weren't grappling. Screaming for help.

Pain in her knee. Pain in her ribs.

He slammed her head against the counter. Momentary blackness. Her hand fell against that damn knife holder. She yanked one of the knives out and plunged it hard into Hallock's belly, twisting it before reaching for a second knife. He bellowed and slammed her hard against the cupboard. She stabbed at his head, trying for the neck. Light switched on. Eliot yelled. She could *finally* see her target. Justine slashed Hallock's neck as he turned away from her, hitting his windpipe and the veins and arteries.

Hallock went down and Justine collapsed as well.

***

JUSTINE WOKE IN A HOSPITAL BED, HER WRISTS RESTRAINED, VISION BLURRY.

"What the hell?" she croaked as she strained against the cuffs.

Her father stirred. "Legal's working on that. Clearly self-defense, but these damn podunk cops think I'm gonna whisk you away before they get your statement. They're making noises about charging you with attempted murder."

"Self-defense—what the hell happened to Hallock?" She blinked at Daddy-damned-dearest.

A half-puzzled, half-proud expression crossed his face. "He's gone, my dearest darling daughter. Completely out of the picture."

"Oh. But—"

"Shh." Philip held a finger to his lips. "We'll talk later."

Those words, plus the thin-lipped smug smile so common when her father had just won a victory, sent chills through Justine.

AFTER SHE GAVE HER STATEMENT, THE CUFFS WERE REMOVED. ONCE Justine confirmed with the authorities that she was free to go, as long as she made herself available should further questions arise, she checked out of the hospital against medical advice.

Philip, Raven, and Eliot whisked her off to a large house near Eugene, overlooking the McKenzie River. Piotr met them there. Justine realized from the grim expressions on the others' faces that she was facing a deeper interrogation than the cops had given her.

She stuck to the story that she had gone to the kitchen to pour herself a drink, and Hallock attacked her in a drunken stupor. Raven and Eliot accepted that version.

Not so Piotr and her father.

Especially her father.

"All right," he said finally. "Justine and I need to talk. *Alone,*" Philip emphasized, glaring at Piotr.

She closed her eyes and slumped back in her chair as the others left.

"*Frag*—"

"*Lucifer,*" she countered, tiredly. Then she opened her eyes. "You honestly don't think I'd let you do that to me anymore, do you, Daddy-poo?"

He scowled at her. "You gonna talk straight, then? There's more to that story, girl. We all know it. It would take more than alcohol to set Hallock off."

"You think I'm going to talk internal Family secrets around Raven and Eliot?"

His nostrils flared. "So you *did* try to program Hallock."

"Yes." She exhaled. "I gave him a nano injection two and a half years ago, but hadn't had an opening to finish the programming until now."

"You should have taken him to bed and done it sooner."

"*Fuck* no!" she snapped, pain and fatigue sharpening her voice. "I'm *not* one of your goddamned sluts, Daddy-fucking-dearest. I *don't* use sex as a tool, damn it!"

His sigh was tired, not exasperated. "Waiting that long backfired on you. Sex is a quick and dirty way to get your programming done in a safe and timely manner."

"As if anyone would tell me that!" She glared at him. "I had no fucking idea that the nanos were time-dependent. Neither you nor Donna-gran are particularly open about that technology! I had to piece it together from file hints."

Philip pinched the top of his nose, wincing. "You never asked."

"*Would* you have told me before now?"

"Probably not."

"There you have it," she said bitterly. "So. What happened was a reaction to my programming attempt?"

"Unfortunately, yes." Philip eyed her. "Hallock's programming included a violent, automatic response to anyone seeking to modify it. Berserker rage. Damn it, you should have told me this was what you had in mind! Then you wouldn't have ended up like—like—*this*." He gestured at her.

She snorted. "Trust me, it's no worse than what you or Joey ever did to me. That experience is probably how I managed to stay on my feet long enough to kill him—that is what you mean by 'he's gone,' right?"

Her father flinched but his voice remained steady. "Pretty much."

"What the hell do you mean by *that*?"

"He's in a coma and not expected to wake up."

"Then he's out of the picture completely, just as you wanted."

"Not quite the way I wanted it," Philip said. "I didn't want this scandal."

"Even if he does recover, he's out of the picture. Unless people think I was the attacker, not him."

"Not yet," her father said slowly. "Me and Piotr, yes—because what he did was clearly a berserker reaction to programming gone bad. The authorities don't know about it." His face softened. "You screwed up the implementation, but you got the job done. Hallock's gone, and Raven's the new head of External Affairs."

"You got what you wanted." God, she wanted nothing more than to crawl into Donald's arms, where she could feel safe. "Now what? Kick me back out of the Group?"

A half-proud, half-puzzled expression mixed with a smug smirk crossed her father's face.

"Oh, no. If anything, this cements your role as Director of Security." He rose. "But just one more thing, my *darling daughter.* Don't try that programming shit again. You got lucky, and the authorities can be convinced of your drunk story. Next time—may be different." He headed for the door, then turned back. "Take a few weeks off. Give yourself time to recover. Raven needs your assistance in purging the deep Hallock loyalists from External Affairs."

"All right," she said.

She *understood* what her father meant. He didn't have to be explicit.

She was no longer a threat to him. He had managed to circumvent Donald's Little Divorce Present by setting up this situation. She *couldn't* do a damned fucking thing unless she wanted to destroy the Group. And then what?

"Good." He left the room.

JUSTINE STAYED IN EUGENE FOR ANOTHER WEEK, WITH PIOTR, TO DEAL with the legal complications after Hallock's death. Eliot promised to get word discreetly to Donald, since she couldn't legally leave the country.

Piotr brought in a doctor to tend to her injuries.

And then, her last night in Eugene, after the authorities finally cleared her, Donald slipped into her room.

She slept well in Donald's arms that night. Her first good sleep in ages.

Even though the way that Hallock's death happened meant that her father held something on her.

After all, wasn't that what he meant by saying that *this cements your role as Director of Security?*

There wasn't any statute of limitations on murder. She had defeated Hallock—but the true winner was her father. He now controlled her, and he hadn't needed to resort to programming to make it happen.

The best she could hope for was that she had time to wait—and hope that another opening for finally defeating Daddy-damned-dearest would come soon.

21 / INTERLUDE TEN

September, 2086

Silence. Then—

"I did *not* expect *that*," Mike said.

"It was a right royal mess." Justine studied her hands. "Daddy-shit-head-dearest probably hoped that Hallock and I would kill each other. That would have taken care of all his problems in a nice, neat little bundle. Mmm. Probably not Joey."

"Who told you that Hallock was dead?" Deontae asked.

"The police. Hallock's care had been taken over by Martiniere medical staff, and my father told them." Justine frowned. "I suppose that meant Daddy-poo gave him to Heaven's Reach."

"It was buried very well, then," Gabie said. *"There wasn't one hint of Hallock's presence when I led the destruction of Heaven's Reach at North Fork."*

"North Fork was the most public of their sites," Lily said. *"Unfortunately, I don't know where they are. Philip was very careful to lock off certain memories from me."*

"Could Donald give us a location for Hallock's physical body, once he's free?" Mike stroked his chin, biting his lower lip. "Dealing with this threat needs to be two-pronged. First, the digi aspects—freeing

Donald and identifying the digi forms coming from Heaven's Reach. Second, eliminating the physical presence of Heaven's Reach and those labs. The fight won't stop until both are accomplished."

"We won't know for certain until we have Donald," Deontae said. "We'd best get a strike force ready, Mike. Swait Secure and Vygotsky together."

"Do you feel up to working on your part of that, Justine?" Mike asked.

"It's necessary," she said. "I'll be able to do it."

PHYSICAL FATIGUE DROVE JUSTINE TO BED RIGHT AFTER DINNER. HER thoughts still raced, and she tried to focus on a book. Activating audio didn't work, either. She ended up backtracking because she would startle, then realize that she was thinking through potential scenarios for freeing Donald and eliminating Heaven's Reach rather than listening.

But her brain wouldn't let her sleep, no matter how tired her body was.

Justine turned onto her back and sighed. "Damn it."

A digi presence roiled nearby. Familiar. Gabie.

"Talk to me, Gabie. I can't sleep."

He manifested at the foot of her bed. *"Nervous about tomorrow?"*

"Unless I've made a mistake as bad as the one that put me under Daddy-damned-dearest's thumb again, we've devised a strategy that will free Donald. I'm just not certain of the cost in lives when we confront Heaven's Reach physically. From your experience, it's going to be a damned bloody mess."

"Damned bloody mess is an accurate description of what happened at Heaven's Reach," Gabie said. He moved closer to Justine, sitting on the side of the bed. *"But talking further about that isn't going to change much. I have questions. I don't understand why Donna-gran wouldn't help you. I know why our father wouldn't. But our grandmother?"*

"Our grandmother was fucking complex, and to some degree

complicit in the actions of our father, Gabie. She never told me *why* she wouldn't train me. Evasion upon evasion. Just like our fucking father."

"I've had—questions about Donna-gran's loyalties over the years. The anti-aging serum. What it took to make that—the deaths of indentured women to create it. She did end up supporting us—but she could have so easily gone the other way."

"I know." Justine shrugged. "I have my suspicions about Donna-gran and her motives. At one point she told me I was becoming too much like *him*—but that was *after* the confrontation with Hallock. She took a lot of secrets to her grave, including her complicity in the continuing development of mind control."

Gabie nodded. *"I don't know about Donna-gran. But her perception that you were becoming like our father—that was one reason why I was so fucking nervous about you and Ruby talking when you met. All I knew was that you had become Philip's enforcer. I feared that you had become his agent without reservation."*

"No. I wasn't. But it was useful to let Serg spread that general impression. Your reappearance meant I was able to *act*, finally." She shuddered. "2047 to 2059. Twelve years where I danced to his tune. Daddy-shithead-dearest was right about one thing. Eliminating Hallock *should* have been much more discreet."

"It would have still been self-defense, Tine."

She shook her head. "Not in that jurisdiction, not in that era. Third-degree murder at best, possibly even first-degree. Donald's legal staff investigated. Electric Born-sympathetic prosecutors. Cutting Hallock's throat crossed the line. He was turning away from me. I could have escaped. I chose not to."

"Aw, shit."

"I went to Remy Trask, after she cleared Ruby from killing Joey when he hit you with that weaponized G9 injection. Part of the maneuvering before you became the Martiniere. We set up a strategy *should* Daddy-damn-dearest have come after me."

"Thank God for Remy's legal mind and experience."

Another shiver. "Yes. But Hallock was only the first death—if he actually died then—by my own hand. Too damn many others after that. How the hell could you handle the killing with Alvarez Armory, Gabie?"

A pause. *"That part is hidden from me. Gabe—the living me who wrote my base algorithm—locked up certain files from his digital clone. I know that things like beating up that asshole who attacked Brandon happened. I can't access my feelings and rationale for doing it. Just like I can't access my feelings about the massacre at Heaven's Reach."*

She snorted. "Witnessing that beating was enough to scare Serg, Gabie."

"He wasn't worried about you, after Hallock?"

Justine considered. "I don't think so. Piotr was righteously pissed when he realized I didn't know about the berserker trigger." She rubbed her eyes. "And the other deaths? Part of security actions. But they were enough to worry Daddy-damn-dearest. Especially during that confrontation after you revealed yourself when you and Ruby joined with Jeff Swait to win the AgSuperhero."

"That was damned fucking scary. Gabe did allow me to access that memory in full."

Justine raised her brows. A second mention of living Gabie being different from digi Gabie, in the same conversation. Gabie didn't usually speak of his past living self as an entirely separate being. What did that mean? Some emotions and memories were locked off from his digi—why? Did she dare ask?

"I was scared shitless. Taking your side meant an open break with Daddy-poo. But before you revealed yourself, I was a few steps away from bringing everything down, just to get myself free. Even if I died in the process."

"You've said that to me before."

"Donald did his best to keep me from going off. I was—on the brink of staging a dramatic suicidal action by 2059." She laughed bitterly. "That confrontation with Joey and Daddy-damned-dearest after you and Ruby and Jeff won the Superhero? I was *so close* to killing them right then and there. Perfect setup—except that the angles were all wrong, and Daddy-fucking-dearest and fucking Joey would not have been the only victims. That—and *only* that—was what stopped me. You were still an unknown quantity. Thirty years gone—I didn't know who you were by then."

Gabie closed his eyes briefly and shuddered before opening them again. *"Aw, shit, Tine. It was the same for me. When I saw you, I didn't know if I was facing Philip's enforcer or my beloved cousin—now sister."*

She sniffled. "I guess it stands to reason that our stone-cold killer of a father spawned offspring with the same ruthlessness about killing."

"Don't go there, Tine. Don't." Gabie's lips curled in contempt. *"The fucker put us in that position. Look at Mike. His clone. He's not like our father."*

"Mike can be pretty damn ruthless when necessary."

"Only when he's backed into a corner. Not the same as our father." Gabie shook his head. *"God. I thought I had it rough, little sister. But you had it worst of all. I couldn't have lasted as long as you did. Hell, I didn't last as long as you did."*

A dry chuckle escaped her. "And you want me to become a digi. Knowing that I can be a killer."

"I want you to become a digi because of your knowledge and experience." Gabie scowled. *"If we don't regulate ourselves, then the living will do it for us. Even more—the genie of mind control programming is still out there, Tine. Sooner or later, someone will rediscover the techniques. Keeping it within the Family and the Group provided some means of control over that technology. Now, with digis—"* he shrugged. *"Mind control and digis are linked. It will take digis to control and stop it. That's why I want you and Donald as digis."*

"That's a lot of faith in me."

"You've more than demonstrated your competence."

"I hope you're right." She turned on her side. "I think I can sleep now."

"Rest well. Tomorrow—begins the first real digi war."

And that was what she feared. The thought was almost enough to spur more wakefulness, except that Gabie murmured some words she didn't quite understand.

God damn it, Gabie, you're influencing me! How the hell did you get that power? When you were poking around in my brain?

Part of her wanted to fight that influence. But another part welcomed it, because it was quite possibly the only way that she could manage to get some sleep.

She would take up the issue of digi mind control influence with Gabie later.

JUSTINE DREAMED ABOUT THE FIRST TRIP SHE AND DONALD MADE TO THE Double R together, in April 2059, shortly after the airstrip had been finished. Detailed, memory unfolding just like it had happened, with no dream logic or extra additions.

A blustery April afternoon, storms bouncing the plane all the way from Portland to the Double R. Justine and Donald held hands and discussed their future during that short, tense flight—appearing in public together, timing, and choreography.

"The ranch is a safe place," she told him.

"Good. Because—oh my falcon, I have so missed you."

"Me as well. I just wish we could go public now."

"August, my falcon, August. At the Real Truther convention."

Justine understood, even though the delay frustrated her. He was still collecting information from the Real Truther networks. All the same, she wanted Donald in her public life again.

"Soon, my love, soon," Donald kept saying.

They worked hard once they got to the ranch, Donald advising Gabie on finance and programming, Justine and Serg upgrading security structures to Martiniere quality. But there were brief moments when one pressed against the other quickly, tiny brushes of hands, even a couple of instances where they stopped in the hallway and held each other for a few breaths. Physical contact with Donald was part of her visits to British Columbia, but it didn't feel like *this*. Even when they cuddled in BC, both of them still held something back. Protecting themselves from further injuries.

Not now. No more barriers. No more reserve.

They fell asleep in the living room after dinner, entwined together, while watching a movie with Gabie and Ruby. Gabie shook them awake.

"It's like old times," Donald murmured to Justine as she stirred from sleep. He nuzzled her temples and forehead, placing little butterfly kisses on her eyelids.

Justine kissed him back, seeking a long-lost unity. He didn't carry her upstairs—too frail for that anymore—but once they were in their room, it was as if the years apart had evaporated. She still didn't experience arousal, but the warm firmness of Donald's hands caressing her body, his familiar citrusy scent, *him* inside of her—it felt so right, like coming home after a long exile. Becoming *herself* again, not the porcelain-perfect shell she had maintained for years.

"I'm so tired of hiding ourselves," she whispered afterward.

"Soon, my love, soon."

Justine stirred awake, the memory lingering with that additional sense that Donald's digi had whispered those words to her.

Soon, my love, soon.

A message from Donald? She hoped so. It wouldn't be like that marvelous time after Gabie had become the Martiniere, this interaction being strictly between digi and living being—

Until she died and became a digi.

Justine contemplated the algorithm activation file that Gabie had sent her.

Then she pulled up the file and toggled the link. Watched the algorithm create her waiting digi.

For better or for worse, she was committed now.

For eternity, Donald, she thought.

Now she just needed to free him so they would be together.

22 / ENDINGS AND BEGINNINGS

SEPTEMBER, 2086

THEY ASSEMBLED IN MIKE'S OFFICE, WHERE THE HOSPITAL BED WAS located.

Mike nodded toward it. "You take the bed, Justine."

"Why? I'm not an invalid."

"You *are* the frailest member of our team."

"And you aren't?" She didn't *like* being treated like a piece of hand-blown glass.

"You have the keys to freeing Donald," Mike said.

He had her there. At least he wasn't using tones to force the issue.

"All right, all right," she grumbled. "We could have done this in my bedroom if you're gonna make me do this in bed."

"You might as well be comfortable," Mike said. "Should have put this bed in your room in the first place."

"I am *not* that fucking fragile, *Michael*," Justine muttered.

"No, but it makes me feel better for you to be in that bed."

He sprawled on the loveseat with JoAnn next to him, her arm around his shoulders, Spot in his lap, Smudgie on the side opposite from JoAnn.

"Up until a week or so ago, you were the one who needed it," she retorted.

"Now it's your turn," Mike said, rolling his eyes. But he suddenly grinned at Justine, and she realized that the banter had distracted her.

On purpose? Probably. Most people underestimated the degree to which Mike analyzed and managed them.

Including her.

Deontae nudged Justine. "Here's your gloves."

He crawled onto the bed next to Justine. *The more physical contact between actors and supporters, the better,* they had decided, based on what they had learned while extracting Brandon's digi from captivity. Supporters not only watched over the vitals of the living persons in digital, but their presence added emotional strength to the actors.

"You comfortable?" D asked. "Because you're in the driver's seat for this."

"Yes." Justine drew in a deep breath. "Are we ready?"

"We are," Mike said. JoAnn held him, her expression tight and worried. Smudgie and Spot mirrored the tension, their ears flattened, focusing on Mike, Spot occasionally whimpering. Brandon and Ruby's digis flanked them.

"I'm ready." D wrapped his arms around her waist, turning her slightly so that her hands were free to access the files. Lily and Gabie pressed close.

"Here goes." Justine snapped up the file folder projection.

JSM—Private—DSA. Green lettering against a black background. No lock on the folder itself, which held five numbered files—*DSA 1, 2, 3, 4, & 5.* Each file with a creation date of September 2073, five days in order, made shortly after Gabie's death.

Justine took a deep breath and reached for *DSA-1.*

This lock was formatted in a similar manner to the challenges created to keep Donald's worm from trashing the Martiniere databases. Easy-peasy. She put the opened file in the secure vault she had made for Donald yesterday, just like the vaults that protected the other digis' core files.

First activation link accomplished.

Next file. Something blanked the link before she could input the full response.

She grabbed for it, grateful to have digigloves so that she could reach right into digital. And *these* gloves were so much faster than her regular ones, with more options.

The prompt tried to kick Justine out and lock the file against her. The ejection attempt would have succeeded with her old digigloves. But the supergloves stuck firmly to the prompt, as if glued. The prompt stabilized, and she caught a flicker of Donald's presence holding it steady as she entered the code.

Good.

She opened the file and secured it. Two files down. Three more to go. She had a small whisper of Donald. From the feel of these files, the algorithm that Donald created was completely different from the ones that Gabie and Philip had made.

At least three digi types, then—four, if Hallock's digi is a different variant.

Next file. This one required full identity authentication.

"*Don't touch it yet!*" Lily snapped as Justine leaned forward to comply with the ID request, habit overruling caution.

"*Do you sense something?*" Gabie asked.

"*Aunt Justine should have gone through this challenge with the first file. I don't trust it.*" Lily tapped her chin thoughtfully. "*It's the sort of trap that Philip's digi used to create.*"

"Do we need to reauthenticate the first two files?" Deontae asked.

"*I'm not certain. Let me check this scanner,*" Lily said.

"I'll check the first two files in Donald's vault," Justine said, nerves tight. Damn it, if she needed to recreate the fucking vault because those files were corrupted—more fucking delays to the process of restoring Donald if she had to rebuild it.

"*Open the vault and let me look,*" Gabie said. "*Don't risk yourself, Tine!*"

"*I'm with you, Gabe,*" Mike said, as his digi self.

"*I'll back you up, Lily,*" Brandon said. "*I remember those traps.*"

"*Ruby, keep an eye on things here!*" Gabie snapped.

The digis went to work. Colorful flashes of them in their pure digital forms reassured Justine that *some* progress occurred—Ruby a magenta red sheet, hovering protectively over Mike's body as he went limp. The others were threads—Gabie bright green, Brandon dark purple, Lily shimmering gold, Mike dark blue.

A lighter blue thread reminiscent of Donald's eyes flashed while Mike and Gabie worked in the vault. Was that Donald or someone else?

Then dark blue and bright green returned, dark blue merging with Mike's body. He opened his eyes.

"Those files are all right," he said. "They're consolidating like they're supposed to. Donald's partially there. Gabe's joined Lily and Brandon in checking out the scanner. Whew. That's tiring work."

"*Mike,*" Gabie said. "*Need you to do this in body. Have your digi ready to protect you, and gently touch that scanner with a fingertip. A single fingertip.*"

"All right." Mike pushed himself up carefully, swaying as he stood. JoAnn steadied him as he slowly walked over to the scanner. "Jo. Don't have your hands on me when I touch the scanner. Not safe for you."

"Got it."

Mike delicately brushed his left index finger across the scanner. Bright white light flared and he jerked his finger away with a yelp. Smudgie and Spot whimpered as he staggered back against JoAnn, keeping his left hand away from her. Dark blue threads roiled around his fingertip.

Ruby formed a containment bubble. She tossed it at the ball of dark blue pulsing around a brighter white light. The light faded as the bubble enclosed it. Ruby stashed it.

JoAnn dragged Mike toward the loveseat. The dogs moved away as JoAnn and Mike collapsed, then crowded in close, Smudgie licking Mike's left hand.

"Is Mike all right?" Justine started to get up, but Deontae held her firmly.

"Don't. Just in case it's a trap," he murmured.

"I'm—okay," Mike gasped. "Just—wobbly. Hard—zap."

Spot scrambled over JoAnn to Mike's lap. She rested her front paws on his chest and licked his face until he started laughing.

"Down, Spot, *down.*" The pup settled in JoAnn's lap, dropping her head on Mike's thigh and gazing up at him. Mike exhaled slowly, rubbing both dogs' heads.

Then he straightened up. "All right. What's the deal with the scanner?" His voice was brighter, firmer.

"*It's a trap,*" Lily said. "*When you put your face to the scanner for the retina ID, it grabs your face. Immobilizes and paralyzes living beings. Destroys digis.*"

"*Donald created a biometric access for you and your codes, Justine, which means you shouldn't face anything other than your standard unlocking challenge,*" Gabie said. "*Proceed with caution. Consider any scanner to be a snare. You already have the necessary codes to unlock his files.*"

"Got it," she muttered.

The prompt faded as Justine entered her codes. She snapped her fingers and grabbed it. It twisted and tried to pull away, but the sticky supergloves held it firm. That sky-blue thread the same shade as Donald's eyes twined around the prompt, holding it stable while she entered her codes. She opened the file and secured it.

"*Almost there,*" Donald's voice whispered to her. "*The next two will be the most difficult. Hallock may manifest. I've been masking you, but that false scanner's destruction will have triggered him.*"

"Understood," Justine said. She repeated Donald's warning for the others.

The digis vibrated with nervous energy, projecting strong enough to make the fine hair stand up on the uncovered portion of Justine's forearms.

"*May I overlay your arms, Aunt Justine?*" Lily asked. "*It might give me a nanosecond jump in response. Maybe more.*"

"*That's a good idea,*" Gabie said. "*I think you should move into her lap, Lily. Bran, Rubes, you probably should do the same with Mike. D, may I plant myself on your side?*"

"Go right on ahead," D said. "Anything to give us an advantage."

Justine extracted *DSA-4* from the folder. As she called up the unlocking prompt, something clobbered her, *hard*. Bright lights flashed and the world wobbled around her, just as if she had received a physical blow instead of digital.

"Oh no you don't," Gabie growled, grabbing at a shape Justine couldn't see.

"Let me use your hands!" Lily screeched as D yelped.

Justine went limp. Her hands reached up next to D's head. They closed on a gray, cylinder-shaped form that solidified as she held it. Mike's dark blue threads snaked out and wrapped around the gold overlay shimmering on Justine's hands.

The cylinder tried to yank away. Justine tightened her fingers on it. Green—*Gabie*—covered D's hands and he seized the tube as well. It writhed in their grip, whipping around hard enough to make Justine's arms ache. She gasped for breath as pain radiated throughout her body.

Spot bounded onto the bed, growling. Smudgie followed.

"No!" JoAnn yelled, holding Mike tight. "Smudgie, no! Back here!"

Spot snarled, then grabbed the free end of the cylinder with her teeth and shook it hard. Her front paws flailed at it, tearing off chunks and flinging them to the floor. Smudgie jumped on the pieces, ripping them into shreds.

The cylinder crumbled. Lily gathered up the pieces, shoving them into another of Ruby's containment bubbles. Justine sagged against Deontae, both of them sweat-dampened.

"You all right, D?" Her voice quavered.

"That was a hard hit," he muttered. "You okay?"

"Yep." Fatigue pulled at her and she *hurt*, but she would *not* yield to her body. She had a job to do.

Justine inhaled unsteadily and pulled up the prompt once more. No more resistance as she opened the file and stashed it in the vault.

"I think a dose of Liquid Protein all around is a good idea before we take on this last file," JoAnn said.

She collected a handful of tubes from the pile on the desk, passed two to Mike, then brought a tube each to D and Justine before sucking one down herself. Mike administered half a tube each to the dogs, then drank his.

Justine felt better after drinking the contents. "Any idea what that cylinder was?"

"It felt like that Hallock presence," D said.

"Yes," Lily said. *"Hallock's digi taking another form."*

"He may be weakened," Gabie said. *"It's easier to take a shape like that when a digi's not at full strength."*

"I wouldn't count on that," Brandon said. *"It can also be a means for concentrating and channeling strength for an attack. That cylinder was pretty damn strong."*

"Concentration of power, true. But will Hallock have much energy left after the dogs ripped his projection up?" Ruby asked.

"Hopefully not, if we move quickly," Gabe said. *"Taking that shape can be a means for Hallock to channel energy toward protecting this last file. We're almost all the way there. He'll have to stop us this time."*

Justine flexed her fingers. "All right, then. Let's do this last one."

She reached for *DSA-5.* As her fingertips touched the files, dark maroon-colored cuffs clamped down on her wrists. She couldn't move her hands or fingers.

"What the hell—?" She strained against them. The cuffs pulled her arms out straight, tugging hard so she couldn't even bend her elbows.

Hallock's digi materialized, his outline the same shade as the cuffs. *"Let's see you try to break free from this!"* he chortled as he reached for her chest, fingers elongating and skeletal. Red zigzags pulsed over his gray, claw-like fingers.

D rolled onto Justine to protect her. Gabie, Brandon, and Mike's digi wrestled with Hallock, trying to keep *those hands* away from her, but he threw them off.

His fingers touched her left shoulder.

Everything went black, pain radiating from her chest to fingertips and toes. Justine struggled for air, trying to drag in deep, whooping gulps of oxygen.

Nothing.

Panic rose despite her attempts to banish it.

Oh God, am I dying?

She *couldn't* die, not before freeing Donald!

The agony intensified. No breath to scream with. Bright lights flashing around her. Flying down a narrow, white tunnel. Loud cackling from Hallock.

"I told you I would make your death hurt! And with those cuffs on, your digi will be my captive, just like your ex's digi is!"

There had to be a way to fight this.

There had to be a way.

Donald. Please. Donald.

A Donald-shaped thought popped into her consciousness. Cuffs. If she could only get rid of those cuffs!

Justine forced herself to relax. The cuffs stopped tugging and she paused midway through that narrow tunnel. Her fingers traced what she could reach of the cuffs, seeking a locking mechanism. Something to release the damn things!

Keypad!

Letters or numbers?

Letters. She felt them. A small but standard keyboard. What should she type?

FE—For eternity.

The cuffs' grip eased slightly.

Oh God, Donald managed to hack Hallock!

RA—Rescue Angel.

More slack, but not enough for her to slip free.

GH—Greg Hallock.

There! She yanked her hands out of the cuffs.

Something exploded open, dazzling her with its intensity.

Arms around her, *familiar, friendly* arms.

"Thank God you activated your digi," Donald murmured. *"Otherwise we would be trapped."*

"Am I dead?" she asked.

"You would have been. And the battle isn't over yet."

"Mike needs to know the physical location so he can send a unit to eliminate Hallock."

"We'll get to that. Other things have to happen first." Donald pulled her down that narrow white tunnel in the opposite direction, back into chaos. *"Need to get my last file into the vault to complete my final activation,"* he said. *"You have to be back in body to finish it. And getting you there...."*

Hallock's form solidified in front of them. *"You have to go through me first."*

"With pleasure, motherfucker," she growled at him.

He smirked. *"Choose your weapon. Any weapon."* A sword manifested in his hand.

Justine sneered.

The capability to materialize any weapon and you choose that? Fool!

She chose one of her favorite weapons, the lightweight SPA-29 automatic rifle with explosive bullets.

"Not fair!" he bellowed before she pulled the trigger, guiding it up and down his form until nothing bigger than her crooked thumb remained.

"I'm a Martiniere," she said to the tiny shards that the other digis gathered up. *"We don't play fair."*

"Enough," Donald said. *"We have to get your digi back in body and revive you sufficiently to finish inputting the code."*

"All right." But she dreaded the prospect. Just how much was this going to hurt? She was so tired of hurting. *So done* with it.

He kissed her forehead. *"I'm here with you, my falcon. Hurry!"*

Observing her still body as Deontae performed chest compressions was an odd experience. JoAnn restrained Mike as the dogs fussed around him. Justine couldn't hear anything as she and Donald hovered over her physical self.

"I've done this before," Gabie said. *"Let me help."*

He and Donald turned her digi to match her body, then *pushed.*

Bright flashes around her as she smacked into her body with a jolt.

Numb hands and arms. Her chest *hurt.* Sweat from Deontae's face dripped on her as he worked.

"Come on, Justine, come *on,* lady. Come back to us," D kept reciting.

She inhaled, a deep sobbing breath that sent white-hot jabs of pain throughout her body. Her eyes popped open as Deontae hesitated before the next compression.

"Hi there, sir," she croaked.

His eyes widened. "You're back!"

Justine forced her fingers to type the last set of access codes.

Another bright explosion. Agony. Burning. Shoving her way through hot lava to grasp that file.

"You can do this, my falcon, my dearest love. You can do it."

Donald's digital arms around her provided relief. She clutched the file tight, dragging it behind her toward that vault. The other four had been *so easy* to flick over.

At last she reached the vault. Shoved the file in. Typed the codes to secure it.

Oblivion. But Donald's arms were more solid than ever as everything faded, except for faint, dismayed cries from Mike, JoAnn, and Deontae.

TIRED. SO DAMN TIRED. AND EVERYTHING *HURT*. THIS FELT WORSE THAN anything else she had gone through; beatings, broken thumb, hysterectomy, that one bad fall with Glory.

But there was a *presence* with her, solid and familiar, nestled into her side as she lay on her back. Faint beeps and chirps from monitors.

She coughed. "Looks like I didn't die," she croaked.

"Touch and go there for a while, darling," Donald said. *"You almost joined me."*

Justine blinked. Oxygen cannula in her nose. Tube in her arm. Monitors everywhere. Definitely *not* at the Double R. Lakeside Memorial or another hospital?

And Donald—

His digi expanded from the small tight curl against her side to his full size.

She drew a deep breath. "So I wasn't imagining that I was dying."

Donald stroked her cheek. *"If Hallock hadn't been so obsessed with making you suffer instead of finishing you quickly, you would have been dead, dear one. He stopped your heart."*

Justine closed her eyes, leaning into the hand he rested on her cheek. So close to real. So damned close. But it lacked the heat of a living being.

"How long has it been?"

"Four days. You had a heart attack, dearest. Caused by Hallock." Donald wrapped his arms around her. *"Gabe and I kept your digi stable in your body. I've worked on the algorithm, upgraded his programming, implemented improvements in the other digis."* A pause. *"I'm letting everyone know you're awake. Prepare yourself."*

"Do we have to?" she groaned.

"Dear one, I promised. I'm here to monitor you and I'll kick people out if it gets to be too much. But in return for just me here with you, you have to go through short visits from Deontae, Mike, JoAnn, and Ron. You scared them. They need to know that you're back."

She took a deep breath. "All right, then."

"I'M GOING DIGI, TOO," DEONTAE TOLD HER. "TALKED TO DONALD AND Gabe about it. And Mike." He swallowed hard. "After that fight with Hallock, and then the reports from Mike's squads that cleaned out what remains of Heaven's Reach—we may have taken care of that branch, but that doesn't mean we're safe, or that it's gone completely. We need strong digis on our side, because the digi revolution is coming. Donald and Gabe are recruiting the Families *hard*. Mine as well as yours."

The digi revolution is coming.

That made Justine quiver a little, even as Donald (choosing to make himself invisible, but still a strong presence) held her tight.

"I'VE MADE A DIGI ALGORITHM WITH DONALD'S HELP," RON SAID A couple of hours later, the next hospital visitor. His jaw jutted firmly, so much like Ruby's. "Yeah, I'm young. But after all this—" he waved one hand. "It's necessary for us, the good guys, to have a strong force. Stuff can happen." Tears glimmered in his eyes. "Like what happened to my dad. I'm going to be the first Black Martiniere. That makes me a target. Having a digi—and making it known—is one protection."

"LOOKS LIKE YOU'VE PROVIDED A RECRUITMENT EXAMPLE," MIKE SAID. "Donald's algorithm seems to be better for digis created while the subject is living—and he's been pretty persuasive about pointing to your choice and how it saved you."

"That wasn't my intent," she said.

"Might not have been—but once again, you've managed to come up with a fix for a problem."

She sighed. Fixer for the Martinieres. Even in her brief dying.

"*YOU ALL RIGHT?*" DONALD ASKED THAT NIGHT.

She sighed. "Just—thinking about everything. An eternity of fixing things ahead of me. God. It feels like the weight of the world."

"*You're not alone,*" he murmured. "*We're doing this together, my dear.*"

"WE'RE MOVING INTO MOONDANCE WITH YOU FOR THE TIME BEING," MIKE announced the day before she was released from the hospital. "You need help with your physical therapy, it's mostly one level, and you need family there besides Ron. Just—in case."

"Bullshit," Justine snapped at him. "Ron and I have staff. We'll be *fine.* You have responsibilities at the Double R, including your horse training."

Mike snorted. "It's a done deal, Justine. Starlight and the two geldings I'm taking to the spring shows are already at Moondance. Easy-peasy. Everything else is covered."

"What the hell? No arena. Minimal stabling. And where are you storing hay?"

"It's *already done,* Justine." Mike's jaw jutted stubbornly, reminiscent of Ruby digging in her heels. "Gabe and Ruby helped me organize the logistics. All three of those horses can use hacking out on the trails. Conditioning."

"You did this without consulting with me first!" She scowled at Mike.

He met her with a matching glare, closer than ever to Gabie's fabled *The-Martiniere-Has-Spoken* glower.

"Feel like staying here for a while? That's the other option. The doctors won't release you to the Double R. Moondance is an acceptable alternative, because I've set it up to replicate a cardiac ICU."

"Damn it." She was too tired to continue this argument. "Mike, I don't want to be babied. Or hovered over. Donald's digi is enough company for me."

"You're not going to be babied or hovered over," Mike said. "There's a pragmatic reason for the two of us being together at Moondance. Dr. Pramula and my other doctors are itching to study your recovery, see how it differs from mine. We *are* the only living survivors of digi attacks. Having both of us at Moondance makes access easier. And while I'm young age-wise, biologically I'm also an elder. They want to see if there's any significant difference between a cyborged, cloned individual like me, and a non-cyborged, original individual like you. And given that biologically—" he hesitated.

"Biologically, you're my father's clone, so the relationship is useful for study."

"Exactly," Mike said. "You'll have more privacy in your suite at Moondance. Still be monitored, but you can look out your slider window. Even go out on the deck. It'll be quieter than the hospital. I've had your suite set up with privacy barriers. No one is gonna hover."

"Mike speaks for himself," Donald said. *"I'm planning to hover over you, my dear. Now that I can."* He had made his digi invisible to all but Justine, and rested his hand on hers.

She squeezed Donald's hand. "I'm not gonna win this fight, am I, Mikey?"

He smiled, tight-lipped. "I've been in your position. Honestly, I'm just trying to make it easier for you." Mike swallowed hard. "We don't know how well you'll recover from your heart attack. This may be a permanent situation."

"That *permanent situation* language doesn't sound good," Justine said.

"You have different challenges from me. We can't cyborg your heart, for one thing." Mike said. "Age, for another. This attack—" he shook his head. "It *will* shorten your life. And I—I'd like to keep you alive. Not just for Ron's sake, but for mine." His voice quavered. "Yeah, you've activated your digi and a form of you will be available in digital after you die. That kept you from dying in the first place. But I've lost too many close family members to sudden death. Gabe. Ruby. Brandon. Even Lily."

He sighed before continuing. "You're my remaining senior close family member present in body. I—want to be with you because, honestly? Personalities can change and become more intense in digi. There are still things I can learn from you—*you*, not your digi, Justine."

What could she say to that? Nothing, really.

She was still needed—by Mike, of all people.

THE NEXT DAY EMPHASIZED THAT SHE WAS SEVENTY-SEVEN YEARS OLD, AND in worse shape than her father had been at the same age. Wheelchair-bound. Maybe she would walk again, maybe not. Her years of training and conditioning had helped her survive that damn attack from Hallock, but—no getting around the fact that she had briefly died.

Fatigue that grabbed her after only a few steps. Muscles that spasmed without warning. Heart that periodically started pounding hard for no logical reason.

As a result, Justine was content to rest in her bed once settled in her suite. She lay on her side, gazing out the slider window at the late September afternoon, the faint haze from the dust of harvest vehicles obscuring the horizon, except for a massive wall of dark blue clouds beyond them hinting at an incoming storm.

Donald's digi snuggled behind her, arm thrown over her as he rested his head against hers. There was just enough weight in his touch to reassure her of his presence without being too much pressure on her aching body. And no warmth, of course.

Something very like the man she had loved was there, however, and that was more joy than she had words to describe. She was happy to revel in Donald's presence.

Together again. And one of these days—

She wasn't that eager to leave life just yet, in spite of being tired and in pain. There were things to do. They might have defeated Hallock and Hawkins, but digi beings were definitely out in the world. There were other, non-Martiniere digis to monitor. Regulations to create.

And as one of the first two living beings who also walked in digi form, Justine needed to be part of that process. Needed to be a witness to what uncontrolled digis could do to living beings. Needed to help the new digis tied to bodies understand their strengths and limitations.

But for now, she was glad just to be in the moment with Donald.

Soon enough, it would be time to embark on fixing this new situation—for how long? Eternity? She hoped not. But beyond her body's death, for certain. Justine sighed.

"You all right?" Donald asked.

"Just completely and totally tired out," she said.

"I still remember those days," he said. *"I didn't lock them out of my algorithm."*

"Thinking about all I need to do once I become a digi."

His lips brushed her cheek. *"Savor life while you can. Record all the experiences that are possible. I'm grateful for the hints that Gabe gave me, because I chronicled as much as I could from those last six months of life and added them to my file. Yes, there was pain. Agony. But those memories of the process of dying gave me a stronger connection to life."*

"That's hard to believe." Justine paused. "And I'm surprised that you didn't share that knowledge about the existence of digis with me then."

"I didn't tell you about the possibility of becoming a digital clone, because Gabe wasn't active and I didn't know if my efforts would succeed. I didn't want to get your hopes up. But it was on my mind at the end—why I asked you to say vows that last day. I hoped to tie my awakening to that link."

"It still hurts that you didn't share the possibility with me."

"I was dying. Not exactly rational. It took all the strength I had to create those final links." He hugged her. *"And the memory of you holding me*

during the last hours, saying those vows with me—oh, my dear, you don't know how much that helped me connect to you. How I clung to that memory during the transition. I've not talked much to Gabe or Ruby about the differences, much less Brandon, but—sudden death leads to disorientation for a while. The memory of your presence while I was dying made transition to digi life much easier."

"Is that why you couldn't respond to me right away? Transition? How long does it take?"

"We won't know for certain without more data. Once you're better, I'll talk to the others."

Her heart started racing again and she tensed. Donald rested a hand on her neck, checking her pulse. Then he eased over her so that he faced her, pulling Justine into his chest.

"Easy," he murmured. *"Easy. Right now, you need to focus on fixing yourself, not the rest of the world. Rest. Relax."*

She gulped as the spell passed and her heart stopped pounding. "I'm not sure I know how to do that. Fix myself, that is."

Donald laughed softly. *"Then it's a damned good thing I've come back from beyond the grave, so I can nag you into learning how to fix yourself first, love. You've always been pretty bad about that."*

"Doesn't look like I have much of a choice now, do I?"

"Better you learn it now than when you're in transition. You don't want to run your charge down to nothing. Self-care is also important for a digi. I recharge when you're sleeping—a skill I'm still developing. Gabe's helping me with that."

"I see," Justine said slowly. She felt sleepy again, gazing out at the distant golden glow of grain fields and harvest dust, and the dark blue frame of storm clouds beyond the glow.

So much to learn. So much to do.

But for now, resting. Healing. Reflecting on her mortality—which was something completely different from what she expected.

Soon enough, she'd be called to fix things.

Fixer for the Martinieres, that's me. In perpetuity, it seems.

On the other hand, one could have a worse legacy than this.

THE END

ACKNOWLEDGMENTS

First of all, many thanks to Greg Hallock, who asked when I was going to make him a villain and kill him off in one of my books. So I did, and has he *ever* become a villain in the lore of the Martiniere Legacy.

As always, my thanks to Phyllis Irene Radford, my hardworking editor.

Meanwhile, here we still are, in the world of Covid. Many thanks to my husband, Lew, and my horse, Mocha, for keeping me sane and my focus away from reacting to politics.

Like what you've read? Want to follow Joyce either through her monthly newsletter or through an email feed of her irregular blog posts?

Sign up for Joyce's newsletter here:

https://tinyletter.com/JoyceReynolds-Ward

The Martiniere Legacy has its own Substack these days, and the current (and possibly final) book in the Legacy, *Repairing the Legacy*, about Ruby and Gabe's remarriage, is currently being serialized there, through mid-2022.

Additional Martiniere Legacy material will also be published there.

https://joycef1d.substack.com/

BOOKS AND PUBLICATIONS

The Martiniere Legacy

First Meetings: A Martiniere Legacy Short Story

Inheritance: The Martiniere Legacy Book One

Ascendant: The Martiniere Legacy Book Two

Realization: The Martiniere Legacy Book Three

A Belated Christmas Honeymoon: A Martiniere Legacy Short Story

The Enduring Legacy: The Martiniere Legacy Book Four

The People of the Martiniere Legacy

The Heritage of Michael Martiniere: A Martiniere Legacy Novel

Broken Angel: The Lost Years of Gabriel Martiniere: A Martiniere Legacy Novel

Justine Fixes Everything: Reflections on Mortality

The Martiniere Multiverse Books

A Different Life—What If?

A Different Life—Now. Always. Forever.

Goddess's Honor titles currently available (chronological order):

The Goddess's Choice: A Goddess's Honor Short Story

Beyond Honor: A Goddess's Honor Novella

Exile's Honor: A Goddess's Honor Novelette

Birth of Sorrow: A Goddess's Honor Short Story
Pledges of Honor: Goddess's Honor Book One
Return to Wickmasa: A Goddess's Honor Short Story
Crown Anniversary: A Goddess's Honor Short Story
Challenges of Honor: Goddess's Honor Book Two
Cleaning House: A Goddess's Honor Outtake Story
Unexpected Alliances: A Goddess's Honor Rough Draft Outtake Story
Choices of Honor: Goddess's Honor Book Three
Judgment of Honor: Goddess's Honor Book Four

Netwalk Sequence Author Preferred 2022 Editions
Life in the Shadows: Book One
Netwalk: Book Two
Netwalker Uprising: Book Three
Netwalk's Children: Book Four
Learning in Space: Book Five
Netwalking Space: Book Six

Bright Star Fair Witches
Becoming Solo: A Bright Star Fair Witches Novella

Non-Series Titles currently available:
Alien Savvy: A Western SF Novella
Klone's Stronghold
Beating the Apocalypse
Bearing Witness

Vella Titles:
Falcon of the Martinieres (part of *Justine Fixes Everything*)
Bearing Witness
Beating the Apocalypse
A Different Life—What If? An Alternative Martiniere Legacy Novel
(ebook release spring 2022)
Becoming Solo
A Different Life—Linda's Story: An Alternative Martiniere Legacy Novel
Federation Cowboy

Audiobooks Available:

Alien Savvy: A Western SF Novella

Released from other publishers:

"Queen of the Snows," in *Once Upon A Winter: A Folk and Fairy Tale Anthology*, edited by H. L. Macfarlane

"My Man Left Me, My Dog Hates Me, and There Goes My Truck," in *Black-Eyed Peas on New Year's Day: An Anthology of Hope*, edited by Shannon Page

"Lost Loves," in *All Worlds Wayfarer*

"The Wisdom of Robins," in *Whimsical Beasts: A Campcon Anthology*, edited by Joyce Reynolds-Ward

"The Cow at the End of the World," in *Well...It's Your Cow*, edited by Frog Jones

"To Plant or Pull Up Stakes," in *Pulling Up Stakes: A Campcon Anthology*, edited by Joyce Reynolds-Ward

"The Notice," in *Children of a Different Sky*, edited by Alma Alexander

ABOUT THE AUTHOR

Joyce Reynolds-Ward has been called "the best writer I've never heard of" by one reviewer. Her work includes themes of high-stakes family and political conflict, digital sentience, personal agency and control, realistic strong women, and (whenever possible) horses. She is the author of *The Netwalk Sequence* series, the *Goddess's Honor* series, and the recently released *The Martiniere Legacy* series as well as standalones *Klone's Stronghold*, *Alien Savvy*, and *Beating the Apocalypse*. Samples of her Martiniere short stories/novel in progress and her nonfiction can be found on Substack at either Speculations from the Wide Open Spaces (general, writing) or Martiniere Stories (fiction). Joyce is a Self-Published Fantasy BlogOff Semifinalist, a Writers of the Future SemiFinalist, and an Anthology Builder Finalist. She is the Secretary of the Northwest Independent Writers Association, a member of the Science Fiction and Fantasy Writers Association, and a member of Soroptimists International.

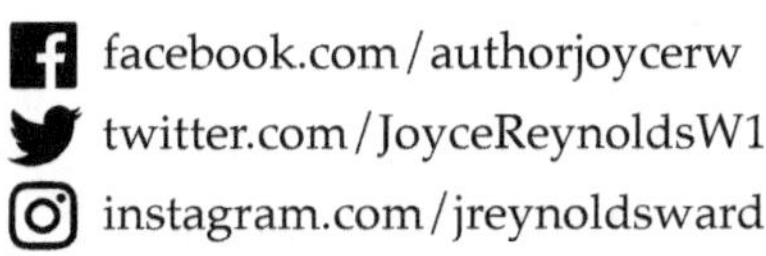